Fawcett Crest Books
by Norah Lofts:

- [ ] THE DAY OF THE BUTTERFLY   24359 $2.95

- [ ] ELEANOR THE QUEEN   22848 $2.50

- [ ] THE HAUNTING OF GAD'S HALL   24272 $2.25

- [ ] THE LOST QUEEN   22154 $2.75

- [ ] NETHERGATE   23095 $2.50

- [ ] SCENT OF CLOVES   22977 $2.50

- [ ] SILVER NUTMEG   24431 $2.95

- [ ] TO SEE A FINE LADY   22890 $2.25

- [ ] WINTER HARVEST   24466 $2.75

Norah Lofts

The Lute Player

FAWCETT CREST • NEW YORK

THE LUTE PLAYER

THIS BOOK CONTAINS THE COMPLETE TEXT OF
THE ORIGINAL HARDCOVER EDITION.

Published by Fawcett Crest Books, CBS Educational and
Professional Publishing, by arrangement with Doubleday
& Company, Inc.

ISBN: 0-449-22948-3

Printed in the United States of America

First Fawcett Crest printing: February 1971

14   13   12   11   10   9   8   7   6   5   4

Contents

A map showing the routes of the THIRD CRUSADE
appears on pages 446 and 447.

The Lute
Player

Author's Foreword

Addressed most particularly to those whose youthful hero worship was extended to Richard Plantagenet.

DURING THE FOUR YEARS THAT IT HAS TAKEN ME TO gather the information and to write this book I have been asked many times that inevitable question, "What is your new book about?" And when, replying with the inevitable reserve, caution, and embarrassment, "Mainly about Richard I and the Third Crusade," I have been astounded by the warmth and enthusiasm with which people have responded, "Oh, Richard I! He was one of my heroes!"

Why do I feel that I owe them, and all those with similar feelings, an apology? Chiefly, I suppose, because I fear that anyone who comes to this book with the pleasurable expectation of renewing acquaintance with the hero of *The Talisman* is bound to suffer disappointment.

When I was at an impressionable age the cinema had not reached the Suffolk countryside, and Robert Taylor, even if he were born then, probably had charm only for his mother; but we had our heroes nevertheless. The war, "the last war," or what I once heard a witty drunk call "the penultimate war," was just beginning and all the girls in my class were in love with Lord Kitchener. Anybody now so young as to doubt that so austere and remote a figure could inspire adolescent passion should read the O. Henry story which tells of a girl who was saved from a fate worse than death by the mere contemplation of his photograph. It was like that. What his pictured features saved my contemporaries from I cannot say; I only know that they were everywhere, rubbed and wrinkled in school satchels, carefully pasted inside books, even, believe it or not, tucked into the taut, youth-bursting tops of gym tunics.

I was immune, salted against this Kitchener fever, for I had just read *The Talisman* and had no room in my heart—or my gym tunic—for the hero of Khartoum. Richard Plantagenet was my hero, though I took care not to reveal this eccentricity. And through the years that intervened, while heroes came and heroes went, I remained, in my fashion, faithful.

11

So, popular and profitable a pastime as debunking may be, I did not set out to denigrate Richard Plantagenet. One must write as one finds, and there is ample evidence, not only in his behaviour to Berengaria, but in the comments and homilies of his contemporaries, to show that in some respects he differed from ordinary men as much as, in other respects, he excelled them. I, for one, am not convinced that one flaw necessarily reduces the hero. His valour, his romantic singleness of purpose remain unquestioned, and that one remark to his traitor brother, "I forgive you, John, and I wish I could as easily forget your offence as you will my pardon," must establish forever both his magnanimity and his wit.

I am told that in this story two things sound very false; they are the reference to the Old Man of the Mountain and the account of Richard halting in the middle of a battle to eat food provided by the Saracens. Both are, oddly enough, as completely vouched for as any incident in the Third Crusade. It must have been a remark of that kind which made Henri Fabre say—with, we are told, a chuckle—

"They fear lest a page that is read without fatigue should not be the truth."

Some incidents, of course, are purely fictional, and many of the people; Anna Apieta has no existence outside this book, and there seems to be a gathering doubt about Blondel.

I offer it all, fact and fiction, surmise and story, with the hope that it will be read without too much disappointment and "without fatigue."

NORAH LOFTS

One

God's Pauper

This fragment of the lute player's story is told by himself. He was called by his given name, Edward, and was a novice of the Abbey of Gorbalze in Burgundy. The incident of which he tells took place in the early spring of the year A.D. 1188.

"ANOTHER PACK OF WOLVES," BROTHER LAWRENCE said as we rounded a curve in the track and sighted the little group of beggars. And I thought how much I would have preferred to meet actual four-legged wolves. One's attitude toward a wolf pack is so simple; one hates, one fears; one attacks and scatters it or one flees in terror before it. No pity is involved. And I, for three days now, had been so wrenched by pity, so appalled by my own lack of power to help those I pitied, that now, seeing the beggars on the path, I thought that I could far more easily have stood still and let a wolf pack tear me to pieces than face a repetition of the scenes at Vibray and Amiche.

"Wake up, boy," said Brother Lawrence, and moved his left leg so that his stirrup struck me on the upper arm. "Listen and kindly bear in mind what I say. No more hysteria, if you please. It serves no purpose and has a very ill effect. I shall give them what is left in the alms bag and pass straight on. I want no more of your nonsense. Remember, hungry men are dangerous."

I turned my head and looked at him, and as I did so he twisted his head and looked straight ahead; but I had seen the expression—almost of gloating—with which he had been regarding me. And I wondered how far my behaviour during these three days had been responsible for his. Once in the old days I had watched a bearbaiting and I had seen, on the faces of several spectators, that very look. A gloating compounded of amusement, ruthlessness, and a kind of speculation: What will this provoke? I made up my mind that this time I would betray no feeling, give him no satisfaction. He pulled the alms bag into an easily accessible position at the front of his girdle and set his face into lines of grave, remote contemplation. So we moved towards the knot of beggars; I limping on account of the blister on my heel and bending forwards a little to ease the ache in my empty belly, while my mind ran backwards and forwards, remembering the events of the last three days and dreading the moment that was approaching.

It was very strange to find myself hating Brother Lawrence. Only three days before I had accorded him the admiration, the hero worship which a young man must extend to an older man extremely skilled in an art to which he

14

himself aspires. To me, on the morning after Lady Day, Brother Lawrence had been the man who had devoted four years of his life to making an incomparable copy of the Gospel of St. John. The manuscript now lay in the library at Gorbalze and was at once the inspiration and the despair of all ambitious young penmen. A visiting cardinal had once said that nothing in Rome or Cassino could equal it, and even that seemed not too high a compliment. There was one page—the opening of the third chapter—upon which it seemed a living spray of wild roses had been carelessly laid. So perfect each petal, each stamen, each thorn; the strong yet slender stems seeming to lift, to make a link between the earth from which they sprang and the heavens of which they hinted; the flowers so fragile, so vital, touched here and there with colours not of this world, colours whose names were known only in Paradise.

Fresh from brooding over this loveliness wrought by pen and brush wielded by human hand, I would see Brother Lawrence pass along the cloister or take his place in the refectory, a solemn, quiet, rather fattish man in no way noticeable or distinguished: yet I looked upon him with awe and admiration and knew that if ever he should speak to me I should sweat and stammer.

On the afternoon of Lady Day I was at work in the South Cloister, painstakingly adding word to word of my own humble manuscript, when a shadow fell over the page and, glancing sharply round, I saw, not our novice master, Father Simplon, but Brother Lawrence looking with interest over my shoulder. I shook out my sleeve to screen my unworthy work from his eyes. He reached over and took up my quill and studied it.

"A trifle too sharply cut," he said, and laid it back. "You are the one they call Edward, are you not?" I nodded. "Then I have a message for you. I am to ride out tomorrow to bring in the manorial dues from Amiche and Vibray; you come with me to keep the reckoning. We shall be gone three days. We leave immediately after Prime and carry food for the journey. I shall take the grey palfrey."

I nodded again and gulped and stammered, overcome with elation. Brother Lawrence glanced once more at my manuscript and said gravely, "You have the makings of a penman." Then he walked away, leaving me dazzled by his cool judicious compliment and by the prospect of spending three days in his company. Perhaps, I thought, I should

15

eventually pluck up courage and lure him into talking about that wonderful copy of the Gospel of St. John.

There wasn't a happier boy in Burgundy, in France, in Christendom, than I when on the morning after Lady Day we set off through the cold brightness of the spring morning. Even Brother Lawrence's choice of mount seemed fortunate to me; I loved Grys, the grey palfrey, and he knew and was fond of me. I was even pleased, God help me, at the thought of the food we carried in the saddlebags; we were to enjoy travellers' indulgence and the meat and roast fowl thus conceded were, for me at least, a rare and special treat, for Father Simplon was a strict adherent to the rule of our founder and never allowed to us novices the evasions and dispensations often openly enjoyed by our superiors.

Brother Lawrence; Grys; good food. All doomed to be the instruments of pain rather than pleasure.

During the past year the seasons had gone awry; there had been a drought in the spring at the time of seed sowing and in many fields the unsprouted corn had blown away with the dust on the easterly wind. August and September had been wet, so that the surviving crops and the fruit in the orchards had rotted as they ripened. Now, at the end of the long winter, there was famine on the land. And beggars on the road.

I was almost eighteen years old, but I had never before seen men and women and children gaunt and wild-eyed from hunger. Until I was sixteen I had lived in my father's castle, dividing my time between a small room where my tutor ruled me and the great hall where food was always plentiful. At sixteen I had entered my novitiate, and though under Father Simplon's rule food was coarse, simple, and sometimes unappetizing, no novice ever went hungry.

Brother Lawrence carried, as was apparently customary on these occasions, a small alms bag of copper coins. To the first little group who accosted us, a man, two women, and a child, he offered his ritual charity, and even as the clawlike hands were extended I heard the man mutter that money was of no use, there was nothing to buy; had we no bread? At that I impulsively reached down into my bag of food and handed out the bread and the lump of meat, and I was appalled by the savage eagerness with which the beggars tore and devoured it.

Brother Lawrence said, "Well, there goes your dinner,
16

boy. And I hope that, having squandered your own, you won't count upon eating mine."

I swear that no such thought was in my mind. I was quite certain that I could, at a pinch, spend three days without eating at all.

Throughout the first day I had indeed no appetite; the sight of so many starving had sickened me. And I had been sickened, too, by the protests of the debtors at Vibray and by Brother Lawrence's ruthless insistence upon the monastery's dues.

By midday on the second day I was hungry. My bag was empty and so was my stomach, and I found that I could not watch Brother Lawrence eat his meal. I had never realised before how gross men are when they eat, how the crumbs fall about, how lips grow shiny with grease. I went away from him and fed the palfrey, thinking of the prodigal son who would have eaten the swine's husks, thinking of the long fasts recorded in the lives of the saints, thinking of our Lord's sojourn in the wilderness and His resistance to the devil's offer of bread. I actually took and nibbled a few grains from the palfrey's nose bag and he nuzzled me, ungrudging, and I felt bound to remind myself that Grys could never have made that lovely manuscript.

The third day was worse. There was an ache in my belly, my head felt swollen and noisy, my legs shook. And my mind rotted. Instead of thinking of the forty days in the wilderness, or the fastings of the saints, or what a good penman Brother Lawrence was, I found myself concentrating upon the capon that was still intact in his bag, and thinking that a kind man, a Christian, would give me a piece to eat and even offer me, because of my blistered heel, an hour's relief upon Grys's back. Outside Vibray, faced with another mass of misery, I had thought, I merely hunger, they starve; this pain which is so sharp after only three days has been theirs for a long time. Then I had broken down and cried, "Is there nothing we can do to relieve them?" And the beggars had taken up the cry and pressed close, perhaps in hope, and clawed us with their hands. Brother Lawrence, with the capon, a piece of cheese, and the better part of a loaf safe in his saddlebag, had urged Grys forward, chiding me for making a scene.

Now, late in the afternoon of the third day, we were moving towards another group of beggars, the biggest group we had yet seen, and Brother Lawrence was saying, "No more hysteria, if you please."

There were between fifteen and twenty of them, and several were children. Some part of my mind, dissociating itself from their misery and mine, noted that in each group we had encountered the women had outnumbered the men. Did women more easily leave their homes and throw themselves upon the charity of the road, or did women, accustomed to denying themselves in the interests of their menfolk and their children, more easily survive in a time of shortage?

They were all quite horrible to look at, clad in tatters, skeleton-thin, their faces touched with an earthy pallor. As they surged about us I found myself staring at one of the women, a tall, emaciated creature, the mother of two children. The little things, pale and thin and dirty, clung to her skirts, and though they looked as no human children should, they had, by contrast with the rest of the group, something of liveliness, of hope. It went through my mind that whatever, in these starving days, had been given to the woman had been passed on to the children, and that was why they looked better and she looked worse than the rest of the mob. I regretted passionately at that moment that I had emptied my food bag on the first day.

Brother Lawrence checked Grys, opened his alms bag, and distributed the few coppers which it held. I saw, I shared, the deadly disappointment of those who had asked for bread and been given an inedible coin. I touched his arm, stretched up, and whispered in his ear, "Brother Lawrence, the children—give them what remains in your bag."

He hissed at me, "No, no! That would cause trouble. Will you be quiet, as I bade you?" Raising his voice, he said, "Good people, I have nothing more. Kindly make way for me." Then out of the side of his mouth he said to me, "Take Grys's bridle and clear me a path."

"They are hungry," I said.

Brother Lawrence turned upon me savagely. "You young fool," he said, "will my hunger mend theirs? Clear me a path before we have trouble." Raising his voice again, he said unctuously, "Good people, I have nothing more to give you save my prayers. Kindly make way there." He jerked Grys's rein, and the meek old horse stood weaving from side to side for a moment, for now the beggars were thick about us. Maybe they drew some faint hope from our argument and delay; maybe they had seen the bag.

At that moment there was no thought in my mind save that Brother Lawrence had eaten fully already that day and would find supper awaiting him when we reached Gorbalze and that there was enough food in the bag to give the children of the party a mouthful or two, enough to ease for a little while that gnawing in the belly about which I was learning. I reached out and laid my hand on the bag, and Brother Lawrence slapped out at me pettishly, like a child defending some treasured bit of rubbish. "You fool," he cried, "what is that amongst so many?"

Through the strange buzzing that had been in my ears all day I heard a great bell, louder and clearer than the St. Denis bell at Gorbalze, ring out. Weren't those the very words which Andrew, Simon Peter's brother, had spoken to Christ just before the feeding of the five thousand? Couldn't I remember the page where those words were written in Brother Lawrence's own copy of the Gospel? It was edged with bluebells, set in a pattern, formal, stylised, beautiful, each bloom a trumpet blown to the glory of God. God, Who had fed five thousand upon five barley loaves and two small fishes, could feed twenty on a roast capon, half a loaf, and a piece of cheese.

A mad elation seized me. I snatched again at the bag, and when Brother Lawrence again fended me off I struck at him. Taken completely by surprise, he rolled from the palfrey's back and lay supine on the bleached winter grass by the roadside. Grys turned his head questioningly, saw me, and stood steady. The beggars pressed a little closer.

I began to pray as I had never prayed in all my life before. Incoherent, passionate, muddled petitions poured through my mind as I fumbled with the string of the bag and plunged in my hand. And I felt something—a vibration, a connection, a surety—something we have no word for, something I had never felt before when I prayed, something that made me certain that God had heard me and would work His miracle.

The capon came out first. It had been trussed and roasted whole, but the skewer had been removed and the flesh was tender, easily broken. Praying, calling, drawing upon God and feeling the deep, calm certainty of His presence, I tore off the leg and thigh of the fowl and held it out to the woman with the two children. She took it, broke it again, and held a piece to each child. The gesture was beautiful; it held all the self-abnegation and tenderness in the world. God saw it too; I felt the throb of His perception. I was dizzy with love for her, for all these gaunt, hungry people, and for God, Who was working this miracle. I heard my own voice, thin, high, exalted, cry:

"Wait, wait, there will be enough for all."

It was answered by a low moaning cry with something of despair, of savagery, and yet of patience in it.

Were they conscious of the miracle? I only know that they stood quietly, watching, waiting. No one pushed farther forward, no hand snatched the portion meant for another. Those to whom I proffered the pieces began to eat with ferocity, each solitary and wary.

The fowl was not multiplied in my hands, but I was not discouraged. At the end, when all was spent, the miracle would come. I broke the bread and the piece of cheese and distributed them, all the time with a faith which, if it were not the perfect faith commended in Holy Writ, was genuine and vigorous and expectant. I did expect that the last piece of cheese would go on being divided, and even when my hands were empty and the bag dangled limp between my fingers I only prayed more urgently and waited. Now, now is the moment when heaven leans towards earth and the veil of sense and reason is rent; now is the moment of the miracle.

Nothing happened. The confidence, the sense of power, the expectancy drained out of me like lifeblood from a mortal wound. I heard a low, despairing "Ah-h-h" sigh through the crowd; saw, through a mist that seemed to redden before my eyes, the pale, thin, disappointed faces. Two or three—one of them the mother of the two children—had received nothing; and nobody had had more than a crumb to tantalise and mock his famine. I had loved them and pitied them and hurt them. A blundering, credulous fool who believed in miracles.

I threw the bag from me. I began to cry. I sobbed out:

"I am sorry, sorry. I thought there would be enough for all. If God had listened there would have been enough for all."

Grys turned his patient head at the sound of my voice and I went forward, meaning to lay my face on his smooth warm neck; but Brother Lawrence's face came up at me from the other side of the horse's shoulder and glared at me through the mist. His face was full of fear and hatred and fury; the mouth in it opened and he cursed me, using words even the roughest archers speak sparingly, words no monk should know. I looked at him across Grys's grey shoulder and said, "God failed me, I tell you. I'd have done better to ask the devil. God can no longer work even a little miracle . . . . "

And then I died and went straight to hell.

I knew where I was before I opened my eyes. I could smell the thick, acrid odour of charring flesh, the greasy smoke of the fire, and knew that I was in the place where the damned roast forever and forever upon the devil's unconsuming grid. And I could hear the wild, jubilant cry of the fiends.

I was not surprised to find myself in hell; I had died with blasphemous words on my lips and rebellion against God in my heart; my sins were unshriven, my soul unhouseled. I was surprised to find that I remembered everything so clearly and that my general feeling was one of calm acceptance. During my lifetime I had several times known, at a vivid description, written or spoken, of hell, an overmastering sense of terror; I did not feel it now. Nor—and this was also surprising—was I repentant. I remember that St. Anthony of Tours, in his *Analysis of the Seventeen Worst Pains of Hell,* had laid great emphasis upon "that agony of mind arising from the consciousness of sin when the time for confession and absolution is past."

Certainly I had died in a state of grievous sin, but now, lying here on the edge of the pit, I was not tormented by any sense of guilt. My mind acknowledged that I had been presumptuous, violent, and blasphemous, but in my heart I could still think: God abandoned me first; He failed me while I was believing and praying to Him.

At that—as had been my habit on earth when visited by a dubious or unorthodox thought—my hand moved to make the sign over my breast, my lips to mutter, "God forgive me!" But I remembered that here there was no need for that. One of the pains of hell is that God has no cognisance of it.

Then it occurred to me that in this indeterminate moment, while I was not racked by torment, or maddened with fear, or torn by pangs of ineffectual repentance, I should look about me and see how near the saints and mystics had been in their forecasts of the exact nature of damnation. The whole idea of hell—the description of which had been so terrifying—was, I realised, constructed upon singularly little evidence. Now I would open my eyes and see how it was that a man whose body had been rendered insentient by death and laid away to rot in the cool moist earth could yet, in his actual flesh and bones, suffer the pains of the undying worm, the unquenched fire.

With a considerable effort I opened my eyes and raised my head a little.

Every single thing that had been written about hell was true. It was all in darkness, save where it was lighted by the glow of the pit in which burned a fire the like of which was never seen on earth; it was at once clear and murky, foul and bright. And outlined against the glow, in a black frieze, were the figures of the fiends, leaping and prancing and yelling, raking with long rods in the fire, turning over the bodies of the damned, so that their pains might increase infinitely. Over all there hung the horrible stench of fire, charred flesh, blood.

I closed my eyes and let my head drop back. Presently one of the fiends would notice me and toss me into the fire. And there I should be in the company of all those men and women whose memories had been preserved because of their iniquity. Judas Iscariot, Herod, Pontius Pilate, all wizards and witches and warlocks, all heretics; Crispin of Châlus, whose fire had started during his lifetime because he had denied the possibility of transubstantiation; Peter Abélard, outcast and maimed for love of Héloïse.

At that thought I raised my head again and looked towards the fire. This time I recognised one of the dark figures with the long rods. It was the thin, skeleton-thin, woman whose piteous plight had, in the final issue, been partly responsible for my last earthly action. So she was dead too. Of course she had been dying of hunger when she made that beautiful life-giving gesture and divided the food between her children. What was she doing in hell? That same old feeling of rebellion moved in my heart and, forgetting that I was now far beneath the notice of God, I thought: O God, whatever she had done before, couldn't that self-denial have been counted to her for virtue?

Then I saw that, to a degree, it had been. For she had been early promoted to fiendship. She was free; she was moving around the edge of the pit, sedulously attending to the business of turning the damned, and when the light from the fire leaped and illumined her face I saw that she looked far happier than I remembered. And the children were with her, still clinging to her skirt as she moved through the murk and the glare and the stench.

Perhaps there were degrees in hell; a social order undreamed of by the mystics.

22

While I watched, the woman used her rod vigorously and then threw it aside. She pushed the children back a little and took the hem of her ragged skirt in her hand and stooped over the pit. Then, carrying something which I could not identify, she moved away, drawing the children within the curve of her unencumbered arm. Gentleness, happiness in hell, I thought, amazed.

Her movement had left a clear space in front of me. I could stare straight out towards the other side of the pit. And on the other side I could see Grys—or what was left of him. The lurid light of the fire shone on the white, bloodied bones, sharp, distorted, horrible, and on the silky flow of tail and mane, the gentle, unmolested beauty of his head. His ribs were a cage of horror out of which the writhing, bloody mess of entrails spilled; his haunches and shoulders were stripped of flesh—even the neck against which I had leaned my sorrow.

The sight of him brought me back to my senses. I realised that I was still on earth and that earth has horrors hell never dreams of.

I do pray to Almighty God for forgiveness of that thought. He had wrought the miracle for which I had prayed, and at first sight of it I recoiled in horrified repudiation. Dear, loving, omniscient Father, forgive me for grudging Grys to Thy poor, as Brother Lawrence grudged the capon .... It was only that I had loved the grey horse and he had been fond of me, and his sudden transformation into a mass of bones and filth lying in a pool of blood was horrible and shocking.

The woman came and sat down near me. Still protecting her hands with her skirt, she wrenched the joint into pieces, blew on them to cool them a little, handed each child a share, and then fell on her own like a wolf. The meat had been blackened and charred on the outside but was still raw within, and as she ate the melted fat, the blood, the very life juices of the palfrey, spurted out and splashed over her hands, her chin, her clothing. The other beggars were following her example and dragging out their portions of meat; the fire burned up more brightly, and the fierce flickering glare lighted the strange, macabre scene.

I had prayed that there should be enough for all, and indeed here was plenty and to spare. I did briefly wonder whether the miracle as I had desired it, the increase of the bag's contents, would not have been cleaner and neater and

23

less horrible, but I put that thought away; even Christ had been content to say, "Not as I will but as Thou willest."

Then it occurred to me to wonder what had happened to Brother Lawrence. I struggled into a sitting position and looked about. I saw no sign of him and after a moment's searching stare I found my eyes resting again on the woman who sat nearest me. She stopped eating, and her hand with the meat in it fell to her lap. I saw confusion and uncertainty come upon her. Perhaps she credited me with some share in the ownership of the horse, or was conscious of the way she was eating. I tried to smile at her reassuringly. She stared back unsmiling for a moment and then rose and, walking jerkily, as though moved by some compulsion which she resented, came towards me. As she did so she pulled savagely at the meat and when she reached me had succeeded in tearing it into two parts. She held one out to me without a word—indeed, she held it out with her face averted; she was looking back over her shoulder to see that no one pounced upon her children's meat during her brief absence.

Even as I leaned away from that dreadful dripping bit of carrion a small quiet voice spoke in my mind, saying that here was a real miracle; that this human creature who had starved through so many yesterdays and knew that hunger awaited her tomorrow, who had borne and must go on bearing the pangs of hunger other than her own—that she should be willing to share this chance-come bit of food was a miracle, straight from the hand of God. I saw the glory of her soul shine over her rags and ugliness and filth, making her one with the angels.

I said, "I thank you from my heart, but my supper awaits me. Keep what you have."

"There is plenty for all tonight," she said gruffly. "And you look hungry."

"I can eat later," I said. She glanced back at her children who were happily worrying away at their meat like puppies; then she looked at me again. Her hands with their burden of meat dropped to her sides. Her eyes took on a most curious look, sly, wary, apologetic, desperate. And I knew that she wanted to speak about Grys; that she thought that I had refused the meat out of distaste; that I was resentful. But she said nothing; nor did I, and after a second she walked back to her children.

I got to my feet, feeling weak and exhausted. I looked out across the mass of gobbling beggars, the fire, the dreadful remains of Grys. And as before my eyes came back to the woman. She was gnawing her meat again; one of the children, satiated, had dropped his head into her lap and lay sleeping, his fist still clenched about an unsightly bone. And suddenly I thought of a way in which I could answer all those things she had not said and at the same time profit her a little. I moved towards her and leaned down as though to tell her a secret.

"There is the tongue," I said quietly. "Smoked over the fire, it would last for a day or two. The tongue—in the horse's head."

Bewilderment gave way to understanding. She was radiant again. "God bless you, God bless you," she said. She shifted the sleeping child, patted the other, and shot me one more glowing, grateful look. Then, furtive and crafty as a wolf, she went sidling towards the carcase. I saw her bend, grim, purposeful, over the supine grey head, the head which had nuzzled me softly while I had nibbled the corn grains. Had I been obedient and laid my hand to the bridle instead of the saddlebag, Grys would now have been safe in his stable. And the beggars—the woman and the children among them—would still be hungry! Oh, it was all too hard to understand; too complicated; too puzzling.

I suddenly remembered Father Simplon's words when I had told him that I had been chosen to accompany Brother Lawrence. "Good," he had said, "it will be a valuable experience for you."

A valuable experience, I said to myself; and, limping away in the direction of Gorbalze, I compared the state of mind and body in which I had set out with that in which I was returning. If I had really died and been resurrected I could hardly have felt more changed.

III

I arrived back at Gorbalze just at midnight, when the bell was ringing for matins; Father Simplon had not gone to bed but was waiting for me in the porter's lodge with a blanket draped over his shoulders. The sight of him told me that Brother Lawrence had reached home safely (I later learned that he had managed to borrow a horse along the road), and the expression with which I was greeted warned me that the story of my behaviour had lost nothing in the telling.

I think that if on my arrival I had been given food and allowed to go to bed I might, by the morning, have recovered

25

some measure of sanity. I expected rebuke and punishment. A novice does not, with impunity, strike his superior and precipitate a situation which loses his monastery a good palfrey. I expected, as I reeled and stumbled back to Gorbalze, that there was a beating in store for me, a stern rebuke from the chapter, and some days on bread-and-water diet. Father Simplon was a great believer in the last-named method of cooling hot heads and hot tempers. I even carried my gloomy anticipations a little farther and visualised some more subtle method of punishment, being forbidden to work on my manuscript, or set to perform some task known to be distasteful. I swear that I was prepared to accept such penances in the proper meek spirit, for I had smitten Brother Lawrence and I had been responsible for Grys's end.

But I had underrated Brother Lawrence's anger and his cunning. He had made a report about me which had created an atmosphere in which, with very little help from me, in my hysterical, exhausted state, far more serious charges flourished.

The first ominous note was struck by Father Simplon when, on his return from matins, he began to question me.

"And what exactly was your intention when you snatched the bag?"

"To feed the beggars, Father."

"Knowing their numbers and how little food was left?"

I nodded.

"How then could you hope to carry out your intention?"

"I hoped," I said, "for a miracle."

And Father Simplon said, "That smacks of heresy."

Later in my life, on the rare occasions when I remembered the ensuing six days, I tried to be tolerant and to remind myself that most of the men with whom I had then to deal were old, were professionally religious, bringing to matters of doctrine all the interest and passion and prejudice which men of the outer world devote to a number of diffuse ends; were all, or most of them, celibate, a state which I now see is not conducive to cool judgment, but rather to hysteria easily provoked and tempers easily exacerbated.

I can forgive them now—can see, in fact, that there was little save stupidity for which to blame them; but when at the end of six days I lay in the punishment cell at Gorbalze, beaten black and blue, empty-bellied, filthy, and despondent, I hated them all.

I could see even then that I had managed badly. I had

26

allowed myself to be provoked into making reckless statements on the one hand and endeavouring to explain the inexplicable on the other. My interview with Brother Gaspard, who, as steward, was responsible for the business of buying a new horse and who was furious with me, opened with a pious lecture upon the estates of man, during which he informed me that since God had laid starvation upon the beggars it was presumptuous and blasphemous to interfere with that state; and it ended somehow with me shouting that it was very wrong for the monastery to demand the full manorial dues during a time of famine and, further, that the whole economy of our community was in direct opposition to the rule of poverty laid down by our Founder.

But to the sub-prior, who came to me quietly and talked in a sympathetic manner, I tried to explain that there *was* a miracle. Not by the multiplication of small viands, not by the fall of manna from heaven, but by the upspring of an idea of killing the palfrey. The sub-prior was smooth, infinitely deceptive; to talk to him after the others was like the ease that follows a bout of toothache. I told him, poor fool that I was, about the other miracle—the woman's holding out of the meat to me. I told him how, for a moment, she looked like an angel.

No lunatic set on self-destruction ever hanged himself more thoroughly. By the end of six days the charges of striking Brother Lawrence and inciting the mob to devour Grys had been almost forgotten. I was charged with heresy, blasphemy, and devil worship.

Dirk, the lay brother who attended to such matters, had laid on the stripes with enthusiasm; it was now nine days since I had eaten a proper meal; the blister on my heel had festered until my leg as far as the knee was purple and puffy, and on the evening when my lord abbot, Guibert of Gorbalze, summoned me to his presence, I was as miserable a creature as any overlord could wish to own.

IV

I had been an inmate of Gorbalze for almost two years, but I had never set eyes upon its abbot. He was confined, by reason of his lameness, to his own apartments, and there had hitherto been no reason why I, a novice, should enter his presence. This remoteness, combined with the story of his past—exciting even to our cloistered youth—made him more

27

of a legendary figure than an actual human being; yet his influence and authority were vital and permeating and everybody in Gorbalze regarded him with awe.

The story told of him was that in his youth he had been a famous knight, remarkable for skill and valour. He had gone to the Holy Land, acquitted himself superbly, and been one of the most favoured nominees for the crown of Jerusalem. But in an affray near Joppa he had been set upon by five Saracens, and though he had fought them singlehanded, left three dead and two wounded on the field and ridden back in triumph, he had been wounded, it was thought mortally. A spear had pierced his thigh and broken off, leaving the head in the wound, too deeply embedded in the bone for any surgeon to remove. He had lain for weeks in the care of the Knights Hospitallers and then, emerging crippled, had taken himself and the moderate fortune gained from looting the Saracens to Cassino in Italy and remained there, an obscure monk, for some years. Legend attributed his sudden promotion to the abbacy of Gorbalze to his indiscreet sponsoring, in the presence of a visiting dignitary, of the claims of Matilda to the throne of England. Matilda, regarded as a better Christian than her cousin Stephen, was secretly favoured in high places, and Guibert's unorthodox opinion, though sternly rebuked by his own community, resulted in his promotion. He was now in the seventh decade of his age and immobile. The spearhead was still embedded in his thigh, and splinters of the bone were said to work out beside it at intervals. It was also said that he suffered perpetual pain and resorted to the use of strange Eastern drugs for its relief.

On the evening when my lord abbot sent for me I wished heartily amidst all my awe and apprehension that I had been able to meet the subject of this interesting history in more favourable circumstances. At this moment my lively curiosity, my tendency to hero worship were, like most other things about me, at a very low ebb.

The cell in which I had been lying was semi-dark even at noonday, and the passages through which I limped on my way to the abbot's parlour were black tunnels in which here and there the sparingly placed candles behind their horn shields cast a flickering, intermittent glow. By contrast the parlour was dazzlingly bright, and for a moment or two after my entry I was blinded and blinking like a bat disturbed at midday. It was a small room, circular in shape, and the stone walls, recently whitened, caught and reflected the yellow light of the many candles, the red light of the fire.

There was a smell of food in the room too—fish, hot butter, fresh bread—and I felt my shrunken stomach move, half tantalised, half nauseated. I stood squinting, violently willing myself not to be sick. And out of the glare a cool hard voice said:

"You had better sit down. There is a stool within reach of your left hand."

I reached out, found the stool, and sat down, wincing on account of my bruised buttocks. Once I was seated, the sickness left me; my eyes adjusted themselves to the light and in a moment I was able to look about me.

My lord abbot sat in a high-backed chair, his lame leg supported on a stool and covered with a rug of wolfskins. On his right stood a table bearing books, an inkpot and several quills, and a litter of parchments; on his left its fellow bore a flagon, some goblets, and a covered dish or two. I saw so much before I ventured to raise my eyes and look into his face.

Save for its colour, a reddish-brown, and the fact that the eyes were open and lively, it might have been a death mask, so harsh and deep and final were its lines. The bones of the brow, the cheek, the jaw, stood out sharply, separated by deep hollowed shadows. Under the bony, jutting nose the mouth was thin, the lips closely folded. Only the eyes, set far back in sunken sockets and yet prominent, were alive, movable, acutely aware. They made me think inconsequently, uncomfortably, of an animal looking out of a den or rock. Altogether a formidable face. I made up my mind that this time I would attempt no explanation, commit myself to nothing. I was briefly thankful for my experience with Father Simplon, Brother Gaspard, and the chapter. This time I would confine myself to expressions of penitence. Even to the question which had tripped me into volubility before, "Do you believe that the devil answers prayer?" I would say, "I am sorry. I expressed myself ill."

In that resolve I faced my abbot, waiting. We looked at one another for what seemed an embarrassingly long time. At last he said, "Well, you seem to have set this whole place by the ears pretty thoroughly."

And I, adhering to my resolve, said, "I am sorry, my lord."

"For your behaviour or its result?"

"Just generally sorry, my lord."

I saw him glance towards the table on his right. I knew at once that somewhere there, amongst the litter of parchments, written in the sub-prior's vile crabbed hand, was a full account of my offences.

"I should like to hear your own story of the whole—episode," he said. "Begin at the beginning and omit nothing."

That was very much akin to the opening used by the sub-prior. Compared with Father Simplon's staccato questions and Brother Gaspard's angry denunciations, it had a friendly sound; but I had been caught on that hook once and was now wary.

"My lord," I said, "the full account would weary you and only confirm the charges laid against me. I am very sorry that I struck Brother Lawrence and led to the death of Grys, and for the other ancillary offences which I committed without full knowledge."

"You talk like a lawman, boy. And the information that you are responsible for a death is news to me. Who was this unfortunate Grys?"

"The grey palfrey, my lord."

"Oh. Of course. Grys . . . . The report merely mentioned a palfrey. I remember Grys. He must have been all of eighteen years old. A toughish dish, I would say. For one moment I imagined that you were referring to one of the beggars either killed in the melee or dead from sudden overeating. That was a very real danger, you know. I have known men, after the relief of sieges, to die from repletion. I suppose you didn't think of that."

"No, my lord."

He sat silent for a little, and I thought, He is old, his mind may be a little vague; that mention of sieges may have sent his thoughts running backwards. He may forget that he asked me to retell the story and so I shall have escaped from further involvement.

"And now," he said, "tell me—why are you so reluctant to give me your own account?"

Startled into frankness, I told him: "Because, my lord, each time I tell the story I worsen matters. Each time something is seized upon and twisted and——"

"Do you think that I am likely to twist anything you say?" The harsh voice was menacing; so was the piercing stare with which he fixed me. I felt cold suddenly and remembered that within the Church a man accused of murder had the benefit of clergy and the "neck sentence" in his favour, while heresy was another matter. I knew that now in my mind; I might shortly know it through my shrinking flesh. . . .

"Answer me," he said.

"Not wittingly, my lord, any more than I wittingly intended to do more than give a few starving people something to eat, but——"

"It may be that by age and experience I am enabled to judge better than you, child. Go on, tell me your story."

So for the fourth or fifth time I recounted all that had happened on the road between Châteautour and Gorbalze. My other listeners had interrupted, either with questions or comments, and contrived to make me angry, or emphatic, or wild-headed. Guibert listened in silence, never taking his eyes from my face; and, oddly enough, this time parts of my story sounded—there was no other word for it—silly.

"I see," he said when I had done. "And now tell me honestly, do you believe that you worked a miracle?"

A trap straightaway, I thought despairingly.

"My lord, I never claimed——"

"Of course not. How suspicious you are! I beg your pardon. Are you still of the opinion that a miracle occurred?"

"At the time," I said cautiously, "and sometimes since. Until now, in fact. Now I am not so sure."

"Naturally. Credulity in one's listener, even though it be tinctured with horror and superstition, is very stimulating to the imagination. I do not believe in your miracle, but then neither do I believe that you are a heretic, a blasphemer, or a worshipper of the devil. I think you're a softhearted, pumpkin-headed boy who has led too sheltered a life and been somewhat suddenly confronted with the problem of suffering. Even your extremely ill-advised outburst to Brother Gaspard upon the immorality of monastic property I can see for what it is—a youthful impatience with a state of society in which things happen to affront your feelings." He paused for a moment to allow these comforting, if rather contemptuous, words to sink in and then went on, "And I'll wager my dinner tomorrow that if Father Simplon and the rest of them hadn't taught you the wisdom of keeping your mouth shut you would now proceed to blurt out to me all that is in your mind. You would demand to know why, if God be merciful, He lets folk starve; and why men like Brother Lawrence and the sub-prior, who have spent their lives in His service, should show themselves in a crisis to be greedy, uncharitable, and even a little cruel. Am I not right?"

He was so exactly right—he had reduced all the dark

31

confusion of my mind to two such simple questions that I gaped at him in wonder.

"Don't look so moon-struck," he said. "Do you think you're the first to ask these unanswerable questions?"

"They are—unanswerable?"

"They are answered every day by arrogant fools who juggle words as tricksters juggle plates at fairs. If we had time and if my memory still serves me I could quote you the whole of St. Blaise's *Thoughts on the Subject of Human Pain,* not to mention a dozen other authorities. But the questions remain unanswerable. Even Christ never attempted to explain. Certainly He said that not a sparrow falls without God's knowledge—not *concern,* mark you, *knowledge;* but that reflection must have been of little comfort to all the blind in Palestine who didn't happen to be blind Bartimaeus; or to the hundreds who doubtless went hungry to bed on the night when five thousand were fed by the lakeside; or to the fathers whose little daughters were dead, not sleeping; or to all the widows who chanced not to live in Nain and so must perforce bury their dead sons. Christ never asked why men are hungry, afflicted, bereaved. Within the scope of His attention He relieved distress when He met it and for the rest accepted or ignored it. An example I commend to you."

"But Brother Lawrence——"

"Bless you, child, Brother Lawrence was just a hungry old man who wanted to get home and realised that you can't feed nineteen people on one capon. By the time you are his age you'll know that, too, and also that if God were concerned with empty bellies He'd have made figs grow on thistles, or so constructed us that we would find oak leaves appetising and nourishing. The fact remains that He didn't and we must accept it without making futile protests which can only result in charges of unorthodoxy."

Both glance and voice had softened into something approaching kindliness. I should have been cheered by that and by his tolerant summing up of my behaviour; yet every cool, reasonable sentence seemed to add weight to my depression. Father Simplon sentencing me to bread and water, Dirk laying on the stripes with good will, Brother Gaspard arguing hotly about manorial dues had, after all, been acting in a known and approved pattern, implying that God was good and that I was a sinner to have entertained even a moment's doubt. But Guibert, under the kindliness, was saying in effect that God was, at best, an enigma, and that I was a fool not

32

to have seen that and kept quiet about it. It was rather as though a physician called in to treat me for a mild form of some disease had suggested no medicine but, baring his own breast, had said, "See, I ail the same thing but I survive, so will you."

"What we must now consider," Guibert said in a brisker voice, "is the practical side of the question. Before we embark upon that, pour me some wine and take a measure yourself. . . . Thank you. Now what I have to say is this. I think it would be very unwise for you to remain here. Brother Lawrence will doubtless do his duty and forgive you for striking him, Brother Gaspard will one day outlive the loss of the palfrey and your revolutionary remarks about church property, but something will remain and for many years, in a community of this size, everything you do or say will be, in a measure, suspect. You agree? I understand that you are a penman of some promise, so I propose sending you to Arcelles, where they will welcome you. In twenty years they have never succeeded in breeding a penman of their own. You should do well there. And certainly the manorial dues will concern you very little; it is the poorest foundation in Burgundy, and as a rest from writing you will doubtless till your own field and fish for your own eels." The mockery of the last words was mitigated by a smile which altered his whole face, making it friendly and conspiratorial. And one small corner of my mind put forth the thought, Oh, I'd like to have known you as a young man, seen that understanding, merry look come into your face as we sat in a pennanted tent planning an assault on the infidel. . . . But the main trend of my thoughts ran another way: This is the moment when I must speak; I must say it now, but what words can I find?

"And now, I suppose," he said, "you will proceed to tell me that you don't want to go to Arcelles or anywhere else; that you don't want to be a monk at all; that you have lost your faith and with it your vocation and propose to rush away into the world and commit all the seven deadly sins at once." He smiled at me again, and I found myself smiling back.

"I hadn't thought yet of the sins, my lord. But—but the rest is what I have been thinking for the past few days."

He became serious immediately.

"Have you taken any orders yet?"

"No, my lord."

"Why did you enter in the first place?"

"My father——"

"Oh yes! Something to do with a vow, wasn't it? A son and a manor out of his many for Holy Church if his leg—was it his leg?—mended. Why were *you* chosen?"

"I was the youngest and, as a child, small. In his opinion I had not the makings of a knight."

"Come here, show me your hands."

I stood up stiffly. The wine I had drunk—sweet and strong—had gone to my head a little, and the floor seemed a long way away. I thrust out my hands, regretting their slight unsteadiness and their more than slight uncleanliness; there was no provision for washing in the punishment cell. Guibert took them in his own, which were thin but of steely strength, and bent back my thumbs and flexed my wrists.

"Your father was right," he said, giving me back my hands as though they were something he had borrowed. "A born penman's hands; useless for anything heavier than a dagger. Do you play any instrument?"

"The lute—a little," I said humbly.

"Would you be welcomed at home? Would your father——"

"He would crack my skull for me and then, if I survived, send me back." That was the truth, innocent of exaggeration. My father was a terrible, fierce man. I remembered my three sisters, packed off one by one as soon as they had reached marriageable age, to marry men they had never seen; they had been terrified, weeping, and, save by my brother William and me, completely unpitied. I remembered William himself, thrown from an unmanageable horse and then savagely beaten for allowing himself to be thrown; and my other brother, whom fat nauseated, condemned to eat fat and fat only for a week, "to teach him to master his belly." More than once in the past I had been grateful that Father had dedicated me to the Church, for my training was left to a tutor, and so long as I minded my book and remained unobtrusive I escaped notice. I had been beaten twice; once for trying, in a moment of madness, to ride the horse which had thrown William, and again when the curtain wall was being repaired at our castle and I had slipped away to watch the masons at work. Horses and buildings had always been a passion with me, but Father considered that interest in either was unsuitable to one destined to be a monk; and a beating from him was a powerful argument. I knew that if I went home now, with some muddled explanation about lack of vocation, my shrift would be very short indeed.

"A cracked skull would complicate, rather than simplify,

34

the problem of your future," my abbot said. "And it may be a problem. A few years ago I could have thought of a dozen noblemen to whom I could have recommended you as scribe and musician, but these are bad times. The idea of a new crusade hangs in the air, and even the greatest are beginning to count mouths at table and practise economy. Also, there are too many young men—and quite a few women—who can handle a pen after a fashion." There was another significant little pause. "It would be rather a pity, don't you think, if your sympathy with the starving poor resulted in your joining their numbers? At the moment you are angry with God for letting some peasants starve, angry with Brother Lawrence for not sharing your anger, angry with me for talking cold sense instead of hot theory. But I would quite seriously advise you not to let these angers—which will pass—ruin your whole career. There is a difference, you know, between a career and a vocation. Inside the Church a good penman has an assured future; outside it he may starve. I would advise you against making a hasty decision."

I knew that he was looking at me with kindly earnestness, but for the first time I found myself unable to meet his eyes. I was afraid that my own sudden knowledge might show in mine. For the course he was suggesting to me, I realised, was the one which he had chosen and pursued successfully. Disabled, frustrated, he had taken refuge in the Church, and to the same refuge he advised me to take my feeble penman's hands.

I looked beyond him, at the wall behind him, which was covered by a large piece of tapestry held out from the curve of the wall by a stretchered frame. It portrayed in horrible and realistic detail the scene upon Calvary; nothing of pain and terror and brutality was lacking. Looking at it, seeing the writhing, tortured limbs, the blood, the crown of thorns, the pierced side of Christ, the broken legs of the felons, the women weeping, and the Roman soldiers detachedly casting dice for the pitiful pieces of raiment, I thought of the heat of the Eastern sun, the flies which would swarm, the thirst, the consciousness of failure, of being ranked with common malefactors, and that final despairing sense of abandonment which had found voice in that inexpressibly desolate cry, "My God, my God, why hast Thou forsaken me?"

And I knew why I had always known an unadmitted revulsion towards all the stories and pictures and crucifixes. That Good Friday represented the very nadir of human experience; as His idealism and kindness and perception were

35

superior to other men's, so His final despair and disillusion-ment were fiercer. And the Church which bore His name had taken this unbearable moment for its very centre—was founded upon the theory of the scapegoat, the universal whipping boy. It advised, prescribed contemplation of this scene of horror. It gloated!

Small wonder, I thought, that a religion founded upon such a human catastrophe breeds on the one hand Brother Lawrence, who can watch other men starve, and on the other Abbot Guibert, who can commend the Church as a career.

Guibert's voice reached me. "Well," he said, "you think things over. I shall tell Father Simplon that I think you have been punished enough and you had better return to your ordinary routine. Meanwhile I will communicate with Ar-celles."

With fluency and courage owing in some measure to the effect of the good wine upon my empty stomach, I told him that I had no need to think any more, my mind was made up: I didn't want to be a churchman, either as a votary or a careerist. I heard my own voice, as if from a distance, giving cogent if rather incoherent reasons. And finally, with a sense of horror I heard myself thanking my lord abbot for his tolerance and kindness, ending, "But then, of course, you shouldn't have been a churchman at all. You should have been King of Jerusalem."

Guibert was startled but unperturbed.

"Small wonder they think you uncanny, boy! Well, what of it? I should have been better than that bag of sawdust they crowned. I could have held——" He broke off. A glint of self-mockery shone in his eyes. "There again, you young rebel, you have an instance of God's inscrutability of pur-pose. Countless good knights have spent their fortunes, shed their blood, starved, and suffered pestilence in attempts to free the holy places from the defiling hand of the infidel. Yet—and I've seen this myself a dozen times—even the wind will work against them. And when at last, despite everything, victory *is* obtained, fools and poltroons are permitted to fritter it away and all's to do again. And a new mass of poverty-stricken, hungry, plague-stricken enthusiasts will fling themselves forward, crying as we did, '*Deus vult*'—God wills it—and having said that, you have said all." He shifted his leg an inch, wincing at the movement. "And it may be that God wills you should cast yourself upon the world. Who am I to gainsay it? The world may have need of you." His voice briskened again. "But I am not dismissing you. I want no

36

trouble with your father. If you obey me you will go from this room and across to the infirmary, where Brother Ambrose will find you useful employment. Do you understand?"

I did, perfectly. At Gorbalze the infirmary lay separate and at some distance from the main building and had its own entrance. Brother Ambrose, the infirmarian, was as deaf as the biblical adder and took no notice of anything or anybody outside his own province. I could walk out by the infirmary gateway where there was no porter's lodge. Father Simplon would hear that I had been ordered to the infirmary, Brother Ambrose would never know that I was sent there; it might be weeks or months before the community at Gorbalze woke up to the fact that it was one novice short. I was going to drop away as unnoticed and unmissed as a leaf from a heavily foliaged tree.

Looking back, I realise that Guibert taught me, without homily, without stripes, a profound lesson in humility.

Two

Berengaria's Fool

This fragment of the lute player's story is related by Anna, Duchess of Apieta, natural daughter of Sancho, King of Navarre.

It was I who found the singing boy, Blondel, playing his lute for pennies in the market place. It was I who took him up to the castle.

Nowadays I derive much of my entertainment from my memories and the speculations and deductions that arise from them. And sometimes I carry my thoughts to the most fantastic conclusions and say to myself, Good God! Not only would so many lives have pursued a different course, but the whole campaign that they call the Third Crusade might have been otherwise if I hadn't chanced to walk abroad in Pamplona that morning.

Easy enough for me to walk out when and where I would. I had, very probably, more liberty than any other female creature in Navarre, for poor women have duties that bind them and rich women are fettered by convention. The rules that govern women are based upon fear, fear of rape, fear of robbery, fear that the woman herself may have a roving eye. Well, nobody would rape me, twisted, warped thing that I have been from birth, with my back curved like a bow and my head seeming to grow out of my chest; it was as much as most men could do to look at me without recoiling; and nobody, in Pamplona at least, would dream of robbing me, for apart from respect for my rank, most people were scared of me and thought me a witch; as for my roving eye, nobody cared where it alighted. What difference could it make?

What difference could it make? I will tell you.

I saw the crowd and heard some notes of music and hobbled up to the edge of the throng. Naturally I could see nothing; but after a moment or two the crowd in front of me began to move backwards and, since I stood my ground, split out on either side of me. I realised why. A little man, not much taller than I, was going round holding out his hat; and those who had pressed forward most avidly to share the entertainment now pressed with equal vigour backwards in order to avoid paying for their pleasure. In the space thus cleared for me I could see a shaggy brown bear tethered to one of the market-place hitching posts; and between the bear and me stood the boy, carefully shrouding his lute with a piece of sailcloth.

The matter of first impressions has always been of interest to me. When one sees another person for the first time one is actually seeing with one's physical eyes the other's physical

40

form. That never happens again. Always after that first moment one's eyes are clouded or distorted by what one knows or what one imagines. That I have proved in my own person. People seeing me for the first time are horrified and repulsed; yet the people who live with and know me are not. The words "use" and "accustomed" leap to the mind in this connection, but what is use and what is custom save the seeing beyond the purely physical? I am as ugly at the hundredth time of seeing as at the first; Berengaria is as beautiful at the end of a year's looking as at the beginning. Nothing has changed save the eye of the beholder; and that, with longer acquaintance, has lost its first sharpness.

To that first glance, unclouded by knowledge or emotion, the boy made an instant and interesting appeal. He did not look like a strolling player; he was very shabbily dressed, but there was a curious look of breeding about him. His hair, cut short, page-boy fashion, was very fair, straw-coloured in the sunshine, and in marked contrast with his tanned skin. His eyes were light, too, and if there had been nothing else noticeable about him they and his very fair hair would have set him apart. But the most striking thing about him was his lack of interest in the situation. Obviously he had done the playing and the little man who was his partner was now attempting to wrest payment from the crowd, but he took no interest in that part of the business. His lute shrouded, he walked towards the bear, which greeted him ecstatically, rearing upon its hind legs, lifting its forepaws, and almost embracing him. He fumbled in the breast of his shabby jerkin and produced an apple, which he placed in its groping paws, rubbed the bear behind the ears, and then stood, remote, detached, waiting.

The little man, observing me, thrust his hat under my chin, and I fumbled in my *aumônière* and found a silver piece and dropped it in.

"God bless you, lady; the blessing of heaven upon you, lady," he gasped, and returned to his pursuit of more elusive customers.

I hobbled forward and addressed myself to the boy, who turned to me immediately with courteous attention, which was followed by a flash of repulsion, which, in its turn, gave way to that look of pity which the sight of me often inspires in people of the gentler sort.

"You play very well," I said.

"It is most kind of you to say so," he said, and made me a bow which no courtier could have bettered.

41

I was, for no reason that I could have named, disconcerted, at a loss for words. I had heard a few notes of music, paid my coin, offered an entirely gratuitous compliment; I should have turned then and hobbled away. But something held me.

"And the bear," I asked, "what does he do?"

The boy's face darkened.

"He dances," he said shortly. "And he balances a ball on his nose."

As he spoke he stepped backwards towards the bear and again laid his hand behind the animal's ears; and the bear again raised itself, put its paws on his shoulders, and thrust its long muzzle into his neck.

"He loves you," I said.

"Poor brute, yes! I believe he does." The musical young voice was rueful.

"And why does that cause you regret?" I asked. It seemed to me a most obvious question, but the boy looked at me with astonishment, as though I had said something profoundly startling.

"How do *you* know I regret it?" he asked with the slightest possible emphasis on the pronoun.

"By the way you spoke," I said.

"Well," he said, and this time I could tell from his voice that he was about to say something very confidential, "to tell you the truth, I do regret it. This bear has a hard enough life without being hurt in his feelings. I was a fool .... When I fell in with Stefan I was sorry for the bear and did my best to ease his lot. Now, as you say, madam, he loves me; and when I leave Stefan he may miss me." The grey eyes looked at me dubiously; the wide mouth curved into a wry self-derisory smile. "Stefan holds that animals aren't human and therefore don't have any feelings. I don't tell him that I stay with him for the bear's sake. But that is so."

"Why don't you buy the bear from him and then leave, taking it with you?" I asked.

He laughed. "That is my dearest dream—though what I should then do with the bear I cannot imagine. But you see, the bear dances and I play—and Stefan makes the collection. Now and again, at a wedding, for instance, I receive something for myself. Given time, old Snout-face, given time," he said, turning to the bear and fondling it again, "we'll get away."

It was at that moment that the idea came to me. I thought of Berengaria, of her waiting ladies, Catherine, Pila, and

42

Maria, shut away up there in the seclusion of the bower; I thought of Coci, our late lute player, so suddenly and so tragically dead.

I said, "I could put you in the way of earning a gold crown. There are ladies in the castle who would appreciate your music."

The castle at Pamplona stands on a mound above the town, protecting, threatening, as you choose to think. I saw the boy look towards it, towards the grey stone walls and battlements outlined against the sunny blue of the sky. I saw him change colour under his tan.

I misunderstood. I thought that he was nervous at the prospect of playing before a more sophisticated audience.

"They are bored," I said. "They will be easily pleased. In fact, you will be doing them, as well as the bear, a kindness!"

He looked again at the castle and then back at the bear and finally said with an air of relief, as though the burden of decision had been lifted from him:

"We shouldn't profit. Stefan would claim the payment."

I put my hand on my *aumônière*, feeling rich and powerful.

"I will give Stefan a gold piece too. One for him and one for you. Will that persuade you?" And without waiting for an answer I turned about and looked for the little man, who was now returning, rather dolefully counting the coins in his hat.

"For a gold crown," I said, "can I hire your boy for an hour?"

"Lady," he said, "for a gold crown you can have him and me and the bear for a fortnight."

"I said the boy for an hour," I said sharply. I took out the gold piece and held it towards him. He took it, thanked me, spat on it and put it in his pocket, and then, calling to the boy that he would meet him there in an hour, went hurrying off to the tavern on the other side of the market place.

"I am at your service," the boy said, and he tucked his lute under his arm and began to walk beside me, curbing his lissom young stride to match my hobble. Before we were out of the market place, however, a little burst of noise broke behind us. The boy turned about sharply and exclaimed, "There, that is what I mean!" in a voice of furious disgust. I turned, too, and saw that about the tethered bear a small group of children had gathered. Some, with sticks in their hands, were poking at the bear, while those unarmed stood farther off, jeering and throwing little stones. The bear, now

43

upright, now on all fours, was lunging at his chain, furious and impotent.

"Stefan never thinks," said the boy angrily. "I'm afraid I'll have to bring the bear with me." He turned and ran swiftly towards the hitching post, pushing the children aside. I watched and saw how the animal changed moods, from fury to fawning, stood up and licked the boy's ear, and then dropped down and back, padding along behind him like a dog.

We must have made a strange-looking trio as we moved, at my slow pace, towards the castle.

I tried to engage the boy's attention and by talking put him at his ease. I am usually adept at that since nobody is immediately at ease in my presence, but the boy answered me shortly and absent-mindedly; and it seemed to me that as we drew nearer the castle he moved more and more reluctantly, until when we came to the dusty slope immediately before the drawbridge it was I, slow as I was, who seemed to be forcing the pace. Finally he halted altogether and stood looking up at the castle's towers and ramparts, and I could see that he was now very pale under his tan and that a fine dew of sweat had broken out on his brow and on his upper lip.

"Don't worry," I said. "I am more critical of music than any of those within, and I think you play beautifully. They'll be delighted with you and probably make a great fuss of you. And if the princess chooses to reward you herself, don't be silly enough to say that I have already paid you."

His face momentarily lost that look of a man bearing physical torment and he gave me a knowing, conspiratorial grin which revealed his white teeth and deepened the sun wrinkles about his eyes. Then the tortured look resumed possession.

"I'm not frightened," he said, "though I am grateful to you for trying to dispel the nervousness which I should no doubt be feeling if I had time to think about it. The fact is, madam, that I am terribly torn in my mind. I want to get us"—he laid his hand between the bear's ears—"out of Stefan's clutches, and the gold piece would take me a long way towards that end. But I don't want to go in there." He nodded towards the castle.

"Could you tell me why not?" I asked.

"I could," he said, and again that very engaging grin shone across the misery of his face as the sun will sometimes on a winter's day flash out across a sullen landscape. "And then you would think me mad as well as ungrateful."

"Shall I guess?" I suggested lightly, trying to help him. "A fortuneteller at a fair when you were a little boy warned you to keep away from castles because unless you did a stone from a rampart would shatter your brainpan, or a drawbridge would collapse under you and you'd drown in the moat."

He threw back his head and gave a great crow of laughter, and between the sun wrinkles his astonishingly light clear eyes looked at me with amusement, and with pleasure, and with relief. Then, with that same abrupt transition to gravity, he said:

"It is quite as silly as that. I'll tell you. Last evening when we arrived there was a red sunset and I looked at the castle blocked in all black and solid against the glow. And I felt that I was not seeing it for the first time and that it boded me no good. It was like recognising an enemy. I imagined that we—Stefan and the bear and I—would have a poor reception in Pamplona, perhaps be chased out of the town. And here I am, invited to enter the castle itself and superbly well paid to do so. Is that just an accident?" He looked down into my face with an earnest scrutiny which made me uncomfortable.

"I don't know," I said. "I can assure you that no ill awaits you within. In what we call the Queen's Tower there are four ladies who lead a dull life and who would welcome diversion. And the bear could go into a kennel and have a pot of honey—they like honey, don't they? But," I added, "I have no wish to persuade you to enter against your will. You must decide." I looked at him and was immediately the victim of a quite crazy impulse. I am ordinarily a little mean about money because, although I have plenty, I am saving towards an end.

"Look," I said, "if it eases your bother, here is your gold piece. Take it and your bear, and go away and avoid whatever it is that threatens you if you enter."

He looked at the coin I proffered but made no move to accept it.

"You mock me," he said a trifle sullenly. "And you have already paid Stefan! To cheat and take charity because a castle looked black against the sunset would be ridiculous. I'd remember and scorn myself as long as I lived. If you please ... " he said, and with the same incongruous grace with which he had bowed when I first praised him, he stood aside

45

and indicated that I should lead the way across the draw-bridge.

Pleased that my little plan to relieve the tedium of the bower was going, after all, to succeed, I led the way in; and once inside, the boy shed his uneasiness and began to look about him with interest. We went to the stables and saw the bear safely kennelled, and I sent a young groom running to seek honey and gave another the strictest instructions that the animal was not to be teased or interfered with.

"You're very kind," the boy said in a warm, friendly voice.

I remember thinking how wrongly he judged me. A genu-inely kind person is kind to everyone; I am not. Something in me—the devil, perhaps—makes it possible for me to be kind only to those who are, if but temporarily, in worse plight than my own. A clumsy young page in disgrace, a young esquire homesick in exile, Blanco, our eunuch, dogs, mules, donkeys—to these I was invariably kind. Ordinary people I could only treat with kindness when they were sick or miser-able and therefore pitiable. And that, of course, was easily understandable; for of every ordinary person, even if it were only a washerwoman, provided she were healthy and formed like a human being, I was jealous.

As we crossed the dusty tourney field on our way to the Queen's Tower and the boy told me that I was kind, I knew perfectly well that a year before I should never have dreamed of bringing him up to the castle in order that Berengaria and her ladies might enjoy his music. A year ago Berengaria, superbly beautiful, legitimate, Father's favourite, adored by everyone who saw her, had been to me the epitome of all that was enviable and hateful. A year ago I should have listened to the boy's music and selfishly delighted in the thought that here was something which I had enjoyed and she had missed.

II

What had happened in the last year to change my attitude towards my half sister was that she had fallen in love, so completely and so apparently hopelessly and in such a ro-mantic kind of way that ever since the evening when she had told me about it I had found it possible to regard her almost as though she were a person in a song or a story.

At Pamplona, immediately after Easter each year, a trial of arms always known as the Spring Tourney was held, and

Father had for years made a point of inviting the most famous knights and of providing the most extravagant prizes, so the event was well renowned and well attended. Sancho, Berengaria's brother (known as Sancho the Bold to distinguish him from Father, who was called Sancho the Wise), took especial delight in producing, if possible, some specially famous contestant, and this year had managed to bring to Pamplona one who was most often engaged in serious warfare and had little time to attend tournaments in outlying kingdoms—Richard Plantagenet, Duke of Aquitaine, eldest surviving son of the King of England.

In many courts his arrival would, I suppose, have caused a ripple of excitement amongst the ladies, but it so happened that in our bower I was the only one who took any interest in jousting. Berengaria was a little shortsighted and found a tournament a blur which was watched at the cost of dust in the nostrils and in the hair, and of din which made her head ache. Pila freckled very easily and preferred to stay indoors; and Catherine had once watched a tourney in which a knight of whom she was fond was killed. Only on the rarest occasions would they venture out into the ladies' gallery, a section of the battlement overlooking the field and always punctiliously prepared with a canopy and flowers and pennons for our occupation. I loved the tourney, enjoyed watching all the famous men and learning their names, nicknames, and histories, but I was self-conscious about being in the ladies' gallery all by myself; I could imagine a visitor going home and saying that the gallery at Pamplona had nothing but a monkey in it! So unless my other half sister, Blanche, happened to be home on a visit from her convent, or one of the other ladies offered to accompany me, I usually watched from a far less favoured and conspicuous spot, amongst the grooms and kennel boys and any scullion who had managed to evade his duties for an hour. Apart from being less noticeable, it was more interesting because the menials always knew everything about all the contestants, and many a choice bit of gossip did I pick up as I watched.

On the third and last day of this Spring Tourney the day chanced to be warm and balmy and not too bright, and Berengaria said that she thought it would please Father if we all ventured out; so, armed with scarves to wave and flowers to drop upon the victors, and followed by pages carrying cloaks in case it turned chilly and jugs of wine and little cakes for our refreshment, we set out from the Queen's

Tower to the tourney field and climbed into the ladies' gallery.

The display that morning was most impressive and exciting and I watched enchanted. We saw one knight in plain black armour acquit himself superbly, unseat his opponent, and then make his horse dance skilfully backwards while he acknowledged the cheers and the shouting in which we women were joining, waving our scarves and tossing our flowers.

In the midst of the excitement I felt a pull at my sleeve and heard Berengaria saying, "Anna, who is he?"

"I don't know," I said, and went on with my cheering. Then two young squires came forward and assisted the knight to doff his helm, and without turning my head I said:

"Oh yes! I recognise him. He is Richard Plantagenet and reputed to be the best knight in the world."

Bareheaded now, the man rode towards us, his horse mincing and curvetting. We screamed our acclamations and threw down the last of our flowers. He lifted a hand and moved his head in salutation and acknowledgment and then rode away.

Berengaria made one of her obvious, flat little remarks.

"What very red hair he has," she said. She spoke casually, and the words might have been taken as an expression of disapproval.

That evening when it was time to retire Berengaria surprised me by asking me to perform the offices of waiting woman. Usually the four of us took turns at this duty and adhered strictly to the rule because Catherine, Maria, and Pila were all inclined to be jealous about it. They regarded that hour or so of intimacy as a privilege. I, to be honest, did not. By the end of the day I was often more tired than I would admit, and it bored me to stand brushing and brushing Berengaria's hair and gently reviewing the day's events, which were seldom very exciting, when I could have been reading by the last light of the guttering candles in the bower. Sometimes I renounced the "privilege" to one of the others, though that was a bother, too, because I had to rotate the favour and often there were arguments and squabbles.

This evening wasn't even my ritual turn and I said so. However, Berengaria said, "But I want to talk to you, Anna." So I repressed a sigh of weariness, and when old Mathilde, Berengaria's woman, arrived with the fresh candles and led the way into the sleeping chamber, I rose and followed. As we helped Berengaria out of her long linen undergown and her shift she reached down, bundled them together, and held them out to Mathilde.

"Wash these," she said.

"Tonight?" Mathilde asked, astonished. "Why, my lady dear, they were fresh only last week."

"Wash them," Berengaria repeated simply. Mathilde, wooden-faced, took them. I knew what was in her mind. She had been waiting woman to Berengaria's mother, who towards the end of her life had been raving mad, and Mathilde was always on the watch for what she called "signs." Berengaria, who was extremely lovely to look at and Father's favourite child, was completely spoiled and given to whims and fancies; and whenever she expressed one, or fell into a temper, or suffered from a headache or a mild fit of low spirits, Mathilde said, "Ah, poor dear, that's a sign." Now she blundered away with the linen which had been worn for a week only and must be washed overnight; and I knew that she would weep into her washtub because such an unreasonable demand was "a sign."

"That's got rid of her," Berengaria said. "No, Anna, leave my hair for a moment." I had taken brush in hand, prepared to get through my duties as expeditiously as possible. "Sit down."

I sat down on the foot of her bed, and she seated herself on the stool near the shelf which bore her silver mirror—part of the loot which our grandfather had brought back from his crusade. Mathilde had already loosened her hair and it now fell over her shoulders, a dark, rippling, silken cloak which ended well below the edge of the stool. She pushed it back from her face with her hands, which she then cupped around her chin, resting her elbows on her knees.

"Now, Anna, you know everything. Tell me everything you know about that knight we watched this morning—the one with the red hair."

"I told you his name. He's the Duke of Aquitaine, and if he outlives his father he will be King of England. He's supposed to be the strongest and bravest fighter in the whole of Christendom.

"Young Sancho persuaded him to come and joust here; he's been trying to get him for years, but generally he's busy with real fighting. I think that's all I know."

"I want him for my husband," Berengaria said.

That made up for the hours and hours I had spent in this very chamber, brushing that mane of hair and listening to trivial chat. I was seventeen years old, almost a year younger than Berengaria, and for the whole of the seven years which I had spent at the court in Pamplona the matter of Berengaria's eventual marriage had been a subject for talk, gossip, and speculation. Sancho, our father, was a man of peculiar notions. Unlike most men of his rank, he had married for love,. and although his lovely wife had become a madwoman he had, with the exception of one piece of dalliance, of which I was the unfortunate result, remained faithful to her. And he had openly stated his intention of allowing all his children to choose mates for themselves. Berengaria, whose beauty had been bruited abroad for many years, had been much sought after, for even princes who must marry within the royal degrees desire to find wives as attractive as possible, but Berengaria had refused every offer so far made, and Father had done nothing to direct her fancy.

Blanche, whose behaviour I privately considered to show far more of the "signs" Mathilde watched for, had at the age of fourteen betaken herself to the convent at St. Lucia, where she lived as a lodger. She was always just going to become a novice, but she never did. Every now and then she would come back to Pamplona and give us little pious talks about the dedicated life, eat her head off, sit out a tournament with me, indulge in a mild flirtation with any man who happened to be handy, and then suddenly retreat again into her convent. And Young Sancho spent his time going from court to court, from jousting to jousting, always falling madly in love with some completely ineligible lady and then falling out of love again. And Father seemed not to mind at all. A very strange royal family, with two princesses who should have been betrothed long since and a prince who showed no sign of his responsibility to the succession.

And now here was Berengaria announcing her choice of husband at last; and I, her crippled, bastard half sister who had spent the first two days of the tourney in company with the grooms and scullions, was forced to say:

"Oh dear. That is awkward. The Plantagenet is betrothed, and has been for some years, to the Princess Alys of France."

Most young women, at such a moment, would have looked disappointed. Berengaria's expression remained almost unchanged. That grandfather who had gone on crusade and brought back many of the ideas and furnishings which made the castle at Pamplona so luxuriously comfortable had one day mentioned, in the presence of Berengaria's mother, then a young woman, the Saracen habit of slitting the eyelids of girl babies in order to give them that doe-eyed, flowerlike

50

look. He said that this custom was responsible for the placid, unchanging beauty of Eastern women, which remained, he swore, unaffected even by a thrust of sword or spear through the body. Years later, when he was dead and Berengaria's mother had borne a girl baby, this curious crumb of information had floated to the surface of her demented mind and nothing would do but that this child's eyes should be slit in the Saracen fashion. And it so happened that Father, back from his Sicilian campaign, had brought with him a captive, a Saracen physician and surgeon—for in the East the two trades are combined—who was competent to perform the operation. Apparently what our grandfather had said was true; much of the expression of the human face does derive from the eyes and the muscles around them. Berengaria's mouth could smile, or pout, or look sour, but her eyes always remained wide open, flowerlike, denying all human feeling; and unless you were used to her and observed her very closely, it was almost impossible to perceive what, or how, she was feeling.

So now she did not look disappointed, or even concerned.

"Who told you that?" she asked.

"Nobody," I said. "But they were talking about it—the servants, I mean—while I watched the tournament yesterday and the day before."

"Then it might not be true?"

"It might not, but it most likely is. Servants' gossip, though sometimes overcoloured, is generally reliable in content." I spoke of what I knew.

"I'll ask Father to see to it," Berengaria said.

I felt a little sorry for Father; it seemed hard that Berengaria, having waited so long, should now have taken a fancy to a man already betrothed; but that was hardly my business.

"Shall I brush now?" I asked.

We spoke no more on the subject until I was about to leave her, when she said, "I should be obliged to you, Anna, if you would treat this as a confidence. I told you because, after all, you are my sister and I wanted to tell someone."

I assured her that her secret—if such it could be called—was safe with me, as it was, for I had seen enough of gossip and the results thereof during my seven years at court; moreover, I am not by nature communicative. I wished her good night and left her.

Her choice of myself as confidante neither pleased nor flattered me—as she had said, she wanted to tell somebody and had chosen me because I was less likely to gossip and at

51

the same time more likely to supply information than any other of her ladies; and having her secret in my keeping did not immediately alter my attitude towards her.

But gradually, over the next month or so, my interest in the affair and in Berengaria herself developed. She had, as she had mentioned her intention of doing, spoken to Father, who had also heard of the engagement between Richard and Alys. "Alas, sweetheart," he said, "you are too late in the field." But under pressure from Berengaria he admitted that this betrothal had been made long since and that it did seem a little strange that, both parties being now well past marriageable age, it should not have been honoured. And finally he committed himself to making inquiries, and what he found out certainly hinted at a curious state of affairs.

Apparently Alys had been sent to England as a mere child in order that she might grow up in the language and customs of the country of which she was to be Queen and had been reared with the Plantagenet children. Ever since she had become nubile there had been repeated efforts on behalf of her French relatives to arrange for the marriage to be celebrated, but always some excuse had been made and the date pushed forward to some unspecified future. Richard, who was on the worst of terms with his father—that was in the Angevin tradition—never went to England, and the young King of France, Alys's brother, had recently expressed himself as dissatisfied and puzzled by the whole business.

This much information Father had obtained by indirect means, and when he reported it to Berengaria she said, "Then there is hope for me! Will you, Father, as you love me, approach Richard himself?"

Father was very reluctant. "To mention such a matter hints at ignorance both of circumstances and procedure. We in Navarre are not so cut off from the world as not to know that the betrothal has never been officially broken, nor so unmannerly as to disregard it." But Berengaria was very insistent and Father, who had never been able to deny her anything, gave in and sent Cardinal Diagos to Richard's headquarters at Rouen with orders to make discreet inquiries and, if the omens were propitious, to put out a cautious feeler.

Diagos, a most courtly and diplomatic old man, must have mistaken the propitious moment, or else the subject was a very sore one indeed, for he sent back and reported that at the first experimental mention of Alys's name the Duke of Aquitaine had reached for his battle-axe and roared out, "By

Christ's Holy Cross, I swear that the next man to mention marriage to me I'll split from chin to chine!"

That most effectively quelled further inquiries. But side by side with this report Diagos sent home a new rumour which said that Henry, very much at odds with Richard over the administration of Aquitaine, was planning to marry Alys to his younger son, John, with whom he was on good terms. It sounded as though Henry regarded the girl as a prize for good behaviour, not as the partner in a firm betrothal.

Berengaria chose to regard this as a most encouraging report and began to beg Father to write to Richard himself.

"He cannot cleave you if you remain in Navarre," she said, and no one could tell whether she meant the words as a joke or as one of her matter-of-fact statements, for her voice and her face remained expressionless.

Father demurred, but by this time he was beginning to be interested in the mystery which seemed to lie behind this situation—as indeed I was myself—and after a little persuasion he did send the letter. The reply was prompt and blunt. It said that the duke was betrothed to Alys of France; and it added, obviously in reply to some remark in Father's letter, that the inquiry had given no offence, since were the duke free to do so he would marry any girl who brought in her hand a good dowry to contribute to the crusade he was planning.

Over this letter Father and Berengaria fell out. Father was furious. "It's the letter of a huckster and an insult to the unfortunate woman he is to marry. It implies that were he free he would sell himself to the highest bidder, as Jaime of Alva sells the services of his Arab stallion. You are well out of any further dealings with a man of so coarse a nature. This letter is typically Angevin; they're upstarts and hucksters to a man and would sell their own mothers to serve their greeds." He said a great deal more, all of it derogatory, and then added, "Let me hear no more about it. This ends a matter that should never have been begun."

"Father, it practically invites you to make him a dazzling offer. And if you love me you will take it in that spirit and write back and say that if he will marry me instead you will make a good contribution to his crusade."

Father looked at her with disgust and dismay. He smashed down his fist on the letter. "You mean to tell me that after *this* you want him? How can you be so shameless? And so stupid? With beauty like yours are you to go to a man who thinks of nothing but the bag of gold round your neck? Good God, Berengaria, you must be mad!"

He had spoken the forbidden word. And while he stood ashamed, his face contracted by the pain of his thoughts, Berengaria began to shed her beautiful tears.

Whether it was a gift from God or a mere result of old Ahbeg's little knife, she could cry as I never saw another woman do. She never sniffed or snuffled, her face didn't screw up or her chin pucker and shake; water just welled into her great wide eyes and spilled over her cheeks and she looked just like a rose with early-morning dew on it. Nobody could resist her then, though any woman watching her must needs be jealous of such a rare weapon. I must admit that she used it rarely, which was perhaps rather clever of her, and hardly ever on anyone except Father and Young Sancho.

However, on this occasion she had come into opposition with something which in Father was not just a formal pattern of behaviour but a deep and vital principle, his chivalry. This whole affair, in his opinion, was a subtle slight upon an innocent lady. I knew that if he had ever been in Richard's place and had to write that letter he would have found it incumbent upon himself to add to the brief statement of his betrothal the courteous, even if untrue, comment that he loved Alys and regarded her above all women.

Father was a romantic and an idealist; that was why he had cherished his mad Beatrice; why he had let his daughters grow up unbetrothed. It was also why he tried to make up for his one most human lapse by treating me so well, making me a duchess in my own right and arranging for my financial independence.

And it is a fact that when the gentle sentimentalist really digs his heels in he can be firmer than the worldling whom worldly arguments sway.

"I'm very sorry, Rosebud, but even to pleasure you there are some things I cannot do. And to offer to buy a man from the lady to whom he has given his troth is one of them."

"But I can never marry anyone else. Unless I marry him I can never be married at all."

"Don't talk like a fool," Father said, beginning to take refuge in rage. "You've never even spoken to the man or looked him full in the face. I'm a bigger fool ever to have lifted a finger to humour such a fancy. And you won't persuade me by crying. You're just obstinate—obstinate as an iron mule—and I ought to take a stick to you."

I approved of that expression, "iron mule"; precise and picturesque, it was worth remembering.

That evening Berengaria began a siege on the time-honoured method of starving one's opponent out, but it was original in that this time the besieger did the starving. She refused breakfast, dinner, and supper; she said she felt sick and the thought of food nauseated her. She ate, at any time, less than anyone I ever knew and would refuse any dish over- or undercooked, or one that had caught the smoke from the fire or been too much handled in the serving. Woe betide the page who sneezed or coughed while he was handing her a dish, however choice; the food was quite discounted, the sneeze or the cough sharply reprimanded, and the dish sent away untouched. I had known her, through an unfortunate combination of circumstances, to sustain life for thirty-six hours on a single crust and be none the worse. So I did not concern myself over a twenty-four-hour fast. Nor was I unduly perturbed on the second day. She must surely, I thought, come to her senses—and one of the senses was the sense of hunger. But no! The third day came. I watched, sceptically, minutely; Mathilde went in and out of the chamber where Berengaria had taken to her bed, but I would swear on the Cross that no crumb was smuggled in. And by the end of the third day her face showed the pinch of hunger and had the wan, hollow look which beggars' faces have.

Pila, Catherine, and Maria, though they made many inquiries and many suggestions, tended to keep their distance lest the illness from which their princess was suffering—as they thought—should be contagious. Only Mathilde, who would have faced the plague itself for Berengaria's sake, and I, who knew what it was all about, would enter the inner room. And my interest, I must confess, was almost purely academic; how far would she go, I wondered, to force Father into taking action against his will? I was interested to see what starvation felt like and managed, without drawing attention to the fact, to abstain from food myself for twenty-four hours. And I did become desperately hungry; so hungry, in fact, that I went to the kitchen and broke a piece of meat off a joint of venison on the spit—it burnt my fingers and my tongue and tasted like heaven and made me most profoundly sorry for beggars.

Yet there was Berengaria refusing calves'-foot jelly flavoured with fresh oranges, turning her head away from bowls of bread and milk flavoured with a clove-stuck onion, rejecting even a glass of sweet red wine from Portugal. An iron mule indeed!

On the morning of the fourth day Mathilde came out of Berengaria's chamber into the bower and said:

"Whatever she says and against her orders, if need be, I'm going to tell the King. This is no ordinary sickness. I know the signs. And this is the way her mother, God rest her sweet soul, started. His Majesty wouldn't take up arms in the cause of Castile against Aragon, and my lady took it very hard and wouldn't eat from Ash Wednesday till the Friday following. And then I took a clothes peg and forced her jaws apart and poured in the broth so that she must either swallow or choke on it. And she lived and was crazy thereafter, to my everlasting sorrow and his too. Now the same thing has happened; I know the signs. But this time I'm not taking a clothes peg. Whatever it is on the *mind* has got to be lifted, or she'll be like her dear mother. Now, Your Grace, would this come better from me or from you?"

In my own way I loved my father. I blamed him for my crooked back and for my illegitimacy, but on the whole I enjoyed being alive, my eating and drinking, my comfortable way of life, my money, my freedom. In the circumstances he had done very well by me. And very often he amused me too.

I felt that it would be better for me to go and talk to him than that Mathilde, with her morbid memories, her grudge, and her grim predictions, should do so. So I went to his private apartment and told him that Berengaria hadn't taken sup or crumb for three whole days and that it was my belief that she would not until he had written to the duke again.

The Plantagenet's reply this time pleased Father and displeased Berengaria. It read, "To my dear brother and friend of Navarre, greeting. Being bound, I cannot be your son-in-law; but when you choose him take care that he be a man of your mind and mine, and we will set your standard, with ours, on the walls of Jerusalem."

"You see," Father said.

And Berengaria said, "I see."

It was to me that Father said, "But being bonded, *why* doesn't he marry the wench? He's always at war and he's heir to England. Why doesn't he marry and get her in whelp? By God, the whole thing is a mystery. I think I'll concoct an errand and send Saturnino to London. He'll sniff it out if anybody can."

56

So Cardinal Saturnino had departed for the court at Westminster with orders to make himself especially agreeable.
And the court at Pamplona had settled down. Something had
broken in Berengaria. She was no longer the beautiful, pampered favourite to whom all things came as by right. She was
the little girl who saw, at the fair, some bright and glittering
toy and cried unashamedly, "I want that, I must have that,
that is for me!" and then learned that an earlier customer
had reserved it.

And I, who had for seven years, ever since I understood
our positions, envied and even hated her because she was
straight and beautiful and a real, royal princess, had come in
the end to pity her. Because it was so plain that nothing gave
her pleasure; nothing mattered save that great redheaded,
hard-hitting Plantagenet who was bonded to Alys of France.

III

It was because I pitied her that I took Blondel home with
me. Emerging with that thought out of the past and into the
present, I became aware that the boy had been saying something about the new way of building outer walls with project-
ing towers.

I said rather vaguely, "And where did you learn of such
things?" He said a little shamefacedly that he had once
watched one being reconstructed.

"One day," I said, "I am going to build a house. With a
glass window."

And why, I wondered, did I say that? I had never mentioned that intention to anyone; but I had, very often, when
the other women were talking about the future and making
much of their hopes and plans, clutched the thought to me,
as one clutches the covers on a cold and draughty night. One
day Father would die and Young Sancho would be King, and
then he would marry and his Queen would certainly not want
me about the court. But I wouldn't be either pitiable or
self-pitying; I'd be off to my own Duchy of Apieta, where
under the sheltering shadow of the great castle I could build
a house without defences, a comfortable house to live in,
with a glass window and a shelf for my books and an herb
garden to scent the air outside the door.

And no steep stairs, I thought grimly, for we were now at
the foot of the Queen's Tower and the steep, badly worn
stairs loomed before me. I knew very well that Blanco, who

57

lived in the little kennel-like room at the top of the flight
would come at a call and carry me up as easily as though I
were a kitten, but such a procedure humiliated me and
never, in health, did I take advantage of his services. Alone,
I swarmed up on all fours like a crab; under observation I
climbed slowly, clutching the wall and hating the place
where it had worn smooth and slippery. Conscious of this
and not wishing to make a spectacle of myself before the
boy, I signalled to him to go ahead of me. "Up here," I said
and waited.

Any other boy picked up in the market place would have
obeyed me thoughtlessly; but this boy, with a little smile
stood aside, flattening himself against the turn of the wall.
Where had a strolling player picked up such manners? I
wondered as I set myself to face the climb.

At the third step he was just behind me, and at the fourth
his hand was under my elbow. I had a vision of that hand as
it had lain between the ears of the bear—slim, young,
browned by the sun, and, I remembered, most noticeably
clean. My elbow fitted into the palm of it and with each
painful effort I made it was there, warm, supporting, surprisingly strong.

Was it at that moment that I fell in love with him? I do
remember that, mounting the stairs, helped by his hand, I
was stricken anew by the cruelty of my plight. Oh, I thought
to be ordinary, shaped like a human being, to be looked at
and touched with affection, desire! Even this crumb of contact, offered from a courtesy tainted by pity, was so sweet!

As we neared the top of the stairs Blanco, the huge black
eunuch, looked, like a guardian dog, out of the tiny room
not much larger than a kennel, in which he spent his doglike
life. He looked at me with dumb reproach because I had
eluded him and gone out alone. He loved to be taken into the
street as escort; it was one of the diversions of his life, which
was, if possible, more dull and monotonous than that of the
ladies he guarded. And at that moment the sight of Blanco
blended most dismally with my secret feelings. He was a
man, unsexed by his fellow men; I was a woman, unsexed by
God. We would both have been better dead.

"Blanco," I said, "I have forgotten to order my new
slippers. Run, will you, and say that I have decided upon red
leather lined with wool. The apprentice who brought up the
patterns will know which I mean."

His great black face split like a melon with joy at the

prospect of a thirty minutes' jaunt into the sunshine. The boy and I went on into the solar.

Having since seen the interior of several castles, I realise—as I did not then—that we women of the court of Navarre lived in circumstances of almost oriental luxury. Our grandfather had brought back with him from the East not only the disease which finally killed him but a great baggage train of treasures as well as a number of notions about comfort. There were no rushes on our floors, instead a great plenty of dark, silky rugs; there were divans, soft with cushions; rich curtains shrouded the bare stone of the walls, and we five women owned among us no fewer than three silver looking glasses.

The occupants of the solar were sitting exactly as I had left them: Catherine, Maria, and Pila idly stitching away at a piece of tapestry. The fourth corner, mine, was held up for their convenience on a stool, so the whole picture was spread out, easily visible, and even as I moved into the room, crying in a lively way, "Look what I've brought you! A lute player who knows all the prettiest songs," I glanced from habit at the amount of progress they had made. They were always at work on their corners in a very lackadaisical fashion, and it amused me to neglect mine for a week and then to sit down and work for a couple of hours in a frenzy of energy and so keep myself even with them. It was only this spirit of competition which made the stitching at all tolerable to me. Their morning's work, I noticed with satisfaction, had done very little to advance them.

As I spoke they raised their heads and with little exclamations of excitement and satisfaction began to scramble their work together. Blondel made another of his accomplished bows and then took the sailcloth wrapping from his lute. He looked quite composed now, and I saw that he had spoken truly when he said he was not nervous.

I signed to him to wait.

"Where is the princess?" I asked.

"Within," said Pila with a casual nod towards the inner door. "Our chatter disturbed her; she said her head ached and she didn't desire anyone's company."

"It's to be hoped," Maria added, "that she won't hear the lute. The boy should play very softly."

Catherine, who disliked me very much, and between me and whom a little nagging war of attrition, waged with sharp words, went endlessly on and on, said, "A lute, of all things!"

The simple phrase was an accusation of tactlessness laid

against me. For lack of any other reason to explain their mistress's recent decline in spirit, the ladies of the bower had fastened upon an explanation much to their taste—which was, in general, morbid. She was heartbroken, they believed, about the death of old Coci, our late lute player. I had never seen Berengaria show any particular sign of affection for the old man, nor, I think, had they; but his death had happened by a most timely chance to occur just when things began to go wrong with her. I was in a position to know that at the time when Coci died everyone in the court could have dropped dead in a moment without causing Berengaria a pang; however, I subscribed to the legend because, satisfied with that, they refrained from further probing; and, living as we did, privacy was a rare and hard-come-by commodity, greatly valued, even when purchased by a falsehood.

I hobbled across to the inner door and opened it, looking into the dim apartment which formed an anteroom to the sleeping apartments. It had a very small window and the tower wall rose sheer outside, so the place was never light enough to work in without candles. In very cold weather, when the solar remained cold despite the heaped fire, we did sometimes use it as a sitting place; with a fire and many candles it was cosy and pleasant. On a bright morning it was inexpressibly dreary.

Berengaria sat on a bench, her elbows on her knees, her chin propped on her linked hands, her eyes fixed on the section of the wall outside the window. She did not turn her head when I opened the door.

"Berengaria," I said.

"Oh, you're back, Anna. What do you want?"

"I want you to come out and listen to some music. I heard a boy performing very well in the market this morning and I persuaded him to come back."

"My head aches," she said, "and the last thing I want is to listen to music."

My natural impulse was to say, "Very well, don't," and to go away and shut the door. But my newborn pity for her was still young and vital at that time, and there were other considerations. In a small confined community a settled melancholy in its most important member is not conducive to cheerfulness amongst the others, and the general atmosphere in the bower had of late been very miserable. So I said:

"Do come and listen. He plays very well, and we shall all enjoy it more if you are there."

She rose with a sigh of resignation and walked into the

solar. I stayed to close the door behind her, and when I turned to face the room I had a feeling that something had happened. Berengaria had halted a few paces inside the room and was staring at the boy; her eyes remained expressionless, but her mouth, which sometimes betrayed her, was open. Across the room the boy was staring back at her with astonishment and admiration writ large on his face. But that was not to be wondered at, for she was extremely beautiful. We were, of course, accustomed to her loveliness, but anyone seeing her for the first time must pay that tribute of the moment's awe which one pays to a cherry tree in full bloom with the sunlight on it, or to one of those scarlet-and-gold sunsets.

The tension was eased when Berengaria took her seat. I signalled to the boy to begin, and he proceeded to play as vilely as anyone I ever heard. Fumbling, missing notes and striking false ones, and singing in a sharp falsetto voice, he blundered through a song and I saw Catherine catch Pila's eye, pull down the corners of her mouth as though she had tasted a lemon, and make a grimace towards me. Ever since Berengaria had chosen me for her confidante and seemed to seek my company there had been jealousy in the bower, and Catherine, least good-natured of the three, had shown her feelings quite plainly. Her grimace now was less a comment on the boy's appalling performance than a criticism of me for bringing him in.

At the end of the first tune I managed to catch his eye and give him a smile of encouragement, and I willed with all the power in me that he should play better. He grinned at me in a way that made me think of someone grinning through physical torment, shook back his hair, and broke into the amusing ditty of "The Dame of Chalon and Her Little Red Hen." That was better. And when he proceeded to play "The Death of Chloris" he was performing almost as well as he had done in the market place.

When that extremely heart-rending song reached its end Catherine said in a voice of sharp challenge:

"Can you play any of Abélard's?"

Abélard's songs were by that time so well known and so popular that spit boys hummed them as they basted the meat and 'prentice boys ran errands to their rhythm, and the question, tossed out that way, was deliberately insulting.

The boy said calmly:

"Yes, my lady. And one I know that is not so well worn as the rest. Shall I sing it?"

He looked to the strings of his lute, moving a little farther into the room as he did so, and then, leaning one elbow against the back of a settle in a pose suddenly easy and negligent, sang:

"To be thy servitor is all I ask;
  To see thee happy is my only joy;
  To do thy bidding is my chosen task.

"Know'st not, thy smiling is my sun at noon,
  Thy voice, e'en when it chides, my singing bird,
  Thine eye, however bent, my sun and moon?

"The world is nought, the future harsh and drear;
  Frail is our hope and threatened is our joy.
  But ah, how dear thou art, how dear, how dear!"

With that song—and it was set to very moving music—he had conquered the ladies, even the prejudiced Catherine. When it ended they broke into little exclamations of praise.

Berengaria said, "You play very well. Thank you. And now you must take some refreshment," and she signalled to Pila, who, because she was greedy by nature and had once run her own household and understood not only food itself but the peculiarities of cooks, had been put in charge of our commissary. And then she called me to follow her and walked into the inner room.

"Anna, where did you find him?"

"In the market place."

"I want him to stay here."

"To take Coci's place?"

She nodded.

Now surely for a strolling player with a bad master to be at one stroke promoted to the position of lute player to the princess was a fantastic piece of luck. Henceforward the boy would have a roof over his head, be certain of three good meals a day, be warm in winter. And he would change a bullying master for a kind and indulgent mistress. Could fate be kinder?

But I thought of Coci, cantankerous, peevish, and yet somehow servile; kindly treated and yet somehow negligible, of little more account than a pet dog or monkey; playing the same tunes over and over to the same audiences; sorting out the silks and the wools for the embroideries; bearing the brunt of the ladies' little moods of irritability; listening to

62

their complaints about their little ailments; running their little errands. Something rebelled in me at the prospect of the boy reduced to that. Instead I saw him out in the open, leading his bear from market place to village green, always welcome, always with a new audience, a free unmastered man. And I preferred that picture of him. Security can cost too much.

I was too wise to voice even a hint of opposition directly.

"Do you think he's good enough?" I asked. "Out in the open I was deceived; indoors I found him fourth-rate. And Father promised to bring a musician from Aragon, you remember. Is it worth bothering with meantime?"

"I don't care if he never touches his lute again," Berengaria said quite vehemently. "I want him to stay here."

"But why, then?"

She was silent for a moment, looking down at her hands. Then she said, "I'll tell you, though I have no doubt you'll think it sounds mad and begin to share Mathilde's suspicions." (That surprised me; Mathilde was very outspoken to me but very discreet, I thought, with Berengaria herself.) "I want him to stay because I once dreamed about him."

"Never having seen him?" I asked sceptically.

"I recognised him at once. I almost exclaimed when I saw him. And he must stay because the dream made him of the greatest importance to me."

My attitude towards dreams, like my attitude to many other things, was extremely mixed. Dreams and their meanings formed one of the main topics of chatter amongst the women of the bower, and I was often bored by the trite, arbitrary explanations assigned them. "Dream of water and you'll hear from your lover ... " Now why should that be? And what happened if the dreamer had no lover? On the other hand, warning and prophetic dreams had an acknowledged place not only in secular literature but in Holy Writ as well; how else was the Holy Child saved from Herod's infanticidal hand but through Joseph's dream orders to make the flight into Egypt? One must keep an open mind on these matters. And my interest was sharpened by the reflection that never before in all our lives together had I heard Berengaria mention any dream of her own, or known her to regard anyone else's with other than mild derision.

"What was the dream?" I asked.

"Oh," she said with an air of making nothing much of it, "it was one of those nights when I couldn't sleep and Mathilde insisted on giving me some of her poppyhead physic. I dreamed I was in the oubliette, down in the dark with the toads and rats. Very horrible. I felt so completely abandoned. I realised for the first time what the name means. I was really forgotten and I knew I should stay there till I died. And then I looked up to where the light showed and I saw that boy. He had a little posy of flowers in his hand and he was looking at me kindly. He threw down the flowers and immediately I was free, above ground, out in the open sunshine. I no more knew how I got out than I knew why I was there in the first place. But just now, when I saw him and recognised him, I knew that it was important that he shouldn't go away again. Sometime, somehow, I'm sure he'll do me a good service."

The simple, undramatised, unemphatic manner of her telling the dream seemed to give it force. I felt a little cold shudder run over me. Was it mere chance that I had gone to the market this morning? Mere coincidence that I had conceived the idea of bringing the boy back with me?

"There's a bear in the case," I said lightly, trying to dismiss my metaphysical thoughts. I told her about the bear.

"Oh, buy the bear then, Anna. Anything so long as he stays. Here, take my purse."

She handed her purse to me in a very lordly way, and I took it with justifiable misgiving. She was extravagant about clothes and other feminine accoutrements and the worst accountant in the world, so she was always hard up and almost always in debt. I was not at all surprised, upon looking into the purse, to find that it contained less than would purchase an ordinary milking goat, let alone a trained performing bear which could dance and balance a ball on its nose.

"Very well," I said, "I'll see what I can do. I'll even lend you a crown, for there's nothing but trash here. But mind, it is only a loan."

I gave her back her purse and went into the solar. The ladies were clustered about the boy, plying him with things to eat. Catherine was even tying a bunch of ribbons to his lute.

"The princess has asked me to pay you," I said to him; and to the women, "Wouldn't you like to see the bear?" I explained where we had kennelled it, and they ran off as excited as children.

Alone with the boy, I looked at him again, pictured him in Coci's place, pictured him as his own man.

"The princess," I said, "has suggested that you stay here and be our minstrel. Would you like to do that?"

"No," he said without a moment's hesitation. "I would

not." He then looked very contrite. "Such a prompt refusal of such a kind and flattering offer sounds ungracious and ungrateful. I'm sorry, but I don't think it would suit me at all."

"If you decide to stay," I said, forcing myself to be fair to Berengaria, "the princess will buy the bear so that it stays with you." And then, to be fair to the boy, I added, "But if you prefer to go I will give you the money to buy it yourself."

"That," he said, "would be perfect. Snout-face and I would be grateful to you all our lives. Madam, you are so kind and so generous I cannot find words to express my gratitude."

I looked at him again and thought of Berengaria's dream. She had dreams of being in a dark place, therefore it followed that lightness would figure in the symbol of liberation. Or it might be that in her sleep-weighted, poppy-drugged mind some memory of a pictured angel stirred. The boy was rather like a young male angel. She hadn't dreamed of this particular boy, I thought, stiffening my mind; any fair-haired, light-complexioned boy would have reminded her of her dream and thus been in a degree recognisable. It was all very silly and very superstitious.

"I think you chose wisely," I said. "By which I mean, of course, that you chose as I would have done myself."

He laughed. "A nice definition, madam."

We settled the price of the bear after a little amicable argument; he was plainly anxious not to impose upon me, and I was anxious that he should have enough to make the purchase without condemning both himself and the bear to immediate starvation. And as he held out his slim brown hand with its long delicate fingers to take the coins I remembered how it had cupped itself under my elbow and the feelings the touch had roused in me. I thought, Perhaps it is just as well that you are leaving. I might, God help me, get to be rather silly about you, and that would be terrible.

I wasn't wise enough then to know that such a thought shows the thought-of thing to be an already established fact.

He thanked me again and kissed my hand and went swiftly and lithely to the door. I heard him humming on his way down the stairs, and I was glad that we hadn't succeeded in trapping the singing bird and condemned it to a cage where, though safe and cherished, it would rub its wings and pine for the open sky.

I decided not to tell Berengaria of his refusal to stay until he had had time to collect his bear and get away from the castle. So I sat down at my corner of the piece of tapestry and began one of my furious onslaughts. I had done only about six stitches, however, when there was a noise on the stairs, and in a moment or two the door was thrown open and there was Blanco, holding in his arms the boy who had so lately gone out of the room and, I thought, out of my life. His forehead was broken and bruised and blood was running down into his eye. His upper teeth were clenched down on his lower lip, and all round his mouth there was a wide white band of pain. As I ran forward he looked into my face, loosed his teeth, and said with wry humour:

"I told you this place boded me no good!" And promptly swooned.

Catherine, Pila, and Maria were clutching one another and gabbling like geese. They had been at the bottom of the stairs when he missed his footing on the worn steps on the curve and tumbled down at their feet.

Blanco laid him down on the divan nearest the window and, rolling his wide-whited eyes, said, "Boy wouldn't faint for knock on head. Other thing." He ran his big black pink-palmed hands over the limp body, shaking his head from time to time until at last he said with a certain satisfaction, "Ah. Ankle broke. Listen."

We could all hear the nasty little grating sound.

Pila with a little scream turned away. Maria said, "I'm going to be sick." Catherine put her arm around Maria and said to me with a defiance that seemed irrelevant, "When he broke his head the blood went on her skirt."

I didn't feel quite steady myself. There is something so completely against nature in a broken bone, and the little grating noise had hurt me, driven a pain into the lower part of my body and down the inner sides of my thighs. But I reminded myself that men had their bones broken every day and that I was a soldier's daughter.

I said, "Run, Blanco, and fetch Ahbeg. Tell him the princess needs him at once."

Ahbeg was that Saracen physician whom Father had brought back from Sicily and who had fixed the expression of Berengaria's eyes for all time. Father had retained him in his service despite the protests of the churchmen and the peculiarities of the man himself. Not young at the time of his capture, he was now very old, almost incredibly eccentric and fantastically dirty. He lived by himself in a small room over what we called the Roman Gate because there were some remains of a Roman fortress in that part of the castle; and there he cooked his own food—people said that Christian babies formed part of his diet—and brewed his physics. Until lately he had always accompanied Father on his campaigns, but this year when the Aragon campaign began he had said he was too old to travel any more and he had given Father some pills, which Father called "horse-balls," to swallow each ninth day. "They will preserve your health," he said, "and should any accident befall you I will be with you immediately, even if it cost me my life." Father had gone off contentedly; he really had the most implicit faith in Ahbeg. I had been angry and accused Ahbeg of gross ingratitude; but at this moment I was very glad that he was in Pamplona and not in Aragon, where Father, according to report, was enjoying superb health. But the old man would only stir from his cell for Berengaria, whom he regarded as part of Father. We had proved that some weeks earlier when Pila had swallowed a fishbone which stuck in her throat. I had been obliged to retrieve that with my scissors!

So now, remembering that I had demanded Ahbeg's presence under what amounted to false pretences, I made the boy as comfortable as I could, at the same time trying not to disturb him, since the setting of a bone even by the most skilful hands is a painful business and best done while the sufferer is unconscious, and then went and called Berengaria. She did not inquire whether the boy had agreed to stay or not, taking it for granted that no one would refuse an offer of such security, and I did not open the subject. She went and stood by the couch and looked down at the unconscious face with a gaze that was intent, if expressionless. Then she glanced round and summed up the situation of her ladies and said mildly, "I hope Gaston retires when you marry him, Maria; knights tend to come back to their wives in worse case than this. As for you, Pila, I thought you went through the siege of Jaca!" Those words, spoken by me, would have given the ladies grave offence and had many small, exasperating repercussions; from Berengaria they were accepted with proper meekness, and within a few minutes Pila and Maria were restored, hovering about, offering suggestions and endeavouring to appear helpful. And within another few minutes Ahbeg arrived.

I realised when I saw the old man that he had had some justification in refusing to accompany Father; he had aged since I last saw him and was now very old, very thin, and very frail. Palsy shook his head and his hands, and from the manner in which he peered at his patient I judged that his sight was failing. He managed, however, to convey his displeasure at being brought from his retreat to minister to a menial, and even as he confirmed Blanco's diagnosis of a broken bone he muttered that any barber would have set it.

"And lamed the boy for life?" Berengaria asked.

Thus informed that the boy's future activity was of importance to his mistress, Ahbeg set to work with his pastes and his bandages and his little wooden splints, and worked with such skilful speed that he had almost finished the job before the boy opened his eyes and groaned. He set his teeth into his lip again. Of all the faces clustered above him, his eyes sought out Berengaria's. As though in response to a question, she leaned forward a little and said almost exactly what I was preparing to say: "You've had a slight accident. But don't worry. The bone has been properly set. And we will look after you." She laid the extreme tip of her finger on his arm and smiled down at him with her own peculiar smile, which always seemed to have something of secrecy about it.

Poor little lute player. I suppose he was lost from that moment. And the strange thing was that she was a woman more sparing of caresses, less lavish with smiles, than any I ever knew.

IV

Of that one day, from the moment when I heard music in the market until the moment when, after long discussion, we decided that the boy had better be bedded in the solar, my memories are perfectly clear and vivid, easily sorted because they run upon a single theme. But of the time that followed, my memories are confused and muddled and untidy, like the back of my tapestry work. Blondel—that was his name, he said—suffered no setbacks and made an ordinary recovery and was soon hopping about on a crutch rigged from a broomstick. Catherine, Pila, Maria, old Mathilde, and even Blanco vied with one another in spoiling him and trying to do him little services. I would gladly have tended—and spoiled—him myself if I could have looked after him singlehanded, but I have always found it tedious to match my behaviour to that of a mob of people, so I stayed a little apart, though I talked to him, and when I discovered that he could read I let him use my books. I had nine of my own already. Berengaria also held aloof, inquiring each morning, very sweetly, how his ankle did and whether he had slept, and thereafter ignoring him.

The bear remained in the kennel, for suddenly in the afternoon of the accident, while we were still discussing whether Blondel should be carried down and laid in the place where the pages slept, or housed in Blanco's little room, which had the advantage of being near the guardroom (with the obvious disadvantage too!), or accommodated in the solar, the boy suddenly remembered the animal and its master. So I sent Blanco down to the tavern to find the man and strike the bargain; and what that bear really cost me I shall never know, for Blanco stayed in the tavern, too, and came back with no money but with a skinful of ale. In many places he would have been thoroughly beaten, but discipline was generally lax in Pamplona.

During all his convalescence I never spoke to the boy of his decision not to stay with us, and he referred to it only once, obliquely, when we were talking of something else and he quoted, "Against the worst of fates the best of men is powerless," and then, pointing to his ankle, said, "Like me!" I waited until he could dispense with the crutch and hobble, and then limp, and then at last walk, and every day, half in hope and half in fear, I expected him to mention the imminence of his departure. Divided, by this time, in my mind, for the thing which I had never dreamed could happen to me had happened; I had fallen in love.

Except upon the tongues of the troubadours this matter of unrequited love makes tedious telling, and even in my own memory I take care to skip lightly over the sore places. Most women, I imagine, suffer this form of sickness at one time or another in their lives, and not one woman in a thousand marries the man she takes a fancy to. Thrice blessed is she who finds herself able to love the man her father chose for her. I believe there are a few such. For most this thing called "romantic love" is the matter of a song, a poem, an ache in the breast in springtime, a sigh, a few tears in the dark. But, lightly as one may regard this matter of loving and being in love, it has its own agonies; and though I had resented and hated the deformity which precluded me from ever being possessed by a man, from ever having a husband and children of my own, I had long ago decided that this same deformity, having bred cynicism and common sense in me, had at least saved me from the ailment called love. And lately, since Berengaria had lost her heart to her redheaded prince and was suffering from lovesickness with all its concomitant woes,

I had rather smugly congratulated myself that this, at least, was a misery I had escaped. Now here I was, waking each morning impatient for the first sight of a boy's young face; jealous, in secret, of everyone who went near him; cherishing, remembering, enhancing every word we exchanged; touching a book as though it were holy because he had handled it. And another symptom of my state was the access of sympathy, as opposed to mere pity, which I began to feel for my half sister.

I still found it hard to understand how one could feel overwhelmingly regarding a man of whom one knew so little and with whom one had never exchanged a word or an idea; but I did thoroughly understand how it was that, having felt the fascination of one particular person and allowed his form, or image, to take grip on one's imagination, the idea of marrying anyone else must needs be extremely repugnant. Berengaria was right, I thought, to put up a fight for what she wanted. In her place I would have fought, too, with just such relentlessness. But of course there was nothing for me to fight about; I had been excluded from those lists from the beginning. I could only preserve—with scrupulous care—my ridiculous secrets, snatch at what small joys came my way, and watch with impotent fury my beautiful, my dear, my singing boy precariously balanced between the bog which was the bower and the rock that was Berengaria.

v

Sometimes in the past I had thought it a harsh custom which decreed that well-born boys should be snatched from their mothers' arms and from the company of women who had tended them since their birth and be sent to serve their time in the halls of strangers. Now I saw the sense of the custom. Without it no boy would grow into a man fitted for a man's world. There is something pervasive and absorbent about a company of women. They receive, they smother, they infect with their own softness. Why, the very pages who attend women are gentler, softer-spoken, more interested in clothes and gossip and less in pranks, altogether more effeminate than those who wait upon men.

Some of this may be due to unwitting imitation or the desire to please, but mainly it is due, I think, to a peculiar attitude of mind in women. They are capable, as men are not, of ignoring the sex of a person who, by reason of age or station, is ineligible for loving. I will guarantee that if five men, living together as we five women did, had had introduced into their company a young female who, though pretty and of engaging manners, was entirely ineligible, they would yet remain conscious of her sex. They would not immediately try to turn her into a male. Catherine, Pila, and Maria did try, from the first, to emasculate Blondel.

"Dear boy, these silks are tangled; sort them for me."

"Blondel, tell me, which girdle is better with this gown, the rose or the yellow?"

And worse things, worse. They talked before him of things they would never have dreamed of mentioning before a man, or before any boy who was to become a man, not merely of shifts and body linen, of bowels loose or bound, but of the punctually recurrent headaches, the pains under the girdle, the ankles that swelled with the regularity of the moon's changes. Nothing was hidden.

I was sickened; shamed for myself and for them. My body was crooked and unfitted for love, but my mind and my feelings were, I had discovered, those of an ordinary woman. I could look on this boy and feel not only love but fierce desire; and often I did so look, when I was safe from observation, and gave my imagination rein, and thought how it would be if I were straight and comely and he my lover. Into such a dream would break some woman's voice, smearing, denying, reducing; making what to me was a man as sexless as Blanco, the eunuch.

In such moments of torment I wished that he would leave. Take his lute and go out into the world and find some girl who would regard him as I did and discover his manhood. But the desire to escape seemed to have died in him, and I could never bring myself to say the resurrecting word. On the other hand, he did not succumb easily to his enchantment. He would often absent himself—giving the bear as an excuse— and go off to the stables and come back smelling of horses, leather, oil, and liniment. The ladies would then wrinkle their noses and complain. And I would lean as near as I could on some pretext or other, savouring the male, outdoor scent which fitted in with the vision I cherished of another Blondel and another Anna.

I knew quite well, of course, why he remained with us almost against his will. He was in love with Berengaria in much the same dumb, hopeless fashion in which I was in love with him and in which she was in love with Richard Plantagenet. Sometimes I thought it was a little comic that there should be three of us under the same roof, all suffering from the same ailment, and all keeping our secrets so well. And sometimes I thought, All this wasted love, all this yearning towards someone who is yearning for someone else, like those figures perpetually pursuing one another around the Greek vase which Grandfather brought home from the East. All that was lacking to make the circle complete was that the Duke of Aquitaine should lose his eyesight and his senses and fall in love with me!

I had to make what mental sport I could out of the situation because I dared not be sorry for myself. For Berengaria, as the year moved on and no news came from England, I did feel sorry, and for Blondel I did suffer vicarious agonies.

Whatever could be done for Berengaria had been done or was being done. For me nothing short of rebirth could do anything. But as the year moved downhill into autumn and my love-sharpened eyes saw new lines carved into the boy's face and I daily witnessed the deadly soft encroachments of the bower, it did occur to me that something might be done to save him. He was young, his attachment to Berengaria was completely fantastical; if he could be got away, restored to a normal manner of life, he would be saved. He'd fall in love, I thought, with the first pink-cheeked, round-bosomed girl who looked at him kindly.

I realise now that I was guilty of supreme egotism, attributing to myself and to myself alone devotion and deathless fidelity and underrating these qualities in others. Be that as it may, during the early days of that autumn I began to cast about me for some way of getting Blondel out of the bower—with his own consent—and away from Berengaria. And it is odd to think that Maria's wedding dress put what I thought was a tool into my hand.

VI

Somewhere, somebody of inventive mind had introduced a new "laced" dress to the feminine world. This did not mean that the dress was trimmed with lace but that the bodice was cut so narrow that the front had to be opened to get it over the wearer's head and then the aperture was laced up with a cord or a ribbon pushed through a number of little pierced holes. This made the gown so close-fitting that it clung to the breasts.

Some high dignitary of the Church—I think in Paris—had been shocked by this fashion and had complained to the Pope, who had promptly ordered that sermons be preached against it in all churches. So one Sunday morning we in Pamplona who had never seen or heard of a laced gown until that moment sat and listened meekly to a homily against this "immodest, iniquitous, and most unchristian device which provoketh vanity in women and lust in men."

Maria was making preparations for her wedding at that time. She had been betrothed as a child and had seen her bridegroom only once and had then been somewhat shocked to find that his mouth would not close over his teeth. So her attitude towards her nuptials was practical rather than romantic, and she craved for a spectacular wedding. The idea of wearing one of the new laced gowns appealed to her, but none of us had the remotest idea how such a gown was made or what it looked like.

On the Monday, Maria very cunningly sought out the preacher of the sermon and begged him to tell what a laced gown was, as she was very anxious to avoid the sin of wearing one unwittingly. The poor man was seventy years old and had probably never looked comprehendingly at any woman's gown, but he was anxious, naturally, that Maria should avoid falling into sin through ignorance, so he showed her a little woodcut which had come with his instructions to preach the sermon. And the woodcut showed Satan, the father of all lies, wearing a laced gown and exposing a pair of breasts of which any nursing mother would have been proud. Maria brought it home with her to show to the rest of us so that we also might be kept from sin.

If you put your thumb over the leering, grinning face of Satan, the effect was extremely seductive; and though I didn't say anything about it, I did wonder to myself, Is this wise? Or kind? So many celibate priests, some of them young. But perhaps they wouldn't think of blotting out Satan with their thumbs!

Having studied the woodcut thoroughly, we wrapped and sealed it and sent it back by Blanco.

Maria then tackled her sempstresses, none of whom, of course, had seen a laced gown or even the picture. And when she was tired of explaining she appealed to Blondel.

"You can draw, can't you? Could you draw just the dress, with the shape and the holes and the cord, to explain how it should look? You needn't bother," she added kindly, "to draw the old devil."

73

Blondel shot me a glance as he so often did. And oh, how dear those little private jokes were to me.

He set to work and eventually handed to Maria a sketch which was, she said, exactly what was needed. Two other sheets of paper he screwed into balls and flung into the fire. They missed the flames and fell into the ashes and later, watching my moment, I retrieved them.

One sheet did show the old devil wearing a laced gown, but not a leering, grinning devil; something far worse, a more dreadful, brooding, tormented devil, consumed by his own fire, gnawed by his own worm. A very nasty little picture indeed. The other sheet bore a lot of straight lines and angles which bore no resemblance to anything I had ever seen.

The picture of the devil I smoothed out and laid flat in a book. Let him think it had been burned. The other I kept openly. And next time I found him alone I produced it and said, "Maria's wedding gown! She will look beautiful." I hoped that would make him laugh, and it did.

"I thought I burned it," he said.

"What is it?"

"Just an idea I had. A sort of mangonel, but improved. You see, I thought that if the stone were projected from *here*, instead of *here*, as is customary, it would fall with greater force. The tendency of everything is to fall, and this way it works with the pulley instead of against it. I don't suppose you know anything about mangonels. . . ."

"I can see what you mean. Like this. . . ." I took up two balls of the tapestry wool and threw them, one after one fashion, one after the other.

"That's it exactly," he said, delighted by my readiness to understand.

"You shouldn't have thrown this away. I shall show it to Father. It's virtually a new weapon and the man who brought it to bear against his enemy would have the advantage."

"May I see it again?" Innocently I handed it to him, and he looked at it for a second and then with a movement that I could not forestall laid it on the very heart of the fire.

"You silly young fool," I cried, bitterly angry because I had imagined Father taking him out of the bower, installing him in the armoury, lavishing favours and rewards on him. "Oh, why did you do such a cursed, stupid thing?"

"I thought I had burnt it," he said. "It was just the idle work of an idle moment. I was only curious to see if the idea were good or not."

"And it was. Even I, ignorant as I am, could understand it. ... Oh well," I said, recovering my composure, "you can easily draw it again. I'm sure Father would be delighted with it."

"Please," he said, "forget all about it."

"Why should I? A mangonel of that pattern throwing a lead ball or a great stone, would be far more deadly than the old kind."

"And who but the devil would wish to make a tool that made war more bloody than it is already?"

"Anybody but a fool. There's a righteous side in every war."

"And could you always be certain that your new tool was in the hands of the righteous, even if you were competent to judge the comparative claims to righteousness?"

"I suppose not always. But Father—this war in Aragon, for example——"

"But the Aragonese think their cause is righteous. Otherwise they wouldn't fight. No nation of people ever went to war believing they were wrong. How could they?"

"Well, then, what about the crusades?"

"They seem righteous to us because we are Christians, but I daresay that to those who follow Mahomet——"

"Be careful," I said. "In another minute you'll be guilty of heresy." I spoke in the rallying tone which one uses when arguing with someone one loves. But he stopped and looked down at his hands in obvious confusion. I then became a little confused myself and took refuge in blunt speech.

"About wars, right or wrong, I know very little. But one thing I do know, Blondel, and that is that it is very wrong for a man of your quality and attainments to waste his life playing sentimental tunes and winding wools and drawing wedding dresses."

Hot angry blood flew to his face, but he said quite calmly:

"Don't we pray for contentment in the state to which God has called us? It may be virtue in me."

"And it may be that in the confusion of our minds we fail to distinguish between the will of God and our own wishes."

At that moment Berengaria and Maria entered the solar; Maria carried Blondel's drawing. Berengaria was saying:

"But think how dreadful it would be if they refused to marry you because they disapproved of your dress!"

"They couldn't make me take it off, could they? Not in church. Besides, the bishop often games with my father and owed him a thousand crowns when last I heard the reckoning. It would ill become him to complain. My mother may, but I shall point out to her how useful it will be later, when I am feeding my baby."

Well, if it were the will of God that Blondel should listen to talk which proved that they looked on him as sexless, it wasn't mine. I made up my mind that evening that I would get him out of the bower.

I made my first move by gaining his interest in the plans for my house, and when we had talked about it and he had drawn several sketches I said:

"Blondel, if the princess would give her permission, would you go to Apieta and overlook the building for me—or at least get it started? You understand what I want and you could explain the plans as nobody else can." I hesitated for a moment and then decided to make play with my infirmity—I think for the first time in my life. "It is hard for me. I couldn't stumble about where they were digging foundations, or climb a ladder to see the roof laid aright. I must have someone I can trust implicitly."

"Yes, of course." He looked thoughtful and then pleased. "I always had an interest in building. Yes, I think I—it'd be a change from the wool winding."

"I'd give you absolute authority," I said. "You could lodge in the castle, and when you'd given your orders for the day you could take a horse and ride in the woods. The woods around Apieta are very beautiful and full of game. Will you do it for me, Blondel?"

"Yes," he said, this time more firmly. "If the princess will consent."

I had a most beautiful vision of him restored to man's estate, his heart mending under the influence of new interests and fresh surroundings. The house would take some time to build, and by the time it was finished he would be fond of it, perhaps, and if he wished to stay in Apieta I would stock a farm and suggest that he look after it for me. He loved horses, so I would hire Jaime of Alva's famous stallion and breed foals of the kind now so highly thought of because they combined the swift grace and spirit of the Arab with the strength and staying power of the European horse. And one day Blondel would marry and have children to whom I could stand as godmother.

When my turn for brushing the hair came round I took it, and I sedulously spent some moments in chat in order to get Berengaria into a good mood. Unfortunately she began to talk about Maria's wedding, which was now imminent and not, in the circumstances, the most cheerful of topics for the princess. However, I said several bright, silly, slightly malicious things and managed to make her laugh, and then I said, "Berengaria, I have a favour to ask you."

"You've done me many," she said amiably. So I proceeded to tell her about my house and my wish to borrow Blondel. I made it sound a very temporary arrangement indeed.

"Oh no," she said as soon as I finished speaking. "I can't spare him. I told you why."

"But surely, just to go to Apieta—two days' ride away. I only want to borrow him. He could come back at once if you needed him for anything."

"I want him to stay here. The world is full of architects and builders, Anna, proper ones. Get some of them to work on your house."

I was so angered by her refusal that I almost snapped out that that wouldn't get Blondel out of the bower and out of the reach of his enchantress; but such a remark would be fatal because it would render my next attempt suspect, and I knew that if this failed I should make another and another. I should never rest now until I had removed him. But I hadn't forgone hope of getting him to Apieta, which would be the nicest way of removing him because then I should remain in touch with him and perhaps one day join him there. So I dug in my heels; I could be stubborn too.

I pleaded for a little while and then I realised that we were merely repeating ourselves, so I laid down the brush and said:

"If you will be so selfish and unhelpful to me, Berengaria, next time Father wants to marry you off to somebody I shan't say a cool sensible word for you. I did last time. Father takes quite a bit of notice of what I say." That wasn't boasting; it was true.

"About that you must please yourself, Anna. I shall either marry Richard or stay as I am, and nothing you say or refrain from saying will make any difference."

That angered me again. "I suppose you realise," I said hotly, "that I have but to open that door and shout what I know to make you the laughingstock of Christendom."

"Oh, Anna," she said mildly, "if I could spare the boy I would, and you know it and know why I can't. What difference does a threat make?"

All at once I understood about martyrs—people about whom it had often puzzled me to read. Berengaria had in her

77

the stuff of which martyrs are made; not necessarily great holiness or mysticism, just a boundless obstinacy. I could well imagine her in Nero's Rome, saying, "I *am* a Christian, so what difference do the lions make?" And no wonder martyrs were so often persecuted! By God, I would have liked to persecute Berengaria just then. I would have liked to beat her over the head with the hairbrush, take her by the shoulders and shake her till her teeth rattled. But I held onto the tail of my temper again and said:

"Look, I promise that if you get yourself magicked into the oubliette I'll fetch him back and give him a posy so that he can magic you out." I thought that might make her realise how silly the whole idea was.

"Oh, I know. Put like that, it sounds ridiculous. But I feel so safe with him about. That dream was a warning, and he did come and I did recognise him. And I feel that if there were a fire or a flood or anything like that he would be the one who would save me. And since that is so, I'd be a fool, wouldn't I, to let him go off to Apieta to build a house which anybody else could do equally well?"

I could see that there was no moving her. To my immense chagrin I found tears of impotent fury filling my eyes.

"Why, Anna," Berengaria said quite kindly, "why do you take this so hard? What can it matter who builds your house so long as it is built? Or why not build it here in Pamplona? Then he could attend to it."

"Suppose I say it's my whim! You should understand that. Why should every whim of yours be pampered? I want my house to be in my own duchy and I want Blondel to build it. He's clever and inventive; he could build well. But no, because you have a poppyhead dream he must stay here and wind wool, as though that were a proper occupation for a man."

"Blondel isn't a man. He's just a singing boy——"

At that I knew that I had better get out of the room before I said or did something regrettable.

Afterwards, when I was calm enough to think it over and not get blind with red rage at the memory of Berengaria's voice saying, "Blondel isn't a man," I realised that though I had been defeated the effort hadn't been entirely wasted. I knew something now. I had been stupid not to think of it before. The way to get Blondel out of the bower was to find him an errand which could in some way be linked with that dream of hers. His only value to her was the fact that he had figured in her dream, and if some errand could be twisted into seeming to fulfill that dream she would willingly send him off to the ends of the earth.

I set my wits to work to think of such an errand.

When I told him of my failure to "borrow" him I could see that he was sorry and relieved. The moth which one catches in one's sleeve and removes from the dangerous vicinity of the candle is probably grateful when it finds itself free, disenchanted in the cool dark, but it may be a little regretful too.

VII

Christmas came and Father was home in time to keep the festival with us. Young Sancho was there, too, and Blanche came home from her convent. Outwardly it was a very merry time, and we prolonged the revels until after Maria's wedding. She wore the laced gown, about which I could see nothing very shocking, and the wedding itself was a very grand affair. Free food was served in the courtyard to the poor of Pamplona, and inside the castle we all ate and drank far too much, and those who could danced until they were tired. Blondel played in the hall and, secure amongst a crowd of people, I could look at him more closely than I dared in the bower, and I noticed that he seldom took his eyes from Berengaria. I could guess his thoughts—they were my own. And Berengaria's too!

When at last, with that odd mixture of the ceremonial and the bawdy which is the peculiar mark of weddings, the bride and groom had been locked into their chamber, Berengaria turned to me and said:

"She cares nothing for him, but they are bedded now." She spoke from the bitterness of her own heart, but she spoke for me and for Blondel—for all poor unfortunate lovers the world over.

Immediately after the wedding Father left for his winter hunting at Grania. On the evening before he left he sent for me. The page who brought the message said that it was His Majesty's special wish that Blanco should carry me across to his private apartment. It was humiliating, but a mark of Father's considerateness, for after a light rain there had been a frost and the ground was slippery.

As soon as I was within Father's own most private room, a curiously austere apartment, I could see that something was

79

troubling him. And as soon as I was seated, with my feet to the fire and a beaker of wine to hand, very snug and comfortable, he told me what it was.

"Look, Anna, I'm off to Grania in the morning, and before I go I want to talk to you about Berengaria. I didn't want to spoil her Christmas or the fun of the wedding, but I've heard from Saturnino and I am sure now that there's nothing to be hoped for. He's an old, tried spy—though he'd hate the word—and in his Christmas letter he said that so far as he could see the betrothal was valid and unquestioned. He even went to the length of asking Henry of England about the matter, but unfortunately, just as he broached the matter, Henry was taken with a fit. I'd never heard that he was subject to fits, had you? Apparently it is so. He fell to the floor and began to chew the rushes. So Saturnino retired and abandoned the inquiry. But he assures me that he pursued it in other quarters and that there is no hope."

"And did he connect the fit with his inquiry?" I asked.

"Why no! It was just an unfortunate coincidence," Father said. But he fingered his beard and looked at me a little dubiously. "Saturnino wrote as though it just happened most unluckily."

"Well," I said, "it all sounds very suspicious to me. You mention Princess Alys to Richard and he grabs a battle-axe and threatens to cleave you; you mention the same young woman to Henry and he falls down in a fit. I may connect the two charming incidents because I have a nasty, suspicious mind. Though what I suspect and what I could deduce from them, Father, it would puzzle me to tell you. However, that is neither here nor there. Am I to understand that you wish me to break this news—gently—to Berengaria?"

He nodded. "She'll cry. And to tell you the truth, I cannot bear to see her cry." He looked at me a little doubtfully. "There's something else I must tell you. Isaac Comnenus, Emperor of Cyprus, is suing for her hand. His emissaries will arrive presently. Do you think, Anna, that you could talk her into some sort of sense before they arrive?" He poured himself some wine and drank it as though it were some horrid physic. "I don't want her to be unhappy; I don't want to force her into marriage. I have done, haven't I, all that a man *could* do to get her the man she has a fancy for? And failed. And now, you realise, she is heading for her twentieth year, the loveliest princess in Christendom, and not even betrothed. It's fantastic. I don't want to force her, but I would like to see her married and settled, for if there's one thing really pitiable and useless on this earth, it is an old maid."

Having said that, he realised that he was talking to one who could never be anything else. He was as embarrassed as a ploughboy. I remembered his many kindnesses, his immense generosity to me, and said hastily, "Sire, an old maid is one left over from the marriage market, and since I never went to market it is a term that cannot apply to me. So use that, or any other term, without thought for my feelings, I beg you. One of the reasons I like to talk to you is that you ignore my shape and my sex and my age."

"Your shape, Anna," he said gravely, "is a reproach to me every day of my life. Had I been——"

"A better man," I finished for him, "then I would never have drawn breath. Sire, I assure you that I am grateful, on the whole, for having been alive. The blame for my shape I lay entirely on my mother."

And that was true.

I had the story once from Mathilde when she was drunk. My mother had been one of Queen Beatrice's waiting ladies; not pretty, Mathilde said, but witty. You couldn't be in her company for a moment without laughing. I could well imagine the sensitive, sentimental King, still young, still virile, meeting this laughing, witty lady as he came from the room where his loved mad Queen was confined, and taking her—not out of love or lechery, but as a refuge. She quickened; and the Queen being then so crazy that it seemed she must soon die, my mother was anxious to remain at court—not be overlooked or forgotten. So she had an iron corset made by a blacksmith.

Berengaria's mother lived for another six years. Mine died in childbirth, having safely delivered my crooked carcase.

I understood her motive, but she had never given me a thought; why should I be sentimental about her?

Towards my father who had given me security, rank, and wealth I did feel kindly, so I now hastened to say:

"But you didn't send for me to talk about me and the past. Berengaria's future is our concern. And I must warn you, sire, that she told me only the other day that she would marry Richard Plantagenet or nobody."

"Well, that's just the sort of pigheaded remark I wish you to counter, Anna. Women understand one another; you'll think of things to say to wean her mind away from this idea. When I talk to her I get angry, and then she cries and we get no further. Make the idea of being Empress of Cyprus sound attractive; ask her if she has really thought what being unmarried will mean for her when Young Sancho brings his Queen to rule the roost here—talk about weddings. You know the sort of thing."

In the privacy of my mind I thought that if he had set me to dismantle the castle's Roman Gate towers with no other tool than my bodkin the task could hardly be more impossible. He had called Berengaria "an iron mule," but plainly he had no notion of the extent of her obstinacy. He wanted everything to be easy and pleasant; he wanted to go off to Grania and enjoy his hunting with a free mind, and he wanted to come back to find an amenable daughter, converted by talk! Poor, unpractical Father!

"And while you are on the subject, Anna, you might just hint to her that this time my mind really is made up. There comes a time when a man must see his duty and act on it. Nobody can say I have not been patient and indulgent; she went to stay with Lucia in Rome and had her pick of the Italian princelings; I took her with me to Toledo and Valladolid and she saw every eligible man in the peninsula. I'd have raised no protest if she'd chosen the poorest if I'd thought he'd make her happy. But no! She must needs take a sick girl's fancy to this Plantagenet whom she saw only once, and that at a distance; and I've gone to lengths no other father would have considered, pursuing the faintest hope. And that has wasted precious time. Now my mind is made up. My mind is made up, Anna. Tell her that from me."

I knew he was blustering. And if Berengaria had been amenable and let me fulfil my plans for Blondel, this was the moment when I would have said two things. One, that to force his will on her now was unfair; if he had ever intended to choose a husband for her he should have done it long ago when she was a child without preferences. The other was that it was a tactical error even to mention Isaac of Cyprus while the disappointment over the Plantagenet was still raw in her mind. I could also have said, "What if she is almost twenty? She's lovelier than ever. We have plenty of time." Father, who would always take the pleasant course if he could square it with his conscience, would have shuffled off the whole business and gone off to Grania thinking that everything would work out well.

But, as I had threatened, I held my tongue.

Father, once started on the conventional course, plunged on:

"There's Blanche too. We're riding as far as Garenta together tomorrow and I'm going to talk to her on the way. She is either going to be married or be a nun. I don't mind which—she's free to make her choice—but I'll make clear to her that this hiver-hovering must end. Whoever Sancho finally picks on won't want to find the place full of——" He broke off, conscious of being on dangerous ground again. His face of kindly concern said as clearly as possible: And then there's you, Anna. Oh dear!

"You know," I said, "it would make everything very much simpler if *all* fathers treated *all* their daughters as you have treated me! My future presents no problem. As soon as I can get the work in hand I am going to build myself a house in Apieta, just a small house, without defences, because the castle is so near. And I'm going to breed horses which will sell for fabulous sums of money. And I'm going to have a candlestand so arranged that I can read in bed, and one room with a glass window. And an herb garden. And I hope, sire, that whenever you come to Apieta you will visit me and see how snug and comfortable I shall be—thanks to your generosity."

As I expected, that pleased him enormously. We spoke for a little while about my house, and then again about Berengaria, and I promised to say to her all the things he wished me to say. Then suddenly he said:

"Could you wear this, Anna? My fingers are thickening; Berengaria has plenty of trinkets and it wouldn't be suitable for Blanche."

He held out to me the great, dazzling diamond ring which the King of Sicily had given him in gratitude for his help in that campaign so long ago. The stone was as large as the nail on a man's thumb and was set in a circle of smaller ones, the whole mounted in a frame of the fine pale gold of Kabistan. It was worth a king's ransom—indeed that is what it was, for if the Sicilian forces had not had Father's support the King of Sicily would have lost his throne that time, no doubt about that.

I looked at it covetously. With that in my possession I should be out of the reach of want for all time, whatever happened to Father, whatever happened to Apieta. In Venice where the spice trade from the East was making princes of little merchants, in Rome where the competition in splendour between dignitaries of the Church had inflated prices to absurdity, I could sell that ring for a sum which would keep me in comfort for the rest of my life. Comfort? Splendour!

But something held me back from taking it. After all, he had two legitimate daughters and a son. I muttered and mumbled a few protests.

"I've just decided to be master in my family," Father said. "Anna Apieta, hold out your hand!" I did so, and he tried the ring, first on my middle finger and then, finding it too large there, on my thumb.

Thanking him, I found myself thinking that it was, in the final count, better to have a hold on a man's conscience than on his heart.

VIII

Next morning Father, taking a tender leave of Berengaria, went off to his hunting, and we were left to face that worst part of the winter with Christmas over and Easter still far ahead. Weeks of trying to keep warm; of too close contact about the hearth with a consequent fraying of tempers; of rheum in eyes and nose and limbs; of unappetising, over-salted, overspiced food.

In that season even to walk abroad on a chance-come clement day, well furred and shod and with a full stomach, was to be made miserable by the sight of ragged, blue-faced beggars. At no time is the difference between wealth and poverty so marked as in winter. And though perhaps no one would have guessed it, I was always particularly susceptible to the woes of the poor, especially those who were in any way infirm. There but for the grace of God and the King's tender conscience go I!

This year, however, safe in the possession of the ring, I had no need to be mean. So I laid out certain sums of money, really comparatively small, and opened a little booth between two of the buttresses of St. Nicholas's Church where the poor could obtain a bowl of stewed meat and vegetables and a lump of bread any afternoon between the hours of two and four o'clock. And sometimes, if it were not too cold or icily windy, I would walk down and stand out of sight and watch the food being dispensed.

I was, truth to tell, more ashamed than proud of my charity. Out of my much—so little; a sop to Cerberus. And yet a visit to that booth was entertaining and enlightening. Piteous as the people might be by reason of their circumstances, they were often cheerful and amusing in themselves; and to see the hungry mouths crammed with the bread, the

84

cold fingers closing about the little clay bowls of stew, gave me a distinct, if unworthy, satisfaction.

One afternoon in late January, Blondel joined me as I crossed the drawbridge on my way into the town.

"I must go down to order myself some new shoes," he said. "If you have an errand I can perform for you——"

"That is kind," I said. "Actually I am on no errand. I merely go down because it interests me to see the dispensation of food to the poor."

"At that booth by St. Nicholas's Church?"

"Yes, it's the only one, isn't it?"

"But I've never seen you there."

"Maybe not. I stand on the far side of the porch."

"I stand on the Market Cross—just where you, madam, found me and the bear that day."

"And why are you interested in it?" I asked.

He looked at me askance.

"And why are you, madam?"

"If you'll answer my question, I'll answer yours. That's fair."

"Well, one afternoon the supply of food ran out before all were served. I happened to be passing. And I thought of all the food that is wasted up at the castle—it was just at the time of the Lady Maria's wedding. So now the best of what would be put in the pig swill up there comes down here instead."

"And how did you arrange that?"

"The chief cook is devoured by a desire to read and write. I teach him. He is more stupid than seems possible; he doesn't yet know his alphabet, but he is honest. He picks out the best bits every day and sends down two tubfuls. And somehow I like——"

"To see them enjoying it. It is the same with me. It isn't that I feel generous or patronising; in fact, mostly I feel ashamed that so little sacrifice on my part should mean so much. But just as one likes to see one's guests enjoying one's hospitality—hospitality is so much nicer a word than charity, isn't it?"

"Then you opened the booth in the first place?"

I nodded.

"Why, were you ever hungry?"

"Only by my own whim," I said. "I once fasted just to see what it felt like. And I didn't like what it felt like at all." I hesitated for a moment and then, in an outrush of feeling towards him, confessed.

"That is the bother about pity. I pity hungry beggars because I might easily have been one. It's difficult to decide how much is pity and how much is fear for oneself—pity could easily be defined as the fear for oneself which one feels when faced with another's plight."

"No." He spoke the word with assurance. "That kind of thought is the kind of choplogic, the unreasonable extension of an idea akin to this argument about how many angels could sit on the point of a needle. That is dangerous. It underrates a generous impulse. Any normal person would hate to be hungry, but that doesn't make every normal person feel pity for the hungry. If it did, booths like this would open in every town and village."

We had reached the place where the booth stood.

"It's all very confusing," I said. "Christ ordered us to sell all that we have and give to the poor—adding that they are always with us." I turned the great ring on my thumb. "If I sold this," I said, "it would feed every beggar in Pamplona for a century—and I'd be feeding with them. But if every person who owned a jewel set out to sell it to give the proceeds to the poor, it's self-evident that there'd be no buyers, the market would be swamped."

"That is profoundly true. But that is because men have, over the centuries, built up a whole series of false values. That ring is very beautiful, but it oughtn't really to represent wealth enough to feed all the poor in Pamplona for a century—in itself it wouldn't keep any living creature alive for a day. The truth is that nothing is of any value except the soil which grows things and man's labour."

"Soil and toil; land and hand; mud and blood," I said.

We stood and watched the booth together and then walked slowly back to the castle. I was tired, and presently, sensing this, he helped me along with his hand under my elbow as before. And we talked and laughed as we walked. He did seem so utterly different out of doors. I wished with all my heart as we crossed the drawbridge that Berengaria had let him go to Apieta.

As soon as we were indoors she began to complain about one of the letters which he had written for her that morning. She could read and, pressed to it, she could write quite a tolerable hand, but she was averse to the exercise and before Blondel's arrival I had written most of her letters. Now that was one of his duties, and for the last day or two he had been kept busy acknowledging the presents which various

86

relatives and envoys in distant places had sent her for Christmas.

Whether there was anything wrong with the letter or not I never knew for certain, for I thought it wise to hold myself aloof lest I be dragged in as arbiter, and I did cherish a slight suspicion that she made the complaint because Blondel and I entered the bower together and had laughed on the stairs. Ever since my attempt to borrow him she had been a little wary and had more than once spoken of him as "my minstrel" with a slight emphasis on the possessive.

Blondel listened to her chiding for a moment and then said calmly, "May I see it?" He studied it and handed it back. "That is perfectly correct."

Berengaria went to the table, took up a quill, scored a line on the sheet and scribbled something, and said:

"Now it is correct. Copy it out afresh with the correction."

His face went dark with anger, and his eyes flashed, and he looked at her with the sudden vast hatred which is love's other face.

"Very well," he said, "if you wish His Eminence to think that you are served by those as ignorant as you are yourself."

There was a sudden shocked silence in the bower. We should none of us have been surprised if she had reached out and smacked his head. I began to quiver. It is an intolerable position to watch the one who is lord of your heart reduced and shamed by something over which you have no control.

But Berengaria said into the silence, "I'm sorry, Blondel. You are quite right." And she smiled at him, her cold, small, secret smile. "And I am very ignorant, though it ill becomes you to say so."

He was now as white as he had been scarlet, and over his jaw on one side of his face there was a twitching. I remembered the old saying about a falling out being a renewal of love—and I remembered how I had for a moment hated and then with renewed force loved him when he had flung the drawing of the mangonel into the fire. I knew exactly how he was feeling at that moment.

He remained in a curious way master of the situation.

"It cannot be despatched like this. I'll make a fresh copy. That is, if Your Highness is really satisfied that the original was correct."

And despite "Your Highness," he spoke as a husband might speak to a cherished wife who had just been a little more than ordinarily silly. Tolerant, indulgent.

Well, he could forgive her; she was the loved one to whom

all things are forgiven. But spite yeasted in me. I hadn't yet told her about my conversation with Father. Tonight—it happened to be my turn to brush the hair—I would.

IX

The parting that ran across her skull was thin and white, like a seam, and the hair under my hands was smooth and heavy, warm near the head and then cool; and it was black with blue lights in it, like a blackbird's wing.

She sat in front of the silver mirror, not looking into it. She studied her reflection less than any normal woman I ever knew.

And in a moment, when I had said the words I was shaping on my tongue, she would cry. Beautifully. She was beautiful, she was legitimate, Father adored her, everyone pandered to her. Blondel loved her. And she wouldn't let him go free to Apieta. Very well, I thought; after all, this isn't pure spite, Father asked me to say these things. So I drew in my breath, and Berengaria said:

"Anna, we've heard nothing from Cardinal Saturnino. I believe both he and Father have forgotten all about it." She spoke peevishly.

I stood there with two words, "forgotten" and "oubliette," weaving themselves together in my mind. They came together, they wrestled like lovers, they were quickly fertile, and their astonishing offspring was produced and matured all in a moment and was there, ready to leap from my brain as Minerva was said to leap from the head of Love.

"I suppose you have forgotten too," she said even more peevishly. "I'm talking about Saturnino's errand to Westminster."

"No," I said, speaking slowly and with care. "I hadn't forgotten. In fact, I have given this matter a great deal of thought, and I have come to a conclusion——"

"That Father never commissioned him at all. Yes, I suspected that myself. Father never took this business seriously enough——"

"That wasn't my thought. I think that it has been a mistake all along, sending great scarlet cardinals to batter on the front door and ask questions. It puts people on guard, and if there is a secret—as there seems to be—naturally those who know it take pains to keep it close. What we needed was to send some humble, inconspicuous person who could go in by the back door and insinuate himself. Suppose now that you could have sent me to Alys and said that I was the best needlewoman in Europe and would she like me to help make her wedding dress. I'd wager my emerald to an old wimple that I'd have known at once whether she needed a wedding dress, and if not why not."

She turned to me with her great eyes shining.

"Oh, Anna, how true! I suppose you couldn't——"

"I said humble and inconspicuous, Berengaria."

I waited. I should have liked the choice and the suggestion to be her own.

"Mathilde would do anything for me and I'd trust her, but her sight is failing and her stitches, look!" She lifted the hem of her gown and showed me an example of Mathilde's needlework. "And Pila is such a greedy gossip, she'd betray herself. Catherine I don't altogether trust——"

Well, I thought, go on! Work your way through the whole household. I've waited so long for this moment I can wait another hour; there's no hurry at all.

"It need not be a sewing woman; that was just a suggestion to show you what I meant. We need somebody trustworthy but observant, and with some qualification which would gain an entry in an inconspicuous way."

Isn't that tantamount to saying the name? Doesn't it cry aloud? Oh, you stupid, stupid woman!

She made one or two other fatuous suggestions; she even mentioned Blanche, who might pretend to be "just a visitor."

"You might as well go yourself," I said. Then I waited another minute and came to the end of my patience and said the thing I had planned from the moment when the word "forgotten" had linked with "oubliette" and I had known that this time her dream would be a weapon in my hand.

I pretended sudden inspiration. I snapped my fingers and exclaimed, "I know! We could send Blondel."

It annoyed me, after all her own ridiculous suggestions, to see her look so surprised and so dubious, as though I had suggested sending Blanco or one of the hound-dogs.

"Blondel?"

"Yes, Blondel. Think—in his lute he has a key that will open almost any door. His appearance is pleasing, his manners ingratiating; with a little contrivance we can get him into Alys's very bedchamber. He's intelligent and observant—and God knows he has enough experience in getting on with women!"

She turned that over in her mind and then said:

89

"But that would be worse than letting him go to Apieta."

I governed myself, pretended again to think and again to be visited by inspiration.

"But, Berengaria, that is what the dream meant! I see it now. You said just now that Father and Saturnino had *forgotten*, and the worst part of your dream was your feeling of what 'oubliette' meant. Don't you see? Blondel will get you out—by means of what he has *in his hand*. The lute." Some inward light seemed to be kindled; she glowed, she shone. She looked so very beautiful and so transported that my heart smote me to think that I should, for my own purposes, be deceiving her so. But if she had let Blondel go to Apieta I wouldn't have been driven to such extremities.

Besides, I thought, who knew? Something might come of it. There was a mystery about Alys and Richard. And everything I had said about Blondel's qualifications as a spy was true, even if disingenuous.

"What you must do," I said, "is to send a letter to the cardinal. Tell him that you are sensible of what he has tried to do, and grateful. Send him a present, just valuable enough to justify the special personal messenger, and add that the bearer is an accomplished musician and that if the cardinal thinks he is good enough perhaps he would introduce him to the ladies at Westminster—you know, a gushing, impulsive, girlish kind of letter. I know just what to say."

"And then we might know! Anna, think. Suppose he really found out something. It is the not knowing that has been such torment. I *couldn't* give up hope while there was this mystery. Oh, Anna, you've given me something to look forward to. I do love you!"

She put her arm about my waist and pulled me to her and kissed me. It was like a sun-warmed rose touching my face.

I was quite horribly ashamed.

"Now," I said a little gruffly, "what shall we send to His Eminence?"

"How about that ring with the sapphire which Aunt Lucia gave me when I stayed with her? She had it specially blessed by the Pope, but it's far too big even for my thumb."

"A combination of the fitting and the unfitting that makes it the most obvious choice," I said.

"And, Anna——"

"Yes?"

"Will you be so very kind as to tell the boy? Not too much, if that can be avoided. I should feel awkward. He's so insolent in a smooth way. It's my fault, I know. On account

90

of the dream I've rather spoiled him. This afternoon, for instance, I was right about that letter and I ought to have smacked his head when he called me ignorant. But I thought, He isn't bonded, he might run away. So I held my hand. And what a mercy I did! Oh, Anna . . . "

I was rather afraid that she might kiss me again, so I moved away and said with sincerity, if with a feeling of guilt:

"I do hope something will come of it, Berengaria. We mustn't hope for too much."

"Just to know, even the worst, would be a relief. If I knew beyond all hope and doubt that Richard was going to marry Alys, I could lie down on that bed and die!"

I could have said, "And that isn't so easy!" When I was thirteen and first realised the full meaning of my deformity—that it wasn't just a matter of being awkward on stairs, easily tired, unable to hunt—when I knew that it meant being ugly forever, that no man would marry me, that I should have no children—then, and for a long time afterwards, I had often had fits of depression when I had cast myself on my bed and longed, prayed to die. I'd lain on my bed and sobbed and writhed and sweated, but I hadn't died! I had just become old. At sixteen I had reached the state which most women attain when they are forty, wrinkled, grey, and past child-bearing. There are blighted peaches and pears like me, spotted, ripe before the main crop, and lying rotting at the foot of the tree while the others mature in beauty. I had sometimes, by a morbid fancy, taken up such a one, bitten into its good side. Not all wasted.

Well, if I could save Blondel from the bower, from Berengaria, from himself, I should not have been all wasted either.

X

A little snow fell that night, and when we woke the bright, unreal reflected light filled every apartment. It was bitterly cold, but the sun was shining in a sky the colour of wild hyacinths.

Berengaria started the day by bidding Catherine fetch out the heavy little ironbound box in which she kept her jewels.

"We'll find the ring and you'll write the letter to accompany it, won't you, Anna?" she said, giving me a significant look.

"All in good time," I replied, returning the look. "First I'm going out to look at the snow. You've never seen Pamplona under the snow, Blondel. If you'd like to come with me I'll show you from my special place of vantage."

We climbed to the place from which I ordinarily watched the joustings. The tourney field lay smooth and untrodden at our feet, and beyond the outer wall were the huddled roofs of all the little houses glistening white in the sunshine. It was quite magical, and for a while we stood in silence, just staring with wonder that was almost childlike.

"It is beautiful," he said at last. "I'm glad that you brought me out. And now, hadn't we better go back? It's rather cold for you."

"I really brought you out because I have something to tell you," I said. "We'll find a more sheltered spot."

We moved around to the south side of the Roman Tower and found a place in the sun, sheltered from the cold wind that came from the mountains—the wind which had brought us the snow—for here so little had fallen that it was no more than a sprinkling. I brushed a clear space and sat down, pulling my cloak closely about me. We were sitting in one of those breaks in the wall designed so that anyone defending the castle could shoot arrows, drop stones, or pour boiling oil or water upon his enemies and then dart back behind the covering wall, and the space was just wide enough for our two bodies. I was nearer to him than I had ever been before. I looked at him and in the bright light saw that the laughter marks about his eyes had given way to others, not graved by merriment, and that there were now some silver hairs amongst the gold on his head.

I remembered seeing similar signs of premature age in a young man, a young knight whom Father had brought home with him from one of his little wars. He had been wounded in the chest and the wound would not heal. He'd been patient at first, submitted to invalid regime and Ahbeg's ministrations, and then rebelled. The wound was hidden when he was clothed, and for about four months he went about pretending that there was nothing the matter with him. But his hair, which had been black to begin with, whitened every day, and his face, in the end, was the face of an old man. One day, dismounting from his horse at the end of a day's hunting, he had given a groan and dropped dead.

He had been buried and forgotten for fully five years, but now I remembered him, his look of defiant endurance and the way he had aged in four months. I had marked him much at the time because I was in a morbid state of mind myself.

He had walked about devoured by a suppurating wound; Blondel was devoured by hopeless love. And so was I. Was the sign set on me too?

"You are hesitating about what you have to tell me," the boy said. "After my rudeness yesterday I shall not be surprised, you know, to hear that the princess can dispense with my services."

He grinned at me quite cheerily.

"It hasn't anything to do with that at all. The fact is, the princess has an errand which you can do better than anyone else. In London. And rather a curious errand."

Interest woke in his face.

She had told me to tell him as little as possible, but he must be told exactly what we wanted to know. I told him, making it all sound rather more official and conventional than it was, saying, "We are wondering . . . we are mystified . . . " I knew that anybody but a fool would understand who was interested and why, and the boy was no fool. He understood.

But even as he accepted the errand his face went white and the lines in it deepened; my heart turned over in my breast with pity and the desire to comfort him.

And then I thought, as in moments of emotion I rather tend to do: How utterly ridiculous this all is. Here is a nameless, landless strolling player suffering the agonies of hell for love of a princess; and here is a woman, completely unlovable, but a king's daughter and a duchess, suffering the same agonies for love of this same lute player.

"You know, Blondel," I said, "sometimes it seems to me that we are born and live our lives in order to make sport for the gods. Not the one great God, but all the lesser ones. Consider Berengaria! So beautiful, so eligible, that in the twelve weeks she spent with her aunt Lucia in Rome fifteen young nobles made offers for her hand. Most of them were ineligible in the strict sense of the term, but no matter. I've lost count of the eligible offers she has received. Crowns roll at her feet like skittles. But the one man to whom she takes a fancy is this man, already plighted. You'd think that alone would satisfy the gods—but no! She must be further tormented by the fact that, though plighted, he remains unwed. And while this goes on every woman who sees her thinks, Oh, to have such hair; oh, to have such eyes; oh, to be so beautiful! That is what the gods laugh about."

And what sport we are making for them at this moment, I thought. But I have saved you, if you will consent to be

93

saved. Once you are out of this place, the enchantment will wane. There'll be a girl, straight-backed, round breasted— and one day you'll say, "There was once in Pamplona a lovely princess . . . " Me you will not remember at all, save as an example of the horrible shape to which the human body can be twisted. Yet twice I have manipulated the strings of your life. I put you into a cage—and I have set you free.

He said, "If there is anything to be discovered I will discover it. Will you tell her that? And if there is anything to be done, I will do it."

I felt the same peculiar thrill, that movement of the flesh against the bone that I have sometimes felt when watching young men take the vows of knighthood. The simple words had that same solemn ring.

"Well," I said, "don't forget to enjoy yourself at the same time. England could be very interesting, especially if you get to Westminster. There's Eleanor of Aquitaine, for instance. She rebelled against her husband and tried to make her son independent in Aquitaine. They say she's in prison some-where. And all these stories about Fair Rosamonde . . . For a minstrel and a song maker a visit to England should be an interesting experience."

We had to climb down from the battlement, and he went before me, his arm stretched up, his hand cupped about my elbow. For the last time!

At that point I realised what I had done. Self-pity washed me. I completed the descent in silence.

XI

The preparations for his departure occupied three days. Berengaria, looking at him for the first time with complete awareness and seeing not just the face out of her drugged dream but the whole person, said that he must have new clothes. As he stood, she said, he would do her little credit. So a tailor was summoned.

I added to the new suit and the cloak which was ordered a pair of shoes and a pouch, into which I put ten gold pieces.

"You planned my house," I said, "and I should have paid so much to anyone else and probably for a worse drawing. This is no more than your due."

He and Berengaria and I were in the inner room together.

94

We were arranging the method by which any information he gleaned should be sent back.

Remembering the episodes of the battle-axe and the rush-chewing fit, I was prepared to believe that the secret, when unearthed, might prove dark and scandalous. So we invented a code. Blondel was to send us back a song; Alys was to be the Lady; Richard, the Knight: the Dragon was to mean King Henry; the King, Philip of France; the Crone, Eleanor of Aquitaine.

Blondel and I were both sunk in depths of secret misery, and even Berengaria at this moment lost heart. And our misery took the form of a crazy hilarity, so that we vied with one another in inventing the most scandalous secrets about the English court and putting them into innocent-sounding rhymes.

Presently Pila put her head round the door and announced that supper was ready.

My heart climbed out of my chest and resumed its beating in my throat. I wanted a moment alone with him—he would be off at first light in the morning—but I knew that he would want to take his leave of Berengaria. His need. My need.

I stood up and stretched out my hand. "Good-bye, Blondel, and may God speed you."

"And may He keep Your Grace," he said. Our hands met and touched and fell apart.

But in the morning I rose stealthily from amongst the sleeping women and climbed in the dawn-dusk to a point where the battlements overlooked the road he must take to the port of San Sebastian. And presently I saw him in his new blue cloak, with his wrapped lute and his little bundle strapped to his saddle, ride clattering out, accompanied by the groom who was to bring back his horse.

At the point where the road turned he checked and looked back for a moment. Once again the castle looked stark and black against the red sky, but it was the red of the sun's rising this time; a good omen.

I remembered then that in all the talk and the planning there had been no word said by any one of us concerning his return. Neither I nor Berengaria had said, "When you come back . . ."; he had never said, "When I come back . . ." His going fulfilled her poppyhead dream, perfected my plan for his release, and doubtless chimed with the secret wishes of his own heart. He would not come back.

So go, I thought, looking my last on him, get away, be

free; go and meet your ordinary young man's life. And God send you happy!

The horse moved on; the turn of the road hid him.

Presently I was calm enough to climb down and take up my pretence at living again.

The first news came from him far sooner than any sane person could have expected, though in the short interval Berengaria had almost driven me mad with her impatience. Every morning without fail she had said, "Perhaps we shall hear today," and every evening she had gone to her bed disappointed. It had taken every modicum of patience I possessed to say, "He is still on the ship, Berengaria"—and I saw the ship, a prey to wind and wave; or "He has only just landed"—and I saw dangerous, robber-infested roads.

So the days passed until the morning came when I could honestly say, "Yes, with any luck he should now have arrived and perhaps been presented to Westminster, but we must allow at least ten days more." Late that afternoon a thin, pale cleric shaken by a terrible cough came to the castle and sought an audience with the princess. He came from England, from Cardinal Saturnino. He explained, coughing the while, that the climate in England had affected his lungs and that the cardinal, a humane man, had sent him home to recuperate and had entrusted him with despatches.

Poor young man, so courteous, so travel-weary, so glad to be back in Navarre, how shabbily we treated him: hardly listening to his greetings, snatching his packet of letters and retreating to the inner room, leaving Pila to perform the offices of hospitality.

The package was bound with thread and sealed. As Berengaria set about tearing it open, like a starved animal with a parcel of food, I felt bound to say warningly, "This cannot tell you anything you wish to know. The boy can but have arrived. You'll find nothing there save a letter of thanks for the ring."

She severed the thread with her teeth, unheeding, and when it broke cast away the outer wrapping with the seals. Inside there were three letters, two slim ones for her, one, stouter, for me. She held out mine without lifting her eyes from her own.

I opened mine gently: *his* fingers had folded it; I had

recognised his writing at a glance. And as soon as the page was unfolded I had seen that this was no ballad written in code but a long, straightforward letter. I was amazed, touched, flattered, and excited all at once. But I had scarcely read the opening words of greeting when Berengaria slapped her two sheets together and exclaimed in a voice of intense disappointment, "You were right, no news of any kind. See for yourself. What does yours say? Is it from His Eminence or from the boy?"

"From Blondel," I said. "Why should the cardinal write to me?" I could hear the asperity in my voice. I felt as though a thousand tiny needles were pricking my skin. Here was Blondel's voice in my ear, unexpectedly, delightfully, and this fool of a girl interrupting.

"Let me see. You're so slow. There might be something." She thrust her two letters under my chin and snatched at mine.

"There could be nothing of interest or importance. Time forbids," I said. But I let her take it.

To distract myself I read her letters. That from the cardinal was a succession of fulsome, grateful phrases. I really only noted the part where he mentioned Blondel. "The boy," he wrote, "is delightful. Sending him was a veritable inspiration, for how could Your Highness have known how sadly I miss the music of my own country? At the first opportunity I shall take him to Westminster, in accordance with your gracious suggestion, and let them hear what music should be. Their own is barbarous."

Blondel's letter to the woman he loved was short and stilted. The letter any young servant might write—having skill with a pen—to any mistress whom he remembered kindly. He thanked her for the new clothes and the cloak because the weather was colder than she could imagine. For the rest it merely announced his safe arrival and reiterated his desire to serve her to the best of his ability.

While I read the two letters, the one so fulsome, the other so stiff, Berengaria had skimmed through mine and now, thrusting it back at me, she said irritably, "What a mass of scribble, and not a word of sense in it."

I tried—I honestly tried—to imagine how I should be feeling if a despatch had come from England and contained no mention of Blondel's name.

"It is too soon," I said as pleasantly as I could. "Have patience. We shall hear. Already the cardinal has accepted your suggestion that Blondel go to Westminster. That is a great stride forward, exactly what we hoped for. News will come."

"You are such a comfort to me, Anna," she said sweetly. I felt rebuked for the pang of hatred I had felt when she called my letter a mass of scribble. And again rebuked when she said in her remote, dreamy way, "I suppose I should go and be agreeable to that young priest."

Left alone, I read my letter from Blondel.

It is the first letter he ever wrote me; the only memento of him that I have. I carry it with me always and have left instructions that it is to be buried with me.

And every sentence in it is addressed to Berengaria. I suppose he thought it would look strange to send her a long rambling letter, yet the desire to communicate, which is one of the symptoms of love, had made him long to tell her of his experiences and impressions. So he had written to me, interlarding the letter with such phrases as "The princess might be interested to know . . . It would amuse the princess to see . . ." Obvious, pitiable device. A mass of scribble!

Maybe, reading it, I should have wept great warm tears of self-pity. Actually I laughed. Only one thing in London, in England, in the world, was of interest to Berengaria, and the idea that she might like to know that in England they drank ale instead of wine, that even the burghers' wives were wearing the new laced gowns, and that no one had yet heard even the commonest of Abélard's songs was amusing.

However, the letter, though not meant for me, brought some comfort. The boy's mind was akin to mine rather than to Berengaria's. He was still aware of other things in the world; interested, receptive. His wound would heal now.

Lent came; always a dull, dreary season, with the spring taking little steps forward and then halting in the teeth of the east wind; with altars and vestments the colour of sorrow; with too much salt fish at table.

This year the dullness of the season was broken in an unexpected manner. Father, who usually contrived to spend Lent in some place and some pursuit where church ruling did not run overhard, this year cut short his hunting in Grania and returned to Pamplona a fortnight before Easter. He appeared to be in excellent health and good spirits, though about the latter there was a slight overtone of joviality which made me suspect that he was not quite easy in his mind about something. And a well-founded suspicion it was, for we were soon informed that he had cut short his hunting in order to receive Isaac Comnenus's emissaries—his brother, the Archduke Fernando, and his cousin, the Archbishop of Nicosia. Two such eminent messengers argued the seriousness of the Emperor's intention, for, as Father said, "Short of coming himself, he couldn't honour us more."

I began to see trouble ahead. It was something new for Father to speak of a would-be suitor's showing him honour: he had dismissed several in the past with very scant courtesy. And my doubts increased when Father began to make high politics an excuse for the lavish welcome he planned to offer the Cypriots.

"With this new crusade ready for launching," he said, "it is of the utmost importance to promote friendly relationships between the East and the West. An unwitting offence now may have most unfortunate effects later, and these fellows have all the Oriental's regard for pomp and splendour."

But the crusade had been talked of for quite a long time, and "these fellows" hadn't recently formed a taste for splendour. No! All that had changed was Father's attitude towards Berengaria's marriage.

Even Lent was to be disregarded. I made so bold as to remind Father of the season when he began talking about a banquet of venison and suckling pigs, of fresh fish rushed up from San Sebastián on relays of swift horses, of peacocks roasted and then redecked in their plumage.

"Oh," he said, "these fellows belong to the Eastern Church; their calendar is different. They keep Easter at some other time, if they keep it at all." I privately doubted whether the Byzantine calendar differed from the Roman by quite so much, but I held my tongue. I was, in fact, a little horrified by the fact that Father could speak about Cyprus as though it were quite outside Christendom and yet be contemplating marrying his darling daughter to its Emperor. After all the years of indulgence, this new attitude seemed suddenly harsh and callous.

"Have you told Berengaria that you intend to consider Isaac's offer seriously?" I asked.

"No, but I intend to do so and to make my intentions perfectly plain before they arrive. And didn't I ask you, before I went to Grania, to hint something of the sort to her?"

"I delayed. We still had some slight hope that the English affair might take a turn."

"It has. A turn in our favour too. I heard from Diagos in Rouen. He said that after a visit from Philip of France,

99

Richard had spoken openly of immediate marriage and was planning to go to England almost at once. That suggests a wedding after Easter, and that news has hardened my purpose. Now that the Plantagenet is disposed of, the next thing we know she'll be falling in love with somebody else, probably even more unsuitable. I can't go through this hoop again, Anna. An unmarried woman of marriageable age is a menace and a nuisance—as the old people knew when they either married their girls at twelve or clapped them into convents."

That word obviously reminded him of his other daughter. He said quite angrily, "I've been a fool with my daughters, a weak, sloppy-minded fool, and no mistake. And with my son. Here I am, well over fifty, with death looking me in the face and not a grandson to my name. One daughter setting her cap at a man who's as good as married, another playing catch-as-catch-can with a religious life, and you—you dare remind me about Lent. You're a saucy minx, let me tell you."

"But, sire, even Charlemagne permitted liberties to his dwarf!"

He winced a little, as I guessed he would, and went on in a slightly more reasonable tone:

"You're saucy, but sometimes I think you're the only one of my brood with a grain of sense. And you must see that this time I must take a stand. I've been patient, I've been lenient. I did all I could to get her the man who'd taken her fancy. But now the time has come when we must be sensible. Otherwise, before we know where we are, she'll be hopping into bed with a handsome young groom or lute player—such things have been known!"

XIII

Even while I hated her there had been things which I was bound to admire about my half sister. Her beauty, naturally, and her dignity, her sense of what was fitting and seemly, and her reserve. But these had been offset by what I can only call a contempt for her character; I had always thought her spoiled and pampered, given to peevishness, indolence, and waywardness. I had often looked at her and wondered what manner of person she would have been had she been born as I was.

Now I knew.

For now she found herself in a position where her beauty

100

and rank availed her nothing; in fact, they militated against her. It was because she was beautiful and a princess that Isaac of Cyprus was suing for her hand, and it was because she had been pandered to in the past that Father had taken this sudden decision to break her will. She had also to bear the sharp disappointment of hearing Diagos's message concerning Richard's imminent marriage.

Nobody could have borne such a shower of blows with more fortitude.

She cried. She cried often and violently, but only in the privacy of her own apartment, alone or in my presence. But throughout the ten days of the Cypriot emissaries' stay in Pamplona she never gave in public any sign of a state of mind that was not assured, composed, serene. And incredibly courageous.

One evening after a banquet of great magnificence, when no one was quite sober, the archduke, who was small and fat and swarthy, very much like an upended pig, finely dressed, approached and laid in her lap a most resplendent rope of pearls. It would have reached to the knees when hung about the neck, and every pearl was matched and perfect. He made one of his speeches, saying that Isaac had sent them, knowing that they were unworthy to touch the fairest neck in Christendom but hoping that she would, out of kindness, accept them. It was a very awkward moment. Father, who had been expressing himself very freely during the last few days, was within earshot; everybody of any consequence at court was looking on. The archduke was actually on his knees beside her.

She picked up the pearls and ran them slowly, appreciatively, through her fingers. Then she said:

"They are beautiful. Very beautiful. Indeed too beautiful and too precious to grace any neck save that of an empress. I pray, Your Highness, preserve them carefully until such day as the Empress of Cyprus may wear them." And she bundled the great shining things together and pressed them into the archduke's hand.

It was not a refusal; it was not a promise. It committed her to nothing.

Alone with me, in the privacy of her own chamber she said, "If I had put them over my head, which was his wish, they would have been a halter, like the bit of rope with which goats are dragged to the market!"

"You evaded the issue beautifully," I said. "But before

101

they take leave they will demand a plain yes or no. There will come a moment, Berengaria——"

"But I have said no! To Father. And he can tell them in privacy. I didn't see why I should say it this evening in the face of them all. He knows that I said I would marry Richard Plantagenet or nobody, and if he chooses to play this game with Isaac's messengers he can't blame me if I play it too. It would be churlish not to. He knows my mind and I know my mind, but since he chooses to be civil, I must be as civil as I can. And despite what Diagos said, you know, Anna, we haven't yet heard from that boy. Another day gone!"

"And when we do," I said, "I am afraid that it will be to the effect that the Knight is to marry the Lady. What then, Berengaria?"

"I'd sooner die than marry the Emperor of Cyprus or any other man on earth. Father knows that. He just thinks that I can be cajoled, bribed with ropes of pearls and flattering speeches. But he is wrong."

There came an evening when after supper Father sent for Berengaria. We had all eaten together in the great hall and had been, on the surface, very agreeable and merry. After the warm, sweaty, food-laden, wine-heavy atmosphere of the hall, the solar had struck very chill, and Pila had offered to brew us a hot posset before we retired and Mathilde was carrying hot bricks from the oven to heat our beds. There was that general feeling of relaxation which comes when people retire to privacy after a public display.

"Tell His Majesty that I shall present myself in a very short time," Berengaria said to the page who brought the message. "Pila, you go on with your posset; I'll drink it before I go. Anna, come with me. Mathilde, fetch the white gown and the gauze wimple. Catherine, my sapphire necklet, if you please. And tell Blanco to get a lantern ready."

She and I went into the bedchamber.

"Well," she said, "the moment has come. I have to tell him again. I've hoped and prayed——" She turned suddenly and, clenching her fists, beat hard and furiously against the stones of the wall. "Good my God," she said in a terrible voice, "haven't I borne enough?"

I took her by the shoulders and swung her round.

"You'll ruin your hands. Look, you've broken the skin already." The blood was indeed starting out in little red beads against the whiteness. She brushed her hands roughly against the stuff of her gown. And then suddenly she relapsed into placidity. She stood like a statue while we brushed her hair and put her into the new dress and arranged the gauzy wimple. When Pila brought in the posset Berengaria said, "A stirrup cup, Anna," and smiled at me as she drank.

She had never looked so lovely; she never looked so lovely again. The new dress was white and made from a roll of the Damascus silk which our grandfather had brought from the East. Its ground was chalky-white and the pattern of roses shone on it, creamy-white. Her wimple was like a veil of mist. Only the black hair, half shrouded by the wimple, the fresh rose paste on her lips, the blue and black of her eyes and eyelashes and the sapphires about her neck mitigated the whiteness. She looked like a woman made out of marble, or snow.

We saw her set off, accompanied by Blanco. We turned back to the fire and drank our possets and warmed our toes. A lively gossip broke out. Pila and Catherine were quite sure that when the princess returned she would be betrothed. Empress of Cyprus.

"And time, too," said Mathilde, going to and fro with the hot bricks. "If her mother, God rest her, had lived, my lady would have been married long since."

"But it was worth waiting for," Pila said comfortably. "Empress of Cyprus. That sounds well."

"The Emperor is elderly—and fat," Catherine said, "and he has been married before."

"Then he is experienced, easygoing, and not too hard to please," Pila said.

They chatted on until they were yawning with weariness.

"Go to bed," I said. "I will await the princess's return. This is my evening for duty."

They demurred; they wanted to stay up and congratulate her. But time went on, the posset had been drunk, and the fire began to die down. Finally they agreed to go to bed. Mathilde and I were left in the bower.

She was asleep and I was almost dozing when there was a clatter at the door and in ran one of Father's pages, scarlet-cheeked and breathless from haste. He gasped out that His Majesty wanted me, nobody else, and immediately. "He said Your Grace was to come in your night gear if you had retired."

Mathilde, struggling up out of her slumber, inquired if anything was wrong. When I told her the King had sent for me she said:

103

"Ah, they're drinking to her health and happiness. The pity is that her dear mother shouldn't have lived to see the day. Drink one sup for me, Your Grace."

But I had a less comfortable and cheerful view of what might await me. I expected to find Berengaria weeping and Father in a rage.

I called Blanco out of his kennel and allowed him to carry me across to the King's apartment, that bleak, austere apartment which nevertheless I regarded as a privilege to enter, so highly did Father rate the privacy it afforded. Only state matters with some element of secrecy in them or family affairs were discussed in that room; it had an unused air which combined with its bare stone walls and floor and its severe furnishing to make it cheerless and forbidding.

When I first entered I could see Father kneeling at the farther end of the room. His back was to me and his head was lowered. Berengaria I could not see at all. I had a momentary ridiculous idea that, having exhausted himself by argument, he had taken to prayer and had sent for me to pray with him. Then, hobbling forward, I saw the reason for his posture. Berengaria lay stretched on the floor and he, on his knees, was bending over her. Then I thought that she had fainted; she had spent herself by argument and either genuinely or tactically swooned. It went through my mind how timely, how convenient, how useful women's swooning fits could be.

A second afterwards I saw the reality. All the bosom of Berengaria's new white gown and the ends of her gauzy wimple were dabbled with blood; and Father, with the end of his long-hanging sleeve, was wiping away the blood which flowed in a steady stream from a long thin wound in her neck.

He had heard my arrival and turned his face to me. It was quite distraught and a horrible grey-green in colour.

"Oh, my God, Anna," he said. "Look at this———"

I thought she had provoked him too far and he had struck her with a knife in his hand. On the table stood a dish of russet-skinned winter apples, and one apple, half peeled, lay near the table's edge.

I enjoy stories of violence, but in real life I shrink from it. And to blood I have an aversion; I don't like the sound of the word or the look of it when it is written. The idea of Father, in a moment of rage, drawing blood on his Berengaria, his favourite and his most beloved, made me feel quite sick.

Berengaria lay there looking like a beautiful white victim of some old ritual sacrifice, and Father's hands were like a butcher's. I said in a very thin, shaky voice:

"Shall I send for Ahbeg?"

"I did. As soon as it happened. He should be here by now. Oh, my God, she'll die. Send again, Anna, or go yourself. I'll kill the old devil if he doesn't hurry." He whipped his other sleeve round his hand and renewed his mopping.

By that time I had had a chance to notice that the blood, though messy and nasty, was not pumping out in the bright red flood that pours from a fatal wound. And as I stumbled to the door I said so. I had got the door open and was shouting to the pages, who were housed a little way down the passage, when I saw the dancing light of a lantern on the curve of the wall and heard the sound of brisk steps and shuffling ones. In a moment Ahbeg, accompanied by a page, rounded the corner.

"He's here," I said over my shoulder.

Ahbeg had one hand on the page's arm and his other fumbling at the wall.

"Don't let anybody else in," Father said. So at the door I dismissed the page, offering my own arm to the old man, and led him inside the room. He peered about blindly, distrustfully.

"The King sent for me," he said in a high quavering voice. "Where is he? What is the matter?"

I realised that he was almost blind. He was older and thinner and much dirtier than when he had come into the bower to set the bone in Blondel's ankle.

"Oh, thank God you've come," Father said. "It's my girl. I was telling her something—for her own good—and she up with a knife and cut her throat. Here, Ahbeg, here. Look . . ." Ahbeg was peering about like a bat. Father took him roughly by the arm and dragged him across to where Berengaria lay.

"Bring a candle and hold it steady," the old man said. He bent over stiffly and looked at Berengaria between harrowed lids.

"Nothing to make a fuss about. A very trivial wound. No more than a cut finger." I heard Father draw in a great gusty breath of relief.

"Cut throat indeed," Ahbeg said grumblingly. "A mere scratch on the neck. And I can't get down on my knees nowadays. Lift her up. Isn't there a table or a settle or something?"

He peered about.

Father, with some of the ghastly colour gone from his face, lifted Berengaria and laid her on the table, and I took the only cushion that was in the room and placed it under her head. By that time the steady red stream, unstaunched, was flowing over her shoulders.

Ahbeg dipped into the ragged, bulky *aumônière* which he wore on his girdle and brought out a needle and thread which he handed to me.

"Thread that for me," he said. "Small things baffle me nowadays. Bigger things I see very well, and where wounds are concerned I have eyes in my fingers. Sire, do not concern yourself. I'm an old man and I never knew any female creature to deal herself a fatal blow yet. They do sometimes jump into water and then scream for help and sometimes they swallow poison—that is fatal. But no woman ever yet knifed herself successfully. Nor ever will." I handed him the threaded needle, which he took without acknowledgment.

He turned to the table, gathered the soiled wimple into a handful, and wiped away some of the blood. Then, as dispassionately as though he were stitching a rent in a piece of cloth, he sewed the edges of the wound together. I felt sick again, but somehow I could not avert my eyes. He was so quick and so expert.

And Berengaria never stirred. I flinched and shuddered each time the needle went home and Father, at the far end of the room, walked about, saying, "My God, my God!"

Ahbeg made eight stitches and cast off—a tapestry term. Then he fumbled again in his pouch and finally produced a small linen bag from which he took a pinch of grey powder.

"Hold your hand," he said to me. I did so and he placed the grey powder in my palm. Then he closed his *aumônière*, carefully putting the little linen and the needle and thread into it first.

"Hold your hand," he said again, and as I did so he spat into my palm. It was horrible. I almost screamed. With the forefinger of his right hand he mixed the grey powder and the spittle into a paste, using my hand as though it were a utensil. And the paste he then smeared over the wound and over the stitches. A little blood was seeping through, and before he had done my palm was something utterly repulsive, Berengaria's blood, Ahbeg's spittle . . . and what was the grey powder, I wondered . . . dried, pulverised toad?

"Now there will be no pain and no festering," he said, wiping his own fingers on the rose damascened gown of his

106

patient. "Make no attempt to wake her. The swoon will pass into sleep, and that will mend the shock. The wound itself is nothing. I would not have wasted the good thread on any but the princess."

"Ahbeg," Father said, suddenly turning from his pacing and his calling upon God, "I want no word of this to get about."

"Am I a hen to cackle in the yard?" Ahbeg asked, and went shuffling to the door. There he turned. "When she wakes she will be thirsty—give her anything save wine. Water, milk, broth, anything. Good night to you, sire." I might not have been present.

"Good night, Ahbeg—and thank you," Father said.

He came and stood by me at the end of the table where Berengaria lay like a dead girl, with the blood already turning rusty-red on her gown and on her flesh and the grey-green paste smeared across her neck as though the wound had festered.

"Well," Father said, "that's something off my mind. I've never known Ahbeg to be wrong. But what are we to do now? What are we going to say to the rest of them? Fernando and the archbishop are expecting an answer; I promised them an answer tomorrow morning. I was just talking to her, I'd have you know, Anna. Just talking. Not raging or upbraiding, though she was being as obstinate as the devil. I was peeling her an apple—that will show you—and she took the knife out of my hand, Anna, while I was peeling her an apple. My dear, this has been a shock for you too! Perhaps I should—I'm afraid I just thought, Anna and Ahbeg. It is at such moments that one knows upon whom one relies. There now, I'll get you some wine, Anna . . . . ."

"I think," I said, "that I would like to wash my hand. What with the spit—and the bood—somehow I want to hold it well away from me and, what with one thing and another, I feel like a crab."

He rushed to the corner where his basin and ewer stood behind a plain canvas screen and brought me the basin of water and a clean linen towel. When I had washed I felt better, more in command of myself. Father took back the basin and, casting a look at where Berengaria lay, still like a dead girl, said:

"It would be a fine story, wouldn't it, for Fernando to take back to his brother—that the princess knifed herself rather than marry him! And how should *I* look? Like a fiend who bullied his daughter into mortal sin—I, the most patient, indulgent father in all Christendom. I swear to you, Anna, I was talking to her most reasonably, saying much the same as I said to you the other day."

He looked at me helplessly. And I remembered all he had done for me. Even the ten gold pieces I had given Blondel were *his* bounty. So I sat and thought and enjoyed the pleasant sensation of a scheme, cunning, complete in every detail, sliding into the mind as smoothly and neatly as a hand slides into a glove.

"We must say that Berengaria was taken ill while she was with you and that you sent for Ahbeg, who said it *might* be plague. That will cause a scare, but you and I have been badly scared this night, and who are the rest that they should escape a little scaring? Plague comes suddenly, and the buboes form in the neck and the groin and the armpits. And plague keeps everyone at a distance. Even the archbishop and the archduke will gladly take leave of Pamplona. After a few days we will discover that Ahbeg was mistaken and that the lump in her neck was an abscess which he lanced in the hope that a clean line would be less unsightly than the ragged hole left by the natural breaking. That, sire, will set a new fashion when the story gets about, and every woman with an abscess will run straight to a surgeon. Meanwhile it will be natural enough that I, having been already exposed to danger, take charge of the sickroom. How does that sound to you?"

Father looked at me as though I had just performed a double somersault before his eyes.

"By our Lady," he said, "you have a nimble mind."

"In your service, sire. And now it would be as well if you left us and went to spread the story and ordered another couch and some blankets and pillows. I shall need two pages in constant attendance, and Ahbeg should come in twice a day."

"If you manage this, Anna, I'll give you anything you wish."

I was most oddly reminded of a morning very long ago when I was on one of my jaunts to the market and had bought some cherries at a stall and, turning, saw behind me a little urchin who had been fishing for tadpoles and held an iron basin full of them in his hand. I gave him a handful of cherries, and with a quite heavenly smile he dived his hand into the basin and brought out one of the little black wriggling things and offered it to me.

"My dear father," I said, "you have already given me so much. This is my chance to do something for you. Go now

108

the whole world knowing that I'd sooner cut my throat than marry a man I didn't love."

"Not just now. But later on you would mind. And there's Father. It would make him look as though he were forcing you."

"His feelings shouldn't be considered. He's been very cruel. If he'd wanted to choose a husband for me he should have done it when I was a baby. To wait until now and then shout at me that I must marry Isaac or be an old maid because Richard was going to marry Alys after all—that was cruel. . . ." She burst into tears again.

Every conversation ended the same way.

Suddenly, on the fourth day of my incarceration, the spring arrived. Through the narrow, unwelcoming windows of Father's little room the sun forced its way and lay in golden patterns on the floor. I climbed onto the high stone sill of the window and looked down over Pamplona. In the past few days the trees in the gardens and orchards had come shyly and cautiously up to the very verge of blossoming, and the warmth of this one morning's sun had coaxed every petal wide open. The pink-and-white blossoms of peach and plum and cherry trees frothed and quivered in the lovely light, and in the background the foothills of the Pyrenees wore their brief, unrecapturable green.

Inevitably I thought of Blondel. Up there in the north the winter would still lie cold on the land, but even there spring would come. He would see a tree in flower and would think of Berengaria and know the ache of love; this year—but next year the flowering tree would speak another name.

Never, even to myself, have I been able to explain why I so persistently underrated his constancy. I knew very well that next year and every year until I died I should think of him whenever I saw a lovely thing, or heard sweet music, or came upon something amusing or interesting which we might have shared. So typically egoistical to think that Blondel was suffering from a curable infatuation; that Berengaria was prey to an unreasonable, obstinate fancy; that only Anna Apieta was truly in love.

Two more slow days passed, and then I fell into a state of panic. I wasn't strong enough or nimble enough to follow Mathilde's example with the mad Queen and hold open Berengaria's mouth with a clothes peg while I poured in the broth, the posset, the wine. And no persuasion, no chiding of mine could persuade her to take nourishment. If I pressed her too hard she would finally push me away, and generally what I offered her ended by being spilled on the covers. Every day her face looked smaller and more grey and her arms were as thin, as brittle-seeming as old dry sticks. What with the starvation and the crying and the sleeplessness, she was in very poor case indeed and, looking at her, I felt both guilty and foolish. The hurriedly devised plan which had preserved her secret, saved Father embarrassment, and got rid of the Cypriots now appeared thoughtless, reckless, and childish. I dared not pursue it any more. So that morning when Ahbeg shuffled in I said:

"The time has come to withdraw this story about the plague. The princess needs more company and better nursing than I can give her. If you will put the bandage on I will go tell the King and he can announce the good tidings."

Ahbeg turned his milky old eyes on me in a gaze of sheer malevolence.

"My lord King," he said, "explained his design and his wishes, and out of the duty I bear him and the gratitude I owe I consented to play a part in this—masquerade. Go, then, run and denounce me as a bungling fool who does not know the difference between an abscess and a deadly bubo. Finish your mummery and strike down with a word my reputation as a physician. Mock your fill. But remember, those who mock at knowledge mock at God, and no blessing attends them."

Little as the old man mattered to me, his words increased my feeling of foolishness and guilt. I had taken no count of his professional pride, and had I stopped to think about it I should have thought that he lived such a lonely, self-centred life that he was immune to considerations of public opinion. Apparently vanity was still active even in this morose, dirty, solitary old man.

"I'm sorry, Ahbeg," I said. "When this thing happened we had to think and act quickly. I see now that it was a poor plan. To tell you the truth, I'm ashamed too. I'm the nurse who failed to persuade her patient to swallow so much as a milksop!"

"You had no reputation to lose."

"I had. The King trusted me so completely that he left me alone to tend her. And now look . . . . Yet where the plaster is beginning to flake off I can see the wound, clean and dry and healing well. All she needs now is more cheerful company and a nurse whom she will obey." And, I thought but did not say, the stimulating society of those who did not know

112

her secret. With me she need make no effort to conceal her misery and her pining.

Ahbeg went over to the bed and looked down on Berengaria. Never did physician and patient regard one another with such complete lack of interest and confidence.

"I would defer the change of story for two more days," Ahbeg said.

He folded his hands into his sleeves and began to move towards the door.

"I dare not do that," I said, putting myself between him and the door. "I keep telling you and you take no notice— for six days now she had taken no sustenance. Can't you see how she has shrunken? If I wait two more days and she remains in this state——"

"She will be dead," he said calmly. "And since I am supposed to have diagnosed plague, that will be understandable and no shame to me. . . ."

I stared at him, shocked past belief at my own hearing. He wanted her to die!

The panic which had been mounting in me since early morning reached a climax. I whisked round swiftly, opened the door, and bellowed for the attendant pages.

"Go and find His Majesty. Wherever he is and whatever he is doing, say that I say he must come at once. Run, run!"

They were, as was their wont, already running away from the plague that poured, as they thought, out of the open door behind me, out of my clothes, my hair, my very breath.

Father had been changing from his soft indoor clothes into his hunting hose and tunic; he had snatched up a cloak and cast it over his shirt and drawers and so arrived, his hair in disorder, his beard uncombed.

"What is it, what is it, Anna? Is she better? Worse?"

I found myself clinging to his arm and gabbling like a frightened child. "She won't eat; she hasn't eaten anything for six days, and she cries and cries. She's wasting away. I can't be responsible any longer, Father. Mathilde would make her swallow, and you or somebody might be able to make her more cheerful. I've tried everything. Father, I have tried, but I daren't be left alone any longer, just watching her waste away."

"Poor child, you're overtired and overwrought," he said, patting my arm but at the same time detaching my clinging fingers. "Ah, Ahbeg's here. Good." Checking the pace of his step and his voice, he moved to the bed and looked at Berengaria. I saw him recoil. "Good my God!" he said.

113

"Sweetheart, what ails you! Why won't you eat? Rosebud, you *must* eat. Even if it hurts your poor throat. You're wasting away. Soon you won't be my beautiful little girl any more. Look, Anna shall make you a milksop, very sweet and soft, and I'll spoon it in for you. And you be brave, brave as a soldier's daughter should be. Rosebud, if you'll swallow a milksop though it hurts you, I'll give you the Order of the Silver Spur. I will, I promise. The first, the only woman in the world to wear it."

I hadn't exactly promised her *that*—it wasn't in my power to give—but I had talked to her in much this same way. And she had responded in the same way, closing her eyes and turning her head from me. One thing he did think of which I hadn't.

"My lovely, if you could only see yourself, thin as a tinker's donkey. Anna, get a looking glass. What, no looking glass here!"

They fetched one; he held it.

But then Berengaria had never been one for looking in the glass except to inspect the set of a new headdress, the fit of a new gown.

Finally even Father was defeated. He rose from his knees by the bed, his face almost as grey as Berengaria's, and walked over to Ahbeg.

"Have you tried everything? Is it the wound? The shock? Or is it——God might have had more mercy! Once, and she so lovely, so much beloved! Christ's blood! Wasn't once enough? What have I done to be punished twice over?" He sank down on a stool and sat there, an old grey tremulous man with his head in his shaking hands. Before I could reach him or speak Ahbeg spoke.

"She will die, sire. She is in no pain; she has been well nursed and the wound is healing well by first intention, no festering at all. But to recover, the patient must have the will to live, and that the princess lacks. Rather she wills herself to die. And when that happens there is no hope."

The sweetest-tempered animal caught in a trap and maddened by pain will try to rend even the hand which releases it. Father was like that. He stood up and wheeled round upon Ahbeg and began to shout.

"The will to live! I never heard such gibberish. Filthy black magic and nonsense! Why, I've seen men stuck through, in dire agony, praying God to let them die, begging their fellows to despatch them to put them out of pain. Had they the will to live, as you call it? They had not, but a goodly number of

114

them lived, all the same." He lashed himself into rage, choosing that rather than despair. "This serves me right for harbouring you with your dark doings and your spells all these years. You call yourself a physician, and then when a sickness defeats you, you blame the patient! Let's take a look at this wound that is healing so well that she can't swallow even a milksop."

Without a word Ahbeg moved over to Berengaria and with the long curved blackened nail of his first finger chipped off the crumbling plaster. Berengaria just stared. Even when he plucked at the thread of the eight stitches and it resisted him and he said, "It is not quite rotten yet," she did not flinch. The wound lay there exposed to sight, the neatest, cleanest wound ever seen, a little red seam.

There was no refuge for Father there.

"I'll call in every doctor in Navarre," he shouted. "I'll send to Valladolid for Escel, the best physician in the world. Do you hear me, sweetheart? I'll fetch Escel to you; he'll have you well in the twinkling of an eye. You've done bravely so far. Bravely!"

He might have been rallying a raiding party which had suffered a reverse. I could see that the feeling of despair which had assailed him a little while since had been too horrible for bearing, so he pushed that aside and was now trying, by means of an angry activity, to forget that he had ever entertained it for a moment. And that was well. Once given way to despair, there was nothing for it but to lie down and die—like Berengaria. Father and I must clutch at straws and by saving ourselves hope to save her.

"You send for Escel, sire, and anyone else whose name occurs to you. And I will fetch Mathilde, who is a better nurse than I."

"And let in her ladies, her musician; she needs rousing, entertaining ... " He cast one more fearful glance at the bed. "The will to live! Bah!" He stamped out purposefully.

Ahbeg took from his *aumônière* a clean white bandage.

"What must be will be," he said. "To humour my lord I have sacrificed my reputation and as a reward I have lost his confidence. But he will learn that the will to live is something more than an idle mouthing of words."

He gave his attention to the fixing of the bandage, handling the princess as though she were an inanimate bundle. Then he shuffled away. Possibly I was the last person to see or speak to him. Three weeks later on a warm day, somebody with a more than ordinarily sensitive nose passed his room in the Roman Tower, somebody curious investigated, and somebody too menial to evade the task took up the body of the unbeliever and buried it in a patch of ground between the armoury and the stable yard, where a succession of Father's favourite hounds had been interred, often with more ceremony. When the news reached me I thought certainly he was old and frail, ripe prey for death; but I could not avoid the thought that without his reputation and without Father's confidence he had found life of no value and had attempted to prove the accuracy of his last diagnosis.

The rest of that day had a curious unreality. With the substitution of the lie about the abscess for the lie about the plague, the room which had been like a leper's cell became a beehive. All day people were coming and going, bringing little presents, posies of flowers, congratulations, commiserations, suggestions for treatment, reminiscent stories of similar afflictions and similar mistakes upon the part of physicians which they had experienced themselves or of which they had heard. And with one exception nobody seemed unduly concerned by the state of torpor in which they found their princess. "I'm glad to see you so much better," "Make haste and get well," they said.

And at least she didn't cry in their presence.

The one person who did not contribute to the general feeling of relief and cheerfulness was old Mathilde.

As soon as she knew that her princess was ill the faithful old woman had offered to do the nursing, and I should have been glad of her help, her company, and the support of her long experience, but I dared not trust her. Sober, she was fidelity's self and would, I knew, have died under torture rather than utter an indiscretion. She did, however, get tipsy, and I had heard from her wine-loosened tongue several secrets concerning those who had trusted her in the past. So I had kept her out and she was vastly resentful. Now, as soon as she was admitted, she avenged herself by attacking me. Looking at the soiled covers of the bed, she demanded to know if this was how an ailing princess should lie, in filth, like a sick hind. Spying out the book with which I had tried to alleviate the tedium of the long hours, she asked how anyone could nurse a patient while she had her head stuck in a book. And to Berengaria she said:

"Mathilde is here now, my lamb. Mathilde will look after you. Mathilde will make you a posset that'd bring you back from the edge of the grave . . . . "

I hoped with all my heart that her posset would meet with a better fate than mine.

Pila and Catherine arrived just then with two pages carrying the rolled-up tapestry.

"We thought you'd like to see how far we have progressed. . . ."

I slipped away, ordered a tub of hot water, and washed and changed all my linen as though I had veritably come from the pesthouse. I walked for a while in the gay sunshine and found the last shrivelled apple for Blondel's bear. But even then, even while I was thinking of Blondel, I was conscious of a nagging, anxious melancholy and presently, with a mingling of relief and curiosity, I found myself back on the sickroom threshold.

The visitors were all gone and Mathilde was alone with Berengaria. A glance at Mathilde's face told me what I wanted to know; it was swollen and smudged with crying.

"It was too late," she said. "If I'd been called in earlier I could have cured her. I tried . . . " I saw her hand go to her pocket and saw the outline of the clothes peg there. "I tried my old trick and I got the posset into her—but it was too late. It just made her sick." She turned away and began to cry.

I went over to the bed which had been freshly spread with fair covers. Berengaria lay with her eyes closed. Her body hardly mounded the quilt that covered her. She looked like a dead girl.

"She's been like that this past hour," Mathilde blubbered. "His Majesty should be told—and a priest fetched."

I stood there staring, facing at last the thing whose ugly face I had tried to avoid, thinking that Mathilde, thinking that cheerful company . . . Now there was no more evasion possible. Berengaria was dying. I thought of all the songs and stories which ended "And she died of love." One accepted that in a song or a story; it seemed logical, romantic, and seemly. But in real life—actually in real life—it seemed unnecessary, ridiculous, faintly squalid. For death, even death in a beautiful girl and death from love, wasn't lovely to look at.

I thought that.

And then I thought: Well, Mathilde with her clothes peg succeeded in keeping Queen Beatrice alive until her mad seasons vastly outnumbered her sane ones. And was it worth it? If Mathilde was to be believed, Berengaria's mother had gone mad over Father's refusal to take up arms in the cause of Castile. Her daughter had apparently gone mad over Richard Plantagenet's betrothal to Alys. Was another broken bowl worth piecing together and preserving?

And then I thought about death—the coldness and the corruption. How death is the last and invincible enemy who will have us all in the end but who must be fought to that end. Nobody should go over to him and say, Take me! And nobody should watch a loved one take that step, say those words!

A loved one!

Was she that? I'd hated and envied her so violently once and later I'd pitied her. But never until this moment had I realised that she was precious and valuable to *me*. That her death would take the light out of the sun. But now I did realise it. I remembered all, even the least, of the endearing things about her: her courage, her good humour—there wasn't a happier court in Christendom until she fell in love— her lack of vanity and pride in her beauty and rank, the way she had of making little shrewd remarks, the fact that she had always been kind to me. Were all these—and all that beauty—to slip away into the wasteful dark, into the irrecoverable past?

"Mathilde," I said, "go make another posset, strong and good. Put everything into it that you know. *Go do as I say!*"

As soon as she had gone I knelt by the bed and put my mouth close to Berengaria's ear and I bellowed my lie.

"I've had a message from Blondel. About Richard. Diagos was wrong! He isn't going to marry Alys. Do you hear me, Berengaria? Richard isn't going to marry Alys. I've heard from Blondel."

Wherever she was, that reached her. The great eyes in their hollow sockets opened and stared at me.

"Blondel," I said. "A message. Richard isn't going to marry Alys. Do you hear? Do you understand?"

If there were any miracle by which blood from a lusty person in full health could be poured into the veins of a man wounded and bleeding to death, those who watched it might see what I saw then. Ahbeg was right—the will to live is a real thing. I saw it revive in Berengaria.

"Say it again," she whispered. Her lips were so dry that they rustled and cracked as she spoke.

I said it again. I said a dozen things. Over and over I said, "Mathilde is bringing you a posset. You'll drink it, won't you?"

"What happened? Is Blondel here?"

"Not yet. I had a message."

"And the news is—sure?"

"Quite sure. But secret. We won't mention it yet. Not until he arrives."

"Richard isn't going to marry Alys?"

"That is so. Now don't try to talk. When your posset comes, drink it and then you will be stronger. Here is Mathilde now."

And now, O God the Father and God the Son and God the Holy Ghost, in Whose hands life and death lie to be dispensed as seems fitting to You, Three in One and One in Three, forgive me that great lie, that trespass on Your province. I couldn't let her die for lack of a lie!

There was Mathilde saying, "My lamb, my honey-sweet child ... " and staring at me fearfully, as though I were a witch; and there was Berengaria trying weakly, like a new-born calf, to pull herself up in the bed. Welcoming the posset, opening her mouth to the spoon.

I stood back, realising what I had done.

XV

I had not been in the cathedral at Pamplona since I was thirteen and had first learned from Mathilde's wine-loosened lips the story about my mother. Up to that time I had thought that the altar there was the epitome of all beauty. It had been set there by Father as a memorial to his dead wife, and it was almost too lovely to look at. It was a filigree tower of ivory so finely carved that it was like lace; and of gold and silver spun out to the delicacy of a cobweb; and of jewels so great and splendid that they dazzled one's eyes. One could only glance at it and think, Oh, lovely, lovely, and then look away. I had taken great delight in it until the Sunday morning after the day when Mathilde, full of wine, had told me about Berengaria's mother being mad and my mother being Sancho's mistress and about the iron corset. On that Sunday morning I had looked at the altar as usual and thought, There it stands and here I stand, one too beautiful to look at and one too ugly, and both of us memorials to a loved, mad, dead woman.

I was in a sorry state of mind then. I had just realised the full meaning of my affliction, and the sight of the altar in its superb beauty and the sight of Berengaria, lovely as an angel by my side, were like blows struck upon flesh already

119

bruised. I made up my mind then and there that I would not enter the cathedral again.

Now, on a night which was cold after the day's sunshine, I stood there alone in the vast dark nave of the church. Some impulse which I could neither understand nor name had driven me out from Berengaria's bedside, sent me hobbling past the St. Nicholas's Church, where I usually attended Mass and made my confessions, and brought me at last to this place which I had avoided sedulously for years.

I dipped my fingers into the icy water of the stoup, crossed myself, and, having made my obeisance to the altar, stood and regarded it. It shone out of the darkness. I knew then that I had come here to abase and punish myself; I wanted to invite the pain which had visited me in this place before. Why? Because I had lied? That wasn't the true answer. I'd lied before; I had involved Father in a lie, and Ahbeg. I'd lied, in a way, about sending Blondel to England. But I had not felt guilty. Where was the difference?

I fumbled my way to the table where the votary candles were and lighted three, one for the Virgin, one for St. Agnes, Berengaria's patron saint, and one for St. Veronica, who was my own. And then I knelt down and began to pray with a passionate intensity which I had not felt for years—not since I had prayed that I might grow straight and whole like other children. And now I was praying for a miracle again, beseeching God and Christ and all the saints, the archangels and angels and all the hierarchy of heaven that my lie might not be a lie at all; that it might be true that Richard wasn't going to marry Alys.

But I did take the precaution to add a petition that, if he were already married and my lie bound to be exposed, Berengaria would not take it too hard, would be resigned at last and go on living.

By the time I reached home again I was, I think, a little lightheaded. The last six days had not been easy, and this one just ending had been both physically and mentally exhausting. But I forced myself up the stairs to Father's room, where I found Mathilde making ready for bed. The princess, she said, had been sound asleep for the last hour.

"Has His Majesty visited her?"

"Yes. He was very pleased," Mathilde said smugly. I could see that she was going to take all credit for that posset.

But tomorrow . . . tomorrow . . .

"Then I think I'll go to my own bed," I said.

120

"You look tired," Mathilde said. Her voice was kinder.

I crawled slowly down the stairs, across the rough tourney ground, and reached the Queen's Tower. The lantern at the foot of the stairs had blackened its horn and gave almost no light. I called twice for Blanco, but there was no reply, so I gathered the remnants of my strength and mounted the stairs on all fours.

The solar was deserted, but the fire had not been thoroughly stamped out and a handful of sticks, ready for the morning's rekindling, lay to hand. My hands were icy-cold from the stone of the stairs, so I laid one stick and then another on the embers, and they burst into flame. I crouched there, warming my hands by the little blaze, too tired to go to bed, too tired to think coherently.

When I heard a movement on the stairs outside I thought it was Blanco coming back to his kennel. And when the door of the solar opened and I looked up, half in curiosity, half in alarm, and saw Blondel standing there, I didn't really believe my eyes. I so often called him to mind; I knew so surely that I should never see him in the flesh again; and all day everything had seemed unreal.

I just stared. He was wearing his blue cloak—I could see that in the light of the blazing twigs—and he had something of the same blue in his hand.

"Your Grace . . . " he said. And though I had doubted my eyes, I believed my ears.

"Blondel! You came back——"

"Yes, Your Grace. I came back. I found out what you wanted to know, but it wasn't a thing that could be put into a letter. And I was—homesick."

The blue thing in his hand was a bunch of wild hyacinths such as gypsy children sell along the roads to passers-by. "He had a posy in his hand . . . " I had lied. I had prayed. I had sent him away to find his own life. And here he was. Homesick. My mind spun like a wheel. I had only a moment left.

"Tell me," I cried, and I could hear my own voice coming as it were from a great distance, coming through thunder. "Your news, Blondel, your news?"

At the far edge of the spinning darkness which bore down on me I heard him saying "Richard Plantagenet," saying "Alys . . . "

The miracle I had prayed for had come about. My lie was true. I had just time to know so much and then the spinning darkness closed in on me.

121

Three

Love's Pilgrim

The story—with some mention of the lute player—is taken up by Eleanor of Aquitaine, the She-wolf, the Lady of the Golden Boot; one-time Queen of France, later Queen of England, mother to Richard Plantagenet.

WHEN MY ONE REMAINING SPY, FAITHFUL ALBERIC the pedlar, brought me news of Richard's landing in Dover I began to reckon my chances of seeing him before the wedding. There was no doubt in my mind that this much-debated, long-postponed marriage was at last going to take place. I thought it likely that I should be summoned to Westminster, have my crown loaned to me for a few hours, be given a fine new gown, have all the nobility of England and France crowding about me, sympathetically, curiously, jeeringly, and saying how fortunate it was that my health had made such a timely improvement. That had happened on one or two occasions before during my sixteen years' banishment; just one or two occasions when Henry thought it to his advantage to show the world that he still had a queen, or to show the people of my own duchy that I was still alive and unmaimed.

I hungered for the sight of Richard; he had always been the favourite of my sons, the one most like me in looks and temperament, the man I should have been if the Almighty had seen fit to make me male. It was, I reckoned, eleven years since I had last seen him, and time drags heavily when one passes it in monotonous confinement. I longed to see what he had grown into, and there were a thousand things I wanted to talk over with him. I could have sent a request, through Nicolas of Saxham to Ranulf de Glanville and so to Henry himself, a humble request that my son be allowed to visit me. But that would have given three men who hated me and whom I hated an opportunity for spite. The two go-betweens would have delayed, forgotten, and finally garbled the message; the fountainhead of authority would have been overjoyed to say "No." So I waited and did nothing, knowing that if Richard wished to see me he would come to Winchester, with or without permission.

A week passed without a sign or a word. I began to harbour some cold doubts. Henry was extremely crafty, and he was also most incongruously sentimental. He might have seized this opportunity of making peace with Richard, and a break with me might be one of its terms. And Richard himself must be in a complaisant or subdued temper ever to have come to England. A truce with his father, a politic marriage with the sister of the young King of France—and thus, I thought, Richard passes from my ken. But he comes

124

into his own; it is a clever and profitable change of sides. I mustn't mind. I hated Henry, I hated the Princess Alys, but I loved Richard. If this change of side were to his advantage—and I was sure it was—I would welcome it, at the same time wondering how long it would last!

On the eighth day, very early in the morning, when I was at my breakfast, Nicolas of Saxham, who was called my resident physician but in reality my gaoler, threw open the door of my apartment and announced, in a manner that denied all the petty cruelties and deprivations which he delighted to impose upon me, Prince Richard, Duke of Aquitaine. I got up, flurried as a green girl, with a manchet of bread still in my hand, and moved from the table a pace or two and so stood while Richard strode into the room.

He said, "Mother!" and came and fell on his knee and took my hand in both his and kissed it, back and palm, and smiled up at me and said, "Thank God you look just the same, not a day older."

And I swallowed and blinked and said: "I hope you do, Richard. Stand up and let me look at you."

He was truly magnificent. Even at that time the minstrels and the minnesingers were making songs about him, and since that time he has, of course, become the subject of many stories, many legends. And for once all the things they say and sing are veritable truth. I am not easily impressed by the stature of goodly looks of men. I was reared amongst tall knights. My grandfather, William of Aquitaine, was reckoned the most handsome man of his time; my uncle Robert, who ruled Antioch and of whom I had seen a great deal during the crusade which I made with my first husband, he of France, was a magnificent man. Even Henry Plantagenet, when as a youth he had caught my eye and my fancy, had had looks and bearing beyond the common. But this, my son, eclipsed all. He had been shaping for size and beauty when I had last seen him, a boy of twenty-one; now he was thirty-two, hardened and matured; a full head taller than I, who am a tall woman; his shoulders broad and square; his hips narrow and muscular like a good hound's; his hair and beard of the true red-gold of the Angevins; his skin tanned and every bone in his face prominent and beautiful; his eyes blue-grey-green, variable as the sea. Truly a most magnificent man. And my son.

He said, "I am sorry to have disturbed you at breakfast."

I said, "Richard, the sight of you does me more good than

any food in the world. Eleven years," I said. "You have grown from boy to man. Eleven whole years."

"Yes, yes," he said, a little hastily, as though suspecting a rebuke, "I should have come. I would have come—but always there have been things in the way. I sent messages——"

"I always received them."

"And I yours. And the gloves." As he spoke he held out the gloves I had made for him out of goatskin and a whole string of pearls. And as he held them out I realised that they were the only thing of any quality about him. If he had taken off his clothes and thrown them into a corner they might have belonged to any common archer. Against the worn, scuffed leather hose and jerkin the fine pearl-encrusted gloves struck a note of incongruity. Not that it mattered what he wore; he had no need for the outward display of rank or state; he would never be overlooked or underrated in any company.

Looking at him thus, I realised that the warmth of his greeting to me, the emotion of the moment, and the pleasantries had been overlaid upon something very different. The whites of his eyes were streaked with red and the pulse in his neck beat hard. I recognised these signs of temper. Connecting them with this sudden visit to me—at the end of a week—I judged that he had yet again quarrelled with his father. Egoistically I thought that it might be about my presence at the wedding. Maybe Henry didn't want me and Richard did. A quarrel, and then this sudden early-morning visit. It fitted. Well, I would say that I didn't want to go to the wedding, that I didn't feel well enough. After all, I was supposed to have been an invalid for sixteen years!

"I must talk to you, Mother," Richard said, beginning to walk about the room and slapping the gloves against his hand.

"I know," I said helpfully. "About your wedding."

He swung round abruptly and said, "You knew, then?"

"I guessed. Henry doesn't wish me to be present and you do, and you've had another quarrel about it. Dear Richard, always so loyal! But this time it does not matter. I'm an old woman now; the journey would tire me and the falseness of my position would be irksome. I am delighted that you are to be married at last, and I hope Alys will be brought to bed of a son within a year, but I shall be happy not to be present at the wedding."

They were beginning to call him Lionheart, Richard the Lion, Coeur de Lion; but there were times when, despite his size, he seemed to me to resemble more a red fox. When he was angry or carried away by enthusiasm he gave the impression of blunt honesty, or reckless candour, or transparent honesty; but there were other times when he looked secretive, wily, foxy. He wore that look now as he turned in his pacing, stopped slapping the gloves, and instead drew them very slowly through his closed palm.

"And is that all you have to say about the—wedding?"

Was his father's sentimental streak yeasting in him?

"Naturally I hope that you will be very happy," I added. "I never cared greatly for Alys myself—but then, in the circumstances, I was hardly likely to. And it is years since I saw her. Besides, Richard, *any* woman would be clay in your hands."

He gave a short sharp bark of laughter.

"And that is all you have to say?"

"What do you *wish* me to say?"

"Have you ever wondered *why*, whenever the matter of my marriage to Alys has been brought up, some reason, always a fresh one, has been found for the postponement? Answer that honestly, Mother."

I answered him honestly. "Many times—with each postponement. At first I blamed you—not too hardly, Richard; you are young and many temptations, I am sure, come your way. And I am not sure in my heart that it is a good thing for both bride and groom to be innocent and untried. I was content that you should have your fling. . . . More lately, I must admit I have begun to cherish a suspicion."

"Yes?" he said, looking at me closely, with caution.

"I have sometimes suspected that it would suit Henry very well if you got yourself killed before you had bred an heir. He dotes upon John. And if someone let daylight into you, Richard, as you are constantly inviting someone to do, before you had a son, then Henry could leave his crown to John and die happy. If during this past week you have made your peace with him and are now his friend, I apologise for speaking so bluntly; but why else has he hindered for years the match which he himself made when Alys was a child and you little more, a match in every respect most suitable?"

"And that is the darkest suspicion you have ever harboured? My poor mother! Well, it isn't news that I would willingly bear to you and I hoped that some inkling of it might have reached you even here. Hasn't it? Hasn't it?" His stare bore down on me.

"Once," I said, "Alberic did bring me word of rumour that

127

was going round London—to the effect that since *you* were not anxious to marry Alys it might be well to let John do so. But nothing came of that," I added hastily.

"What Alberic and the London gossipmongers didn't know I must tell you now, Mother. My father and my betrothed are paramours!"

If a mangonel had hurled a great stone into the room I should have been less surprised. Surprised, not shocked. I was not shocked, for I did not then believe it. But I could see that Richard did.

"That," I said, "is the most malicious piece of gossip I ever heard. And it isn't true. I don't care who told you, Richard. It isn't true. Do you think I should not have known? How could such a thing be kept secret? Besides, Henry wouldn't dare. The princess of France, sent over here as a child and entrusted to Henry to bring up; his son's betrothed! Why, such a scandal would rock Christendom. No, Richard, whoever dropped that poison in your ear was acting from some ulterior motive, anxious to set you against your father again. Though it confounds me," I said after a second's reflection, "to name anyone who could have thought of such a story. Unless it was John. Was it John, Richard?"

"No," he said. "Nobody told me the story; I discovered the fact for myself, with some slight help from a French lute player who never guessed what he was about. The evidence of my own eyes, Mother, does that convince you?" His lips drew back from his teeth and his eyes glinted in a grimace that I recognised as his angry grin. "As for your not knowing, there is the best of reasons for that! Even if all England knew—which isn't this time the case—the old devil would have taken care to keep *you* in ignorance. He hasn't been outstandingly lucky with his lights-o'-love, has he, Mother?"

Not even at that moment was I going to admit anything. Not even to Richard. The stairs of Haverford Grange had collapsed under Huldah of Leicester, and the woman they called Sweet Edith of Ely had eaten oysters that had been overlong on the road from the oyster beds at Colchester. Rosamonde Clifford had died suddenly, but there were physicians who had attended her for the lung rot ever since the birth of her second son. I looked Richard straight in the face and said:

"That sounds like a cheap balladmonger's gibe, Richard. I hope you didn't intend it so."

Richard looked straight back and retorted, "When I made the discovery I remember thinking, even in the midst of my rage, that you must be either ignorant or very helpless, or there'd have been some strange porridge brewed for that little drab."

"I should be interested to know how you happened to make the discovery."

"It's a long story," he said impatiently. "I came over to please Philip. I want him with me on this crusade and he wants Alys married. So I came, meaning to despatch the matter as quickly as possible. His Majesty received me very genially. . . . Mother, you know his way when he chooses, smooth and slippery as oil. He began by suggesting that I should go to Windsor; he talked of hunting, as though I were here for pleasure. I made myself plain about that. I explained about Philip and told him why I had come. He then said that the princess was sick; she had a rheumy cold and had been abed for a week or more. But God gave him those eyes, Mother—clear as Venetian glass, aren't they? The deceit looked straight out at me! I countered with deceit; I changed my mind; I said I'd go to Windsor—she being ill and unable to receive me. So I left him. In the evening I went to William's Tower, where she lay, and it was true, she was abed with a cold. But they let me in, all fluttered and excited— you know how women are. And I had presents for her from Philip. Two of her ladies were there in the bedchamber— and we talked. I gave her the presents, and we talked about where and when the wedding should be and who should be invited. Very proper and formal. I took the opportunity of looking at her; I'd never seen her since she was full-grown, you know. A pretty wench, even with a gruesome cold—all that yellow hair. But uneasy. Very pleasant, agreeable to everything, but very uneasy and anxious to have us all away—not only me—all of us. One of the ladies yawned, and she seized on that. I left her with them, setting things in order for the night.

"In the anteroom there was this lute player, very softly trying over a new song. He said that sometimes he went in and played for her until she fell asleep. We talked for a little and then I borrowed his lute and went back. The women had gone, and when I opened the door she thought I was the boy and said, "I don't need you tonight," and then saw me and was most mightily confused. . . . Oh, why am I spinning this long yarn? Mother, there is a secret door to her room, opening on steps from the river, and before I had played three stanzas *he* came in by it, cock aloft, if you will forgive

129

the expression! And she began to scream. What she said in fear and what he said in rage made it all perfectly clear."

"You mean they admitted—— Richard, surely you must be mistaken. Alys was almost a baby when she came here. He's always regarded her as a daughter, like Joanna. I find it difficult to believe even now. Look, Richard, are you quite sure? You have never much wanted to marry Alys; if you had you would have done so years ago. Now Philip has tried to force your hand. Are you sure that you are not seeking an excuse, and finding one, because you looked so hard?"

"I want Philip's allegiance. For the crusade. Should I jeopardise that because of what I imagined? You, Mother, shrink from believing this because it is too shameful. If you could have heard them, she squalling like a scalded cat and he raving ... And now at last I have a grudge against him that will bring all Christendom to my side. Even that pious half monk, Philip, who thinks it such a *pity* that a son should raise hand against his father—though he hates Henry as the devil hates holy water—will see the justice of my cause."

"If he believes it, which he won't. Richard, I know Henry— he's faithless, he's lecherous. I hold no brief for him at all, but even I have the greatest difficulty in believing that a combination of circumstances and your state of mind haven't led you to a mistaken conclusion."

"There's no mistake. If you could have seen and heard them. Not that I grudge him the white-faced, yellow-headed little whore. He's welcome to her—as I told him. What angers me is that he should plan that I should marry his leavings. It's all of a piece with his behaviour. Anybody'd think he was God Almighty. Always the same. Henry, Geoffrey, and me. Duke of this, Duke of that—fuel for his vanity, titles and nonsense, none of it real. Always one of his long-nosed Normans hanging on our elbows, telling us when to go to bed, when to change our linen. . . . All false! And this is the ultimate falsity. He counts his sons so little that he thinks he can take first cut at my joint and that I shall not mind. Well, at least I gave him to understand that I do not take his leavings—even though it costs me Philip's friendship. And between him and me there will be war henceforth until one of us is dead. The world shall know why. All Christendom shall know what a lecherous old—— Henry the Law-giver—Lawgiver, forsooth—is."

With that I pulled my muddled, shattered mind together and began to think quickly.

I still found it incredible that Henry and Alys should be

lovers and not a whisper of the fact have stolen out. But Richard was prepared to believe it, did believe it, and was about to shout the dreadful news to the whole world.

For myself I minded little if at all. There had been Huldah and Edith and Rosamonde. . . . Men whispered that I had poisoned all three, but they were whispers, not shouted accusations. And it was one thing for a king to take a mistress, quite another for him to debauch a young girl, his ward, committed to his care as the betrothed of his son. That fact, bruited abroad by the son himself, would have results horrible to contemplate.

There had been a time when, if I saw something more clearly or more quickly than other people, I let fly straight at the bull's-eye of the argument, rapping out my reasons. That way I had gained the hatred of two husbands, reduced one son to spineless subjugation. Now I was wary and cunning.

"It is a horrible story," I said. "And if you proclaim it, Richard, everyone in the world will think your quarrel a just one. And how they will laugh!"

"Laugh? By God's toenails! Why should anybody laugh?"

"Because everybody dreads old age, Richard; therefore, anything that diminishes the value of youth is pleasing to them. Have you never noticed how, if an older man unseats a younger in the lists, men laugh? I have. And the prospect of a father cuckolding his son—for that is what it amounts to—will make them laugh till their ribs crack."

He stood stock-still and glared at me; then he said sullenly, "That's true. I hadn't thought of that."

"You've had little time for thinking," I said.

He brooded for a second or two and then burst out with renewed savagery: "But I *wanted* a good excuse against him. He's played the injured father often enough. 'A nest of rebellious vipers'—that's what they say of us. 'Honour thy father,' they prate. And," he added, turning on his heel and slapping the gloves again, "I've Philip to think of. I never was sure of that unclipped monk's allegiance, even when I was going to marry his sister! Now I'm in worse case. If I don't marry her and don't give the rightful reason, the shifting poltroon will be making terms with Henry within a week."

I spoke slowly, gently, adding word to word as though the thought I uttered had just occurred to me; concealing from Richard the fact that my mind had run ahead of his, for that is a thing, I had learned, that men abhor.

"I think you should tell Philip. And if you pretended that you concealed the truth from the rest of the world out of

131

chivalry, that would be an excellent thing. That would appeal to Philip. But for the rest, for many reasons, I would leave them guessing. For one thing, the sight of two princes, father and son, squabbling over a girl's body is not a very edifying spectacle."

I could have said much more, but I waited.

"*He* said that," Richard muttered. "He offered me the satisfaction of meeting him in single combat. I told him I wanted a fuller revenge than the making of a hole in his great carcase would afford me. He also offered—if I kept silence—to withdraw all supervision from my duchy. I told him that any man of his who showed his face in Aquitaine after this would withdraw without waiting for *his* order. I meant to expose him, shame him before the world. And now—if I must hush up the story ... " His face darkened ominously.

"There's no *must*," I hastened to say. "But there is another reason for keeping silence. Will you be offended if I explain it to you?"

"When you offend me, Mother, I'll tell you. I'm not Harry, you know."

"Poor Harry, God rest him," I said, and spared a thought for my eldest son, who, entirely intractable towards everyone but me, had been pliable as thread in my hands. But Harry was dead, and this angry man before me was the heir to England—it was to him I must speak.

"These English of yours, Richard, are a peculiar people. Coarse, ignorant, bloodthirsty, but very *moral*. And this country is English now, not Norman any more. William conquered England, but he did not vanquish the English people; a few retained their manors; many women married Normans and imposed their peculiar standards upon their children. They're sly and they love to cloak a practical expediency with a well-sounding idealism. I realised that long ago and knew that if half Henry's misdoings were noised abroad there were many men who would rise up and say, 'Shall this fornicator rule us?' And they'd really believe that it was the fornication and the adultery that they hated and not his Angevin blood and his reforms of law. And the English are very susceptible to the rule of women; look how they rallied to Matilda; look how they still sentimentalise about 'Good Queen Maud.' Any time in these last twenty years, Richard, I could have raised a queen's party in this country and had all the best men in England on my side. Joined by every little tyrant whose castle Henry has dismantled and every noble whose authority he has undermined."

"And I wonder you haven't," Richard said. "By the Rood, in your place I would."

"And to what end?" I asked. "To what end? To set all England in a ferment of a Saxon revival? To make smooth the way for the kin of the Atheling? No, I wanted England for my son. Once—before I acquired wisdom—I tried to take it by force. I misjudged that time. I thought that Harry and I—— But that is old history and I have paid the price of my mistake. Sixteen years, Richard, I have been confined here, and I shall stay here until I die or he does. And I have learned wisdom. We must wait now and let him rule England, *whole and entire*, until he dies; and you must survive him and you must get you an heir. You can rise against him in Aquitaine, where men are sensible, if rise you must; but do not speak the word which might make your moral English say, '*All* these Angevins are evil men!' Leave England intact, for this small island is the brightest jewel in your crown. Aquitaine, dear to my heart, Gascony, Brittany, Normandy are great and glorious; but they are vulnerable, always dependent upon the good will or the weakness of their neighbours. England is, or could be, an impregnable fortress that could defy the world."

"Yes," he said, nodding his head. "In Harold's place I could have held it. Harold was a good fighter but a poor strategist who fought the wildcat while the tiger mustered for the spring!" He stood still for a moment, running through his mind the battles of Stamfordbridge and Senlac Field as *he* would have fought them. Battles, the muster and disposition of men and weapons were to him a mental playground.

I moved quietly back to the table and into one of the coarse horn beakers which had long since replaced the silver on my table I poured a measure of the bitter English ale with which it pleased Nicolas of Saxham to serve me instead of the wine I loved.

"This is quite horrible," I said, "but I can say from experience that it is harmless and even sustaining."

He took the beaker and drained it, set it back on the table, and then walked beyond and seated himself on the seat below the window.

"You argue just like a woman, Mother," Richard said. "With one breath you tell me that if men knew about my father and my betrothed—damn them both to hell—they'd laugh till their ribs cracked, and with the next you predict that the same news would lead to bloody rebellion. Now you can't make that team pull in the same yoke."

I had been accused of almost everything in my time, but never before of lack of logic.

"You say that because you don't know your English, Richard. The very ones who laughed at you, the cuckold, would be the first to rise against him, the lecher. And you must admit that between the two there'd be very little royal Angevin dignity left."

"Nimble little tongue," Richard said with sudden good humour. "No wonder he keeps you locked up!"

"I keep myself locked up," I said proudly. "When Harry and I rose against him I could have gone to Aquitaine and bleated out the true story of Rosamonde Clifford, justified myself, and ruled there. But that wasn't what I wanted. I wanted England—all of it. And I didn't want it for John; remember that. Harry first, then you. You are my sons. Were; are. Harry was; you are. John is Henry's man."

Richard was silent for a moment, then he said:

"Well, you have muddled the argument, but you have convinced me. I'll tell Philip and nobody else. Then I'll make an excuse to fight Henry, and this time I'll fight him to the end. I'll begin by attacking Le Mans, which he regards as another Bethlehem because, forsooth, he was born there."

"And for Christ's own sake, be careful when you fight," I said. "I live in dread lest anything should happen to you."

Everything, every conflicting expression went out of his face, leaving a great clear shining.

"Nothing can happen to me," he said, "until I have taken Jerusalem. Begin to worry about me when my colours fly over the Holy Sepulchre. Then I may tread on a rusty nail or swallow a fishbone; and die, the happiest man on earth! Until then nothing can touch me. I've proved that. I've taken special risks to prove it. Mother, you must come on crusade with me. The Lady of the Golden Boot must ride again! We'll ride into Jerusalem side by side and feast where Solomon's great palace stood. And then you shall repeat your exhortations—and I will listen. For when I have taken Jerusalem I shall be vulnerable like other men."

"Richard," I said, forgetting my role and speaking motherly, "that is wild talk. And dangerous. You are vulnerable *now*. You have great strength and great skill—but you are flesh and blood, prey to sword, or axe, or arrow. What you have just said sounds—so reckless. And it smacks of witchcraft too."

"And isn't that natural enough?" he asked with a teasing laugh. "Aren't we all, according to legend, descendants of the devil?"

"Hush," I said. A little shudder ran down my backbone. This was not the moment to remember the woman who was great-grandmother to *my* brood. The woman who went to Mass so seldom, and then was always careful to leave before the consecration, and whose husband finally ordered four strong men to hold her down at the moment when the Host was lifted. They said that the four men were left with the cloak of the countess in their hands. She had vanished, and there was the scent of burning brimstone in the church.

"Richard," I said firmly, "who is talking like a woman now? We are settling policies and campaigns. Let's leave the chatter of broomsticks and magic to the old women huddled over the fire on winter nights. I have thought of something useful. If you do decide to fight your father there is that which he regards more highly than the town of Le Mans— the loss of which would deal him a shrewder blow."

"He loves that town beyond all."

"No, he holds one thing more precious."

"And that is? Mother, tell me. It shall be my first target."

"Your brother John," I said. "John is the heart of his heart. If you could persuade John to join you . . . "

I felt, even as I spoke, that I was suggesting the impossible. John was Henry's man. I myself regarded John as a hen might regard a duckling which she had hatched or as a briar might some graftling. Out of my flesh he sprang, of my blood he was born, but he was no child of mine. He had lain at my breast in his suckling days, a dark-skinned, dark-eyed baby, inclined even then to fattishness, the stranger. Henry, Geoffrey, Richard, even my gentle daughter Joanna, had courage from the start; they thought nothing of a nipped finger, a broken knee. John was a born coward. My children had no conscious charm; they did what they willed. If it was wrong, they were in disgrace; if it was good, they were in favour, but they never tried to please.

John had great charm, deliberately exercised. All through his youth he behaved as though he were a peasant child suddenly transported and, conscious of his inferiority and his alienness, was endeavouring to please while at the same time, peasantlike, he pursued his own advantage. Even I, puzzled as I was to realise that I had produced him, could not hate him with any thoroughness. I disliked him, I distrusted him, I was very jealous because Henry preferred him to any of his legitimate sons and rated him almost as highly as he rated the other Geoffrey, Rosamonde Clifford's bastard, but there were times when something he said, acutely intelligent, or witty, or flattering, would disarm me. Several times during my banishment—but always when his father was overseas—John had arrived at Winchester to pay me a visit; always he brought some present, most carefully chosen—wine, preserved fruit, game, trivial yet showing that he understood exactly my circumstances. I would be on my dignity with him at first, but he would ignore that, or rather use his awareness of it to spur him to greater efforts, and he would retail me all the gossip of the court and reel off every funny story he had heard and be, for an hour or so, a most charming companion.

"Brother John," said Richard quite softly, "little Brother John Lackland! That should be easy. Little Greedy-guts sticking to Father because Father has the key to the pantry! We'll see! I'll make a bargain. I'll tell him if he joins me *now* I'll leave him in control when I go on crusade. If I am King, as I hope to be, I'll make him regent of England; if not, I'll give him power in Aquitaine. Given authority anywhere, he'd wring himself out a fortune in six months! And just to make the bargain sweeter, I'll promise him not to breed an heir until I return from the Holy Land. And that will give him something to pray for."

So many vehement protests formed in my mind then that I hardly knew which to voice first. John in the saddle in England would mean trouble within a fortnight; John in the saddle in Aquitaine would drive my duchy into the arms of France in seven days. Hadn't this great, magnificent silly perspicacity enough to see that? Of course it was a bribe which was certain to bring John to his side, and Richard, being what he was, had no thought of anything but the immediate fighting; he was taking John up as a man lifts a weapon. I could see all this. But it would be dangerous to say so. I would leave that, I thought, until later. I merely said:

"Oh, Richard, that would be an ill thing to promise. You should get the crown on your head and at least two healthy boys at heel before you go crusading at all."

At that he gave a hearty laugh in which there was no tinge of bitterness.

"A fine thing to say to a man who has just lost his betrothed!"

"A small loss," I said, "and the world is full of young women." I said it absent-mindedly, for, thinking back to the

136

affair of Alys and my husband, I had remembered something.

"Richard, a while back when you spoke of discovering this business you mentioned a French lute player who aided you. If we're going to keep this affair secret and tell only Philip the real truth, what of that fellow? Is he clacking all over London at this moment? How much does he know?"

"Not being deaf, everything. He was in the anteroom—I'd borrowed his lute and he waited to recover it. The King and I both bellowed at the top of our voices, and Madam squealed like a stuck pig. At that moment I didn't care who knew or who clacked—I meant to clack myself."

"He must be found and his weasand slit at once," I said. I thought rapidly. "I'll attend to it. Alberic is at hand. He brought me news of your arrival some days ago, and I asked him to remain in the district so that I could send you a message if you failed to come. If the fellow has blabbed already, his throat being cut so promptly will give pause to —others who think to spread the story, and at worst it may find its way into a ballad, like the Fair Rosamonde tale which already they call a legend. What was this lute player like?"

"He had white hair," said Richard, frowning in an attempt to remember. "But he wasn't old. I noted him little at the time. He played very well and spoke French like a Frenchman."

"He should be easy to find," I said. "Alberic shall go to London this morning."

"I also, in search of John," Richard said. He rose and came towards me and laid his arm across my shoulders. "Be of good cheer, Mother. Before we meet again things may have altered. If God has any justice I shall win this time. We'll enjoy our freedom together!"

I found myself repeating my pleadings with him to be careful, not to take unnecessary risks. That made him impatient and our leave-taking was, in the end, abrupt and lacking in sentiment. As soon as he was gone I sent for Alberic, pretending that I was in need of sewing materials. He took my strange order with his usual calmness and set off. It was some weeks before he wandered in again, bringing as his excuse some lace which, he said, was too good and expensive to offer to any but the highest ladies in the land.

He had failed to find the white-haired French lute player, though he had learned his identity and made a thorough search for him. But he brought, he said, news of all kinds. The poor little Princess of France had fallen into such a state of ill-health that all thought of her marriage must be aban-

137

doned. She was leaving London. Some said that she was returning to her own land, others that she was going to the nuns at Rumsey, others that the King was making her a permanent establishment at Windsor as though she were his own daughter. Of the true reason for the breaking of the betrothal arrangements Alberic had obviously heard no whisper of rumour, for even when I had plied him well with my detestable breakfast ale, saved for the purpose, and he was in the maudlin state in which any natural delicacy he possessed which might have held him silent on that subject to *me* would be abandoned, my most cunning and leading questions drew a blank. The lute player had vanished and he had not clacked. Putting those two facts together, I came to the conclusion that Henry himself had taken steps to ensure his silence.

Meanwhile I had other things to think of, for Alberic brought other news. Duke Richard, he told me, had had another quarrel with the King about the supervision kept on him and the authority imposed by the royal officials.

"Unless they are withdrawn," he is said to have shouted, "they shall all share the fate of Salisbury and his lickspittles who were sent to hold my mother down in 1168!" (In that ill-omened year Henry had sent me back to my duchy ostensibly to control and consolidate, but he had sent the earl and a great horde of officials to do the real ruling; and my fierce people, insulted on their own account and on mine, rose and made mincemeat of Salisbury and his men, all in one bloody day.)

"And if they share his fate—nay, if one of them is so much as touched—you shall share your mother's fate," Henry bellowed back.

That was their last talk together. Richard went back to Aquitaine, and already Henry was mustering men and making arrangements to leave England.

II

Soon there was no need for me to depend upon Alberic for news. Every tongue wagged with it. The young French King and the young Duke of Aquitaine, "united as never before"— a noteworthy phrase—began the attack; Henry of England rode to meet the challenge, but something was wrong with him from the beginning. Age? Disillusion? The carelessness bred of long dominion? Whatever the reason, he took only a small army, largely composed of mercenaries, and the young allies, "united as never before," very soon established their superiority.

It may be grossly sentimental of me, but I always believed that the affair of Alys destroyed something in Henry. The seduction of his son's betrothed, a young girl who had been entrusted to his care, who had literally been like one of his own children, was something which, in the heat of passion, he could square with his own conscience and with his own peculiar attitude towards God—so long as it was secret. But now he knew that Richard knew and he must have guessed that, since the two young men were now firm allies, Richard had told Alys's brother the reason for the breaking of the match. And I think Henry was ashamed, who had never known shame in his life. The three met, we are told, in a farcical attempt to arrange matters peaceably, and Richard and Philip, after some puerile chat, marched out of the conference place laughing, with their arms linked. Henry must have known why they were laughing and why they were so firmly linked against him.

They took his most beloved town, Le Mans, and burned it. Henry, defeated, wounded, and in great pain, sat on his horse and looked back at the flaming town and then vented his fury in words of unparalleled audacity. "Since God has seen fit to take from me that which I most valued, I will take from Him that which we are told He values most—my immortal soul!"

After that, tended and comforted by his bastard, Geoffrey, Rosamonde Clifford's son, he rode to his lodging, and there he received the insolent, domineering terms upon which his son and his son's ally were prepared to make peace. Amongst the demands was the forgiveness of all his subjects who had taken arms against him. He roused himself to ask who, and how many, they were. And the son of his mistress took list in hand and read out the names. Amongst them was the name of John. Just as Richard and I had planned.

It was the final blow. They said that he groaned out, "John too. My well-beloved son. Now my cup is full." With that he turned his face to the wall, refused food, medical attention, the priests' ministrations, and so died.

And Richard was King of England and lord of the whole Angevin empire, just as I had hoped and planned. And I was free to leave my prison at Winchester and take my rightful place in the world after sixteen years of exile.

But something had happened to me too. Just as the exposure of his love affair with Alys had made an old man of Henry, so Henry's death had made an old woman of me. For so many reasons that even the long night watches when I lay wakeful were hardly long enough to suffice for me to sort them out.

I lay in my new bed, most comfortably feathered and covered, and I mourned for Henry. He had treated me ill and I had hated him and had waited for his death these many years, yet I mourned the manner of it. There was something about that defiant outcry of his against God that roused my blood. It was admirable, manly, and it fitted the young Henry as I remembered him when he first visited the French court with his father and we looked at one another, he a youth of seventeen, I, a queen, twelve years his elder. I would think of that and sometimes I actually found myself wishing that I had been a woman of another sort, cut to the pattern of his paramours, meek, pretty, feminine counterparts of the man who could go to his death defying God. If I had been such a woman I might have held him, but the very part of me that made me appreciate his daring made it impossible for me to live with him in peace and endure his lordship meekly. That was the paradox. Any one of his women outside that burning town would have cried, "Oh, Henry, oh, my dear, don't, you'll surely go to hell!" I should have cried, *Bravissimo!* But then, any one of his women, told to do this or that, or not to do anything at all, would have said, "Yes, Henry." I always said, "Why?" or "Have you thought . . . ?" or "In God's name that is folly!" We were ill matched, and we came, as husband and wife, to an ill end.

Other times in the night I lay awake and thought about the price Richard had paid for his victory.

And if my mourning for the lost days and the failure of my marriage may have been feminine sentimentality, my fears for the future were every one of them logical and well founded. Time proved that. Richard had gained the allegiance of Philip and of John. And between them they brought him to victory. But at what cost!

I have lived long enough to see the final result of that alliance which made Richard and Philip "united as never before" and sent them swaggering out of Henry's presence laughing, their arms linked. Implacable hatred, that was the result. And for a very curious reason, a reason which seems to be unknown to all the makers of ballads and the singers of songs who go jingling on about the Third Crusade and the differences which arose between Philip of France and Richard of England. They all attribute Philip's hatred of Richard to jealousy, jealousy of his size and strength, his valour, his skill in fighting, and his popularity with the common soldiery. All of that may be true, but I believe that the trouble between them began, though it lay dormant for a while, on the day when Richard found Philip hunting, drew him away from his entourage, and said:

"My father and your sister are lovers. I shall not marry her, and him I shall fight to the death. Now, Philip of France, will you side with me or with that lecher and that whore?"

Richard told me himself that those were his words. Blunt, tactless, inconsiderate, and to the point. And the question naturally put Philip in a very awkward position. It would have been a difficult question for any man to answer, but for Philip it was peculiarly so. For Philip had inherited from his father, my first husband, a pious streak, and he took very seriously such a choice between his personal inclination and his moral obligation. In such a situation a man, according to whether he is hedonist or idealist, must make his choice; and Philip found the choice hard because in him the two were balanced. His sound good sense bade him to keep out of this quarrel; his piety forbade him to side, even by neutrality, with a lecher and a whore. Richard's blunt words had left him no loophole and in the end he came out on Richard's side and for a time drowned his doubts by a violent partisanship. But he always, I think, cherished a resentment against the man who had forced the decision on him. He repeatedly proposed, after Henry's death, that Richard should let bygones be bygones and marry Alys after all.

"Had you not been so tardy a lover that accident would never have happened; and it is no worse than marrying a widow," he said on one occasion, when the question of Alys's future cropped up. Richard, with an ill-timed humour, replied that a man was forbidden by Holy Church to marry his father's widow! That kind of joke went down ill with Philip, who was monkish and had all the monk's outward attention to form and inward sly evasion. Philip may have disliked Richard for many reasons and he may have regarded him with deadly envy, but many little signs, particularly Philip's attitude towards the woman Richard did marry, point to an enmity beginning on the day when Richard made his blunt decision and then used a moral lever to force Philip to make an equally blunt one.

And then there was John. No evasion of the promise and

the bribe was possible now. Richard had said that John should be his regent if he were King before he went on crusade. He was King and he had taken the Cross side by side with Philip in the new crusade which William of Tyre was urging throughout Christendom. So in a matter of a few months England would lie at John's feet and suffer all the misrule that can spring from authority without responsibility. Just at the moment when the most sound, most cautious government was needed to hold the country in trust for its absent King a reckless, selfish, greedy savage child would be in control.

I worried incessantly and I resented it, for, apart from such mental discomforts, my life had come out into a pleasant place. In some ways the change was comic. When the breath went out of Henry's body Nicolas of Saxham, erstwhile my gaoler, became my subservient slave, and Glanville, who had never taken his overseership seriously enough to care whether I lived or died, became most attentive. There was no more brown ale; the wine appeared on my table almost as suddenly as it did at the wedding in Cana; all my clothes and a good many of my jewels were returned to me. Did I wish a fire, the day being chill? Would I care to ride, the day being fine? Overnight I changed from being an unwanted, unloved wife of a king to a cherished queen mother. Sometimes I thought wryly of all the women whose sun had set over their husband's graves; mine had known a belated but brilliant redawning. Before ever Richard had come back for his crowning I was besieged by fawning suitors and I lost count of the petitions and requests which came to me—often accompanied by gifts—as a means of reaching the King's ear. I ignored them all, and the only request I made to Richard at that time was a purely personal one.

("Nicolas of Saxham, Your Majesty, presents a solemn petition and begs that he may be suitably rewarded for the faithful discharge of his duties as your mother's warden all these years."

"And what would my mother suggest as suitable?"

"His head would look mighty well at the top of a pole; and if excuse for such extreme reward were needed, I think a close scrutiny of his accounts would provide it."

"Aye, and teach the rest of the knaves that I take count of pennies. A timely lesson and one they must learn soon."

So Nicolas of Saxham went to his account and Richard permitted me to give his forfeited Suffolk manor to the faithful Alberic, only stipulating that the feudal dues on the property be raised from four fully furnished men-at-arms to ten. Alberic was demented by pride and joy. He took for his coat of arms a pedlar's pack with ten lances sprouting from it!)

Richard was crowned in September with more pomp and ceremony and magnificence than had ever been seen before. It was such a pity, I thought, that he should take so little pleasure in the welcome extended to him by his English people or from the efforts they made to display their fervent loyalty. He spent no penny of his own and grudged the extravagance of others. "If they have no better use for their money, I have," he grumbled. "Does a canopy that costs enough to arm ten knights make me more a king than I am already? ... So the Tailors' Guild is providing free wine for every sot in London! By God, before I'm through with them they'll wish it back for the sake of their own dry throats."

Only the gifts which came to him pleased him, and for any king less devoured by single-minded ambition they would have assured wealth for many years. Not even I had guessed the immensity of England's wealth or of Richard's popularity. Apart from his size and beauty—always sure key to the heart of the common people—there was his reputation as a fighter to commend him. The streets of London rang day and night with songs of his prowess, many true, some exaggerated, some invented. And the gifts poured in. Simple common people who saw in Richard the son of Henry the Lawgiver and the symbol of their security dug into their greasy purses and wooden coffers; the nobles and barons who saw him as the knight-errant who would shortly go off on crusade and allow them to return to the lawless power of the old days opened their silk purses and jewel boxes. Even the Jews ventured out of their protective obscurity and brought him presents, a move which resulted in a small immediate tragedy and a great future one. Richard received their presents graciously, even eagerly—he would have taken a present from Satan himself, I think—but some officials, mindful of the law forbidding women and Jews from participating in the ceremony, and some of the rabble who needed no excuse for disorder set about the Jews and there were riot and massacre, both on a small scale. Richard was vexed, but the matter was easily forgotten in the general rejoicing.

As soon as the ceremonies and the feastings were ended Richard came to my new and most comfortable apartment in Westminster, greeted me briefly but warmly, and threw himself into a chair. "There," he said, "God be thanked, all the mummery is over. Four days we've been at it, and now I think everyone is satisfied that I *am* King of England. And now Mother, I want to talk to you."

I said lightly, "I am all attention, Your Majesty," but something warned me that he was here on a serious errand; and, looking into his face, I was aware of a faint, pricking concern for his health—the first, I think, that I had ever known. Boredom and his own boundless impatience, both of which he had been compelled, in some measure at least, to restrain, had exhausted him more than any physical effort could ever do; he looked tired and strained, almost distraught. I determined there and then that whatever it was that he was about to ask me—and I suspected that a request was forthcoming—I would do without question and without hesitation.

"You know, don't you," he began abruptly, "that I intend to go to Palestine as soon as I have gathered men and gear sufficient? I've just seen Longchamp and Hugh of Durham, and they are off to raise money quickly. Longchamp has a stupendous plan for turning the Jew riot in York to advantage—but I won't go into that *now*. If you choose"—he wagged a finger at me—"you can gather me in a considerable sum in a short time. But I won't deny that it entails some inconvenience to yourself."

My jewels, I thought with a slight pang. Ludicrous! I'd gone decked like a shrine in the jewels of France, forfeited them all when Louis divorced me, and gone to Henry as bare as a tinker's bitch; Henry had loaded me again, fingers, wrists and ears, throat and brow, as became a queen; then he had taken all away. Some had recently been restored to me, and now . . .

"My jewels," I said. "Well, luckily I haven't yet got into the habit of wearing them! Several of the best pieces have vanished too. But to what I have you are welcome, Richard."

His strained face softened into a grin, boyish, but not quite at ease.

"I don't ask your trinkets, *yet*. It might come to that! I'd rather save them against the day when we ride together into

Jerusalem. Remember? No, Mother, what I ask of you at this moment is a feat of exertion and no small measure of diplomacy." The uneasy, boyish grin, the cajoling way in which he had said, "Remember?" and above all this beating about the bush—so unusual with him—puzzled and disconcerted me. What was he about to demand?

"I want you to go to Navarre—to Pamplona—and do an errand for me there."

"Holy Mother," I said, "that is quite a journey for a woman of my age!" But I said that because that was the first sentence I could form in my confusion. Behind it my thoughts ran wild. It *was* a journey, but if Richard knew anything about me at all he must know that journeying was my delight, and after all those years of captivity to be made free of the wide world ... No, it wasn't the journey, it was the errand that made him hesitant and furtive. Surely he didn't want me to marry Sancho! Or did he? Did he secretly, like Louis and Henry and Harry and John, fear and detest me? Had he so soon planned such a subtle way to be rid of me? And I thought, I won't do it. I've suffered enough from husbands! I'll go to some small estate and live as a private person; as a peasant, rather.

"Yes," Richard said, "it is quite a journey, and that is the least of it! It's when you get there——"

"For God's sake," I exclaimed, "speak out, Richard. What do you want me to do in Navarre?"

"Convince Sancho," he said, "*convince* him that my intentions towards his daughter are honourable and persuade him to send me the money immediately. I can't marry her yet. I haven't time. But I will, as soon as I get this business well under way, and to do that I want the money. If you go and talk to him and bring her to meet me somewhere and get him to send the money to me at once, I'll be everlastingly grateful to you, Mother."

I saw my hands moving as though they had been detached from my body, weaving about in the air before me. Hysteria, I thought, and clasped them firmly in my lap.

"You're going to marry one of Sancho's daughters?" I asked. "Which one, Blanche or Berengaria?"

"Berengaria—if it can be arranged."

"But, Richard, in heaven's name, *why?* You're free now, you're King of England, lord of Aquitaine; you could marry any princess in Christendom."

My mind broke into froth and I groped about in it to pull

145

out certain facts I remembered as poor people grope in the surf of breaking waves for driftwood.

"Her mother was mad," I said. "I well remember when my godchild, Marie-Maud, was married at Limoges—and, Richard, that must be almost twenty years ago—all the gossip in the bower was about the Queen of Navarre having conceived in a moment of sanity and whelped in a fit of madness. They joked about it and said usually it was the other way round! And since then I've heard that this Berengaria is superbly beautiful. Richard, she's beautiful and twenty years old and not yet betrothed! Doesn't that suggest anything to you? She's probably mad too."

"She can be as crazy as all Gadara for all I care," Richard said.

"You mean you fell in love with her pretty face when you were in Pamplona some time ago," I said bitterly. "Richard, my dear one, my darling son, the only son I have left— please, just this once, just this one time, listen to your mother. . . ."

"If my mother would just listen to me for a moment, if she had listened at all," Richard said coldly, "she would remember that money was mentioned. Not madness in old queens or pretty faces in young princesses, money, gold coins which a man needs to equip an army and conduct a campaign. So stop squawking for a moment while I tell you the situation. I never saw the girl; I daresay she was there amongst the other women during that tournament, and events seem to suggest that she took a fancy to me. Sancho began to make approaches a long time ago when I was tied by the heel. Then lately—in fact, before I'd told anyone but Philip that I wasn't going to marry Alys—there was Sancho's emissary again. He'd offered me a substantial contribution towards my crusade once before; this time he doubled it, and this time I was in a position to accept it. But breaking with Alys after so long a betrothal and no reason given hasn't exactly enhanced my reputation with scheming papas, and Sancho, before he parts with a penny, needs some assurance of my good faith. If you go to assure him and collect the girl, all will be well. But if the job isn't to your liking, say so now and I'll ask Joanna to go. She's kicking her heels in Sicily and would be pleased to help her brother."

"I'll go, Richard," I said hastily. "If anybody goes, I'll go. But I wish you would think, just for a moment. Lightly as marriages are arranged, they *matter*. And so few people are free to choose. You are. You are the most eligible man on

146

earth, I should think. Is it really necessary for you to *sell* yourself"—I used the word deliberately and repeated it—"to sell yourself for a sum of money, like an apprentice marrying his master's buck-toothed daughter?"

He rose from his chair and stood over me until I rose, too, and pulled myself up and faced him.

"Should *you* talk?" he asked, not rudely; if anything, a little sadly. "You *chose* Father! You could have stayed with Louis or had any man in the world. Every man who looked at you lusted after you. You chose! This mad, this destructive notion that one person matters more than another, this devilish worship of personality—where did it land you? I don't want a certain woman or even a certain sort of woman in my bed; I don't crave a face or even a certain sort of face at my table. I want to get to the East quickly and beat Saladin. Sancho's money will be a means to that end. That is all I want, all I've ever wanted since I could remember. I've never drawn sword, lifted axe, or couched lance without thinking: Beware, Saladin, here I come! But thinking and wishing and praying are not enough. In these days nothing counts but money, and of that I have always been short. I've scrimped and saved; if you could see my headquarters at Rouen you'd see them poorer and meaner than your prison at Winchester. I keep no state, no musician, no court fool. Soldiers I feed, no others. Look at me! My mail is good; that goes to Jerusalem; the gloves you gave me—the rest is rubbish. Four days ago they set Edward's crown on my head. This morning I broke it up and sold it, piece by piece, to the Jews. By God, I'd sell London itself if I could find a buyer."

The vehemence of his speech had flushed his face and brought the sweat out on his brow just below the line where the red-gold hair sprang crisply. I looked at him and thought: London, that fair rich city which I saved for you! But there was nothing to say; any protest I might make would only alienate him from me without in the least affecting his resolution. Edward's crown, London, England itself, were worthless to Richard because he had a nature which could never appreciate a gift; the only thing he could accept was a challenge.

I felt a little unwilling nudge of pity towards this Berengaria, mad or sane. For she would love him, soon or late; no woman could see him and not feel the prick of desire; and he

· · ·

"And you," I said irrelevantly, "write love songs!"

147

He looked surprised and uncomfortable for a second, then he laughed.

"Quite another thing! Well, Mother, will you go to Navarre for me, or must I send Joanna?"

"I'll go," I said. I must not miss the chance of putting him "everlastingly grateful" to me. For in matters of that kind Richard was a man of his word; he executed his threats and he honoured his promises. I could foresee a time when it might be necessary for me to have some hold on him, and I could always remind him, say, "Who went to Navarre for you?" and gain at least his attention.

"Then listen," he said. "Explain the situation to Sancho and tell him that the sooner I have the money the sooner I can make my arrangements, and the sooner they're made the sooner will his daughter be Queen of England. If he balks at that condition, if he says he'll pay after the wedding or wants me to waste time on a wedding at Westminster or any such nonsense, don't parley with him. Loss of time, to me, is as bad as loss of money. Let me know by swift courier and then make what excuse you like and come home. But if he is amenable, bring the girl to Marseilles or Sicily—I cannot tell yet. So much depends. And keep her quiet and contented until I am ready. And another thing—this is where you will be valuable—at all costs prevent her from bringing a horde of women with her or much baggage. You've been on crusade; you know the conditions. Frighten off the waiting ladies, as you love me. Now, how soon can you leave?"

"In an hour," I said. "I must change my clothes and tell Barbara to get ready."

He laughed. "It will take me a full day to arrange your escort. And I think you should aim to make a good impression. Say the morning after tomorrow. Can you really be ready by then?"

"I can," I said.

He looked at me curiously. "A woman in a thousand," he said slowly. "I shall always remember that you did me this great service."

"I hope you will remember it with gladness." I heard the doubt in my own voice; he heard it, too, and answered it.

"Young Sancho, the girl's blood brother, is whole and sane enough, Mother."

"God send the girl is."

There and then I made up my mind that if I found otherwise I would so contrive and arrange that the money would never be despatched; I would throw it into the sea, rather. Yes, I'd save Richard from himself; I'd not have him marry a madwoman. But that was all in the future and uncertain; there was something quite certain and immediate which I might be able to do.

"I'm not one to collect wages before the job is done, Richard, but if you are really grateful to me for going to do your errand there is one thing you could do that would pleasure me more than any other thing on earth."

"Tell me," he said.

"No. I'll leave a letter. When I have sailed and you know that my going is not dependent upon your humouring me and that I have your ultimate good at heart"—and how much at heart and to what lengths I will go you have no idea, my son!—"open the letter and give it your serious, unprejudiced consideration."

"I will," he said solemnly.

With that we took leave of each other. And as soon as he had gone I sat down and did a strange thing. I wrote to Richard beseeching him to bring back Geoffrey of York, his father's bastard by Rosamonde Clifford. Geoffrey was lingering overseas, afraid to set foot on Richard's domain, afraid that the wrongs and the insults of many years might be avenged now. Only Almighty God knew what I had suffered through this man; he had been a thorn in my side since the moment of his conception. Henry had named him, illegitimate, after *my* son, Geoffrey of Brittany; he had favoured, preferred, loved him before all his sons save John. In a public assembly he had put his hand on his shoulder and said, "You are my true son, the others are the bastards." Truly the very bitterest memories flocked round me as I wrote; Rosamonde Rose-of-the-World—had been my first supplanter; the scandal of her death had ruined my marriage. Yet now I sat and wrote beseeching my son to show favour to hers. For though I hated the young man I respected him and knew that in favouring and trusting him Henry Plantagenet had shown shrewd good sense and judgement.

Geoffrey of York was the one man with ability and integrity and personality enough to hold Hugh of Durham and that little rat Longchamp in leash. In Rosamonde's son the Angevin virtues had emerged untainted by the Angevin vices; he had courage without recklessness, high temper without rashness, determination without obstinacy. Given an opportunity, he could control even John. If Richard showed him kindliness and favour now, before exile embittered him, before his devotion, unfocused since his father's death, had found another object upon which to expend itself, he would have gained himself an adherent without peer. So, brushing the ghosts and the memories aside, I wrote and begged my son to give authority to the son of his father's mistress. I wanted Richard to have the best.

IV

I have lived to see Berengaria's beauty become a byword. The songs and the stories about her give her credit for that rare type of loveliness which makes instant appeal to men and women alike and which remains vivid in the memory of anyone who has ever looked upon her. All that is true—in a way; but although the first feeling evoked in me by the sight of her was one of astonished admiration, disappointment followed so hard on its heels that the two were almost inseparable.

She was wearing, I remember, a gown of pale blue-green colour, cut low and tightly laced; and halfway up her long throat, worn in a way I have never seen a necklet worn before, was a wide band of gold studded with sapphires which incongruously called to my mind the heavy leather collars studded with spikes which wolfhounds wear for protection when they hunt. A gauzy veil of the same blue-green colour, fastened by ornaments of sapphire, covered her hair, which was very black and glossy and dressed in plaits which fell over her shoulders and bosom to far below her waist. Her skin was white and quite without blemish, and her eyes remarkable, large, clear, blue-green in colour, and fringed by long dark lashes.

At first sight breath-takingly lovely, but at second, disappointing. There was something lifeless and cold, almost inhuman, about her. Even when she smiled the smile never reached her eyes; the smooth red mouth stirred, the plane of her cheek took on a different, still lovely curve, but her eyes never lightened or warmed.

She had great natural dignity; that and the cold remote beauty would be becoming to the Queen—but to the wife? Especially to the wife of such a turbulent, virile, lusty man as my Richard? I had doubts. Doubts, too, about her capacity as a breeder. That long slender neck, those frail wrists, those narrow hips gave no promise of fertility. I had seen them before on childless women.

150

And always, of course, there nagged at the back of my mind the memory of the mad Queen Beatrice.

With these thoughts in mind I took no care to present Richard's demands pleasantly to Sancho; indeed, I hoped that he would refuse them outright. My first interview with him, however, quelled that hope and left me with the suspicion that Richard might have demanded much more and still been accommodated. Sancho was almost pitiably eager for the match.

"To tell you the truth, madam, since the moment when my daughter looked first upon your son, two years, three years ago—time passes so swiftly it is difficult to keep count—I have not had one easy moment. These minnesingers and strummers who chant about the glory of love at first sight should stand in my shoes for a while; they'd alter their tune. I doubt whether any woman in Christendom has had more or better offers made for her hand—but no, nothing would do. She must have Richard Plantagenet or die. And by the Virgin's hair, at one time death did seem the only alternative. Thanks be to God all that is over and we have attained a safe deliverance."

"You should have betrothed her long ago, sire," I said, deliberately making my voice light and playfully chiding. Why had he not?

"I know. And had I my time over again, by God's throne, I would. But, madam, I could never convince myself that these cradle matches are just or kind. Expedient, certainly, as I have learned to my cost. Nevertheless ... " He let the subject drop. "In this one case, at least, all has ended well."

I reserved my judgement. And I was cunning. I set the date for the sending of the money a full week ahead so that I might have time to observe, to come to a decision. "She must have Richard Plantagenet or die" seemed to indicate that some fire smouldered beneath that icy exterior, but it might also indicate the inexplicable whim of the insane who must demand strawberries in March or fresh peas in October.

But I was wrong. At the end of a week which I had used cunningly and well I gave Sancho word to send the dowry to Rouen. I had talked to Berengaria often and seen that she warmed undisguisedly at the mention of Richard's name. Those strange eyes never altered their expression, but they lit up from within; and she was eager to hear the least, most unimportant thing about him, anecdotes of his childhood, his preferences, his prejudices.

I had talked also to members of the household, my ear

alert for any word or even any silence which might give a clue. There was one garrulous old woman named Mathilde who had nursed Queen Beatrice and tended Berengaria since her birth. She was too stupid to suspect the reason for the questions I asked her, but she answered them all to my satisfaction. With the two waiting ladies also I had long and intimate conversations without gathering anything which justified suspicion.

And Blanche, Sancho's other daughter, came home, in honour of my visit, from the convent where she spent most of her time. She was a pleasant, quite ordinary young woman, against whom all that could be said was that she had difficulty in making up her mind to take nun's vows, a fact which I personally took to be a sign of sanity rather than otherwise. The third member of the family, Young Sancho, I wholeheartedly liked. Save that his colouring was darker and his temper one of easygoing good humour, he might have been one of my own brood.

Gradually and cautiously I came around to the opinion that the match was a good one.

Once the dowry was despatched and the betrothal made certain, I began to talk to Berengaria about the future, the travel, the possible hardships and deprivations she must face. Drawing on my own experience, I explained the folly of taking too much baggage, too many ladies, and her docility endeared her to me.

"I need only Mathilde to look after me, Pila for appearances' sake, and of course Anna and Blondel."

"That would be too mean an entourage," I said. "Who are Anna and Blondel?"

"Anna is Duchess of Apieta, and Blondel is my musician. They are away now, in Anna's duchy. She is building a house there, and since Blondel can plan and draw I lent him to her to help her. But they will be back soon."

Anna and Blondel, thus defined, sounded welcome additions to the party. Richard had boasted that he kept no minstrel, but even his single-minded parsimony could hardly extend to a refusal to retain one who came in his wife's entourage, and everyone knew how much a good minstrel could contribute to the happiness of a household. As for the duchess, I felt that Berengaria's bower could well do with such an embellishment. I have never been one for pomp and show, but even I thought that her establishment was meagre and unworthy, typical of a court which lacked a queen. She had two ladies, a jolly greedy widow and a thin embittered spinster, neither very well born or well travelled or learned. They lived together in circumstances of comfort and in an atmosphere of amity which I had noticed to Berengaria's credit, but although they were suitable enough perhaps to attend the princess of a small obscure kingdom, they were not quite right for a queen of England.

Therefore, the mention of the duchess interested me, and I tried to make Berengaria talk about her. Building houses is a hobby which ordinarily only women of sense and substance pursue, and I visualised Her Grace of Apieta as a large, dignified, middle-aged noblewoman. And this idea Berengaria did nothing to dispel; she lacked, indeed, all that made a good gossip. Her conversation gained fluency only when she was talking about Richard, though occasionally she brought out little shrewd remarks which proved that despite her remote and detached air she was more aware of what went on than one would have suspected. Nor, indeed, was she so lacking in humour as her cast of countenance suggested. As day followed day and I found her docile, surprisingly without vanity, and very good-humoured, I found myself thinking that Richard, choosing blindly, had chosen wisely. If he could avoid the thought that if he touched her she would break in pieces, they might do very well.

All the arrangements went smoothly; the sempstresses set to work on the wedding dress; presents and messages of good will began to pour in. Sancho selected a number of knights and ladies who were to travel with us and to attend the wedding, and a series of pre-nuptial banquets was given, including a great feast to all the poor in Pamplona. It was on the evening after that feast, the last of the series, that the Duchess of Apieta and the minstrel came home and stabbed through the complacency into which I had relapsed.

Blondel was the French lute player with a young face and white hair whose throat I had commissioned Alberic to slit.

Anna, Duchess of Apieta, was a horrible hunchback.

Now I have suffered, from earliest childhood, from a reprehensible but uncontrollable aversion to the maimed and the malformed. When I was four, they say, I went into a convulsion at the sight of a one-legged old soldier whom my father, out of charity, had employed as a groom. This aversion is completely unreasonable and for that reason irradicable. In the presence of a cripple or deformed person my flesh crawls on my bones, I become physically sick. While I was Queen of France and again while I was Queen of England I founded various homes—"retreats," they called them—for

153

afflicted persons; I was credited with Christian charity, but my sole desire was to rid, as far as possible, the streets and highways of sights which made me shudder, lose my appetite, and which spoilt a day or a journey for me. I was not *sorry* for the objects of my aversion; if I could have momentarily overcome my disgust I would have smashed them to pulp; I hated them for the malaise with which they afflicted me; I wished them out of existence. I suppose God has His strange reasons and purposes and some unfortunates must therefore be born misshapen or suffer mutilation through no fault of their own; but they should not be allowed to expose their infirmities and so torment the rest of us.

The duchess arrived back in Pamplona just at nightfall. She had been expected two days previously, and for the last forty-eight hours Berengaria's placidity had been replaced by a fidgety impatience. It was she who first heard the clatter of horses' hoofs on the drawbridge and cried, "Here they are at last!" A few minutes later the door opened and there was a huge Negro bearing in his arms what looked like a large overdressed child. A sharp-featured, pallid little face peered out from beneath a richly furred hood, a velvet cloak bordered with fur covered the whole body, and two tiny feet in shoes of softest leather dangled in the air. Berengaria rushed forward, crying, "Oh, Anna, I thought something had happened to you. I expected you two days ago. Oh, I have missed you."

"Dear me," said a musical, slightly husky voice, "such a greeting would put anybody back on his feet. Set me down, Blanco."

He did so, and once again I felt the sickness which deformity evokes in me. This was the Duchess of Apieta, who was to come with us to Sicily, to Cyprus, and on to the Holy Land! Not if I could help it, I thought.

Controlling with difficulty my shuddering repulsion, I took her little clawlike hand in mine and said that I was delighted to see her. She made me a curtsy, very competent, considering her disability, and made some reference with just the right touch of light courtliness to my almost legendary past. She had heard so much about "The Lady of the Golden Boot," she said, and was honoured to see me in Pamplona.

"And where is Blondel?" Berengaria asked.

"Gone to see the bear. I trust it has been well seen to in his absence."

"Then everything is all right," Berengaria said. And her placidity dropped back over her like a garment. But across the hunchback's little white face there drifted an expression which most irrelevantly reminded me of Richard when he wore his foxy look.

Berengaria turned to me and said happily, "We can set out now. Perhaps the day after tomorrow." To Anna she said, "You must come and see my wedding dress, Anna, it is beautiful. Laced, like those they preached against."

"I'll see it tomorrow," said the little duchess. "I must go to bed now. I am exhausted. In the end they had to rig me a litter." She brought out the last words in a wry, self-derogatory way.

After supper the minstrel, Blondel, appeared in the bower, bringing his lute. I recognised him instantly and without pleasure. Without any undue stretch of the imagination it was possible to fill in the little gap which had hitherto existed between the breaking of one betrothal and the making of the next. Richard had told me that Sancho's emissary had arrived in Rouen with a renewed offer of marriage before anyone save Philip knew that the engagement with Alys was ended. The lute player had posted straight back to Pamplona with his scandalous bit of news; and although I must in honesty admit that no one about this court had given any sign of secret knowledge, doubtless they had all been regaled by the story of how the King and Prince of England had denounced one another and the Princess of France, subject of the dispute, had "squawked like a stuck pig."

This knowledge made me uncomfortable; more uncomfortable than it would have done some weeks before, when I was on the alert for signs that the secret was out. When one has lived for some time watchful for rumour and then has gradually sunk back into complacency, there is a sense of shame as well as a sense of shock in discovering that all the time one has been living in a fool's paradise. But I tried to be reasonable, telling myself that it was stupid to resent an action which had borne such happy results and brought Richard such a lovely and suitable bride as well as the money which meant so much to him. At the same time I felt that Sancho was to blame. Assuming that he had used the boy as a spy and made use of his discovery to further his own ends, then he should not have left him alive and free to tell his tale where he would. We managed these things better in Aquitaine!

It was a jaundiced eye which I turned upon the inmates of the bower that evening, and especially upon the handsome,

155

white-haired boy with his sweet voice and his nimbly strumming fingers.

I made up my mind that I would not set out or share the close proximity of shipboard, tent, and march with two people, one of whom filled me with physical nausea, one of whom caused me mental uneasiness.

I was confirmed in this determination when next morning I found myself taking my breakfast next to the duchess, who seemed none the worse for her overnight exhaustion. The meal was spoiled for me, and to tell the truth, after sixteen years of Nicolas of Saxham's providing, I was taking a delight in gluttony. There were so many things for which from increasing age and long abstention I had lost the taste that I held hard to what was left to me to enjoy, and food was one of them. The thought that for months to come I might be obliged to share board—and possibly even bed— with this deformity was not to be borne. Nor was the thought that probably our sole source of entertainment might be the white-haired lute player who knew too much.

I intended to speak to Berengaria immediately after breakfast, but as soon as the meal was over she and Anna disappeared into the dark inner room which led out of the bower. I took a piece of bread, smeared it thickly with honey, and sat myself down to wait until the duchess, having—as I supposed—inspected the wedding gown, emerged. Once I heard voices from within the room, voices raised to the pitch where the sound of them, but not the sense of the words they uttered, penetrated the thick walls. Then after a short time the door opened and the duchess came into the bower. Her small face was very white save for two bright feverish patches high on her cheeks. I had already, in such short time, developed the trick of staring at her face whenever I was obliged to look at her. It was not unattractive, with small clear features and lively, intelligent eyes, but her usual expression, like that of all cripples, was sharp and defensive. She recognised my presence but did not speak and hobbled out of the room.

I licked and wiped my sticky fingers, brushed a crumb or two from my gown, and went in to Berengaria, who was sitting bolt upright on a stool in front of a silver mirror but not looking into it. Her hands, half hidden by her long trailing sleeves, were clasped across her bosom so that each hand gripped the upper part of the opposite arm. Her expression was just as usual, one of sweet, calm, almost blank placidity, but there was something almost triumphant about her pose, the lift of her head, the folded arms. I have seen successful jousters draw back and sit their horses in somewhat the same manner.

She rose from the stool as I entered and invited me to sit, but I motioned her back and took a seat on the bed, whose covers had not yet been shaken and spread anew. And rather than attack her too suddenly on the matter of her entourage I asked:

"And did the duchess approve of your gown?"

"I did not show it to her. We had something else to talk about." And again, although her face remained expressionless, there was that look of triumph.

I tried another opening.

"It is agreed, then, that we set out tomorrow?"

At that she smiled her small, sweet smile.

"Tomorrow. We are to lodge at Vecchia and then Jaca. There Father will turn back and we shall go on. Madam, how long will it take us to reach Marseilles?"

"That is almost impossible to say. So much depends upon the state of the road and what pace we can keep." Here was my chance. "With regard to that, my dear, there is something which I feel compelled to say, and if it is distasteful to you I beg you to remember that I speak out of long experience and from a concern for the good of all concerned."

"What is it?"

"I think the Duchess of Apieta should not accompany us."

"Has Anna been talking to you?" she demanded. Out of the sweet blank face the voice came suddenly, shrewd, a little vicious.

"No indeed. Why? Surely her incapacity to take such a journey was obvious when she returned from Apieta in such a state of exhaustion. On that comparatively short journey she was obliged to take to a litter and two days' time was lost. We are setting out on a journey five hundred times as long, and the loss of time may well be proportionate."

"Anna is far stronger than she appears. That delay on the journey and her retirement to bed were not due to exhaustion, madam. She was afraid to face me with her nonsensical proposal. You know how one postpones an unpleasant task."

It was not the first time that Berengaria, who so often seemed inattentive, unobservant, a little blank of mind, had surprised me by making a remark that was shrewd and perceptive.

"And what was her proposal?"

"Nothing new. For a long time now she has been thinking of building a house in Apieta—her duchy—and ever since

157

she discovered that my minstrel could draw and plan she has been fretting for him to go and supervise its building. Before you arrived she 'borrowed' him, and naturally as soon as she had him out of my sight she bribed him and cajoled and flattered him into saying that he would stay in Navarre and build it for her. She came in this morning to tell me that, with my permission, both she and Blondel would stay at home."

Relief, a most comfortable sense that I was lucky, flooded my mind. The two of them disposed of, without any effort on my part, without any acrimony.

"She was very wise," I said. "A woman so infirm and a minstrel who would sooner be building a house in Navarre would be poor company on a venture such as we are undertaking."

"I'm sorry to be obliged to contradict you, madam. They two are the only company I need. I would sooner leave everyone else behind."

"But why? A crippled little woman who will be nothing but a drag on us, and a minstrel who will be homesick and sing songs about it and make everyone within earshot homesick too. You can have no idea of the power a minstrel wields, Berengaria. A sad song can depress, a gay one enliven the spirits of a whole camp. Sometimes, I'm told, when things go wrong with Richard's men he takes a lute and plays a rousing song."

That reached her real attention, as any mention of Richard could always do. She asked quite eagerly what his favourite songs were, and we chatted for a moment with intimacy and animation. Then at her remark that Richard would appreciate Blondel's playing I was forced to say:

"I wish you would think over what I have said and be persuaded to leave them behind."

"I shouldn't consider doing so for a moment."

"But why?" I asked again.

"I couldn't explain. You would never understand, madam. For reasons of my own they matter to me more than anyone else—in Navarre. And you concern yourself needlessly. I would sooner have Anna's company, especially in a crisis, than that of anyone I know. She has sharp wits and great spirit. And as for Blondel, he only gave way to Anna's nagging. He'll come gladly enough."

It was a deadlock. I was anxious not to offend her, if for no other reason that that she had been so complaisant and amiable about her train and her baggage; but I found myself

158

wishing most heartily that she had been obdurate about everything else and tractable now. I looked at her sitting there, so beautiful, so unruffled, and so stubborn, and rage rose in me. I should have liked to set my hands on her shoulders and give her a good shaking. But argument seemed useless, and to lose my temper would be disastrous, so there was no point in prolonging the interview. I said:

"I hope most earnestly that you will think over what I have said. Time is short."

She smiled.

I went away to seek Sancho. He was her father and he had impressed me as being a reasonable man.

Sancho and his son, known respectively as Sancho the Wise and Sancho the Bold, were out in the stable yard inspecting the horses and mules with which we were to set out next day. It was a scene of great activity; grooms and pages were running to and fro with pieces of baggage, animals were being trotted round the yard, harness being tested and polished. Sancho, made aware of my presence, turned, took my elbow in the cup of his hand, and said:

"Come and drink wine with me, madam. This is a sad day for me, albeit a happy one too. Let us drink to our sorrowful joy."

He conducted me to a part of the castle I had never penetrated before and into his own room, which, in contrast with the general appointments of the place, and especially of the women's quarters, which were extremely luxurious, was bleak and bare to the point of austerity. His wine, however, was excellent, and when we had drunk to a successful journey and to Berengaria's happiness and to Richard's well-being, my temper was smoothed and sweetened and Sancho's sorrowful joy considerably mitigated. Talk ran easy and free, and when the time came for me to mention what was on my mind I found myself speaking the words with just the right touch of light detachment.

Sancho's hand went to his beard.

"Oh dear," he said. "Pray believe me, madam, when I say that I understand your point of view. As you put it, a cripple and a malcontent do appear to be unwelcome additions to any party, but Berengaria has reason on her side. She and Anna have been inseparable since childhood, and the boy Blondel once rendered us a signal service. I can understand that, setting out on such a venture—for it is, you know, marriage, for a young innocent girl, even when she has the good fortune to be marrying the man of her choice—she

159

wants with her the tried and familiar companions of her youth. Added to which Anna is most excellent company. I shall miss her very much. I have often"—he smiled at me engagingly—"been glad to take Anna's advice. And, as you say, she could always travel in a litter if necessary."

He smiled at me again, but it was plain that no support could be expected from him. All I could hope now was to investigate, as far as possible, the mystery of how much Blondel knew and how much he had told. I drained my wine cup and held it out for refilling, hoping that Sancho would drink with me, *in vino veritas*. I talked of the journey for a few minutes and then said casually:

"And the minstrel once proved himself useful. In what way, sire?"

The wine was in his blood now and he laughed. "In a manner of speaking he and Anna between them made the match, madam. You have seen my daughter when her mind is set—and this, remember, is a matter comparatively trivial—impervious to argument, deaf, blind, obstinate as an iron mule. Well, some time back . . ." And he proceeded to tell me the story of Berengaria's falling in love, refusing other offers, and finally despatching the boy to discover what he could about Alys and Richard.

"And he came back," he concluded, "having travelled night and day, with the news that the betrothal was at an end. Such early information, madam, enabled me to reopen negotiations before every other father in Christendom could do so—with the happy result that you are here today."

I mixed truth with falsehood and said, "At that time I was in Winchester, completely cut off from all communications, and Richard was never one to be explicit about his own affairs. What exactly did your lute player tell you? I have so often wondered." Now I should hear the ugly words. My hands knew the need to clasp themselves together, braced. But I kept them hanging loose, the hands of the idly curious.

"Of all the mysteries, that is the greatest," Sancho said, reaching for the flagon. "If Blondel knew, he never would tell. He said that he was certain of his information; where and how he had gained it he would not say, and short of putting him to the torture, which in the circumstances would have seemed ungrateful, to say the least, I could extract nothing but the bare facts from him. In the desperate case which I have described to you I was ready to snatch at the most unlikely chance, so I acted upon the information without more ado. With the happiest results."

Was he deceiving me as successfully as I hoped I had deceived him? Or had the boy shown discretion beyond belief? I thought for a moment and began to feel more kindly towards the minstrel, for it seemed to me that if he had told anyone it would be Sancho, and if Sancho knew he would assume that I knew, too, and would be unlikely, especially in his present mood, to attempt to conceal his knowledge. Why the minstrel should behave with such peculiar delicacy and reticence I did not try to explain even in my thoughts. I could only be grateful that he had.

However, even my gratitude could not make me welcome him as part of our company. And as for the hunchback! But what more could I do?

"I'm afraid you must be thinking, madam, that I have sadly spoiled my daughters, and indeed I often think I should have taken a stick to them long ago."

"Perhaps," I said, anxious to part from him on an agreeable note. "But I frequently took stick to my brood, and all but Joanna grew very headstrong." A sudden thought struck me. "I hope to God," I said, "that Berengaria never sets herself to oppose Richard's will, because then the sparks will fly."

"Don't worry about that." He laughed. "She will be wax to his hand."

v

She seemed, in fact, to be wax in anyone's hand during the following weeks as we made our weary and sometimes painful way towards Marseilles. A better-tempered, less demanding princess never travelled out to meet a husband. She seemed to move in a dream and to be oblivious to the discomforts and inconveniences that are inseparable from travel.

Even at Marseilles, where we met the disappointing news that Richard and the English fleet had sailed for Sicily a week earlier, she kept her composure.

"A little longer to wait, that is all," she said.

A little longer. Poor girl! There were times when I almost forgave her obduracy over Anna and Blondel.

Richard had left me a letter which was typically his. It opened with a brief formal greeting to me, the princess, and all her company; he trusted our journey had not been too arduous and that we were well. He said that it seemed likely that he would have to winter in Sicily, as there was more to do than Michael and all his angels could attend to in a twelvemonth. (Richard Plantagenet, single-handed, would finish it in six was the implication!) He directed me to go to Naples, where Joanna, my daughter, the widowed Queen of Sicily, would meet us, and then I was to take the princess to Brindisi and "rest her there contented" until such time as he should send for us.

Having thus disposed of us in a few lines, he proceeded to write volubly upon a matter weightier on his mind, if not nearer his heart—the business of prising Joanna's dowry from the new King of Sicily, Tancred, who had given proof that nothing short of violence should wrench from him the golden table, the silken canopy, the two dozen or so gold cups and platters, and the sixty thousand mules' burden of corn, oil, and wine. If Tancred wanted war over such a petty matter, war he could have and in plenty. I was to assure Joanna that when Richard had finished with Tancred not a barrel of oil would be withheld from the count, and every slight and insult which she had suffered would be adequately avenged.

Berengaria was with me when the letter was delivered to me; and when I had perused it I felt obliged to hand it to her, though it embarrassed me that she should find herself and her affairs dismissed in a few lines and so many devoted to the disputed property. I could tell by the set of her shoulders and the way in which she let her hands fall into her lap with the letter that she was disappointed. Her face being so expressionless, her gestures had a peculiar eloquence, I had noticed. She was disappointed, but not in the least affronted. There was no doubt about it, at that time she had no will but Richard's and was so infatuated by the idea of him that she could not see a fault in him. I found myself saying apologetically that if the whole muster of the crusade was to gather in Sicily the place would be vilely overcrowded and that it was considerate of Richard to arrange for us to be accommodated elsewhere. But I knew why we were being sent to Brindisi. Richard was busy and he didn't want a clutter of women about him.

So we proceeded to Naples, where I was overjoyed to see Joanna, whom I had not seen since her wedding, and to whom Berengaria showed such instant and unquestioning affection that I suspected she was all the time seeing Richard in Joanna—than whom no two people could be less alike, save for the hair. Joanna's hair was the same bright colour

162

and of the same texture as Richard's, and time, bereavement, and worry had neither dimmed nor thinned it. I noted a little cynically that though Berengaria never brushed her own blue-black tresses she was always eager to brush Joanna's. However, wryness apart, that was all very pleasant and commendable; though from my point of view it had one great disadvantage. Berengaria's taking such a fondness for Joanna, their sharing a piece of tapestry, huddling together on the same settle, going to Mass together, and so on, threw me and the crippled duchess more than ever into one another's company.

I tried. For my own peace of mind's sake, I tried to overcome my aversion to the little hunchback, but I failed; and that was not her fault, for she tried too. Everything that Berengaria and Sancho had said about her was true. She was self-contained and independent, making claims upon nobody's pity; she was shrewdly intelligent and her wit was just on the sour side, so her conversation was extremely entertaining. If she had only been made in normal human shape I should have found her a fascinating person, as she, for a time, seemed to find me. It sometimes seemed a little hard that the one person whom I had lately met who took an active, vivid interest in me as a character, who had evidently heard and remembered things about my past and was eager to talk of my doings, should be a woman with whom I found ordinary easy conversation well-nigh impossible and whose company I was bound to avoid as much as was compatible with good manners.

Settling into our apartments which Richard had arranged for us in Brindisi and preparing to stay there, as we then thought, for a week or two, the easy camaraderie of the journey had to be abandoned and the matter of precedence considered. Berengaria was blissfully vague about such things, so the task fell to me; and in my allocation of sleeping apartments and places at table I cunningly endeavoured to keep a distance between the duchess and myself. I had done this to my own satisfaction when Berengaria took notice for just long enough to say, "Madam, Anna must come before Carmelita; she ranks next to Joanna, does she not?"

"Carmelita is Duchess of Avosola," I defended myself, conscious of guilt in the matter.

"But Anna is my sister. What I mean, madam, is that she is my father's daughter. Did you really not know? At home I suppose it was so much taken for granted—but at home Anna always ranked immediately after me and Blanche."

"Naturally," I said. I was stiff with anger. I should have been told. It was all very well for the Navarrese to take the situation so much for granted that it was no longer even a subject for gossip, but how could a stranger guess? Though perhaps I should have done or, if not guessed, suspected something, had I not been so disappointed at finding my respectable house-building duchess a misformed chit, had I not been so much absorbed in my own feelings towards her. It was certainly unusual for a young girl to be a duchess in her own right; and Sancho had said that he was very fond of Anna and had mentioned his daughters' wilfulness. Blanche, I am sure, had never needed a stick in all her life.

I had certainly been very unobservant, and perhaps a little deluded by Sancho's reputed devotion to his crazy wife, and by the wonderful memorial he had reared to her in the cathedral at Pamplona. Of what sly misdoing, I wondered savagely, was that crooked little woman a memorial?

There was nothing for it, of course, but to move my eyesore a place nearer to me by bed and board. And presently she seemed to guess that she was obnoxious to me and ceased to press her society on me. Presently, too, I had other things to worry me.

The weeks sped by, and there was no summons from Richard. I had sent him a message acquainting him with our safe arrival and telling him about Berengaria in such terms as would, I thought, make him anxious to see her. Richard ignored that letter, though I knew it had reached him. Towards the end of November I began to feel impatient, and though I hid my own impatience I could see its counterpart breaking out here and there amongst the members of Berengaria's suite. Berengaria seemed contented enough, rapt in her dream, emerging now and then to make some shrewdly sweet remark, breaking into animation whenever Richard's name was mentioned, and spending most of her time in fashioning him a jewelled belt as a present when they finally met. And Young Sancho, who had some of his sister's placidity, was contented, too, taking much exercise in neighbouring tilting yards and organising boar hunts in the forests behind the town. But the ladies and gentlemen who had ridden out of Navarre to see their princess married and who had counted on a short absence, and that filled with enjoyable activity, were naturally irked to find themselves stranded in Brindisi and no limit fixed for their exile. Complaints and questions increased from day to day. Finally, when the change of month from November to December had quick-

164

ened everyone's sense of the passing of time, Young Sancho himself came to me and pressed the general question while ostensibly pleading the cause of one young noble, Garcia, who wanted to return home because he himself was due to be married during Christmas week.

"I gave him leave to go, madam, but the others are fretting. Often in January it snows and then the road is closed, sometimes for three weeks together." What he left unsaid I understood and answered.

"Richard has given no sign," I said. "He was anxious to bring his quarrel with the King of Sicily to an end before we went. And perhaps the rogue put up more opposition than he expected. But I have heard nothing." I looked at the handsome young man and remembered that he was Richard's friend. It was he in the first place who had brought the pair together; the idea of using him occurred to me.

"If I were younger and more apt for travel," I said, "I would go to Sicily and remind my son of his unmartial obligations. For the truth is, when Richard has a war, however petty, on his hands, he thinks of nothing else until his opponent sues for mercy."

"I know," Sancho said, laughing. "I know my Richard—the best fighter since Charlemagne!" He grew serious again. "How would it be, madam, if *I* went to Sicily? I have never seen the island, though I have heard my father talk of it. And it is a long time since I saw Richard. I might see some fighting, and they"—he indicated with a wave of his hand the discontented courtiers whose mouthpiece he undoubtedly was—"would be more content if they thought that some action was being taken."

(The old woman will never move! Prod her, Sancho, or we shall be here next year at this time. Remember what happened to Alys of France! And what is all this talk about Tancred's pretty niece?) I knew very well what was being said!

"Go with my blessing," I said. "The sooner they are married and Berengaria with child, the better shall I be pleased." I wanted to let him know that my impatience had more vital roots than my personal boredom. "But be tactful. Richard has in the past been so bulled about and ridden by chancellors and cardinals and their ilk that at the slightest hint of coercion his bile rises."

"I know my Richard," he said again.

Maybe he did, maybe not. The sure thing is that he did not know himself. I saw him leave with the unexpressed determination to tell Richard that though he was King of England he couldn't keep the princess and half the court of Navarre hanging about as a housewife keeps a pedlar waiting at the back door. And I saw him return, his errand forgotten and nothing in his mind save the urge to take the Cross and join Richard's crusade at the first possible moment. For Richard had greeted him with affection, put his arm across his shoulders, led him about through camps of men and pickets of horses, showed him his muster of stores and ships, and talked to him until the boy was bemused and bewitched. He came back to Brindisi to tell Berengaria that Richard was busy, that Richard was wonderful, and that he was going back to Navarre to seek their father's consent and support because he meant to go on crusade himself.

Berengaria listened to every word he said about Richard, but she was not interested in his own plans. It was left to me to draw him aside and confront him with the question:

"And what of your errand?"

"Oh," he said, "I could see that Richard had too much in hand and in mind. I forbore to bother him. Madam, if you could see what he does in the course of a day! He will throw off his doublet and work with his men; I even saw him dressing sores on pack mules! He says he will attend to the wedding when he has time, and that, I judge, will not be before spring." He began to talk of his own plans. I interrupted him.

"Your going home will worsen the situation, Sancho. They will all want to go with you. They'll believe that the betrothal has gone awry; whatever you may say, they'll prefer to believe that you are going home because you have discovered Richard is philandering with Tancred's niece!"

"I assure you, there is no truth in that rumour. The man is too busy. If you could see him as I have seen him, you would believe."

"I can believe without seeing. I know Richard. I believe that he is busy and that he will marry Berengaria in the spring. But the others ... No, Sancho! They were all very restive when Garcia went; when you go they will go with you. And your sister will go to her wedding worse attended than any merchant's daughter."

"If she went barefoot in her shift she'd be a damned lucky woman, and so I shall tell her." He laughed. "Berengaria knows that. As for the others, I shall explain."

But he hadn't the personality to give his explanations any force, and the thing turned out as I expected. It was as it

166

says in the Bible, "They began with one consent to make excuses." This one remembered a daughter due to be brought to bed, this one a son who was to be married, another an old father about to die, another an old mother left in charge of estate; two or three ladies discovered that they were suffering from ailments only Navarrese physicians could deal with; several young gallants recalled the charms of ladies left in Navarre. And who could blame them. They had come out to attend a wedding; the date was still unfixed, the bridegroom was too busy even to discuss it, and the prince was going home. To be sure, he had a high-sounding excuse—but everyone knew better. And they all wanted to go home.

So far as I was concerned they could all have gone and jumped into the sea; I didn't care a groat whether they went to Navarre or to hell, but I did fear for the effect of the general exodus on Berengaria, who had behaved up to that moment so impeccably.

However, I had misjudged her. "Let them go," she said when at last the matter came under open discussion. "Without them, when Richard does send for us, we shall travel more quickly." And on the day of leave-taking there was no shadow, not even of homesickness, over her mood. When the bowing and kissing of hands was done she embraced Sancho and sent her love to her father and sent him a message that he was to let Young Sancho join Richard as soon as possible. Her last words to her brother were:

"I will see you in Acre." Then she turned back and was soon at work on the baldric. I was filled with admiration and affection for her and thought for the hundredth time that Richard was uncommonly fortunate. I also thought that he had but to see her to love her.

Winter closed in upon our narrowed company. We were comfortably housed and well fed, and although there were the inevitable little squabbles which must arise in any company kept in close quarters for protracted lengths of time, we were, on the whole, happier than we were before Sancho and the discontented contingent had left. The members of our company now, with a few exceptions, were going on crusade together and were bound by an unspoken unity of purpose. The little duchess and I avoided one another by common consent. Blondel, of whom I had taken a more tolerant, if mystified, view since my talk with Sancho, I might have come to like had it not been that Berengaria and Anna and Pila and Joanna all vied with one another to spoil him.

So Candlemas passed and winter began to wane. I began

167

to feel impatient again, and the feeling grew until the pleasant, aimless days following one another seemed as long and tedious as the days of my imprisonment at Winchester.

VI

Everything comes to an end, and one bright mild morning when spring seemed near at hand a small ship put into port and presently a little scrubbed page, wearing Richard's livery, was brought into my presence and delivered into my hands the letter for which I had so long waited. I broke the seal eagerly and looked at the page which was written in a good clerkly hand, not Richard's hasty scrawl. The phrases too were pompous and polished, though the directions were Richard's entirely, very abrupt and very clear. The small ship, *St. James of Padua*, would wait and carry us back to Sicily, where we were to board a more seaworthy vessel, *Mary the Virgin*, and proceed to Cyprus. I was to tell Joanna that Tancred had capitulated and that her dowry was safe. The consumable goods Richard had commandeered and would pay for at current prices; the golden table and cups had been sent back to England and deposited in various religious establishments, where they would be safe. So far, so good, a very cheerful letter. For me the sting lay in its tail.

"I have arranged with Isaac of Cyprus to receive you and to aid you in preparing for the wedding, which will take place as soon as I join you there. Since your stay in Sicily will be brief and I am much occupied, I trust that the princess will excuse me from waiting upon her. Philip of France is with me now, and for reasons which you will understand it is advisable for me to concentrate upon the business of the crusade. . . ."

I understood that well enough. Philip was still sore and in a touchy mood; the less said about or seen of the new bride, the better. Richard at his foxiest! But it wasn't Richard who had to tell Berengaria that we were off to Sicily, or saw her hands fly to her breast or heard her voice, for once expressive and ecstatic, say, "I shall see him at last!" And it wasn't Richard who had to say, "My dear, I am afraid not. Not until we reach Cyprus."

I thought it inconsiderate, if not positively unkind, of Richard to have arranged for us to go to Sicily at all. Why not, I wondered, let us ship for Cyprus at once in the small ship? But before we reached Messina I changed my opinion;

168

St. James of Padua was an unhandy vessel and rolled like a drunken tinker even on the calmest day; and her master, apologising for our discomfort, promised us many things of *Mary the Virgin*, a fine new ship, he said.

It was a pity that she could not have been sent to Brindisi to carry us direct to Cyprus, but it seemed that she was at the moment bringing a contingent of French soldiers from Marseilles and would land them, reload with stores, and be ready to sail as soon as we reached Messina. It was, in fact, a reasonable, sensible, and time-saving arrangement if one could ignore the feelings of the girl who had set out from Navarre, waited long in Italy, and was now to go to Sicily and leave without so much as a glimpse of the man she loved.

Berengaria earned my astonished admiration anew on that voyage. She never questioned the arrangement; even in the throes of seasickness she uttered no complaint. And I believe that if *Mary the Virgin* had been ready to sail as soon as we arrived, we should all have gone on to Cyprus together in good heart, and everything would have been entirely different. But the ship was not ready.

It is grievous to a thinking person to reflect how many troublesome things arise from the best intentions.

At that moment, when all Christian Europe was afire with ardour to recapture the holy places, a markedly communal spirit was abroad and gifts from groups, orders, communities, and guilds, all of them most well intentioned and almost all bound to be the subject of fierce dissension, came pouring in. For a short time the Cross on a man's shoulder set him apart, a dedicated man. The Pope, with tears running down his face, had blessed the leaders and they had all sworn to hold faith as brothers; old feuds, differences of rank and language were momentarily forgotten in a great spiritual afflatus which, because it took no count of realities or of the experience of centuries, held within it the seeds of disaster and disillusion.

We read in the Gospels that the early Christians "held all things in common." We are not told for how long or short a time such an idealistic affair lasted, nor in what confusion it ended, but we know that it did end. To the ordinary well-meaning Christian person this crusade appeared to call for a return to communal effort, communal ideas of property. So the imaginative (and singularly well informed) nuns of Brittany all combined their resources and forwarded a considerable sum of money "to be used to provide camel transport in the desert." The Guild of Clothworkers in Amsterdam contributed eight scaling ladders "to be reared in our name against the walls of Jerusalem." Every woman in Aquitaine whose name was Mary contributed a coin great or small, and sent the total "to be used to liberate the places where she whose name we bear walked and sorrowed." There were thousands of such offerings, worthy, touching, mostly wasted. "Devil take the camels, I want a hundred donkeys *now*," Richard is said to have shouted at one juncture, and that summed up the whole situation. If every gift could have been labelled, "For Richard Plantagenet, to use as seems him best," nothing would have been wasted or misused. A communal spirit is an excellent thing; all men and women of good will pouring all their efforts and all their resources into a common cause could be invincible, but only if such efforts and such resources are at the command of one person, the most capable and vigorous, and in complete authority.

Mary the Virgin was one of six ships contributed to the crusade by the mighty and wealthy College of Cardinals. One of the six bore an English name and was manned chiefly by English sailors; one was entirely French; one German; one Italian; one Flemish; one Spanish. They were the largest and most modern ships afloat, and they were all under the vague but comprehensive authority of "The Leaders of This Crusade." Richard, who found the entirely English ships of the fleet rather small and in need of different rigging for the Mediterranean, had settled on the English-flavoured *Mary the Virgin* as the vessel to carry us to Cyprus. But the ship's master, a surly misogynist, the illegitimate son of a Bristol archdeacon, demurred at the arrangement and said that his commission was to carry crusaders and their armourments, not women and their gear. Richard, who could never bear any hint of opposition in a menial, said bluntly that the master's trouble was that he was afraid to set sail ahead of the main fleet and ordered him an escort—of baggage vessels. The man, extremely offended, mustered the five other masters of what was known as the "Cardinals' Fleet," and the six waited upon Richard to tell him that since their duties were undefined they would welcome the decision of the College of Cardinals, who had commissioned them and in whose pay they were. The College of Cardinals had a nominal headquarters in Rome, but the full body met only at the election of a new pope, so heaven knows to whom, or exactly where, they would have lodged their appeal. However, Richard was resourceful. He asked, "Which one of you has a

170

grievance?" The man from Bristol—Saunders, they called him—stood out.

"And the ships were to be devoted to the service of . . . ?"

"The leaders of the crusade, sir."

"And they are, at this moment, in this island?"

"Yourself and the King of France, sire."

"Very well, you, the aggrieved, and we, the leaders, will meet at supper and discuss that matter. Is that agreeable to you?"

Master Saunders said that that was fair enough.

He spoke no French; Philip of France spoke no English. Richard could understand English, though he spoke it rarely. But over the meal, while he plied Master Saunders with strong wine, he acted most agreeably as interpreter. What he said to Philip nobody knows, but at the crucial moment he called in Robert of Boxford, who spoke both French and English, and asked him to translate to Saunders Philip's decisive word, which was:

"This crusade cannot be pursued without all sorts. Your ship and every other ship must carry all sorts. The leaders of the crusade decide that in the name of God you must carry all sorts."

"Women and their gear?" Saunders asked.

Robert of Boxford put the question in French to Philip, who obligingly said again, "All sorts." And Philip was known by everybody to be more than half a churchman; the nearest thing to the College of Cardinals that Saunders was likely to reach with any ease. So he gave in, albeit ungraciously. And Richard compromised by packing the vessel so full of crusaders' gear that she lay low in the water and shipped it in the slightest wind, and he crammed the stern with archers who lived in supreme discomfort, envying, no doubt, the ladies who, equally cramped, were to live on the foredeck, with a canopy for shade and curtains for privacy. The cardinals had meant well, Richard had meant well; possibly Master Saunders had meant good rather than evil, but the ladies would have been far happier on a small, entirely English ship where the captain would have welcomed them. A trivial and silly business, but typical of much that took place.

VII

My trouble began as soon as we found ourselves lodged in a half-ruined castle on the inland fringe of Messina, not more

171

than half an hour's ride from the camp, which lay on the other side of the town, a short distance along the coast. The tents and the pavilions with their pennants and standards had been clearly visible as we sailed into the harbour, and Berengaria had looked towards them with great intensity and said, "Isn't it strange to think that Richard is there?" And Joanna, who should have known better, for I had warned her—but she was always a simple fool at heart—had gasped out, "And doesn't it seem hard that we shall not even have time to *see* him?"

At that moment time—or the lack of it—was my ally and friend. I still thought that as soon as our gear was shifted we should be off for Cyprus, where both young women could amuse themselves with arrangements for the wedding. But Master Saunders, little knowing what he did, put up his protest and time ceased to be my friend. There we were, with some days of waiting ahead of us, and there was Richard within easy distance, and the whole situation became very awkward indeed.

Joanna was easily quelled. I could say to her, "I forbid you to mention the possibility of seeing Richard. And if you forget my orders I shall forget that you are a woman and clout your ears as I did when you were a disobedient child." But I could not speak thus to the Princess of Navarre. So the war of attrition started.

As soon as it was known that our sailing was to be delayed Berengaria began, very sweetly and gentle, with, "Surely, madam, now that there is time, we could visit Richard or he could visit us. You know it is two years or more since I saw him, and then only once for a moment."

She said this in the presence of Joanna, the duchess, and the Lady Pila, and although they held silence I could see by the expression on their faces that they thought she had reason on her side. I couldn't say bluntly that Richard didn't wish to visit her or be visited by her, or that flaunting the new betrothal would rub salt into Philip's wound and make him difficult to handle. So I fell back upon procrastination, that dangerous device, and said that if our stay in Messina were really prolonged I would see what could be done. I had a frail hope that when Richard knew that we were waylaid here he might, if only from curiosity, suggest a meeting. But so far as he was concerned a thousand miles might have stretched between the camp and the place where we were lodged. And Berengaria kept worrying the subject as a dog worries a bone. I remembered, against my will, all that

172

Sancho had told me; how she had seen Richard and wanted him, and pined and fretted and refused the Emperor of Cyprus, taken to her bed and seemed as though to die. This wasn't the conventional betrothal with the bride shy and reluctant, dreading the moment of meeting. Strange as it seemed to be a spectator and participant in such an affair, one had to admit that the whole thing was a little like the stories which the minstrels sang.

Finally I was driven to say that I would send and ask Richard to sup with us. I had no alternative, for Berengaria had said bluntly that if I didn't, she would. At least she didn't *put* it so bluntly; she made the suggestion with that sweetness which I was beginning to suspect: "Madam, would the invitation not sound better coming from you, his mother?"

I made it sound as well as I could. I even mentioned the lute player and invited Richard to enjoy our music as well as our food. I sent the letter by my own page, Gascon, who was soon back with a verbal message that we should be hearing from His Majesty. The girls, less experienced than I, spent the day bullying the cooks and preparing the table and their dresses. Blondel was dragged in to practise the songs they thought Richard would like. Joanna called to mind the ditties Richard had favoured in his youth. Anna, pestered by Berengaria to think up "something new," rattled off in a matter of moments some lines, so witty and so topical—they dealt with Master Saunders, his ship, and the College of Cardinals—that for a moment we all forgot ourselves and were united in gusts of hearty laughter. Blondel set the lines to music very admirably. Even I found myself thinking that when Richard did come he would be extremely and most pleasantly surprised. So beautiful a bride, an atmosphere so gay and so informal . . .

An hour before the time for supper Berengaria and Joanna disappeared to brush one another's hair and make themselves beautiful. Lady Pila went with them, but after a time came out, declaring that they needed none of her help and sniffing greedily at the food scent which was beginning to reach us from the kitchen. The Duchess of Apieta, most sumptuously dressed and bejewelled, joined us, and I noticed with interest that she shared my nervousness.

Presently there came the rapid clatter, the sudden halting of hooves in the courtyard; one horse, but then Richard was quite likely to come unattended. The Lady Pila, unheeding, lolled on the settle, picking at the small sweetmeats, thinking of the meal; but the duchess and I, moved by the same impulse, were on our feet, and as our eyes met I realised that for once we were entirely, and without reserve, in sympathy. We waited. In a moment or two a man was ushered in. He went on his knees to me and then, rising, stood bolt upright and gave his message in a flat, wooden recitative:

"To the Queen Mother of England and the Princess of Navarre, greetings from His Majesty of England. He cannot wait upon you. A boat loaded with casks of beef capsized this morning in the harbour and we hope that with the turn of the tide this evening some may wash in." He hesitated, began to fumble, changed foot as it were. "Madam, the King said that the great ones about him scorned such little things and the lesser men did not understand that one day a cask of beef might make all the difference. And, madam, he gave me a word for your ear alone."

The little duchess laid her claw on Pila's shoulder and they went out together.

"Madam, the King said you knew his wishes and bade you not trouble him again."

I said, "Will you tell him that I know his wishes and that I will try not to trouble him again but that I find myself in a very difficult position? Very well. You may go."

I pretended that the private message had consisted of apologies to Berengaria. She accepted them placidly, seeming quite unmoved. It was Joanna who cried from disappointment. I could have cried too. It all seemed such a pity. But at the same time I could visualise the moment when a cask of beef might make the difference between victory and defeat; a siege, a forced march; here you are, my lads, food for another day, we aren't beaten yet; this is a cask that I dragged out of the turning tide and it will turn our tide! I could see romance in that; not the romance of candlelight in the wine, pretty faces, pleasant songs, but the stronger, tougher romance of complete devotion to one cause, of the negligible detail that changed the whole course of a campaign.

I tried to make Berengaria understand. I tried to make her see the drama of her situation: the hard, virile, preoccupied man who had taken a great cause so much to heart that in its service he could deny even his own inclinations; who would, when the right moment came, turn to her with the same single-mindedness.

"And when you ride by his side in triumph into Jerusalem, you will forgive him," I said.

"I forgive him now, if there is anything to forgive. But I do want to see him," she said.

From that moment the words "want to see him" or "like to see him" were continually on her lips, either in their artless simplicity or with reinforcements.

"I don't wish to disturb him or waste his time. I only want to see him."

Once she added, "Not that he should see me," words which, coming from a woman so lovely, who must have been aware of her loveliness and its effect upon all who looked at her, were peculiarly disarming.

Then she said, "If I could just look down on him from the musician's gallery . . ." And I said, "My dear, where Richard is there is no such thing. By all accounts he lives in a tent like a common archer."

But she was never convinced. In other circumstances I might have been amused to see how a young woman of such natural dignity and impeccable manners could become so brash and outspoken under the prick of desire, but as it was, every reference to Richard made me feel uncomfortable and obscurely guilty.

There came an evening when Berengaria and Joanna were huddled together over the baldric, work upon which Berengaria, out of her affection, allowed Joanna to share; the little duchess was reading and I was stitching a tuck into the bodice of a gown. Barbara would have done it far more quickly and expertly, for I was unhandy with a needle, but Barbara and I had recently had an argument. She had said that despite all the food now at my command I was growing thinner, and I contradicted her. But it was true; I knew that every dress hung on me slackly, so I was taking in tucks unbeknown to my woman.

The girls murmured softly over their work; the log on the hearth crackled. Then suddenly through the quiet I heard Berengaria say, "I must see him. I can't leave for Cyprus without seeing him. One of us might drown on the way, and then I should never see him again. It's not to be borne!" There was a new wild note in her voice. I looked up and was astonished to see that tears were running down her cheeks. Not a muscle in her face moved, her eyes were not screwed up, her mouth was not contorted. I had never seen a woman cry so beautifully. Joanna, of course, immediately began to cry, too, square-mouthed, shaky-chinned, snuffle-nosed. I sat for a moment thinking. What a weapon! To be able to cry without becoming repulsive, for most women take to tears as a final resort and thus defeat their own ends.

"Anna," Berengaria said in that same wild voice, "you must think of something. Think of some way to let me see him before we go away again."

Joanna said, "Mother can do it. Mother will devise a way."

And suddenly it was as though a line had been drawn across the room, with Berengaria and Joanna on one side and the duchess and I on the other. She looked up, put a finger in her book to mark the place, and waited. I said:

"Really, Berengaria, you make it very difficult for me. Richard is busy, and it is his wish to defer the meeting until you are in Cyprus. We asked him to come here and he was prevented; if he had wanted—I mean if he had been free to come another day, he would have suggested it himself. Begin now, sweetheart, to be a good wife and make your husband's wishes paramount. In a few weeks you will be married and see him every day."

I was conscious of a failure in me. I should have moved towards her at that moment and taken her in my arms, administered little deft pattings of the shoulder and strokings of the hair. Meaningless gestures, but time-honoured soothing to the one in distress and giving the observer something to do other than stand and stare. But such actions do not come easily to me. Joanna, however, got up and put her arms about Berengaria and said, "There, there," and things of that kind, and tried to draw her back to the settle. Berengaria shrugged her off and took a step or two towards Anna.

"Anna, you say something. Help me."

The little duchess said coolly, "Madam of England has explained the situation, 'Garia, and really there seems nothing to do about it. Unless you emulate Esmeralda . . ."

Berengaria looked blank for a moment; the tears that were in her eyes spilled over, but no more came. Then she smiled her sweet small smile. "Esmeralda . . . Of course. Oh, Anna, why didn't we think of it before?"

"Oh, I wouldn't advise it. It wouldn't work in real life, you know."

I had never heard of Esmeralda, so I had no idea what they were talking about, but something in the duchess's voice was disturbing to me. It had a falseness; she was saying one thing and meaning another, and usually her voice was very genuine. Now, though she said, "I wouldn't advise it," she was really saying, "Go ahead and do it."

176

"What are you talking about?" I asked quickly. "Who was Esmeralda, and what did she do?"

"She was only in a song," Berengaria said.

"Oh, I remember now," said Joanna, brightening and blowing her nose. "Oh, that would be very romantic. Just the sort of thing to appeal to Richard."

"It'd be madness," said the duchess. Deliberately, ostentatiously, she took her finger from the page and resumed reading. But the arrow was shot, and the harm had been done.

There was at least one person in the room whom I could address with sharpness and authority. I did so.

"Joanna! Will you please answer my question and tell me who Esmeralda was?"

"Only a girl in a song, Mother. Don't you remember? The one who took a lute—no, a harp, I think. It was a harp, wasn't it, Berengaria?"

I snapped my fingers impatiently, and Joanna hurried on, "Took a harp and went to the place where Sargarossa was holding her husband prisoner and sang a song that sounded just like a song to everybody else but was so cunningly fashioned for his ear alone that he understood that Gilbert Falaise was coming to his rescue."

"Oh," I said. "And you are lunatic enough to believe that if Berengaria went in for such mummery Richard would find it romantic! I always knew you were a fool, Joanna, but I should have thought that even a fool might have more sense at your age!"

I knew that I was making poor Joanna the scapegoat because I could upbraid her without actual breach of etiquette; and I thought even in my irritation that later on I could explain to her that everything I said to her I had actually meant for Berengaria and the duchess.

"No wonder men despise women," I said, "and choose to keep them at a distance whenever serious business is afoot. Richard is so busy with things that are real and important that he has no time to call upon us, and you think it would be romantic to go acting like somebody in a ballad. Wearing cap and bells, I suppose."

Joanna's chin began to shake again and her eyes filled with easy tears. The duchess closed her book with a little snap and said:

"Madam, please remember that it was I, not the Queen of Sicily, who made the suggestion; she may not have understood that I made it in jest."

"One should be careful of the jests one makes in the presence of simpletons," I retorted.

Berengaria stood up again.

"Joanna is not a simpleton, and Anna is not jesting," she said. "I cannot go to Cyprus without seeing Richard. And since he cannot come to me, I must go to him. And I must go in such guise that I neither waste his time nor distract his attention. Anna had wit enough to see that and to devise a way."

"Unfortunately you haven't Esmeralda's gifts," said the duchess, repudiating the compliment. "You can't sing, Berengaria."

"I can strum on a lute well enough; Blondel can do the singing," Berengaria said, quite unruffled. "And I can wear his better suit of clothes." She appeared to become aware of my consternation and turned to me, saying sweetly, "I am sorry, madam, to act against your wishes and without your approval, but this is a matter of great concern to me, and for once I must judge for myself." With that she moved to the door, opened it, looked out, and said, "Find Blondel. Tell him I want him at once."

I said, "Berengaria, if you do this thing you may regret it all your life. Something will happen. You will be discovered and Richard will be angry beyond words. In songs and such rubbishy tales disguises are always perfect—but, my dear girl, whoever heard of them in real life? Your breasts, your hips would betray you in a moment. You'd never reach Richard's tent. The archers would take you for some camp follower up to a prank, and God alone knows what might happen. Rape, probably. A camp is not a convocation of monks, you know."

I thought to frighten her. I succeeded only in frightening Joanna, who gasped out.

"Mother is right, Berengaria. Besides, what would you do with your hair?"

Berengaria lifted her hands and touched the long black plaits which lay over her shoulders, followed the curve of her bosom, and ended well below her waist.

"Cut it off," she said calmly. "It will grow again on the way to Cyprus."

"For God's sake, don't talk like an idiot," I burst out. "Before the boy comes and you make yourself a laughing-stock before him, Berengaria, listen to me. The whole idea is insane. You shan't do it. I forbid it. Do you hear me? Until you are married you are in my safekeeping, and I forbid you to say another word or make another move about this mad notion." I swung round to the little duchess. "You started this," I said hotly, "in jest! Now end it! Go on, use your famous wits and say something that will bring her to her senses."

Before she had time to say anything there was a gentle tap at the door; it opened and there was the lute player. He was breathless and flushed, as though from haste, and his hair was all misted from damp so that it stood out, silver-gilt, like a halo.

"Go away," I said, "we don't want you after all."

"Come in, Blondel. And shut the door." That was the duchess's voice, so low that it was almost gruff.

He included us both in a sweeping glance and then, still on the threshold, his hand still on the door, looked towards Berengaria.

"Madam, you sent for me." The words rebuked me and the duchess.

"Yes, I did, Blondel. I want you to fetch your lute and your better clothes—not for you to wear them, to lend them to me. I'll explain everything afterwards—as we go. Hurry now and bring me the clothes."

I had always thought him an effeminate young man, a pretty boy. Generally he fitted in so well into our female company with his songs and his lute, his handiness with the tapestry wool, his knowledgeableness about women's attire. But tonight, quite suddenly, as he stood looking not puzzled but cautious and entirely unflurried by the strange order, I became aware of the male quality in him. Masculine, reasonable ... He might be my ally. Before I could speak to denounce the plan anew to one who might be in sympathy with me, the duchess spoke.

"The princess has taken a fancy to emulate Esmeralda, Blondel. It is entirely my fault. I joked about it and said that was the only way of getting into the camp."

"The camp?" he said.

I could see that there was no need for further explaining; he was familiar with the story of Esmeralda. I shot a venomous glance at the duchess and noticed that her eyes were bright with malice. Through some part of my mind which held aloof from the immediate problem there passed a strange thought: She has something up her sleeve! From the moment when she made that apparently idle suggestion she has been moving towards *this* moment! Now why? To what end?

I gathered myself together and spoke direct to the boy.

"This may have started as a joke," I said, "but it has now gone too far. Princesses masquerading as goose girls or minstrels are all very well in stories and songs, but to think of it happening in real life is nothing short of madness. If you lift a finger, Blondel, to assist in this prank you will do your mistress a very ill service and——"

He broke in quite rudely: "That was in your mind, my Lady?"

"It was, and it is," said Berengaria. "Madam of England has voiced her objections and absolved herself of all responsibility. Any blame that comes of it I will take on myself. Now, Blondel, there is no time for further talk. Go fetch the things."

He made no move, and with a sudden uprush of relief I knew irrationally, but with certainty, that this could be left to him for handling. I was so sure that I turned away and began to kick the logs on the hearth nearer the heart of the fire.

"My lady," he said, "that was an order, and it goes against the grain for me to disobey you; but I cannot, in this case, both obey and serve, so I must disobey. The King of England lives in a tent surrounded by common soldiers, and what private life he has goes on behind a screen in a space about a third as large as this room. Any unknown player forcing his way in would be well below the salt—where the talk alone would scald your ears. For that reason, if for no other, I would not dream of taking you there—even if disguise were possible, which it is not. No woman over the age of twelve could really masquerade as a boy, despite all the songs in the world."

"You refuse to come with me?" He did not answer. "Very well, then I'll go by myself. I can find a minstrel, and doubtless I can hire some clown's clothes which *his* master provided."

"Madam, the clothes which you gave me are yours by unalienable right. But whether you go in those or in those you wear now, when you go into the tent of the King of England you go heralded so that your rank and your sex are accorded the respect due to them. If needful I will announce you at the very top of my voice."

He said all this very firmly but quite casually, and it was exactly as a husband, indulgent but sensible, might counter some outrageous whim in his wife.

I stared at him admiringly; Joanna gaped at his effrontery; the duchess looked slightly, very slightly, amused; Berengaria

180

seemed stunned. Four women, one man. And the man had spoken!

Berengaria, for all her stunned look, found words first. She said, as coldly and calmly as though she had had him in to answer some trivial question:

"Very well, you may go."

His face flew a sudden banner of scarlet; in all his spoilt days nobody had used that tone to him before, I gathered. But he bowed to us all and made his exit without any loss of dignity. And as though the closing of the door behind him had released some restraining spring, Berengaria's rage broke.

VIII

My nerves were still throbbing with agitation at the memory of that rage and the scene which it precipitated when, two hours later, I mounted a mule and set off through the dark drizzle to go to Richard's camp. I was once again heavily conscious of my age and of the fact that I had been completely routed and forced into taking an action at odds with my will.

Complete loss of self-control is as contagious as fire, and when Berengaria stared at that closing door and then flung round and gave way to her temper, it was as though someone had thrown a blazing brand into a dry haystack. In a moment, it seemed, we were all afire with rage, rashly exposing our hatreds and prejudices and grudges with the same demand for attention and thoughtless self-exposure with which a beggar will exhibit his horrid sores.

Who would have thought that my gentle Joanna hated me so much? That the same voice which had so recently said, "Mother is right," should now be shrieking, "The sons, always the sons! Richard is busy, so he mustn't be disturbed! Except by her, who sends the messages and gets them back, even when they are about *my* affairs! Women don't matter. Only the boys. It's been like that always."

It was, in a way, true. I was fond of my girls, but they hadn't mattered as the boys had.

On the turbulent flood of memory another piece of flotsam appeared. Myself, rounding on the little duchess and saying:

"It's all your fault, with your jest that wasn't a jest at all! I always knew that your sort would work me ill! For years I've known it. I thought it was physical aversion, but it was

181

prophetic. Your sort brings bad luck. We were happy enough and all was going well until you weighed in with your jest. Damn your wits, they're as crooked as your carcase."

Much of that was true too. And the saying of it, the understanding of that premonition released me. I hated her for her part in this affair, but I no longer shuddered at the sight of her. I could have touched, shaken, smacked her as though she were whole and sound. And she hadn't spoiled my supper tonight! That was over. I knew why I had hated cripples—they were just unlucky for me.

And there was Berengaria screaming at her half sister: "You sat there dumb! You knew he would do anything you said. You sat dumb. You only suggested it in the first place so that he should be able to make a fool of me! Because I didn't want him to go and build your accursed house."

Truth there, too, now that I had time to think of it. The suggestion was made in malice, the result regarded with amusement; the one had been deliberate, and the other foreseen.

The only one of us who had not lost her head or shouted or exposed herself was Anna (I could think of her as "Anna" now). And it was she who, when Berengaria had lashed herself into complete frenzy, used her puny strength to restrain her and turned to Joanna and said, "Fetch Mathilde and tell her to bring the physic, she'll understand."

Joanna was completely hysterical by that time and said, "Yes, that's my part—to run other people's errands! I'm Queen of Sicily, not a page boy." It was then that I smacked her face. And she came back to her senses and dropped back on the settle, crying helplessly, while I summoned the waiting woman.

With Berengaria's removal, clasped to Mathilde's voluminous bosom—"Come, come, my lamb, what have they been doing to thee?"—and with Lady Pila's face, changed from greed to curiosity, poking round the door and saying that supper would soon be ready, we all, Joanna, Anna, and I, gathered the rags of our dignity about us and were fain to cover not only our long-festering sores but also our newly inflicted wounds. Joanna had thrown her arms about my neck and begged forgiveness.

"I love you, Mother. I admire you above all women. I meant nothing; it was just—it was just——"

"It was just enough," I said, making play with the word. "And when you have sons, as I hope you will, and daughters, you will understand and forgive me." I took a bracelet from my arm and pushed it onto hers. She was pleased as a child and went away to wash her face and tire her hair. I was, for a moment, alone with Anna. We stood in embarrassed silence. Then she said:

"Truth is like wine, isn't it? You can get drunk on it."

"I'm sober now," I replied. "And for anything that I said in the heat of the moment to hurt you, I beg your forgiveness."

"Nothing you could say could hurt me. And I was to blame."

"You were," I said, countering frankness with frankness. "Why did you do it? Why did you mention this—Esmeralda at all?"

"If I told you, you'd think I was raving too." She looked at me with so much kindness that I thought she was about to take me into her confidence. But finally, with a little lift of one shoulder, she said, "That is not important. What matters now is this desire of Berengaria's to see Richard before we sail."

And Berengaria, on Mathilde's shoulder, had cried, "I only wanted to *see* him, just to *see* him. Is there anything so very wrong about that?"

It was there that I took my decision.

"I will go to Richard and see what can be arranged," I said. "Tonight, after supper. But do not mention it to anyone. We must not raise false hopes."

So here I was, with my own page, Gascon, holding to my stirrup and swinging a lantern, riding on a mule to Richard's camp. It was a dark night and long before moonrise, but almost as soon as we set out we could see the camp: the smoky rose of the fires where men were cooking their meal and the bobbing points of the lanterns. Then we dropped down into the cavernous streets of the town, and the mule's hooves slid and slithered on the damp cobblestones. We emerged on the other side and the camp was visible again, and soon I thought, or imagined, that I could smell it. The unmistakable, unforgettable smell of a great company of men, with their horses and their leather and their canvas— the smell of the camp.

I began to feel better. A most curious excitement moved in me, as though a butterfly had been trapped in my chest. I forgot not only the recent scene but a great stretch of years and found myself thinking of that long-ago time when I had ridden out to war, slept under canvas or under the stars, taken no thought for the morrow, carried no burden of memories. Nothing, nothing in all this world—and I doubted whether there was anything in the next—could make up for the joy of being young, with all the future stretching in sunlight before you. Time passed, with quarrels and sorrows, expedients and compromises, and there you were, suddenly an old woman looking backwards, with all the past blurred in a shadow; even those sunlit expectations revealed for what they were, marsh lights, delusions.

Oh, if only I were a young man riding down to put my hands between Richard's and take the oath.

This camp by the sea outside Messina was only a temporary mustering place, but it was a good camp, arranged as though to last forever. Alert sentries swung lanterns in our faces before allowing us to pass. The tents were laid out in straight rows, with wide paths between them, not in a shapeless huddle, and now and then the acrid, pungent effluvia of a slowly burning muck heap informed me, through my nose, that Richard had his sanitary arrangements well in hand. I remembered how often in other camps, during the former crusade, I had urged some such measure upon Louis.

"The dung heaps are too great," I said. "The earth can only absorb so much, and when it is saturated it spews out the rest and we sicken."

Louis said, "That is women's talk! Every farm door opens on a muck hill, and who is healthier than a farm boy?"

But I knew that camps were different, and Richard knew it too. His muck had been gathered and was being consumed by fire. Such a good organiser, oh, my Richard; and I come into the midst of all your organising to bother you with such a little matter.

It did seem such a little matter then. Whether he saw her, whether he married her here or in Cyprus what real difference could it make?

Already my mood had changed so much that if Richard and I had been under the same roof and I had gone, say, to his apartment to tackle him about his attitude to his bride, I should have shrugged my shoulders and turned back from the door. But having come so far ... Besides, now that I was within reach of him I was bound to admit that my desire to "see him" (horrible words!) was almost as urgent as Berengaria's own. So I pressed on, past a silken pavilion which the standard of France—once, strange to think, my own—marked as the lodging of Philip of France and on to an open space in the centre of which stood a large plain canvas tent with the Leopards of England hanging limp from its centre

184

pole. The flap was pinned back and the opening shone golden. A tall bearded man-at-arms stood on guard beside it.

I got down from my mule with a wry grimace at my stiffness—a fine crusader I made nowadays—and picked my way over the stones which had been placed in the mud before the tent opening. The guard dropped his lance with a practised gesture across my path and asked me my business. Gascon let the mule's rein drop free and ran forward, announcing me in a loud, challenging voice. The guard put his hand across his mouth in a confused, uncertain manner and hesitated for a moment. It was plain that he had been told to be careful whom he admitted. Then he peered into my face and reached out a hand and caught one of the attendant pages by the shoulder.

"Her Majesty the Queen Mother to see His Majesty," he mumbled, and swung the lance aside.

I, in turn, caught the page by the shoulder and said:

"Make no fuss. I can go in unannounced."

It was a large tent, oblong in shape, and wide enough to take three trestle tables set parallel with one another and running lengthways from the opening to within about ten feet of the upper end. These tables had obviously just been used for supper; broken bits of food and puddles of spilt liquor lay about their tops, and below them the hound-dogs worried the bones which had been thrown to them. Three or four serving-men, moving with concentrated quietness, were clearing away, and at one side, between the table and the tent wall, two young squires, also unnaturally quiet, were polishing mail.

At the upper end of the tent, where the tables ended, a rough platform of planking had been raised and some slight attempt had been made to transform this into a dais. A rug or two had been laid over the planks, and on it stood a table of a more permanent kind, though mean enough. On one end of the platform stood a screen, but that was now pushed back, and I could see a low plain bed and a wooden stand bearing a basin and ewer. I had been right in telling Berengaria that Richard lived amongst his men and not much more comfortably. A stinking oil lamp hung from the roof of the tent just over the table on the platform, and there were candles at each end as well, so that, coming from the dark outside and standing in the dimly lighted body of the tent and looking into the brightness, I was for a moment like a spectator at a morality play in a church. But no church and no play ever offered any observer such a curious spectacle as now met my eyes.

My eyes sought Richard first, naturally. He was sitting in a chair behind the centre of the table, and the light of the lamp fell directly upon him, touching the red-gold of his hair and the yellow-gold of the simple circlet upon his head, and making all the hollows of his face look deep and grey. He looked tired and old, even ill, an effect increased by the fact that he wore only shirt and drawers, though a cloak of red velvet was cast over the back of his chair. The heat in the tent, where many men had lately crowded over hot food and where lamp and candles were burning, was quite stifling. Walking from the farther end, I had already loosened my damp cloak and thrown back my hood and I could feel the sweat breaking out on my face.

Richard's head was bent over what looked like a toy made of firewood which stood between his hands on the table. Standing behind him, with his head almost resting on Richard's shoulder, was a small pale-faced fellow in a black gown with a white-tabbed collar. And at some distance, towards the table end, but also peering at the toy, was a big burly man in the buff coat of an archer. As I approached, the little man fumbled in his pocket and brought out something which he handed to Richard. Richard fitted it into the toy, and a second later something came flying through the air towards me. I put up my hand and by the merest chance caught it. It was a little clay pellet, just like those which boys roll in the gutter every spring. Marbles, the game is called, and many times I had watched the game from my window at Winchester and wondered that it should always be played in March and April and then abandoned until next year.

Richard, following the flight of his marble through the air, looked at me and said, "Mother!" He stood up, reached one hand behind him for his cloak, and succeeded in pushing it off the chair. The archer and the man in the black robe rushed to retrieve it, and I heard their heads crack.

I laughed. "Never mind your cloak, Richard. I've cast mine," I said, dropping it as I spoke. "Give me your hand." He came to the edge of the dais and stretched his hand, which I took, and pulled myself up beside him. He kissed me, and I ran my hands over his shoulders and over the place where his hair grew harsh at the back of his neck. The old weak tenderness ran over me. My son, I thought, my son! And in the back of my mind I heard Joanna crying that only the boys mattered. Could she but have known. Of all the boys—my beautiful boys—only Richard! Or rather Richard most of all.

"What brings you, Mother? Is anything wrong?"

"No. Nothing wrong, Richard. And I have no wish to disturb you. I can wait. Go on with your game of marbles. Look, I caught this one. You can shoot it again." I opened my hand and offered him the pellet. He took it between his finger and thumb and turned back to the man in the black gown, saying gaily:

"Just my luck, Escel! This is my mother with whom I refused to sup the other evening, pleading lack of time. And she comes to see me and finds me playing, as she says, at marbles!"

The man made his obeisance, at the same time letting out a little nervous titter to show that he appreciated the King's joke.

"But it works, Escel! Let's try again. Here, Mother, sit down and watch for a moment. Now, Escel, swivel it round and aim at the farthest candle."

Escel fiddled with the firewood contraption, and in a second or two another pellet flew out, striking the candle with such force that the flame was extinguished and candle and stick were borne downward and outward, over the edge of the table and to the ground.

"Accurate, too," Richard cried, pleasure and awe mingling in his voice. "And to think that we've been working it the other way all these years."

"It will certainly do damage. The pellets I made to exact proportion; they are the equivalent of a ball of lead weighing a hundred-weight."

"That'll make the Saracens jump! Escel, I'll knight you for this here and now, without formality, as though we were on the battlefield."

Escel became very flustered. "Sire, should you not wait until the engine has proved itself in battle? And I would remind you—the idea was not mine in the first place."

"What of that? If I wait I shall be atop the walls of Acre and you'll be dispensing your pills. I'll reward the boy, never fear. Kneel down."

He moved behind the screen, fumbled about for a moment, and emerged with his great sword in one hand and in the other a pair of spurs caked with mud. "Go on, man, kneel down; I haven't got all night! Now, I call on all those here present—and that means you, too, Dickon, so leave that table alone for a moment—to witness that I here and now

187

confer the order of knighthood upon this man, Escel, with all the privileges and responsibilities appertaining to the rank. I think that qualifies. Rise up, Sir Escel," he said, striking the bowed, black-covered shoulder. "Here's a pair of spurs for you, and I'll find you a horse in the morning. And keep your eyes open for suitable timber, will you? We must take it with us. I'm told there's not a tree left standing within twenty miles of Acre. I'll talk to you further in the morning. Good night, Sir Escel."

"Good night, sire. I wish——I can't——Oh, sire——" said the new-made knight, looking as though a whirlwind had struck him.

"All right, Escel. Good night." His voice was kind but dismissing.

Sir Escel bowed to me, blundered off the dais, and went hurrying away through the tent, his spurs and his wooden toy clutched to his breast. Richard sat down on the edge of the table and drew a couple of deep breaths.

"Now," he said, putting his hand to his hip and looking past me, "let's have a look at this beef. You brought it, didn't you?" His voice, jovial to start with, sharpened at the question.

The archer came forward. I could see the sweat start out on his brow and his magnificent beard wobble with the shaking of chin.

" 'Tisn't fitting to put it under your nose, Your Majesty."

"You were supposed to put it in your mouths, weren't you? Bring it here."

"My lord, I never meant no harm. I meant it more as a joke like! I never thought——"

Richard looked at him with a gaze which was frightening, less on account of its sternness than of its immense concentration. Slowly, reluctantly, the man lifted onto the table a chunk of beef, quite black, except where the white maggots crawled, and so rotten that it stank. I turned my head away, but Richard got up and leaned over it with the same fascinated attention that he had given to the little wooden engine.

"And you were served this at midday?"

"Yes, my lord."

"Who served it?"

"The sergeant served us, my lord. Rolf the Dispenser opened the cask."

"Fresh opened today?"

188

"Fresh opened. But they've all been the same the last week."

"Cover it. I've known a dead horse to smell better! You were right to complain. I'd be glad to know what sort of joke *that* could make you crack!"

"I only said, my lord—— Well, it wasn't much of a joke neither. I said they was feeding us this to get us ready to eat the old infidel, like."

Richard laughed. "We'll eat them, you and I, eh? Now go and find Rolf and tell him I want to see that cask and its brand mark. Somebody's going to smart for this! I'm glad you complained and drew my attention to it. We'll all eat rotten meat before we finish in all likelihood, but on the battlefield and all together! Good night."

The archer dropped down on his knees and kissed Richard's idly swinging foot, stammering incoherently. Richard gave him a little gentle push with his toe and bade him good night again. The archer got up, jumped down from the dais, and was striding away, a man much relieved in his mind, when Richard called after him:

"Hi, you. You, the eater of infidels! What *did* you eat today?"

"I didn't. Some of them got some green stuff in the market. But I'd opened my silly big mouth and was bid wait on you, my lord."

"Dickon," Richard shouted, "take and feed this good fellow. Give him the best we have. And then bring us some wine. Give us the best of that too. Well, there now, Mother, I've done. No, by the living God, I haven't. There's a despatch from England. Alwyne brought it just as Escel came in with the new mangonel. He was dead on his feet and I sent him away to sleep. Ah, here it is. Urgent, he said, and bad news." He jerked his head like a horse tormented by flies. "We'll have our wine first and then read it." He looked at me and smiled. "I'm glad to see you, Mother. You managed things well in Navarre. Smooth as oil. I'm very grateful to you." There was a barely perceptible hesitation. "And how is the princess?"

Suppose I said: Madly in love with you and only just restrained from bashing her head against a wall because you won't see her? There were men who would be pleased and flattered—but little men, the sort who needed a woman's adulation to bolster up their self-esteem.

"As I told you, very beautiful, and of a most agreeable nature. Really, Richard, a girl in a thousand; and better than you deserve. . . . You should have come to supper, you know. Berengaria and Joanna are eager for the sight of you."

But even while I was saying this my eyes and my thoughts were on that despatch from England. Urgent and bad. What had gone wrong? Alwyne I remembered. He had a manor at Pant Glas in Shropshire, on the border of Wales; and twenty years ago he had repelled a Welsh raiding party with such ferocity and such success that Henry had called him to Westminster and presented him with a gold cup. Later he had married a younger sister of Rosamonde Clifford. So he was, by marriage, uncle to Geoffrey of York. And his urgent bad news might be something trivial and local about the Welsh border—or it might be from Geoffrey, and urgent and bad indeed.

Richard put down his wine cup and said, "Well, this can't be deferred any longer." He broke the seal, shifted so that the light fell onto the page, and read silently for what seemed a long time. Then he said not uncheerfully, "Ha-ha-ha. Who advised me to get Geoffrey Whoreson back? Who was quite certain that he'd keep everybody in order? God's eyeballs, you'd have done better yourself. And nobody could have done worse!" He read on and presently gave a great snort. "Whose flag, do you think, flies over my keep at Windsor this moment?"

"Not Geoffrey's?" I faltered. A sick feeling of shame and remorse came over me. I had advised—more, I had pressed Richard to appoint Geoffrey; I had been so sure of his ability and his integrity. Why had I been? What dementia had led me to trust the Rose Bitch's whelp? She had set her cap at being Queen; what more likely than that her son, with his half-royal blood, should covet the throne while its rightful owner dressed sores on pack mules? I should have known!

"Richard, tell me," I exclaimed in agony, unable to bear the suspense any longer.

"On your life, no! It's better than that! Geoffrey sent me this letter. It's my Master Longchamp who sets up to be King in my absence. Master Longchamp's flag flies over Windsor!"

"That ferret," I said, astonished; and at the same time a little ashamed of the relief I knew. Longchamp was never my candidate; I'd been against leaving him in authority from the first! I couldn't be blamed for his behaviour, though it was the measure of the failure of the man I had sponsored.

"Three bonny fellows I left in charge," Richard said. "They let him get the upper hand, and what do they do about it? Send me a letter. As though I had nothing else to

190

do. Castrated asses!" He resumed his reading and then thrust the letter under my nose. "Here, read for yourself."

I read that Longchamp had summarily dismissed almost everyone whom Richard had left in office and who was capable of being dismissed, replacing them with creatures of his own, mainly his relatives, or relatives of his numerous mistresses. That he had set up a private army of his own, with its own uniform. That he had tampered with the coinage. That he never went abroad without an escort of fifteen hundred armed men. That he signed orders with his private seal, as though despising the Great Seal of England. That he sought out occasions to insult and diminish all of rank or standing, save only Prince John, who, although he spoke of the chancellor with hatred and contempt out of his presence, was much in his company and often of one mind with him.

"Well?" Richard said as I finished reading and stared with dismay into his face.

"This is terrible," I said. "The little rat, born in a ditch and reared on a dunghill! Ruler of England. Richard, you must have left him enormous powers."

"I left him in power to raise money for me. His devices for getting money were brilliantly conceived and executed. He has more brains in his little finger than Geoffrey and Hugh have in both their great skulls. And it's a pity I must lose his services because I have no man capable of restraining his nonsense. Lose them I must, because it's plain to me that if he rides out with fifteen hundred men at heel he's raising money on my authority and putting it into his own pocket! *And* flying his flag over Windsor. That is intolerable!"

I looked at him with growing dismay and no little bewilderment. Was it possible that he had missed the ominous sign which pointed to a worse state of affairs than the loss of a little revenue and an insult to prestige? Couldn't he see the game Longchamp and John were playing? Longchamp, leaping from power to power, would wait until he was unassailable, and then he and John would strike a bargain; the crown for the rogue with the royal blood, the power behind it for the rogue with the brains and ambition. Both would be perfectly suited; John craved the glitter without responsibility; Longchamp itched for authority. Richard was fretting over the loss of money and a flagpole and seeming to ignore the fact that he might lose his crown. Or was he seeing the reality, and was I being overimaginative?

"If I had time," Richard said quite pleasantly, "I'd go back and impale the little upstart on his flagpole! But that is out of the question. I'm damned if I know whom to send." He studied a slight abrasion on one of his knuckles and then sucked it thoughtfully.

I hesitated for a moment, then said: "I know this advice will be unwelcome—but frankly, Richard, you should go yourself. Not because of the money or the flag flying; they're trivial things compared with the general situation. You see, Geoffrey says—— Where is it? Here. Listen. 'Every day sees his party strengthen and ours weaken as men go over to him out of fear or self-seeking.' You see, England is already divided; the very thing we dreaded and tried to avoid." At least you didn't, I did, but "we" sounds better. "Whoever you send," I hurried on, "will only be one man more on Geoffrey's side. Only *you* are above both parties. Only you have the power and the courage. And, Richard, think of the effect of your arrival. Longchamp will collapse like a pricked bladder from sheer surprise, and every man in England will see that though you have this great enterprise on hand you still have time and thought to spare for your own country." I watched him carefully. "The crux of all this," I said, tapping the letter, "is that the cunning little swine has got him a good bodyguard. They fold their hands and say, 'What can we do?' He has fifteen hundred men at heel? You are the only one whom fifteen hundred men would not deter. I can think of nobody else."

Flattery of the basest kind, though not without an element of truth. I saw Richard's eyes brighten as he sensed the challenge. For a moment I thought I had persuaded him. Then he suddenly smacked his hand on the table and said:

"No. Mother, this is the ultimate trick of the devil!" His voice took on a curious edge. "Every possible thing that could delay me has conspired to do so." Each word came out, slow, sharp, distinct. "It would take an hour to tell you all the obstacles, all the delays that I have borne. Sometimes it has seemed to me that God Himself must be a fool, or impotent to let such things happen to me. There is the Holy City in the grip of the infidel, a thing you'd think He'd shudder on His throne to see; and here am I, the best soldier of my time, asking nothing more than the chance to go and fight for its freedom. And from the awkwardness of Philip of France to the obstinacy of a mule, everything has worked against me. Now I am ready, and the devil, having played every card but this, brings it out with a flourish! I will not go. I tell you, Mother—and you can hear me too, Satan—I wouldn't go back to England if it were on fire from coast to coast and I could put it out by blowing on it." The dark red colour had crept over his face, and against it his eyes looked like pale pebbles. He was breathing quickly, and the sweat shone on his brow.

"I know," I said soothingly. "Your patience must have been strained to breaking point. But, Richard, England matters too."

"Matters? Of course it matters! England provides the sinews of war. And I can't have Longchamp nibbling at them. I'll stop his depredations. Alwyne must go back with orders to Geoffrey to stiffen himself. 'Loyal and incorruptible' Father called him once; what's the sense of being loyal and incorruptible if your backbone is like a wet plaster?"

"He is both those things," I said. "He informed you at once, though he must have felt shame at confessing his failure." And why, I wondered, should I be defending Geoffrey, the son of Rosamonde?

"He squealed for help!" Richard retorted harshly. "Well, I'll help him, the pusillanimous dummy. I'll send somebody fresh and independent with new orders and with authority to override him and Longchamp." He gnawed savagely at his sore knuckle and then looked up. "I know. I'll send Coutances!"

"Oh, Richard," I said, speaking out as I had done in the past days, "such an old man!"

"Well, you're an old woman," he said with a bark of laughter. "You're none the worse for that, are you?"

Either much better or infinitely worse; by what standard should one judge? And this is no time to choplogic.

"Why that particular old man?"

"He's honest. And Geoffrey and he know one another. Geoffrey goes a little in awe of him. Whatever orders he carries Geoffrey will try to carry out."

"But, my dear boy, Geoffrey's obedience has never been in question. We may assume, surely, that he has already done his utmost, else he would never have written this—this confession of failure in the first trust you have ever laid upon him. He has his pride. This despatch must have cost him blood to write! Sending Coutances to bully him will be beating a dead horse. If he'd had a bolt left he'd have shot it rather than appeal to you. And Coutances will have no effect upon these people who go over to Longchamp day by day. He hasn't a word of English to his tongue. And you know how they feel—at least *you* don't, but I *do*. 'Another bloody foreigner!' That's what they'll say. And the mass of them

193

have little taste for churchmen. If you won't go yourself—and I say won't, Richard, because it sticks in my mind that you could if you had a mind to; one more month of the infidel's foot in the holy places can do little damage; he's been there for years; one more month of Longchamp in England may lose you your kingdom—but if you won't go yourself, at least send a man, a soldier, an Englishman."

It was just as it had always been. There was Richard looking at me with the very same cold distaste which had shone on the faces of Louis and Henry whenever I had argued with them. And he spoke with the same harsh voice.

"Any man, any soldier worth his salt is here with me and going forward with me to hunt bigger game than a cheating little pickpocket playing at king of the castle. I have no man to waste on him! He's frightened Geoffrey Whoreson, and by God he's scared you. He hasn't brought me to the point where I'd waste an untried knight on him. Coutances and a scorching message from me are all he'll get. I'll go and see Coutances now."

He stretched a long arm behind the screen and hauled out a plain linen jerkin into which he began to struggle. I knew it was the worse moment to pursue an argument; I knew that whatever I said would anger him further, but this thing mattered. So I waited until his head was free and he was buckling the leather belt about his waist, and then I said:

"Richard, don't be in such a hurry. Don't send an old foreign cleric, I beg of you. What you need is not just another man on this side or that—you need somebody above the lot of them. Somebody capable of *ruling* England."

He stood still, his hand on the buckle. "Look, Mother. Once before I took your advice and called back Geoffrey of York. Did that profit me?"

"It got you an honest report of the state of affairs. Your Hugh of Durham and your brother John haven't bothered to tell you that the Great Seal of England is tossed aside and the guttersnipe's standard waving over Windsor, have they? Have they?"

He looked at me with pure hatred and then, just like the others in the early years when they loved me, took refuge in a typical male attitude. "Little woman, don't worry." He struck me lightly on the shoulder. "Cheer up, Mother. You take this too seriously. It was the devil's last throw. He'll leave me alone now. You'll see."

I was momentarily speechless. In the silence he picked up

his great sword and then, after a second's thought, laid it down again and went back behind the screen.

"I'll come part of the way with you," he said, "the mule pickets lie that way. Tancred kept his bargain, but a third of the beasts are lame and all of them rotten with sores, and my fellows say that the muleteers will *eat* the bran poultices I ordered. So I drop in now and then when they least expect me and I keep a little stick. Where in Christ's holy name is my little stick? Ah! 'Mule in front,' I say, 'mule behind,' and I wallop their arses." He emerged again, tucking a thin flexible cane under his arm and pulling on the gloves I had made him. "Dickon! Dickon! He's always underfoot when I don't want him and a mile away when I do. Oh, there you are. You know where Sir Alwyne lies? Take him a hot posset and a dish of frumenty, well spiced; wake him and tell him it is my order that he eat and preserve his strength. Now, Mother," he said, leaping down from the platform and reaching his hand to me. "Coutances and Bavister and my lord of Rheims lie out by the mule pickets—the men call it 'Pets' Corner'—and I can make one errand of it."

Sir Alwyne's hot posset, a poultice for a mule, an archer's jest, threatened insurrection in England—all one! All little grains of dust on the long road to Jerusalem! Equally important. Equally inconsiderable.

IX

Outside his tent, where Gascon waited with my mule, he gave his immediate and concerned attention to the fact that I had travelled by night with so poor an escort.

"I thought you had more sense," he said. "Every Sicilian from Tancred down is a thief and a robber."

"I'm not worth robbing," I said.

"There's the mule! Since I made Tancred hand over Joanna's dowry a mule is worth its weight in gold in the island." And he had detailed six stalwart fellows to accompany us home.

The escort slowed down our progress. Gascon could hang onto the stirrup and trot along at a good pace, with little pauses now and then to gather his breath; it was thus that we had come. But now the six fell into marching order on either side of the mule, and we must perforce match our pace to theirs. The mule, with its head towards home, moved more briskly than on the outward journey and needed some restraint. Pulling against its hard mouth, thinking my thoughts about England, and running my mind over the interview just past, I had covered at least two thirds of the distance back before I remembered joltingly the reason for my visit to Richard. It seemed unbelievable, but from the moment when the despatch from England was mentioned, Berengaria had dropped out of my mind altogether.

Was I getting old and muddle-minded? Not that my forgetfulness mattered in this particular instance, for had I kept my errand in mind I doubted whether I should have broached the matter. This was hardly the evening for tackling Richard about affairs matrimonial.

Nevertheless, the sudden stab of memory gave me one of those physical jars which would have halted me in my stride had I been afoot; being on the mule's back and already bearing on the rein to maintain even pace, I bore harder, and the mule, resenting the pull, lashed out with its heels, turning sideways. My escort was thrown into confusion, and before we had recovered ourselves—I had been almost unseated—there came from behind us, from the direction of the camp, the call of a trumpet, the sound sweetened and muted and made sad by the distance.

One of the men said, "My lady, if you would wait for a moment ... That is the signal, and the rule is, wherever we are, whatever we are about, if we hear it——"

"What signal?" Nobody answered. The six were shuffling into position until they stood shoulder to shoulder along the side of the path. Then as one man they lifted their arms and cried loudly:

"Help, help for the Holy Sepulchre!"

Three times they cried it; and though any solemn ritual intended to be performed by a mass of men can become ridiculous when performed by a small number, this was not ridiculous. It was, on the contrary, impressive and curiously moving. Gascon had lifted his lantern high and inquiringly, and in the uncertain light I could see the six faces, with disconnected features leaping to prominence as the glow touched them, a beard thrust forward as its owner threw back his head to make the call, a row of white teeth gleaming in a square-opened mouth, an eye, absorbed and earnest. I was abruptly conscious that these were dedicated men, soldiers of the Cross. A moment before we had been moving along as one body; now Gascon and I were set aside, an old woman and a page, outside the mystical union. Something in that thought made my throat thicken.

196

They dropped their arms, and the spokesman said in his cheerful English voice, "Thank you, my lady. At your service again."

"Do you do that every night?" I asked, making no move to proceed.

"Every night, my lady. Last thing before lights out. But only within sound of the trumpet. If we'd topped this next hill I doubt if we'd have heard it, then we needn't have stopped you."

He spoke the words in a cheerful, matter-of-fact way, just explaining to me. Afterwards, looking back, I often wondered exactly why they should have affected me as they did.

At the moment I heard there the very voice of England. The punctilious observance coupled with the complete lack of sentiment. One of my Aquitainians would either have considered a lady's convenience sufficient excuse for ignoring the rule—thus being entirely practical; or, if he wished to observe it, he would have done so wholeheartedly without considering her convenience or the nearness of that hill—thus being completely sentimental. There was the difference, and if there were a single word for it, it would describe all the English, gentle and simple, rich and poor. Scrupulous about the rules, but sceptical too. Stop because you are in earshot, but cynically note that in another moment you would have been over the hill and free of the ritual. Exactly the same attitude as that of the London crowd, the loyalest on earth, who interrupt their cheering with ribald and audible comments about royalty's little physical peculiarities and who really liked Henry all the better for his red nose and potbelly. This apparent inconsistency in the English has made people of other nations call them two-faced and perfidious. I remembered that when I was trying to explain the English to Richard I had called them sly. I had almost said "hypocritical." Both words were wrong. They had the peculiar capacity of facing both ways. Of seeing all round a subject.

I have noticed repeatedly that though the English crowd could be very savage it was never deadly as a crowd of my own Aquitainians could be. Sooner or later something would provoke its mirth, and through the purifying laughter some lonely voice would say, "Poor old bugger!" and with those words the mob's sentence of death upon the subject of its interest, baited bull, chased pickpocket, discovered forger of coinage, brewer of bad beer, would lift. Even in the full heat of a hare-coursing, when the blood in dogs and men reached fever pitch, a hare had only to make one gallant or comic turn and somebody would cry, "Live hare!" and somebody else would beat off the dogs, and that hare would live to run another day.

The English were never extreme. And that made them, up to a point, a very exploitable people. At this moment they were bearing with wry humour and patience the exhortations of Longchamp's regime. When he fell they wouldn't tear him to pieces. They'd handle him roughly, no doubt, but somebody would say, "Poor old bugger. He's lost his flag and all his pretty soldier men." And the crowd would laugh and let him get away. Next day they'd regret it and spend hours describing what they ought to have done to him.

That was my England. My? I was Eleanor of Aquitaine, and there was no doubt that individual Englishmen, such as Nicolas of Saxham, had treated me ill. But although, or perhaps because, I was alien I could look at these people and understand them and love them. And I could see what Richard could not, that the sending of one more elderly cleric, however honest, however well-meaning, would mean nothing, less than nothing, to the ordinary mass and mob of people who made up the English nation. What they needed in this moment of confusion wasn't orders or even support for either party, but a rallying point, somebody outside—if possible, above—the quarrel between Geoffrey and Longchamp.

Pursuing this train of thought, I had not noticed that we were on the move again. I became aware of external things to find that we had topped the hill which the man-at-arms had pointed out. On the downward slope, and with the smell of home in his nostrils, the mule renewed his efforts to brisken the pace, and the soldiers were almost running, skipping, and slithering on the loose rain-worn surface of the road. I had that feeling, which sometimes comes in a nightmare, of being momentarily powerless, pushed or dragged towards some dreadful yet obscure danger, and unable to lift a finger, unable even to voice a scream of protest. The only difference was that in the dream the sensation of helplessness, of being carried forward, is accompanied by a sense of fear. That now was lacking. I wasn't frightened; I was just being carried forward, futile, helpless, as inconsiderable as a leaf that the wind blows.

Richard had brushed me away, first in anger and then with good-humoured contempt, and this mule was rushing me down to Messina, back to the women, back to the trivial exasperations, to a way of life and a pattern of behaviour which was a negation of all my understanding—and of the power which I knew I had in me.

Conceit is the belief in a power which one does not possess; all too often it is confused with self-confidence, which is belief in the power one does possess as surely as one possesses two eyes and two hands and two feet. I *knew* at that moment, without a trace of conceit, that, given the chance, I could put things right in England, and that, after Richard, I was the one person who could. I knew that just as I knew my own age and height and the colour of my own hair. I wasn't frightened of Longchamp; I stood in no awe of John; I understood the English and they had affection for me; I had proved that when I reappeared in London.

Even by virtue of my rank, I thought cynically, I was the best person to send. I had only to go to Windsor to spend a night and Longchamp's flag must come down, or he stand convicted of open insurrection—and he wasn't ready for that yet!

I wasn't blown up with self-esteem. I sat there on that pulling mule and knew that I was over seventy and that everything I had ever previously attempted had miscarried: my crusade with Louis, my rebellion against Henry in support of Harry, my attempt to rule in Aquitaine. All failures. And a thousand lesser things too. But now suddenly it seemed to me that all my long life of failure had been a preparation for this task; I had been forged and tempered and sharpened as a good blade is; fired by enthusiasm, plunged into the cold water of despair, beaten into shape by hard circumstance, and finally edged by conviction.

Was I now to let this mule carry me down to Messina where I must say, "My dear, Richard is too busy to see you, there, there! Come, let us pack our embroidery and our little disappointments and go to Cyprus. There, there! Blondel will sing us a little song and Anna will make a little joke and Pila will arrange a nice little meal"? While Coutances went bumbling off to England with a letter, at which John and Longchamp would laugh, and Longchamp would go on filling his pockets and John his empty pride by wringing out my English people as a housewife wrings out a rag?

By the Rood, no!

I tugged at the mule and cried, "Halt!" to the soldiers. It was again like that nightmare where, in the last extremity, the dreamer cries out and wakes.

"I must go back to the camp," I said. "I have remembered something of importance."

199

The soldier whose peculiarly English attitude and cheerful English voice had affected my decision (or not? Had not this moment been approaching step by step since they laid me in the arms of my mother instead of the son she had craved? Who knows?) said kindly that if it was a message or anything that he could carry back to save me the exhaustion of the return journey he would attend to it. And thanking him for his offer, I thought: My poor good man, I am not a woman weakened by her seventy years and her grey hairs, but strengthened and perfected.

The soldiers accepted the change of direction cheerfully, but Gascon sighed, and I heard him and sent him home. The mule sighed, too, but I turned it to face the hill and the rising moon.

The camp was very quiet; the fires were dowsed now and the lanterns out. But the men knew their way, and we came expeditiously enough to the open space outside Richard's tent where soldiers and servingmen and pages, wrapped in blankets against the chill of the early spring night, lay sleeping and looking like corpses. But the guard was wakeful. This time he gave me a look of recognition and respect.

"His Majesty is within and not yet asleep."

"That is well," I said. I could indeed hear from within the tent the sound of music, of little broken melodies, the desultory, experimental plucking of the strings that comes before the lute player settles down to his song.

The body of the tent was dark and empty, but the oil lamp still shone above the dais. Once again it was like being in the nave of a church when the miracle play was about to begin.

This time there were two players: Richard, who lay propped on his elbow on the bed, his head and torso visible, the rest of his body hidden by the screen, and the lute player, who sat on a stool, holding his hands and his lute into the lamplight, with his back to Richard. I knew him because the light shone on his white-gold hair and made a nimbus of it. It was Berengaria's minstrel, the boy Blondel.

I had entered the tent briskly, meaning to say what I had to say before my courage failed me. But surprise halted me. What was Blondel doing here? Had Berengaria sent him?

At that moment Richard's voice reached me.

"That's it! Perfect. Now, from the beginning!"

The boy turned his head with a quick, delighted look and then turned back, bent over his lute, struck up the music, and started to sing. I had never heard him sing so well, so sweet, so clear, so true and tunable, and so merry, like a blackbird

200

singing on an April day in England when the sun shines warm after a shower and the hawthorn buds break white in the hedges.

The song was new to me.

> *"Sing of my mail that was dug in the darkness and*
> *fashioned in light*
> *That I might go armoured by sunshine and secretly*
> *move as the night.*
> *Link on link, chain on chain, polished and bright;*
> *Sing of my armour, dug in the darkness, forged in the*
> *light.*

"Now, sire, this is *your* verse. You must sing it."

Richard pulled himself from his reclining position and sat up on the bed's end. His voice rang out, as tunable as the boy's, but deeper and harsher.

> *"Sing of my sword, heavy and sharp as fate,*
> *Sing of the sword that shall batter the Holy Gate.*
>
> *In the good enterprise*
> *Blood shall this blade baptise*
> *And leave immaculate.*
> *Sing of my sword."*

I was by this time close to the edge of the dais, ready to speak as soon as the song should reach its end. Blondel began on the next verse.

> *"Sing of my shield . . ."*

I had been looking at the boy as I moved towards the dais; my eye, first startled by the sight of him unexpectedly encountered, had been arrested by the fact that he looked different from the Blondel of the bower. Ordinarily he wore a hangdog look. I had once or twice wondered at it, for he had a very pleasant life; all the ladies spoiled him; he ate and lived very softly for one of his kind. But now and again his face reminded me of the faces of men who had borne some shocking experience—some of the Christian prisoners whom we released from Saracen hands (and our crusade, if it did nothing more, set scores of them at liberty) had worn that look; and I have also seen it on the faces of men stricken with moral sickness and soon to die. But tonight that look

201

was gone; his face was merry and young; even the white hair shone gold in the lamplight and lost its frosty incongruity; and his eyes took on a lustre and his teeth shone when he opened his mouth to the singing. One could imagine an archangel—not Michael, for he, being a soldier, would wear a sterner look, but Gabriel, perhaps—looking somewhat like that.

And I remembered that earlier this evening—though it seemed much longer, years and years ago, in fact—I had had reason for gratitude toward him. Although in the confusion that followed his withdrawal I had lost sight of the fact, he had prevented Berengaria from making a fool of herself. And now he was doing well too. Richard, after the music and the singing, would be in a softer and more amenable mood than he would have been coming straight from the interview with Coutances or from the mule pickets. More likely to listen to me.

How you do seem to crop up, I thought quite kindly, looking at the back of the silver-gilt head bent over the lute. And then, coming back to practical things, wondering who sent him, Berengaria? Anna? Once before he had spied out the land—was he spying again? But the whole thing had a remoteness, an unreality which it would not have had if I had found Blondel in this tent before I had heard those soldiers say, "Help, help for the Holy Sepulchre!"

I stood there, waiting for the verse to end and thinking these oddly assorted thoughts. Then it happened.

Richard's hand, lean and brown, cupped for caressing, reached out until it almost touched the back of that silver-gilt head; it hesitated, hovered, and fell away, as Eve's hand must have fallen away once, twice, before it closed at last about the deadly apple.

And I looked into Richard's face and saw there what is perhaps the most shocking, most humiliating thing any woman—let alone a mother—can see on any man's face: naked, hungry, lustful desire directed at another man.

Quite unmistakable to anyone, and to me horribly recognisable, for as a young woman I had spent some time in the company of my uncle, Robert of Antioch, the most charming and handsome man of his day, but a notorious lover of boys.

One can think many things in a second of time, and I thought then: How odd that I should remember Robert this very evening. For when I was thinking over my thousand failures I had thought of how, full of the pride of young womanhood and beauty, I had flaunted my charms at him, exerted myself to be witty and companionable, not in jealousy exactly, but certainly competitively with the favourite of the moment. And Louis had been angry, had accused me of misconduct—and how could I say that Robert hardly noticed me because I was not a pretty page boy? That was one of the thousand failures, remembered just before I had halted the mule.

And now I saw in my most beloved son the taint. And knew that it had been transmitted through my blood. Henry and his kind had vices enough, God knew, but the vice of Sodom was not one of theirs.

The full weight of my understanding and my knowledge fell on me like the lead that falls on the wretch condemned to *peine forte et dure;* and I stood there, within arm's reach of Richard, so shocked and stunned that if he had looked up and seen me I could not have spoken to him. If a lion had come rampaging through the tent I could not have stepped out of its path.

Alys, I thought, and the long delay . . . Berengaria and the absence even of curiosity . . . It all fitted.

So did that damned boy's reluctance to accompany Berengaria on her innocent, girlish escapade.

If there had been anything to sit on I should have sat down; if there had been anything to cling to I should have clutched it. But the trestle tables and the benches had been moved away, and I stood there in the empty space, and the darkness and the emptiness whirled round me and over me and through me. I was alone in the infinite night.

But blows fall, and none but the last is fatal; from the rest we reel and recover ourselves and go on. Presently my mind began to move again and I thought: This thing which I have stumbled on by chance in no way affects what I came back to say. England stands where she stood. And Richard, whatever he may be, is still my son.

Just then the song ended. The boy swept his fingers across his lute in a final triumph-burst of melody; leapt to his feet, and, facing Richard, said, "Sire, that was magnificent!" And though my heart's beat reverberated in my ears and made all my limbs unsteady I forced myself to move forward and say, before Richard could speak, "It was indeed."

That startled them both. The boy looked confused and guilty, Richard surprised and concerned. He got to his feet and with an exact repetition of his former gesture assisted me onto the dais. This time, however, instead of embracing me he peered at me earnestly. "You should have been safe home ere this. What happened?"

"Nothing amiss." I was surprised to hear my voice, so light and easy and ordinary. "It was just that on my way, like Saul of Tarsus on his way to Damascus, I saw a great light and came back to discuss what it revealed to me."

"Then," he said jovially, "you're luckier than the saint to whom nothing was revealed. If I remember rightly he lay blind for a fortnight. Is that correct, Blondel? You're the bookman. Good God, boy, don't stand there looking as though you'd been caught picking a pocket. Madam, my mother, will overlook your being out of bounds after dark."

The haste to set the boy at his ease was significant. And if I had been blind, the very way in which he had said the word "Blondel" would have informed me; nothing is more revealing of love or hatred or indifference than the way in which one's given name is spoken.

"I have one or two other things to occupy my mind," I said ironically, "and perhaps I also am out of bounds after dark."

The boy shot me a look of understanding. "By your leave then, sire, madam . . ."

"All right, Blondel. Tomorrow, if you can elude the watchdogs. I may have a little time after supper."

Exactly in that manner would Robert of Antioch dismiss and make further assignation with the favourite of the moment. Deceiving no one but himself, poor fool. And I wondered whether Richard would fall into the usual pattern of behaviour by watching the boy out of sight. He did.

The only thing that was different was the boy himself. Robert's favourites had all been conscious, pert, slyly flaunting. There was nothing of that about Blondel; no flicker of the eyelashes, no knowing smile, no smugly wriggling bum. He walked away into the dimness and out of the tent as a young squire might walk. However, I remembered from my talk with Sancho that this was a young man who had kept one secret well. And that was Richard's secret too!

I sat down heavily on the end of Richard's bed, and he turned from watching the boy's exit and bent over me with concern.

"Mother, you are worn out. You shouldn't have turned back. What was it you thought of that couldn't wait until morning?"

I found myself wishing to God that I hadn't turned back. As he stood leaning over me, tender anxiety on his face, and the whole of him so handsome, so virile, I wished with all my heart that I had not turned back and so escaped the hurt of this dreadful knowledge. I said involuntarily, "Oh, Richard, my dear boy . . ."

"Mother, what is it? What ails you?"

The Dead Sea poured its bitter waters in which no fish breeds, no weed lives, the very symbol of sterility, over Sodom long ago. Fertile green England is my concern. I will not be circumvented.

"Richard," I said, "on my way back I was thinking about Longchamp and John and about your plan for sending Coutances to settle things. Look," I said, "I know this is going to make you angry and I know that no man, you least of all, likes being told what to do by a woman; and when I came out of Winchester I vowed that I would never offend you by opposing or advising you. But I must. I saw this thing so clearly that, as I told you, it was like a revelation, and so I came back to tell you that Coutances isn't the man to send——" I hesitated because he was staring at me with that same immense concentration which had disconcerted the archer. And I hesitated also for the supremely ridiculous reason that I had got my sentence in a muddle. "Coutances isn't the man to send; I am," didn't make sense; it might make him laugh and turn the whole thing ino a joke. I should have said "person."

And while I hesitated Richard began to speak.

"I've been thinking this over too," he said. "I saw Coutances; he's willing to go, but dubious. And while he was humming and hawing I thought——" He broke off and, reaching along the table, produced a letter, folded and sealed. "While the scribes were at work writing to Geoffrey and to Longchamp I got this ready to send to you. I thought the boy could deliver it to you in the morning. Here you are, read it and spare me saying it. It sounds so ridiculous said out loud." He broke the seal and handed me the sheet, open. And then, "Ha," he said. "The boy forgot his lute; he must have been thoroughly disconcerted." He took it in hand and while I read the letter he picked out with one idle finger the simple outline of the melody they had been singing.

I took in the gist of the letter at a glance and thought: He isn't a fool, nor is he so indifferent to England's plight as would appear.

Aloud I said, "Stop that noise, Richard. And tell me, what is *ridiculous* about this proposal?"

"I meant no offence by that, Mother," he said hastily, and

threw the lute aside so roughly that its strings twanged and thrummed. "But after your saying that Coutances was too old—that I must send a man, a soldier—to say, 'Go yourself,' did sound a little——"

"Fantastic," I said. "But it was, in fact, the thing I came back to suggest myself."

He began to laugh, and after a moment I joined in his laughter. I was so relieved that the argument had been avoided; that he himself had suggested my going. It made my position so much more assured.

We laughed together, gasping out that we must both have thought of this thing at the same moment, trying to fix exactly the time when the thought struck us.

And then another thought struck me and I said, "But I actually came to strike a bargain, Richard. You know me, nothing for nothing and damned little for a groat—that's my motto."

Keep him in this good humour for as long as possible. And think—marriage might save him even yet. Marriage carries certain obligations and it curtails time and opportunity. Only the very depraved—and he wasn't that, surely, only tainted—O God, let it be only tainted and recoverable!—could pursue both courses at once. And this thing that has happened to him is a thing which does, they say, happen to men who live almost exclusively with men, soldiers, sailors on long voyages, monks. It's like vines left unstaked which twine about one another, substituting and pretending. Berengaria is so beautiful and she is so passionately inclined towards him; she could save him.

(But at that moment—so mixed is the human mind—there flashed into my mind the memory of Uncle Robert turning from a troupe of lovely Arabian dancing girls to fondle a nasty, positively cross-eyed little page.) But one's thoughts can be enemies and must be dealt with as such; Robert wasn't married then, I reflected resolutely; and he was older, more set in his ways.

"Well," Richard said, "what's your price, Mother?"

"I would like to see you married before I go."

"There isn't time. I want you to go back with Alwyne."

"When?"

"The day after tomorrow."

"Then there is ample time. Berengaria doesn't desire a spectacular wedding. She has her gown. If I go back this evening and say that on account of my leaving for England the wedding is to be tomorrow she will be in the seventh heaven of delight. You have no notion, Richard, how much that young woman adores you—or how lovely she is. And you know, I would like to finish off one job before tackling another. I did set out to bring you your bride and see you safely bedded with her. Give me that satisfaction. You set to work and get the bishops and archbishops prepared and I'll go and tell Berengaria to shake out her wedding dress."

"I'd do it out of gratitude to you, inconvenient as I myself should find it," Richard said, "but for one thing which I am rather surprised you should have overlooked. Lent, Mother. Lent started last Wednesday."

Months later, when Richard was lost to the world, cast into some nameless prison, and years later, when he was dead, beyond the reach of praise or blame or irony, I was glad that I did not then round on him and say what was in my mind. It was so very scathing. As though Lent mattered to him! As though he didn't know that any priest—English, French, Sicilian—on the island would have performed the ceremony and known that the dispensation was certain. Richard Plantagenet pleading Lent as an excuse!

A dozen scalding remarks formed in my mind, but I uttered none of them. Not because I hesitated to offend—that was all over, and in future I was determined that I would always speak my mind; and not because at that moment I wished to spare his feelings. What held me silent was utter weariness. I felt as a man might crossing a mountain range, climbing one pass and another and yet another, and then finding that one more confronts him and that his vigour is completely spent. Quite suddenly all my strength drained away as lifeblood drains from an unstaunchable wound. There'd been the emotional strain of the scene with Berengaria, which now seemed as though it had taken place a hundred years ago; then the mule ride; then the wrangle with Richard over Coutances; then another ride and the further emotional demand of making my own decision; and finally the torturing weight of my discovery. Now, faced with this last evidence of Richard's determination to have things his own way, I capitulated without any struggle.

That is what it is to be old. Some power remains, but it must be husbanded, not squandered.

After a moment I said quite gently, "The wonder is not that I should have forgotten, Richard, but that you should have remembered."

And so at the end we parted tenderly. Our paths lay in opposite directions, and neither of us was bound on a peaceful errand. God alone knew how many things might so conspire that we might never see each other again. And he was my best beloved son; flawed by a fault I had never suspected, less perfect than I had believed all these years, but no less dear.

I hung on his neck and kissed him and cried a little. He rallied me cheerfully. "Settle this business quickly, Mother, and take no risks for yourself. Remember—we are pledged to ride into Jerusalem together."

Exhaustion had made me weak and fanciful. I stood there and I knew with a certainty past all question that we should never take that ride together. I thought then that the failure to keep the tryst would be on my side—I should be dead or too infirm. I never doubted that he would take Jerusalem; even as he spoke I could imagine that triumphant procession, the ultimate aim and object of his life. But I could not imagine myself by his side: no, the woman who rode there would be Berengaria. And that was as it should be. However, I answered him stoutly:

"You make way for me in Jerusalem, Richard, and I will keep London open for you. We will ride together not once but twice!"

He kissed me again with great warmth and said:

"We'll meet outside Jerusalem!"

And then there was nothing left to do but to wish one another Godspeed.

Four

Richard's Troubadour

Blondel gives his own account of the Third Crusade.

I AM WRITING THIS HISTORY OF THE THIRD CRUSADE at the bidding of Anna, Duchess of Apieta, who has always been my true friend and patron.

I know quite well why she set me to it. It distresses her that I should so often seek oblivion in the wine pot, and now that the house is finished she has cunningly—but I see through her—found me another occupation.

But why should I complain? Should I not rather gloat? I sit here in the sun, with the shade of a vine to shelter me at need; I have quills and ink and fine Chinese paper for my work. By my side is a butt of that strange red Palestinian wine known as the Blood of Judas, and I have time to write, time to remember. No scribe could ask more.

I am going to tell the truth as I see it about this crusade. Too many stories, each with that grain of truth that makes the falsehood palatable and dangerous, are already rife. "When Richard Marched through Holy Land," "Jerusalem, I Die for Thee," and "Crossing the Holy Headland" are sung in every hall and tavern. And for the great mass of Christian men they tell the whole story.

The very word "crusade" has something of magic, and even men who have no skill in music and who lack voice for singing, provided they also lack an arm, a leg, an eye, or have some scar to show, can stand up anywhere and recite one of these three songs and know that however they gabble and garble men will forgive them and reward them with alms. Why, once in Poitou I heard "When Richard Marched through Holy Land" being declaimed at three street corners simultaneously, so that a man might make a round of the market and never lose track of the tale. Very few of these minnesingers know or care whether their tale is true or false. I, at least, as Anna says, was there.

My story begins on a night in Messina when Richard of England was bidden to sup with his betrothed, his mother, and his sister, and at the last minute failed them, sending some excuse about dredging beef barrels out of the inwashing tide. There were thousands of men in Messina at that moment who, at his bidding, would have drowned themselves, walked out and let themselves drown in that tide at a word from him—such was his power. Why must he stay and thus disappoint her?

When the news came I was in the kitchen of the palace in

which we were housed, steadily and carefully drinking, sip by sip, waiting for the moment which I knew would eventually arrive—the moment when, with all my senses numbed by wine, I could face the ordeal of seeing the meeting between the woman I loved and the man she loved. Ludicrous and fantastic as it may seem—and irrelevant as it may be to this story—I loved, and had loved for a long time, my mistress, Berengaria of Navarre, who looked on me as a dog. The spirit, as it says in Holy Writ, bloweth where it listeth. There is no more to say, and do not fear that I shall trouble you here with a story of unrequited love.

This story, indeed starts with anger. I knew better than any man alive that Henry of England, father to Richard, was a lecher unmatched since Herod Antipas, who debauched Salome, his stepdaughter. And now I thought: Like father, like son; and what is all this we hear about the niece of Tancred? So that evening, my lady not being in a mood for music, I took my lute and, falling back to my old wayfaring gait, ten steps walking, ten steps running, made my way to the crusaders' camp. And as I travelled I remembered the stories I had heard in England about Queen Eleanor's way with little harlots. Tomorrow, if my suspicions proved well founded, she and I would be allies, most strangely yoked. She wanted an heir for England; I wanted my lady's happiness.

So, hot in pursuit of the hare of my suspicion, I thrust my way into the camp and by showing my lute and saying that I had come to play to the King of England I gained access to his very tent. He was not within it, and a glance informed me that it was no place in which any intrigue of a secret nature could be carried on. It was a large tent, and the lower end was just like the lower end of any castle hall. If Richard of England intrigued with Tancred's niece he did not do it here.

Supper was over; a few latecomers were still at the trestle tables; a few satiated men lingered over their drinking, watching two young knights put their hounds through their paces for a wager. One fellow, very drunk, stood unsteadily on his feet and gave voice to a ribald song which was received with enthusiasm and sly exhortations to further bawdiness.

My lute, as always, assured my welcome. A sober-visaged squire removed the bone upon which he had been gnawing from his mouth and beat on the table with it. "Now we shall have some proper music, and time too," he shouted. The man who was already singing took objection to this and spoke his mind freely. The grave man stood up and dealt him, without rancour, a stunning blow, and then, taking him around the middle like a sack, attempted to throw him out of the tent. Those who had been applauding the song joined in the fray. The two hounds, leaping and baying, added to the confusion and the noise.

"Strike up, for the love of God," someone said in my ear, "or there'll be fighting in a minute; and fighting amongst ourselves is one thing the King will not tolerate."

So I struck up as lustily as I could, choosing a song which I knew—having once been in England—was immensely popular there. Within a moment every Englishman in the tent was roaring out the stanzas of " 'Twas on a Fair May Morning" with their peculiar mixture of sentiment and bawdiness, and the Frenchmen present joined in by humming or beating out the measure on the tables. Even the hounds were clouted into silence.

By repetition and by inserting trills I made the song last as long as possible, for I knew I had no other which would be so well favoured here. But at last I was bound to end it.

There was some applause, and through it a loud voice said:

"I am glad to see a company in such good heart."

We all scrambled to our feet and faced towards the tent entry.

I had seen Richard Plantagenet, Duke of Aquitaine and King of England, before in circumstances which have no place in this story. I had seen him first in a dimly lighted anteroom in William's Tower in London, and there my jealous eyes had sought his face and his body for the beauty or the grace which had so commended him to my lady that she had fallen in love with him at first sight. I found none then, and tonight I found none.

He was a tall man, certainly; his shoulders were broad and his hips narrow; but his legs were slightly bowed from long hours in the saddle and his arm muscles so overdeveloped that they looked clumsy. Christ once gave sight to a man blind from birth and he, looking on his fellows for the first time, said, "I see men like trees walking," and that exactly describes Richard Plantagenet. Minstrels sing of his red-gold hair and beard. Red-gold is a colour which shows to advantage from a distance; close at hand, it was the raw crude colour of a scraped carrot. And it accorded ill with his complexion, which was so red that it wore habitually the look of a skin flayed by harsh winds or newly sun-scorched. Amidst all this florid colour his eyes, which were blue, looked startlingly pale, prominent, which gave him an unsettled look. He had, too, very thick eyebrows of the same colour as his hair; they grew outwards in tufts and upwards in points and were unusually mobile. His nose was short, hooked, with great flaring nostrils full of red hair, and his mouth was wide, paler than his face, and slightly crooked. His mouth wronged him; it gave him a sardonic look, as though he mocked. And mockery was never one of his pursuits; his approach was always very simple and straightforward. The tree walking!

It is to be hoped that Anna never gives this manuscript to my lady, Berengaria, to wile away an hour of tedium. But if she does ... there you are, my dear. That is how Richard Plantagenet appeared to the impartial observer. (O God, forgive that word "impartial"! I lie. I hated him.)

But it was quite plain that the story about dredging up beef casks had not been a fabrication. When he walked into his tent and I saw him in full light for the first time he was soaked from head to foot. The thin linen jerkin and hose which he wore clung to him like a skin; the red-gold hair was plastered to his skull; the red-gold beard came to a point like a rat's tail and rippled water onto his breast. And I never in all my days saw a man look so radiantly, so beatifically happy and contented.

He said, genially chiding, "I thought I gave orders that this tent was to be cleared thirty minutes after the supper bugle! Feed you I must, put up with your hullabaloo I will not. Get you gone. You all have duties or beds. Get to them."

He looked at the company, and I had an odd feeling that he knew exactly what the duties and where the bed of each individual would be. His eyes rested on me. Duty undefined, bedding place unknown.

He strode through the tent until he was level with me. Then he put his hand, cold and rough from its contact with salt water, under my chin—just as a man greets a petted child, raising the shy face.

"You play very well, boy. Welcome to our tent. Come along. Presently, when I am more at my ease, you shall play for me."

For a moment his pale eyes gazed at my face, and I wondered whether he remembered that dim anteroom, the borrowed lute. But he strode on, saying, "Yes, Raymond, go on now, I am listening," and one of the men with him broke into gabbling speech.

I could have turned and gone then. I had satisfied my curiosity. I was free to go and puzzle out some means of telling my lady that it was true about the dredging of casks. But something held me. It was just like another moment I remembered, a fatal, decisive moment when I had been free to go, free to stay. I could have turned on the market place at Pamplona and joined Stefan in the tavern and never set eyes on Berengaria; never in this world have looked on the Princess of Navarre. A staggering thought. And I was equally free, as men reckon freedom, to turn now and go from Richard Plantagenet's tent. He might have remembered and asked: Where is that lute player? Where did he go? But no one could have answered him because nobody knew whence I came or whither I went.

But I believe that we choose as we are meant to choose. Here I set it down in black and white and in my best writing. We do what we are ordered to do. By God or the devil. (Dear Anna, you understand; you wouldn't publish that heresy while I was alive, would you?)

I followed to a rough sort of platform which had been reared at the end of the tent and furnished with a rug, a table and chair, and a screen.

Standing near the edge of the platform in a waiting attitude was a small man wearing the black robe and the white tabs of the physician, and as I drew near I recognised with a little shock of surprise Escel, the doctor from Valladolid whom Sancho, King of Navarre, had summoned in haste to Pamplona when Berengaria had lain a-dying. Escel had arrived to find his patient well on the way to recovery, but he had borne no grudge because he was on the road to France to take the Cross. "The crusade will need those who can mend wounds as well as inflict them," he had said.

Richard stopped by Escel's side.

"I'm sorry to interrupt you again, Raymond," he said, "but this is urgent. Well, Escel, what news?"

"Four more died today, sire."

"God damn it! Why? Escel, why? Young lusty men, well fed, well tended. And all in that quarter. That's how many—fourteen, fifteen—this last week?"

"Fifteen, sire."

"And you bled them?"

"Yes, sire."

"And gave them the new draughts?"

"Yes, sire."

"Then by God's blood the place must be cursed or it's bad air, as I said. They must be moved. Ralph." He looked round inquiringly, and an elderly, responsible-looking man pushed

214

his way forward. "Ralph, I want every tent between what they called Pets' Corner and the water moved. There's something wrong with that site. Move the whole lot up here into the meadow at the back of this tent."

"My lord, in that meadow His Majesty of France has picketed his horses," Ralph said diffidently.

"I know. But with all due deference, my archers are of slightly more importance. Nevertheless, Simon——"

"Here, my liege."

"Simon, put on your most formal manner and go and wait upon His Majesty of France. Give him my greetings and tell him that I propose, with his kind permission, to set some tents in his horses' pasture. Tell him the exchange will benefit his nags because down by the water the grass grows very green. No, wait a bit. Better begin with the horses. Say that I've noticed that the high pasture behind my tent is grazed to the ground; ask him whether he'd *like* to make the exchange. No. By the sacred wounds of Christ, he won't like that either; he'll take it as criticism. We've had words already about the French way with horses. Oh, devil take the lot of them. Ralph, get those tents moved; Simon, round up the French horses and drive them down. I'll go to His Majesty of France in the morning and explain. That way my archers will have the benefit of the better air while we argue the matter out."

The solution seemed to me to be sensible, though some of the remarks preceding it reflected rather ominously upon the state of relationship between the two leaders. Richard reverted with scarcely a pause to whatever it was that Raymond was telling him. Finally he said, "Tell him I said so, and I don't propose to discuss the matter any further. His conscience, forsooth. Tell him I have a conscience, too, and that it has teeth!" Raymond and two others who had not spoken bade their King good night and went away.

Richard leapt lightly onto the platform and went behind the screen. I climbed up, too, and took my place at the end of the table, laying down my lute until such time as it was required. From this position I could see his bed, a canvas pallet stuffed with straw, protruding in places, set upon a wooden frame. I could see also two iron tripods, one holding a basin and ewer, the other his mail. My cell at Gorbalze had not been barer.

He talked on, and all the time an apparent half-wit called Dickon was clumsily wielding a towel and fumbling about for dry clothes. Not without surprise and some inner amusement I found myself thinking how much more nimbly I could have ministered to him; and when one of the remaining men started to make some complaint in a high raucous voice I thought: Oh, couldn't you wait until the man is dry and reclothed?

But at last he was. Only he and Dickon remained behind the screen, and to Dickon he said, "I can fasten my belt. You go and fetch me something to eat." He emerged from the screen, buckling his belt, and immediately began to talk to me.

"Now, boy, we'll have some music. By God's toenails, I'm so sharp-set I could eat an old woman, provided she were well roasted. And if you play to me I shall feast like Jove on Olympus, whatever Dickon choose to bring me. I'll wager you a crown to a groat it'll be pease porridge. It is a most remarkable thing, but a fact, I swear. If you demand a proper meal it will appear—on shipboard, in the middle of a march, anywhere—but once let it be known that all you ask is *food* and you'll get pease porridge, certain as death itself. Ha, here it is, and what did I tell you? Pease porridge, lukewarm and something that looks like dead donkey. All right, Dickon, if you say it is beef, beef it doubtless is. Run away. And tell that fellow on guard not to admit anyone except Escel. I'm going to have some music. And by God, I've earned it. Fifteen casks I brought in with my own hands tonight; and the men with me, just to outdo me, landed twenty. Good fishing, thanks be to God." He took up his knife, then halted it. "Boy, have you had your supper?"

"Yes, my lord." And how much better I had supped! I thought of the little pasties, the fresh broiled fish, the tender young fowl, the oranges and the candied grapes, the cheese, the little sweet cakes all prepared in his honour. It had been a wonderful meal, and nobody save the Lady Pila had really done more than pick at it.

"Then play for me," he said, and began to eat the stodgy wedge of cold pease porridge and the slab of beef which really did look very much the colour of a donkey. He ate voraciously at first, and then more slowly, while I played "The Death of Roland."

When I finished he said, "That would be a timely reminder—if I needed it. Once you depend on a man, you lose him; while he depends on you he is yours. Not that I'm prone—— Tell me, boy, where have I seen you? It sticks in my mind that you once did me a service."

"I have never done you a service, sire, to my knowledge."

I had lent him my lute, but at that moment the service I owned was to Berengaria of Navarre, not to Richard of Aquitaine.

"Where do you hail from?"

"I am a minstrel in the service of Her Highness, the Princess of Navarre. But I am here without the knowledge or the permission of my mistress."

He wiped his knife, first upon the edge of the table, then on his sleeve, and sheathed it.

"So you're straight from the women's quarters, eh? Tell me, are they all well? All in good heart?" I thought there was something almost deliberate in his lumping them all together. Knowing that I had just come from the place where Berengaria was, wouldn't any ordinary man have asked——

"All the ladies are well in health, sire," I answered with equal deliberation. "The princess and the Queen of Sicily were sadly disappointed over your failure to sup with them."

He made a gesture of impatience. "It was impossible. Not only on account of the casks washing in; other things, a dozen of them. You heard Raymond and Escel, didn't you? Women don't understand. Even my mother, who *should* know! When I am actually storming the walls of Jerusalem nobody will expect me to stop and clean myself and put on fresh clothes and go out to supper and make pretty speeches. What they cannot and will not understand is that the storming of Jerusalem has started here and now. If moving those men tonight has saved one life—by the grace of God, that man may be the one who will speed the arrow into Saladin's heart. Just as one of those beef casks might provide rations for the one day that means the difference between defeat and victory. Nobody understands! Down to the last inch of a bowstring, down to the last nail in a horse's hoof, everything is important and everything has to be seen to." He breathed hard through nostrils that were suddenly white against the red of his face, and continued more calmly: "Women seem to be incapable of understanding such matters. But there, I don't suppose you understand either. Play me another tune, boy. Then run back to your mistress, and for the love of God tell her that I am indeed very busy."

But I did understand. He might push me aside, dismiss me, send me back contemptuously with a message for the women. But the very way in which he had said the word "Jerusalem" told me more than a thousand explanatory sentences could have done. He was in love with an idea. And a man has room in his life for only one love.

I knew that. Christ Himself knew it. "No man can serve two masters"—they were His own words. And, while my fingers busied themselves playing a little trio of songs which I had played so often during my itinerant days that I could have played them in my sleep—"Caps on the Green," "Gathering Peasecods," and "The Merry Windmill"—my mind was slowly accepting the thought that when he had taken Jerusalem Richard might turn to Berengaria and love her, but not until then.

Tinkle, tinkle, the last little tune ended.

"You play very well," he said. "Do you ever make tunes of your own?"

"Very often."

"So do I. While I walk about, or just before I fall asleep. One has been dinning in my ears for days now. I'll see if I can pick it out. Lend me your lute—though it's long since I handled one." He reached out his hand.

The gesture and the last sentence were exact repetitions of the action and the words with which he had borrowed my lute in the anteroom of William's Tower. As our eyes met across our hands and the lute I saw memory and recognition dawn in his. He dropped his hand and said slowly:

"You are *that* boy! I knew I had seen you before. Is that the very lute?"

I nodded, apprehensive. After a moment's thought, as though he were making up his mind how to take this news, he broke into laughter.

"Well, well, an odd situation indeed. Tell me, what happened to you? After we had decided to hush up the scandal there were vigorous plans afoot for cutting your throat as a means to still your tongue. Did you guess that? Is that why you fled to Navarre?"

"No, sire. I returned to Navarre because I then had the information I had been sent out to acquire. The king was anxious to know about your marriage."

"I see. So that was how he knew!" He brooded and I hastened to say:

"I never mentioned to anyone what happened, my lord. There was no need. That the betrothal was at an end was all anyone cared to know. My tongue has been as still as though you had indeed cut my throat."

"Oh, not I, not I," he said hastily. No, I thought, your gracious mother! I understood now why she had always detested me.

"Were you never tempted to make the whole sorry story

218

ino a song?" Richard asked. "I would have been, in your place. What a subject! Listen. . . . " He reached out again and took the lute and without hesitation broke into a song which, if ever it had been sung in public, would have been more popular than " 'Twas on a Fair May Morning." The tune was catchy and memorable, the words excessively bawdy but extremely witty. If he were indeed extemporising he was a musician and a maker without peer, but it seemed more likely, I thought, that the song had been ripening in his head for a long time.

"One could go on for hours in the same strain," he said at last, "and may I rot in hell if I understand why you——"

He broke off abruptly as, close at hand, a trumpet began to sound raucously. He pushed back his chair and stood upright. I got to my feet too. The four or five men who had remained in the tent after it had been cleared of the crowd were all standing, and the servers who were swabbing down the tables ceased their labours. Evidently it was some sort of ritual but one I had never heard of.

Richard lifted his right arm high in the air and, anxious to do the proper thing, I moved to imitate him, but when my arm was level with my shoulder I became aware of his eye on me, warning, sternly disapproving. I cast a furtive glance into the body of the tent and saw that the only arms uplifted were those of the soldiers; pages and servingmen merely stood still.

Then all the men cried together, "Help, help for the Holy Sepulchre," three times in loud, solemn voices. And for as long as it took to utter the threefold cry one realised that they were united, all dedicated men, followers of the Cross, not in the wide-embracing sense of being Christians, but in the enclosed, esoteric brotherhood of crusaders.

And I had moved my arm! I, who ranked with the swabbers of tables.

The whole thing was over before the hot blush which my mistake had brought to my face had died down; the man who had been fondling his dog went back to his stroking; the man who had been polishing his mail began to ply his pad again.

"I had no time to warn you," Richard said quite kindly. "It is the custom for those who have taken the Cross and for those who follow them into battle to make that call every night. Just to remind them that crusading isn't all guzzling and looting and whoring. A sound practice. Do you know, at

219

this moment I'm ashamed that *that* trumpet call should have caught me singing a ribald song."

Then he snatched up my lute again, plucked at it for a moment, and broke into a song that was new to me, "Jerusalem, on Thy Green Hill."

I hadn't hated him because he was to marry Berengaria; in my craziest moments I had known that she must marry some king or prince, and he was the one she had chosen and the one to whom I had, in a mean small way, helped her. But I had hated him ever since we had arrived at Marseilles and found him gone; a week, seven little days, too long to wait! And I had hated him when he kept her waiting in Brindisi all through the long winter. Most of all I had hated him for disappointing her this evening. I had come to his camp in hatred.

But as he sang, all that feeling—hatred, resentment,—jealousy, call it what you will—fell away.

I'm getting old now; my wits are rotted with wine bibbing, my heart withered by sorrow, but if at this moment I could hear for the first time that voice singing that song, I think I should be affected as I was affected then.

Some of the words were taken straight out of the Psalter. "If I forget thee, O Jerusalem, let my tongue cleave to the roof of my mouth, if I remember not Jerusalem above my chief joy." But I assure you that the words of the passionate exile by the waters of Babylon were matched, exceeded, by the new words of a passion that spoke not of a backward-looking homesickness but of a pressing forward to a goal, and of the desire to be worthy of reaching it.

I listened and I understood. More, I was lured into becoming a crusader. I sat there, thinking: I could be an archer, or a groom, or, with training, a smith.

By that time I was, so far as wine was concerned, completely sober, having drunk nothing since I left my lodging. And in all sobriety I sat and yearned to contribute to the crusade.

The song ended, and the last lingering notes died on the silence. I brushed my wet face with my hands, and when I could trust my voice to speak I asked:

"My lord, who made that song? He is the master maker of all. I would know his name to hold in reverence."

"No, no, that is praise too high! I made it, and I am not even sure that it is a good song. It moves me to tears—you, too, my boy—but that alone is not the measure of a good song."

"It is beyond all praise," I said. "Any moderately good minstrel armed with such a song could win more followers for the crusade than are gained by all the preachers, including William of Tyre himself."

Richard laid down the lute and laughed.

"If ever we lack men I will remember that. At the moment there are men in plenty; too many, I sometimes think. No, boy, what we need is more money, more gear, better weapons, sounder baggage animals, and fewer old women in men's garb in high places, fewer gold plates and scullions and cooks to move about, less of the inflamed pride that seeks insult and then festers!"

He had jumped to his feet when he began to catalogue what the crusade needed and was now pacing about behind the table. At one turn he halted.

"But once I start on this subject, I talk for hours and all to no avail. Besides, I swore I would not get excited, especially at night; it holds me back from sleep. I lie there sometimes for hours"—he jerked his head towards the little bed—"and it's as though a fever gripped me. It is as much as I can do to restrain myself from getting up and rushing out to right something I know is wrong or facing somebody and really speaking my mind. They call me rough-tongued, but oh, my God, You know, unless You're as blind and daft as some of the things You have made and are pleased to call men, that twenty times every day I control myself more than some men do in a lifetime." He seemed to be in a frenzy; his whole face, the very whites of his eyes had gone red. But he stood still and breathed hard, and presently said in a less violent way, "I was thinking about the change of meadow. God alone knows how long I must waste tomorrow convincing my brother of France that the change will benefit his horses as well as my men. And even when he is convinced he'll add it to his long sour list of grudges. But this is no concern of yours, boy. You trot along and get to bed."

Then I knew what I must say.

"One thing you said, sire, is, in a way, my concern. You spoke of better weapons. I once had an idea for making a mangonel that would throw a stone farther and straighter and harder."

That stone fell short, crooked, and soft.

"Did you indeed?" he asked, and laughed a little, not mocking exactly—one does not mock a child—but gently sceptical. "You'd be surprised to hear how often ideas for the improvement of engines of war are brought my way, thrust

221

under my nose, in fact. Perhaps one in a thousand works, and I'm still ploughing my way through the nine hundreds——"

"But this does work," I said sharply. "At least I'm sure it would. It's a matter of reversing the way the pulley lies—making use of the tendency all things have to fall downwards. Oh, it's hard to put into words and I burnt my drawing, but I could show you in a moment——"

"Well, you bring the drawing to me when you have made it. I promise to give it full attention." Still sceptical, still gentle.

"Sire, if you will wait a moment . . ." I said. I jumped off the dais and ran to the fire, which was almost out, ready for stamping, and drew out of it three or four sticks which had burnt and then fallen outwards and smouldered into blackness.

"May I draw on the table?" I asked, jumping up beside him again. He nodded, laughing at my enthusiasm. I drew rapidly, explaining as I did so. I felt him go rigid with concentration.

"You see?" I asked at last.

"I see. By God's eyeballs! Virtually a new weapon. And so simple. Why has nobody—— No, boy; there must be a hitch somewhere. I've been using mangonels all my life and never thought—— They're as old as time, too. Could it be left for *you* to see what was wrong with every one? Let's look at it again. Yes—yes." He leant over the rough drawing, wishing to be convinced, but cautious, afraid of showing too much credulity. "It sounds all right and it looks all right," he said at last, "but we must make a model to scale and see if it does work. Sweet Christ, if only it does!"

I would have offered then and there to make the model, but before I could speak Escel, with his long robe girded up into a belt of rope about his middle, revealing his thin shanks ending in enormous muddied boots, came into the tent, walking more briskly than is usual with his kind.

"I half expected you," Richard said, advancing to the edge of the dais to meet him. "More dead?"

"Two more," Escel said in a voice not far from tearful. "We wrapped them well and carried them very gently, sire, I assure you. But for all that, two who were living when we lifted them were dead when we set them down. And that makes seventeen in a week."

There was a moment's silence. Then Richard said in a resolutely cheerful voice:

"But this may be the end. Don't lose heart, Escel. It was a

222

bad place. And you know, war does mean dead men, God rest their souls in peace. Come and see what I have here."

I took up my lute and said, "By your leave, sire," but he did not hear me. I went through the tent where the hound and his master, the man who had been polishing mail, and one or two others had settled down to sleep, and I had reached the door when Richard bellowed after me, "Wait! I don't even know your name."

I turned and told him my name.

"Come back tomorrow, Blondel," he called. "Good night."

II

That was the effect the crusade had on sober men throughout Christendom. It dragged me, the lute-playing, wool-winding peace lover, down to that camp every day, patching leaky tents, digging drains, blowing the smith's bellows.

The day came when my lady wished to go to Richard's tent in minstrel's guise, and I prevented her, not entirely for her sake, as would have been the case a few days earlier, but also for the sake of the crusade. Richard Plantagenet, whom I saw then only as a crusader, was busy and occupied with many things, and I was willing to save him from distractions.

A few days later the camp at Messina, which had been mustering point for all crusaders, began to disperse. The old Queen Mother of England, called back on urgent business, was the first to go. Then Philip of France, with his right-hand man, Hugh of Burgundy, and seven thousand men, sailed for Acre.

Richard was still cutting and shipping timber. He had heard that there was no tree standing within ten miles of Acre, and he was determined to take all that he needed for mangonels, arbalests, trebuchets, and storming towers. So he stayed behind till last, but on the night before I was to leave with the women he said:

"My new galley, *Trenc-la-Mer*, is very swift and I may overhaul you. I may be making music with you, Blondel, before you expect."

I relayed this message to the ladies; and since the long-delayed, long-awaited wedding was now definitely arranged to take place in Cyprus, throughout the voyage their spirits ran high and they were able to ignore the cramped quarters and the manners of the master of our vessel, who did everything in his power to make us feel out of place and ill at ease.

We sailed into the harbour at Limassol and were forbidden to land. Sir Stephen de Turnham, who was in charge of our party, confident that some misunderstanding had arisen, had himself rowed ashore and sought audience with the Emperor of Cyprus himself. He returned very flushed and agitated. There had been no misunderstanding. When the Emperor had promised to welcome and cherish Richard of England's bride, he had not known that she was Berengaria of Navarre; he had been under the impression that Richard of England was betrothed to Princess Alys of France. He was sorry, but on a certain occasion some emissaries of his had been very scurvily treated by the King of Navarre, and even to oblige his friend and brother, Richard of England, he was not disposed to welcome Sancho's daughter.

Berengaria, having listened to this report, said with her delightful placidity:

"What matter? We can wait in the open sea until Richard comes. Not that I think that Isaac Comnenus has cause for complaint. His emissaries were royally entertained"—she looked at Anna of Apieta and gave a little laugh—"up to a point."

"But he promised," said Joanna of Sicily, something of her brother's bright fury in her eyes. "He *promised*. Richard will be very angry when he hears of it. Did you make the Emperor understand that?"

"I did my best, madam. I threatened and I pleaded and I exhorted," said Sir Stephen. "The Emperor was adamant. He said that if we attempted to land we should be sunk by missiles from those towers. And the whole beach is lined with people, very hostile."

"And by my reckoning," said Master Saunders gruffly, "we're in for a storm, the like of which I've seen only once before, and that in these waters fifteen years ago, when I was in Famagusta taking on a cargo of spices. Same purple sky, wind in the same quarter. I mind it well. Within four hours she'll be blowing the devil's own hurricane. Would his great almighty tin-pot highness listen to me, sir, do you think, if I went in and asked as a common sailor man for shelter against the storm?"

"I should doubt it; I should doubt it very much," said Sir Stephen. But he looked at the sky, which had taken on a very strange colour. "You could try, of course. I did not mention the weather, having no knowledge——"

224

So Master Saunders set out, but he was not even allowed to land; a shower of stones and other missiles, nastier if less harmful, greeted his approach, and one enormous stone cast from the tower that guarded the harbour narrowly missed his boat.

Then this surly, unpleasant man showed his mettle and his skill. He hauled in his anchor, brought the ship about, and made off "running before the wind," he said. The storm lasted for four days before it blew itself, and I began to think we should run at last into Alexandria. Then the wind dropped and the sea calmed, and in a peace that was like the peace of heaven we turned again and sailed back until we could see within the harbour of Limassol. The *Trenc-la-Mer* was not anchored there. The two ships which had sailed with us and whose masters, if they had been wise, would have followed Saunders's tactics, had been wrecked. The beach was strewn with wreckage and goods, which the Cypriots were busily salvaging, and with dead bodies of drowned crusaders, which they pushed callously back into the sea again.

Yet Isaac of Cyprus had vowed to give help and succour to all who had taken the Cross, counted himself and was counted by others as within the ranks of the Holy War.

There was now the question of what to do. It was possible that Richard, in his fast ship, had reached Cyprus and, not finding us there, had proceeded to Acre. Master Saunders chose to think this most likely, for he had gear and archers aboard and was plainly disposed to consider their safe delivery of greater importance than the keeping of a tryst, even though it were between his King and his future Queen.

Sir Stephen, whom the storm had shaken, was likewise anxious to reach port and land his precious charge safely. But my lady Berengaria said that Richard had promised to meet her in Cyprus and that unless he had gone down in the storm, which Mary and all merciful saints forbid, to Cyprus he would come. They argued about it until she said flatly that if they attempted to sail for Acre she would fling herself overboard. Then the master of a Venetian ship which had been allowed to go into the harbour and leave again steered near us as he departed and shouted that there was no evidence that the *Trenc-la-Mer* had passed that way.

So we waited, suffering no more than boredom, acute anxiety, and a great shortage of water, until after ten days what looked like a forest of coloured sails rose out of the water. Richard had arrived, and not alone. After almost everyone had left and when he himself had been on the point of embarking, two ships from Wexford in Ireland, the Ardri-ach's contribution to the crusade, had come limping in. They had been badly battered by a storm. Richard had waited until they had rested and refitted, and during that interval two longboats manned by wild Norwegian barbarians and one laggard ship from London had arrived. These, with the ships which had arranged to sail in Richard's company, made a very imposing fleet. And while Berengaria stood weeping tears of joy and relief because the *Trenc-la-Mer* had arrived safely, Joanna said jubilantly:

"Now we shall see. Isaac is about to be very, very sorry for his behaviour."

The minnesingers chant about the taking of Cyprus as though it were a jousting, a half-comic revenge taken by a knight upon one who had offered some insult to a lady. True enough; it was that.

"Tonight you shall sleep in Isaac's palace, my lady, and he shall walk before you in chains." Those were Richard's words. He said them while he was still on his knees in the act of greeting the woman who had loved him with a lonely, single-minded devotion for years, who had travelled many weary miles and waited, waited in Brindisi, in Messina, and outside Limassol. Those narrow white hands of hers had only just fallen out of his; the touch of his lips was still moist on them. She was saying, "It does not matter, my lord. Nothing matters now." But his mind was already away, waging a battle, exacting a vengeance.

Oh well, I suppose we can only give what is within us, what is ours to give.

He gave her Isaac's palace to sleep in; he gave her Isaac's daughter to be her waiting woman and musician; he marched Isaac himself, laden with silver chains, before her. And after their wedding he set the crown of Cyprus on her head.

Serious historians debate the ethics of Richard's behaviour towards Isaac. The German monk, Ulrich of Salzburg, who cannot be entirely unsuspected of prejudice, speaks of it as an act of unprovoked, unwarranted aggression, just one more proof of Richard Plantagenet's greed and bloody-mindedness; Sebastián of Cordova, a secular writer who often, almost flippantly, hits on the truth, asserts that, having made sundry new mangonels in Sicily, the King of England could not refrain from testing them in a minor engagement. It remains for the Saracen historian, Benamed, to say that the conquest of Cyprus was the action of a clever strategist. Nobody but a fool, he says, leaves an active enemy in his rear. Isaac had proved himself a false ally and was justly and sensibly dealt with. It is just possible that they are all right. These reasons and motives are not mutually exclusive. The battle which we watched from our ship, the battle which lasted for three days, may have been fought from a mixture of chivalry, bloodthirstiness, curiosity, and strategy. We didn't think about Richard's motives; we were too busy watching his actions.

Twice I thought him a reckless fool. The first time was when he landed alone on the beach. His Londoners and some of the barbarian Northmen were tumbling from boats and following hard on his heels, but he did land alone and for—well, possibly no longer than five minutes, though it seemed an endless time—was alone on that beach, wielding his battle-axe amidst a shower of arrows, stones, logs, and knives. By sheer weight of numbers the Cypriots, if they had so chosen, could have overwhelmed him and trampled him to death before help arrived. But it is a fact—I saw it happen—they flung at him what was in their hands and then fled like sheep. Those who were lucky and quick got into the city before the gates were slammed to and bolted; those less lucky remained outside and were butchered—like sheep.

Next day he landed a battering-ram, a great tree-trunk shod at one end with iron and mounted on a platform which ran on twelve wooden wheels. Iron handles were fixed at intervals along its sides, and men seized these and at a given signal propelled the whole thing forward so that it smote its objective with great force; then they dragged it back and thrust it forward again. The target of the ram was the sea-facing gate of Limassol, a sturdy copper-plated structure reinforced by iron bars. It was flanked by tall round towers from which it should have been easily defensible.

Two mangonels were also landed and assembled, and while the ram thudded backwards and forwards the mangonels hurled over stones to disconcert and disable the defenders within.

When I saw the pulleys drawn and released, the great stones soar over, pitched short and high, I could not but be pleased with my innovation. By the simple process of reversing the pull and the thrust I had made the machine twice as easy to work and twice as deadly in action. But I wished that I had seen it used for the first time against the infidel. The people of Cyprus had certainly driven us out into the teeth of a storm, and latterly we had suffered from lack of water. But somehow . . .

However, this is no place to tell of my heart-searchings. Let me record that the defence of the city was feeble and puerile. At long intervals a shower of arrows would spatter down from the two flanking towers, but they seemed never to fall when the men who handled the ram were within range; whereas the English archers, only ten of them, picked off with deliberate accuracy any Cypriot who exposed a fraction of his person for so much as a tenth of a second. Everything that is said about English archery is true. The compulsory attendance at the butts every Sunday afternoon for every male between the ages of twelve and fifty, the constant, reckless poaching in the King's forests have left their mark. They say that all the best archers have had an eye put out for shooting deer, and I later verified for my own satisfaction that the ten marksmen who helped to take Limassol had only sixteen eyes among them! Is it squeamish to spare a thought for all the superb archers who have had the misfortune to be caught twice?

By midafternoon on the second day the ram, when it struck the gate, changed its note. There was just that difference which there is between a good coin and a counterfeit one thrown down. And an hour before sunset the copper gate gave way, opening, under a final thrust from the ram, far enough to admit two men, two slim men, abreast.

From our point of vantage out in the harbour we could see that at the very moment when the sea-facing gate gave way the one to the rear of the town opened, as though the one blow had struck it also; between twenty and thirty men on horseback, oxcarts, a long string of donkeys, and then a great crowd of people on foot began to move out from the rear of the town, seeking the hills and safety. But the King of England, on the seaward side, could not have known that the retreat had begun.

Then he performed his second act of recklessness. Leaping upon the ram, which had been left this time to stand where it had been thrust, he ran along it and threw himself through the narrow breach in the gate. Any one resolute man or any one desperate woman standing on the other side with even so slight a weapon as a stout stick could have despatched him then, for he had been helping to handle the ram and had discarded all his armour. Bareheaded and clad only in the soft leather jerkin which knights wear under their mail to save their skins from chafing, he flung himself into Limassol.

Berengaria, her face the grey-white of ashes and so wet

228

with sweat that it looked like the face of a drowned woman, said:

"Oh, fool, crazy fool. Now they'll kill him!"

"But they never do," Joanna cried. "This is his way. They're too surprised."

That evening we all went ashore and through the broken gateway and up to the strange pink palace from which Isaac had fled. It was a beautiful place, quite unlike any building in the West. One entered through a single gateway set in a long blank wall and found oneself in a courtyard full of fountains and dark trees and flowering shrubs and great marble vases brimming with flowers. Eighteen wide stairs on its farther side led to a deep verandah reared upon marble pillars, and within there were rooms of great size and magnificence, almost empty save for low cushioned divans or cushions laid on the floor, and tables of marble or silver, none more than eighteen inches high. The space and the emptiness and the strangeness were a little intimidating, and as I moved about in the Cypriot palace I could not help thinking how lost, how very homesick Berengaria would have been had Sancho succeeded in making her marry Isaac. This evening, with Richard safe and within arm's reach, she was so happy that the strangeness was merely another excitement.

For lack of ordinary furniture we were all bound to sit on cushions or squat on our haunches, according to our degree, and take our food from the little dwarf tables, and that fact alone gave rise to great hilarity. Amidst all the jollity, trying not to dwell too closely or with too jaundiced an eye upon the pair who sat together on one divan, he eating and drinking heartily as a conqueror should, she with an unwonted banner of scarlet flying in her white face, I thought now and again of the outer world and found little comfort in my thoughts. There was the old woman, thin and brown as a stick, who had been carrying water when the stone from the mangonel struck her; the bucket had rolled from her grasp and lay there, side by side with the stone which had split her old skull and spilt her brains.

Not that the mangonel had done all the damage. In the very road where the palace stood I saw a little Cypriot boy, seven, eight years old, stretch his arms from post to post of his house door and defy one of the Northmen to enter. He was spitted like a fowl. And there was a thin yellow dog, writhing in a ball of agony as he bit at the broken arrow in his flank.

What pity can I spare now for the old woman, the child, the dog? I who have seen 2,844 men killed in cold blood in one day. I who have lifted my own arm and slain men in hot blood.

III

Of the wedding of my lady Berengaria to Richard Plantagenet I cannot write as an eyewitness, for I was lying drunk in the kitchen yard when it took place. I had had my hair cut and I had donned my best clothes. I had the music ready to play. I meant to do her credit. At the last minute I went into the kitchen, which was full of pages and servingmen, and guards drinking, snatching morsels from the spits and the ovens, helping one another dress, and all very merry. And I remembered her as I had just seen her, all white and gold. The white gown encrusted with gold lilies, the golden cloak bordered and lined with white, and a deep collar of filigree gold, spun by the same family of craftsmen who had made the golden spider-web altar in the cathedral at Pamplona, encircling her throat, covering the scar. So very beautiful, so radiantly happy. And I knew, because of my dreams, just how that black hair, cool yet warm, warm yet cool, and with a fragrance all its own, would tumble loose over the breast of a lover; how the curved pink mouth would break open and the kiss would begin, soft, then hard on the teeth, and finally soft and sweet on the tongue. I knew all but one of the intimacies of the flesh, knee, belly, breast, and thigh; but always at the point of consummation the dream would leave me and I would awake and rise in a sensuous langour to seek the well, for in cold water, blessed or unblessed, there is great virtue. And often I have gone into my lady's presence subdued, cleansed, a little damp, but not forgetful, and thought: Could you but know, how angry, how infinitely shocked, offended, and insulted you would be!

All this I sat thinking as the hourglass dripped its sand towards the moment when they should be made man and wife in the sight of God. And I drank, seeking the numbness which a sufficiency of wine usually brought me. It eluded me and I drank more. Then suddenly I found myself blinking and retching under a bench in the kitchen; the wall torches were flaring, for night had come, the meats were hissing on the turning spits, and the wedding was over, the feast in full swing. From the hall came the loud, jubilant sound of a harp skilfully and masterfully played.

I caught a servingman who was bringing empty dishes back into the kitchen. "Who is making the music?" I asked.

"Old Ikymo's daughter," he replied with brief discourtesy.

I listened for a moment. Then I turned away. At this her wedding, my lady, had no need even of my music.

IV

Most of the songs and some of the serious accounts of the crusade make mention of Isaac of Cyprus's daughter, and in more than one there is a hint that she was responsible for the failure of the marriage between Richard and Berengaria. That story, which people eagerly believed and ardently spread, was an attempt to explain the inexplicable, and there is as little truth in it as in the earlier story which accused him of dalliance with Tancred's niece and the later one which accused him of being in love with Saladin's sister.

That the marriage was a failure from the beginning was all too plain, but no other woman can be blamed for that. Unless she be some nameless, unrecorded woman who took from him, in time past, all the woman-love that was in his nature. I can vouch for the fact that he never spent a moment alone in the company of the Cypriot princess whom we called Lydia. She had eight given Christian names, all of them lovely, but to the rank and file she was always known by the name which the English soldiers bestowed on her. The English always have a great affection for their enemies, especially after they have beaten them, and indicate their fondness by the giving of nicknames. Isaac was always Old Ikymo, and Lydia was always Ikymo's daughter or Princess Ikymo.

She was a small, swarthy, voluptuously curved young woman with a vivacious manner and a talent for entertainment; she sang; she played the lute, harp, and dulcimer; she danced. To my taste her face was spoiled by a growth of dark hair on the upper lip, but I have heard men of some discernment in such matters count that as a charm rather than a fault. She came and gave herself up to Richard some forty-eight hours before her father was brought in, and Richard received her chivalrously, raising her from the ground and saying to a knight nearby, "Conduct this lady to the princess"; and with Berengaria, Joanna, Anna Apieta, and Carmelita Avosola she spent the campaign. She had no importance, and I mention her at such length only to refute

231

the scandalous story and because her presence in the household had two effects, one small one on my personal history,
one larger and more far-reaching. She superseded me as
musician to the ladies. And she was niece to Leopold of
Austria, who, after his quarrel with Richard, accused him of
robbing, ill-treating, and debauching her and made this part
of his excuse for his subsequent behaviour towards his former
ally.

It is quite amusing to reflect that Richard, to whom wom-
en were profoundly unimportant—the only woman to whom
he cared even to talk was Anna Apieta—should have had his
relationship with two of his allies, Philip of France and
Leopold of Austria, marred by innuendoes concerning
women.

This recurring rumour that he was a lecherous man is
understandable. His father's reputation was evil, his own
marriage a disaster. Why that should be only God, Who
made them both and brought them together, could explain.
She was so beautiful, one would have thought that lust, if not
love, would have held him to her for a little, for long enough
for him to get to know her and appreciate her worth. Every
man who looked at her loved her, and most women too, and
women are not usually devoted to one who outshines them in
every way. It was surely the most cursed fate that the one
man she loved, the man whom she had chosen and fought
for, should be impervious to her looks and her qualities.

It may be because she loved him and had neither the skill
nor the wish to hide it. There was a perverse streak in him;
he could only appreciate what he had to struggle for; the
fiercer the struggle, the more value he set on the object. To
run to him and say, "Here I am, take me," was to make
oneself negligible to him.

Dear Anna, when you read this, will you be astonished
that I noticed how he sought your approval? Will you
remember how often on those few occasions when he favoured the ladies with his company he would turn to you and
say, "What does Anna think?" or "Anna, this will interest
you." Berengaria, and not she alone—any other of the ladies
would have her ears for so much evidence of his notice—but
they were for you.

However, the wedding feast lasted for three days, and
there were three nights when they went to bed together. She
had so much, three days and nights in Cyprus in the spring.
And she was Queen of England and of Cyprus, for Bernard
of Bayonne crowned her after the wedding with a double

232

crown and gave her both titles. And she knew, I think, what the world did not, that whatever took him from her was not another woman. No. He left her lonely, unsatisfied, bewildered, never jealous. God help the woman who inspired jealousy in her! Or maybe I should say what a pity, no woman did! Jerked out of her meekness, her subservience, her piteous submission, she might then have shown Richard the other side of her nature, the ruthlessness, the fury, the determination that lay under the lilies and the white roses which were all he ever saw. But that never happened, and their story proceeded as I tell it.

On the morning of the fourth day, with that same boisterous, almost childish air of escaping back to his own world, Richard went out to the stable yard where Isaac, through panic or muddle, had left several horses. There were two special chargers of some fame, a bright yellow named Flavel, and Lyard, a grey. Richard intended to choose one of these for his own mount. Since I was interested in horses and the morning being fair and warm, I went out with the motley crowd to see him make his choice.

The grey accepted him as though he had been its master since it was foaled; the yellow resented being mounted by a stranger. In the first moment it threw him and went snorting and charging about the yard like a crazed thing. We ran towards Richard, who lay on the stones partially stunned, but he bellowed, "Catch the horse, you clowns, never mind me!" And he got up and mounted again. This time Flavel tried other tactics; bucking and rearing, standing on his hind legs and striking as he had been trained to do in battle with his heavily shod forefeet, he rampaged round the yard, at intervals rushing towards a doorway, a wall, or a gatepost and trying with devilish cunning to crush his rider's leg. But Richard stayed in the saddle and fought with grim good humour, and presently from the doorways or tops of walls where we had taken refuge we saw the change come. Flavel ceased fighting and began showing off. He charged, he stopped in half his own length, he pivoted on his hind legs, turning on a space no larger than a dish; he smote down an imaginary enemy with his forefeet and then, lowering his head, lifted him in his teeth and cast him away. And presently they were no more a horse and a rider but some other entity, half human, half equine, like the legendary centaurs, fused into one by the heat of their battle, melted together by their sweat.

"This is mine," Richard said as he dismounted, "but I'll take the grey too. I have a use for him."

He stood catching his breath and brushing the sweat out of his eyes; the knuckles of one hand had been grazed to the bone by one of Flavel's wall-rubbings, and some of the blood, together with a good deal of dirt, was transferred to his dripping wet face. And there he stood, a grubby, happy, carefree boy, when Sir Stephen de Turnham and Sir Bertrand de Verdun entered the yard.

"What brings you abroad so early, my lords?"

"A letter from His Majesty of France, sire. This moment arrived by swift ship," said Sir Bertrand.

"News travels fast in these parts," Richard said, shaking a sweat drop from his nose. "Pious protest against putting Isaac in chains! No way for one Christian monarch to treat another, dear me, no!" He began to break the seal, but the stickiness of blood and sweat on his fingers hindered him and he rasped out, "God's name, can't somebody spread this for me? And you dolts, get that horse rubbed down! Shall he take a chill while you gape?"

Sir Bertrand broke the seal neatly and spread the letter. Richard took it and gave it his reluctant attention. Then like a hound that has scented his quarry, he stiffened, read on, absorbed. Finally he crushed the missive in his hand.

"But I *told* him," he cried, "I told him to do nothing until I arrived except widen the beachhead. The one thing that mattered. The one thing he didn't do! Dear my God, what are our enemies? It is our allies we should be saved from. Sir Bertrand, run. Have the muster sounded; send criers through the town. We start embarking in an hour. The French went and surrounded Acre, and now the Saracens have surrounded them and are trying to cut them off from the sea! Sir Stephen, will you warn the ladies and take charge of them as before? Boy, boy, run and find Sir Guy de Lusignan; bring him to me at once. I shall be on the beach."

He swung round and hurried away. I ran and found Guy de Lusignan, the man whom Richard had unavailingly supported in his candidature for the crown of Jerusalem. When we reached the beach it was, to the lay eye, a scene of complete chaos, but Richard was moving about there as unruffled yet as watchful as a housewife in her kitchen. With exactly the same air—ah, here is a pan just on the boil, I will attend it—he turned to De Lusignan and said, "Guy, it's a poor substitute for Jerusalem, I grant you, but Cyprus is yours. And at least not subject to the surveillance of the

234

three blind mice! The water supply in this town—and probably all over the island—should be looked to. And this harbour needs dredging. Isaac's brother Fernando is still at large; deal with him how you will. If I were you I'd bargain with the Archbishop of Nicosia—he's a cousin; he might be useful. If he'll crown you, well and good; if not, have no truck with him, get him out of the way. Good God, man, I don't want your thanks; I want your loyalty behind me— you've always had mine, you know. And while I think of it, *my* wife is Queen of Cyprus, don't forget! So if you think of marrying again—— Hi, there, you son of Satan!" He turned to pursue an archer who was forcing his way into a boat already overladen.

Having watched a kingdom thus casually given away, I went back into the palace to make my bundle and offer my services to the ladies. And there I learned that generosity was in vogue that day.

"Oh, Blondel," said my lady, "the King and I were speaking together last evening after you had played, and since we cannot hope always to be together in the Holy Land, and since he has no minstrel of his own, and since the Princess of Cyprus can always play for us when we desire music, I told him that he could have your services in future."

Sire, would you accept this dog? It fetches and carries and is a reliable guard. Sire, would it please you to own this monkey? It has several amusing tricks.

I stood silent for a moment. Anna Apieta said into the silence:

"Perhaps you should add, Berengaria, that the King begged and beseeched you. . . ." There was something more in her voice than a desire to soothe my feelings, and whatever it was flicked something tender in Berengaria's memory.

"I could add that. I could also say with truth that you put the idea into his head, Anna." She waited and then went on: "None of that matters. I have had time to consider it and now think well of the plan." She came a step nearer and laid her narrow white hand on my sleeve. "It isn't only a question of making music, Blondel. You can look after him; see that he doesn't sit down in sweat-soaked clothes and take a chill, or go out bareheaded into the sun. Or neglect to eat. You know, the small but yet important things." Her small secret smile which never disturbed the grave sweetness of her eyes shone on me for a moment as her hand dropped away. "And, Blondel, you could always bring me news of him."

How pleasant! How convenient! "To do thy bidding is my

chosen task." I had meant that each of the many times I had sung it in the past. And I had enjoyed every one of my stolen visits to Richard's camp, every moment of the time I had spent in his company. Even now as I stood there not saying a word, a feeling of freedom and excitement was rising in me like yeast. But I hadn't come back from London, I hadn't come this far on my way to Palestine just to be given away like a pair of old gloves! They were both waiting for me to say something. I said it.

"Perhaps my new master," I said, "will give me a collar with his name on it. It is convenient to know to whom one belongs."

Some devil in me had made me want to hurt her. But the shaft misfired. She looked at me blankly and said:

"Don't talk nonsense, Blondel."

It was Anna Apieta who suddenly and for no reason I could see burst into tears. Dear Anna, why?

v

So I sailed on the *Trenc-la-Mer* as we sped to the rescue of the French and Burgundian troops who had surrounded Acre and then in their turn been surrounded by Saracens and were now in grave danger of being cut off from the sea.

We found the harbour still in Christian hands, however, when we sailed in on the evening of St. Barnabas's day. But the danger had been real enough for every thinking man in that great company to look upon Richard's arrival as the end of a great peril and to behave towards him as children, terrified of the dark, would behave toward a grown man who arrived bearing a torch. Indeed the welcome accorded him would have turned the head of any other man, however modest and self-effacing he might be. French, Burgundian, German, Spanish, Norwegian, and Italian, they crowded about him as though they owned no other leader; the trumpets shrilled out their notes of welcome; every musical instrument in the camp gave of its best; a great avenue of torches lighted his way from the shore to the place where his tent was being reared. Richard is here! The Lionheart has arrived! All will be well! It was a crazy, intoxicating welcome.

It evoked in Richard Plantagenet a most typical response.

"This is an undisciplined mob, not an army. Suppose Saladin struck now! By God, in his place, I would."

The shouts, the plaudits, the trumpets, the torches meant

236

nothing to him. They hindered rather than helped the crusade. And how far they hindered only God could say. For there were four men at least in that camp on that evening who thought themselves the Plantagenet's equal or better. "The Lionheart has arrived. All will be well!" sounded ill in the ears of Philip of France, Leopold of Austria, Conrad of Montferrat, and Hugh of Burgundy. The danger inherent in that glorious, spontaneous welcome to the newcomer lay not in well-timed sudden assault from Saladin, that most generous foe, but in the slow, sour rancour, the fatal jealousy that it fostered in Richard's own allies.

But of that, too, much has been sung already. The tale of jealousy can be told by those who have never left their own hearthside. Let me tell of what I saw.

I saw Acre on a brilliant sunny morning. It looked like a posy of flowers wrapped in a stiff white napkin and set down on a squashed dung heap. The town had white walls, and within their circling whiteness were the roofs of the houses, the minarets of the mosques, rose-pink, lemon-green, primrose-yellow, hyacinth-blue, the bright ochre of marigolds all shining in the sun, and, from a distance, beautiful.

Between the white walls and the crusaders' camp lay a wide, desolate belt of filth and ruin. Once there had been gardens there and vineyards and fruitful orchards, but every tree had been cut down, every bush uprooted for fuel, and now in all that space there was no single blade of green, no living thing save the vultures and the rake-ribbed dogs pecking and grubbing in the dust, the dung and the rubbish, the ashes, the bones, the bits of broken harness.

This girdle of desert had been laid about Acre and steadily widened during the last two years, for the siege was no new thing. An army of Germans and mercenaries, ill organised and of late virtually leaderless, for Barbarossa had died, had been camped there for two years. But the siege had never been hard pressed, and until the arrival of Philip of France and his fresh army the Saracens in the town had never been completely cut off from their fellows in the hills. Philip, newly arrived, ardent, had closed the gap, and Saladin had retaliated by besieging him and by making repeated attempts to take possession of the harbour and so cut off the Christian army from the sea. It was this threat which had brought Richard hot-foot from his bridal bed.

He was now riding around the camp alone save for me, and he had curtly forbidden me to speak until I was spoken to. He had refused all other company. "I think better when I am alone," he had said. He had come out of his tent, looked at Flavel, the yellow horse which awaited him, and asked:

"Where is the grey?" They told him and he ordered it to be brought and then bellowed for me.

"Look, boy," he said, "I never rewarded you for your invention. When Escel's model worked I knighted him, but I regretted it. A knight without armour is neither flesh, fowl, nor good red herring. But here's a mount for you. Hop up and see how you like him. You can ride around with me. But don't talk."

That was how I came into what proved to be a pretty brief possession of a trained battle charger.

I was sorry that Lyard was grey. A grey horse still had a place in my dreams and in the even more horrible hours of lying awake in the night, and though there was a world of difference between this gaily caparisoned entire and the gentle old monastery palfrey, there was a likeness too. However, this was no moment to think of that. I was suddenly the owner of a horse so good that when the King of England had had to choose between him and the one he rode he had been puzzled and had simply chosen Flavel because he had fought him, being worse-tempered. And I was riding round with Richard on his first inspection of the camp, and that was a thing that many great and important men would have been glad to do, because first impressions are so sharp and durable, and a word here, an excuse there, the apt word at the right moment can be so very effective.

I realised within ten minutes that the only camp I had ever seen—the clean-swept, austere collection of tents at Messina—hadn't been a camp at all. This was a camp—this disorderly jumble of tents, dung heaps, broken casks, drinking booths, quarrelling idle men, heaps of rotting food, women half-naked lolling in the sun.

Later on when I walked through the poor quarters of Acre, Arsouf, and Jaffa and saw the filth and degradation I wondered whether there might not be such a thing as spiritual contagion. For throughout the whole campaign it seemed to me that the filthy foulness of these Eastern towns which looked so pretty from a distance and which, in closer contact, were so shocking and offensive to eye and nose and ear had spread out and affected, not by imitation or contact, but by some imponderable means, the manners and morals of the crusaders.

Even Richard never succeeded in making a good clean camp in Palestine. He tried, by precept and example and finally by savage punishments. He closed the drinking booths, but they sprang up overnight and often numbered one to every six tents. He issued endless orders against women—but as soon as we had settled for a week, there they were, drabs and doxies of all kinds, the dregs of the European seaports, the survivors of rape and massacre of the Eastern towns. He organised small armies of dung carriers and refuse collectors and set the great stinking fires alight on the outskirts of every camp, but still the filth mounted and still the crusaders lived in circumstances exactly comparable to those of the lowest of their enemies. Even in the consumption of that product of the poppy which we were beginning to call opium we copied the Saracens, more and more as time went on and men suffered from wounds which would not heal, from recurrent fevers, agues, open running sores which the heat and the dust exacerbated. As soon as a camp was established, there on its outskirts were the furtive pedlars of the drug which could banish pain, cradle the spirit in soft peace, delight the mind with rare bright visions, all for the price of the hard-earned coin, the sick awakening, the tremor in the bones, the despair of the soul.

However, this was a bright morning, and all these things were still to be learned. Richard was vastly disgusted but cheerful. "All armies rot in disuse," he said. "When we rear our ladders against those walls there'll be no time for drinking and whoring." He rode on, his intent glance marking this to be altered, this to be mended, until we came to the place where the Archbishop of Canterbury, Baldwin, had his headquarters. He and Hubert Walter, Bishop of Salisbury, had come on with a force of Londoners and men of Kent while Richard was in Messina.

Over the buff-coloured tent the Leopards of England flew side by side with the standard of Thomas à Becket, whose murder Richard's father had ordered in a fit of passion. A man ran forward to take Flavel's head, and the yellow horse immediately reared.

"Leave them. They are trained to stand," Richard said. And I took that as sufficient invitation to dismount and follow him into the tent. I was curious to see Baldwin—one of the few men who had gained a reputation for saintliness while pursuing a career of worldly activity.

A narrow bed stood just within the doorway, and on it, propped high with many pillows, lay an old man. His eyes were closed and he might have been dead but for the fact that his dark, cracked lips were moving and a stream of words, uttered in a low husky voice, issued from them. A young cleric, hunched on a stool near the head of the bed, was scribbling rapidly, leaning down to catch the words which went on without any of those pauses so necessary to the scribe who takes down dictation. Standing a little apart was a short, thickset man wearing a coat of mail covered by a rough canvas jerkin. He was watching the man on the bed and listening to his words with an expression of sorrow and yet of contempt.

On Richard's entry this expression gave way to delight and surprise. He came forward, dropped on one knee, and took Richard's hand between his.

"My liege lord, I had not hoped to see you so soon."

"I looked for you last night," Richard said.

"And gladly would I have been there," the man said. "But"—he nodded towards the bed—"he was violent. He wished to speak with you the moment you arrived. I had to stay and restrain him. This morning he is calmer. He is writing what he wishes you to know."

The husky voice murmured, "Evil can never be overcome by evil, and do not think that drunkards, lechers, and blasphemers can take the Holy City. Who shall ascend into the hill of the Lord? Or who shall stand in His holy place? He that hath clean hands and a pure heart; who hath not lifted up his soul unto vanity, nor sworn deceitfully . . ."

The poor scribe, having given Richard a distraught glance and a dip of the head, went on scribbling for dear life.

"They told me he was sick," Richard said. "What ails him?"

The man in the canvas coat shrugged his shoulders, and his mail rattled.

"Nothing they have a name for. He should never have come, the saintly, gentle old fool!" He spoke with the anger of hurt affection. "What did he expect to find? A company of militant angels? My lord, soldiers guzzle wine, they steal, they swear, and if on a hot day an infidel girl comes to the camp with a donkey and two panniers full of cool melons and pears, they buy her wares and then, given a chance, tumble her——"

"Well, what of it?"

"What of it?" The man jerked his hand towards the bed. "He must stop it, that's all. He must charge against human nature like a bull charging a wall. He broke his heart first, and then his mind gave way. Weeping, fasting, praying, and now raving——"

240

"The doctors?"

"What could they do? His ill lay too deep for their probing. He should never have come." His shoulders moved again under the rattling mail. "In Canterbury," he said, "he was known for a humane man of tolerant understanding. Here he became a martinet and a saint. God alone knows what I, what we have all borne in these last weeks."

Richard stood quite still for a moment and then took three strides towards the bed. He lifted one of the limp waxen hands which lay like the hands of a dead man outside the covers.

"My lord of Canterbury," he said in a voice which was quiet and of surpassing sweetness, "I am here. Richard of England. Your Grace, I am here; you can tell me whatever it is you wish me to know. My lord, open your eyes. Give me your blessing—and your instructions."

The discoloured eyelids in their sunken sockets did flutter, but there was no recognition in the eyes thus opened.

"I am writing my last letter," the husky voice said, "pray do not disturb me." The eyelids closed, and the stream of words flowed on: " . . . better, my lord, a thousand times better that these holy places remain defiled only by the infidel for whom Christ can plead—O Father forgive them, they know not what they do—than that they should be taken in triumph by men who, bearing the symbol of His passion on their shoulders . . ."

Richard stepped back from the narrow little bed and stood silent, looking on while the husky low voice continued, denouncing, exhorting, and the clerk scribbled. I could see that he was listening attentively.

"For delirium," he said at last, "it makes wonderful good sense and matches exactly some thoughts I have entertained this morning. But he—he's finished, Walter. And the war only just started. You must take his command."

"I've had it for some days past," Walter said gruffly.

Richard looked at him measuringly, approvingly; then he turned and looked at Baldwin in a way which, had Hubert of Salisbury been either more vain or more perceptive, would have galled him.

"I'm very sorry about this," he said, turning back again. "He was"—he sought the just word and found it—"ardent."

"He was an idealist. They always break first," Hubert Walter said with the air of one stating a plain and incontrovertible fact. In the background the voice went on and on, talking now about sincerity of motive being matched by

241

purity of conduct. "The only army he could have marched in step with is that of Michael and all his angels!" Walter said in a voice which mocked and yet betrayed an inner hurt. Then with a shrug of his broad shoulders he went on: "Sire, what is this I hear about a new mangonel?"

With an air of great relief Richard said, "It is a fact. A new weapon to our hand. A boy—he's here somewhere, I brought him with me—Blondel, he discovered it—something so simple that it's unbelievable nobody ever hit on it before. He'll explain. Get yours altered, Walter, as soon as possible. I intend to strike at once. This army has sat here too long."

"It has lacked a leader; there's nothing else wrong with it at all," Hubert Walter said steadily. "Now that you are here, my lord——"

No doubt that was just the look which I used to turn on Brother Lawrence.

"Poor Baldwin," Richard said.

"It is a pity," Walter agreed gruffly. "And you know, sire, the men greatly reverenced him until he began——"

"I know," Richard said hastily. They stood together for a moment in silent communion. Two strong men mourning one who, though better, was weak.

VI

The move against Acre was not made immediately, however, for Richard lay in his bed, smitten down by a fever which was never entirely absent from the camp and which attacked almost every newcomer. His limbs alternately shuddered with cold and burned with fever; he complained that his head was bursting and he had an unslakable thirst. He was the worst patient in the world. Twenty times a day he would attempt to struggle out of bed and sometimes succeeded in staggering to the tent door and would stand there swaying, clutching the post or the shoulder of whoever was nearest. Then, cursing horribly, he would allow himself to be led back and covered, and sometimes in as short a space as half an hour he would try again. There were times when he lay supine and other times when he would start up and send us running with messages, orders, requests for information. He took it hard that, though he sent messages inviting Philip and the other leaders to come and discuss the imminent assault with him, none came. They had—apart from their own disinclination to invite contagion—the best of excuses for their refusal. Escel

242

forbade all visitors, but Richard raved furiously about their cowardice and apathy.

Each day I found time to scribble the latest news of his condition and send it across to the small house by the harbourside where Berengaria had her temporary lodging. I was glad that I did so and that I was in a position to know and report the truth, for on the third day a rumour that he was dead spread wildly round the camp. He was certainly quiet on that day, for Escel in despair had administered a strong opiate and he slept for fifteen hours.

He was better when he woke and immediately set about the renewal of his plans. He forced Escel to admit Hubert Walter.

"Tomorrow, Walter, we can at least get the storming towers into position, and by the next day I shall be well enough to lead the assault."

"I doubt that," Walter said bluntly. "Your face is the colour of a dirty clout."

"You'll see," Richard said. "I shall be out and about in the morning."

And in the morning, despite all protests and expostulations, he had himself carried out on a mattress, after he had proved that his legs would not support him, and throughout that blazing day he lay in the dust and the shadeless glare giving directions and watching the luckless attempts of the men who were manoeuvring the great storming towers into position.

A storming tower—sometimes called "a bad neighbour"—is a light but rigid wooden structure consisting of several platforms one above the other, connected by ladders. It is mounted on wheels and pushed into position against the walls of the besieged town and counteracts the advantages which the besieged derive from their permanent towers. There are three great problems in getting the "bad neighbours" into position. Relatively too high for their bare area, they tend to topple over when pushed, especially on yielding ground, such as sand or mud. The men who push them are extremely vulnerable while they are pushing. There is a moment when the tower stands near the besieged walls and is not yet manned. At that moment, while men are mounting the ladders and preparing to defend their temporary tower, really determined defenders thrust out great timbers and often succeed in overturning the whole structure, with consequent damage to the men under and within it.

All these problems had to be met and overcome before the

243

siege towers were in position by Acre walls. When three in succession had overturned owing to the ill balance of the wheels in the sand and dust Richard called a halt, and for the rest of that day and the whole of the next gangs of men toiled at making four comparatively hard roads, one on each side of the town. There was no spare timber, nor tree within reasonable distance, but Richard gave orders that every house in the little colony by the harbour was to be demolished and the stones and beams from them used.

"That," he said as he was carried back to his tent, "will take at least a week. I shall be fully restored by that time. Meantime I must think of some means of protecting the men who push."

For the garrison at Acre was very unlike the defenders at Limassol. From every tower and slit in the walls the arrows poured down, deliberately and carefully aimed, seldom missing their mark. And the one storming tower which had by luck almost reached its position that day had been burned when the defenders had flung out in the space of two minutes forty short staves with bundles of flaming tar-soaked tow bound to their heads. Men pushing the tower had been horribly burned and fled screaming; the tower had flared up, a monstrous outline of red fire.

That evening Richard said, "Tell Gilles to cut the throats of the thirty worst mules and keep the hides whole."

The hot fit was on him then and I thought that he was raving, so I replaced his covers and said some of the senseless, soothing things one does say in such circumstances.

"Don't be a fool, Blondel," he said, pushing the covers away. "Go do as I say. Do you imagine that *you* are the only one ever to have a good thought? I want thirty mules' hides, stretched flat. And don't look at me as though I were crazy! Go and tell Gilles."

But mules, I knew, were precious. Thirty mules—God pity and strengthen them—carried an immense amount of baggage. If he were now even ever so little out of his mind and came to clarity to find thirty mules killed with my connivance ... But he began to struggle out of bed, and I thought: Better at this juncture thirty mules than the King of England— and went and gave the order.

Next day, when the road making started in earnest—men had been up at first light tearing down the harbour houses and carrying material up to the town—there was fought the short, sharp civil war over the matter of armour.

It was plain from the first moment that the garrison at

244

Acre was not going to stand by tamely and see those roads made. Down came the arrows; out in great flaming arcs came the fire-headed staves.

"Sound the retreat," said Richard from his mattress to the bugler who stood beside him. "This road must be made by men in armour." He gnawed his thumb. "At least hauberk and helm."

Later on we were all to see armoured men, whose horses had died or been killed, ploughing along through sand and dust, over rocks; but at that time, when the war was young, an armoured man was a mounted man, and a mounted man was a knight, or the son of a merchant, or at lowest some yeoman's eldest son whose armour and steed had been bought at the price of his family's penury for five years, and all such were privileged and proud.

Few of those who had shouted, "Richard has come. All will be well," had reckoned on a scorching day when he would issue the ultimatum that the armoured men must build the road or lend their helms and hauberks to the unarmoured men. But he gave that order, and there was a great confusion.

His understanding was limited and highly eclectic, but he did understand men.

"I have two coats of mail," he said, raising himself on his elbow. "Blondel, choose me from amongst those buff-coated fellows one about my size."

"A difficult task, sire," I said without any intention to flatter.

"The nearest, then. Where is the man who caught the burning brand by its handle and flung it back? He was a stout fellow, and I'd lend him my mail with pleasure."

He noticed everything—within limits.

I found that man—six inches too short and four inches too narrow—and we dressed him.

"Now help me into my other harness," Richard said. And he stood up, donned hauberk and helm, and, wobbling like an unweaned pup, went out to the road's beginning and took up the hammer which one of the men had laid down when the retreat was sounded and began to beat a slab of stone into its bed of sand. An arrow hissed down, struck his helm—the Saracens are marksmen of a quality matched only by the English at their best. Richard, hammering away with his right hand, waved his left with a gesture that said, "Ha, missed, you see!"

And within the space of time that it takes for a man to

strap on his harness all the choicest knights in Christendom, the very flower of chivalry, men who had never handled any tool save those of war, never done a menial task in all their lives, were out there in the sun and the dust, working like villeins.

Having no mail and failing to borrow, I joined myself to the gang of men who carried stones and timbers up from the demolished houses. I broke all my nails, which are essential for the playing of a lute, and so bruised and lacerated my fingers that it was with pain and difficulty that I wrote my daily report to my lady that evening. And if the bad penmanship was compensated by a somewhat hysterical enthusiasm, I hope I may be forgiven. For I had helped to unharness him. He had risen from his sickbed and worked in hot heavy armour for eight hours. The sweat gathered about his feet in pools as we unlaced him—one would have thought that he had stepped undried from a bath—and he trembled like a poplar. Even hatred and jealousy had, perforce, to give way to admiration.

The hard narrow tracks were made more speedily than seemed possible. And then I saw why he had ordered the hides. Nailed slant-wise to the edge of the lowest platform of the storming tower, they afforded almost complete protection for the men who pushed. They were hard enough to repel an arrow and green enough not to flare up under the touch of the flung torches. Fifteen on each side, they gave sufficient shelter, and as each "bad neighbour" rolled into position under the walls of Acre the hides were ripped off and nailed onto the next. And the day came when I watched men climb those ladders, muster on the platforms, and leap upon the walls, while the mangonels thudded and the arrows darkened the sky.

Twice during the attack the Saracens from the camp in the hills swooped down in an attempt to relieve the pressure on the city. And twice Richard, turning gladly to a form of warfare more to his taste, led the force which drove them off. Those repulses doubtless added to the despair of the besieged, and on the eighteenth day after the completion of the roads they hauled down their flags and sent out emissaries to discuss the terms of surrender.

An awed silence fell as the gate of the city opened and closed again behind the three men who emerged. Two were Saracen emirs, turbaned and dressed in fresh white clothing; the third was a Frank with hair so sun-bleached that it was almost as fair as mine. From shoulder to heel he was covered by a long scarlet cloak of a hue so vivid that in the blazing sun it afflicted one's eyes with pain. When they first emerged he walked a little behind the Saracens, but as they drew near to the spot where Richard stood, awaiting their slow and dignified approach, he ran forward suddenly, dropped to his knees at Richard's feet, and seized the hand extended to him, bowing his head over it. The action had enormous significance, the eloquence of the mummer.

Had Richard been wise or tactful or even ordinarily cunning he would have sent men running to bring out the other commanders or made the gesture of taking the emissaries to the tent where Philip nursed his little fever. As it was, he beckoned to Hubert Walter and to the old Count of Algenais and thus, companied by the two men he most trusted, stood in the sun and personally accepted the garrison's surrender and personally dictated the terms. The man in the cloak stood up, straight and arrogant, and acted as interpreter. It was arranged that the garrison of Acre, about twenty-four hundred men, were to go unharmed in return for a similar number of Christian prisoners; until the Christians were brought in the garrison would be held as hostages.

It was the briefest, most straightforward bit of bargaining, and when it was concluded one of the emirs drew a piece of cloth from his sleeve and signalled towards the tower that overlooked the city gate. Immediately two mounted men, each leading another horse, magnificently caparisoned, came out. The Saracens, with a final obeisance and some speech which the fair-haired man translated scornfully, stepped back, mounted, and, accompanied by their grooms, galloped away to carry the terms to Saladin, whose camp lay in the hills. As they left the man ripped off his bright cloak and flung it after them in a gesture of final repudiation. He stood for a moment quite still. He was naked save for a piece of cloth about his loins, and his body was beautiful, slender, muscular, sun-tanned—and yet delicate, capable, in some strange way, of conveying things other men need words for. At this moment it spoke of pride and triumph, release, repudiation, scorn. Then he fell to his knees again and I saw his shoulders move as he sobbed.

Richard, looking a little confused, stretched out his hand and then touched him on the shoulder. "Sir," he said courteously, "I know not your name nor your degree, but I bid you welcome in the name of all Christendom." The man sobbed on and Richard's confusion became embarrassment.

"Come, man," he said, "tears on such a joyous day!" And "Come," he said, "you must be clothed and fed." And then, "Be of good cheer, sir; you shall come with us to Jerusalem."

But the man went on kissing his hand and sobbing, and I could see impatience prick the King. He looked about and saw me.

"Boy, take this good man and make him welcome to our own tent. Give him of our best." To the man he said:

"There, there, weep your fill—and this evening we will make merry together. You are the first of the many! We will all rejoice in due time. At the moment I have much to do. ..."

He turned away to complete the taking of Acre, which he did with as little fuss as he would have brought to the plucking and eating of an apple.

So I was left to deal with Raife of Clermont while Richard went on to make the first of his deadly blunders.

It is true that he had laboured like a serf on the road making, true that he was actually exchanging blow for blow when the garrison hauled down its flags, true that he was out in the sun glare and the dust when the emirs walked out to make the surrender. And nobody could deny that at that moment Philip of France lay on his bed and that Leopold of Austria was with him, eating peaches and pomegranates. But there had been Frenchmen on the storming towers, and Austrians. And one would have thought that Richard, with his curiously tender consideration for the common soldier's feelings, would have refrained from tearing down the Austrian flag which those who had fought had proudly set up on the section of wall they had captured. But moving round, satisfied, triumphant, on the evening of that day, he said, "What is that flag doing there? Take it down."

Leopold never forgot the insult; never forgave it.

The ordinary men-at-arms, oddly enough, did. And both French and Austrians began to try to sidle into Richard's company. Leopold and Philip spoke of desertion and of bribery, but I, moving about amongst the men, heard other words. "I joined the crusade and I follow the man who most ardently leads the crusade," reasoned the man capable of lucid statement. "He fights, they don't, and he's the leader for me," said others.

And I would think of William of Tyre, who had preached this crusade in Europe, and of His Holiness, who had blessed all wearers of the Cross. To them the crusading army was just one great closely welded company where individual nationalities, preferences, talents, achievements, and ambitions were melted down into the common cause. But men never are thus melted into a mass. Out of the womb they come, separate and dissentient, and until the greedy grave engulfs them, separate they remain. Even the cause of the Holy Sepulchre can hold them together in spirit for no longer than it takes to make that evening call.

One day when all the idealists are discouraged, an army of mercenaries under a single leader—— But I digress.

VII

After the taking of Acre the ladies were moved from their wretched lodging by the harbour into a small white palace beside the blue-minareted mosque in the centre of the town. Hubert Walter found time to make a formal visit to the Queen, whom he had never seen before, and Richard sent her kind messages, but he was too busy to go himself. There were three days, loud with recrimination, insult, explanation, and excuse, and then old Algenais suggested that there should be a feast—in honour of the victory, in honour of the ladies, and in honour of the first released prisoner, Raife of Clermont.

During these three days I had been much in this man's company, for he slept and ate, as I did, in Richard's tent and had been entrusted to my charge. I had heard his curious history. He had been taken prisoner when he was an esquire fifteen years old, and had spent ten years in captivity. He had been circumcised against his will and sent as slave to the Sultan of Iconium—the man who was reputed to have fallen in love with Eleanor of Aquitaine when she was on crusade. He had been set to work as a gardener. Once the Sultan's second wife had walked in the garden and desired a certain flower. Raife had cut it for her, trimmed off its thorns, and put it into her hand. The Sultan had seen him, been moved to jealousy, and had ordered that he should be castrated. "But the man who was to do the job was a—friend. There was some mutilation, and I suffered the pains of Purgatory, but he spared me." When the Sultan's daughter married the Emir of Damascus, Raife had gone with her; and although he hated all Saracens and had never a good word for one of them, I gathered from one or two things that he let slip, and also from his omissions, that his new master was reasonable and humane. In his service Raife had risen from groom to steward, an office which included some secretarial work, and in that capacity he had come to take part in the defence of Acre.

Although he was so little older than I and had spent so many years in circumstances little conducive to the development of personality or the cultivation of intelligence, he was, compared with me, mature, worldly-wise, immensely gifted, confident, complete. The Count of Algenais, who, after the first flush of sympathetic enthusiasm, came to regard him with slight disfavour, once said that he had lived so long in the East that he had become as subtle and wily as a Saracen.

"And that," Raife had retorted in an easy, unabashed way, "accounts for my long survival and my early release."

Richard had laughed. He liked Raife of Clermont, both for himself and for what he represented. He was the first fruit, an earnest, a token of the deliverance that this crusade would bring. And he had many things to commend him to any leader—he knew the enemy; he spoke and wrote Arabic; he knew the Saracen way of life, customs, prejudices, trend of thought. He would be very useful.

And as Richard doted on Raife as his first recapture, so Raife doted upon Richard as his deliverer. With everyone else he was almost fantastically proud and touchy, insolent, sharp-tongued, and hasty-tempered. Once I mildly expressed astonishment at the disrespectful way in which he answered some question asked him by the Duke of Burgundy. He had laughed in his bitter fashion and said, "I have lived, Blondel, where the flicker of an eyelash at the wrong moment could result in torture you never dreamed of. What could Burgundy do to me?" But towards Richard, who would avenge his lost years, his many wrongs, he was different. Not meek, not subservient even there, for many a heated argument, many a sharp exchange of verbal buffets took place between them; but he did regard Richard as a person apart; he was prepared to be the lion to Richard's Androcles.

On the evening of the celebratory feast the tables—and again I detected old Algenais's tactful hand—were arranged in a great circle, without head or foot, and the most important guests were spaced out with considerable discretion. No one had refused the invitation and everyone had donned his best clothes and finest jewels. It was a highly coloured, a magnificent scene; a little awesome if you chose to see it as the gathering of the very flower of Western chivalry, apparently united. I took my place behind the Queen, ready to play at a sign from her; and to keep my thoughts from straying I worried deliberately about my broken nails and the fact that I had not touched my lute since we landed. Her hair, now that she was married, was gathered into a great knot that seemed to tilt her head. pridefully. She was lovelier in her hyacinth-coloured gown than even I remembered her. All the old hungers woke and stirred.

Resolutely I turned my attention to the conversation at the table.

Somebody had mentioned the Old Man of the Mountain.

By this time we were all familiar with the name and dreadful reputation of this mysterious potentate. He ruled in a mountain fastness in the Lebanon, and his subjects were murderers by profession. They were known as Assassins, and the word was beginning to make its way into the everyday polyglot language of the crusading army. "A real old assassin, you are," one man would say to another, or to a mule, or even to an unhandy tool. In the same way the title Old Man of the Mountain had crept into common use. "Savage as the Old Man of the Mountain," as a measure of ferocity, or "Oh, tell that to the Old Man of the Mountain," as an expression of incredulity.

Yet despite his penetration into our consciousness and our talk, the Old Man was wrapped in mystery, in legend, in doubt. Nobody had ever seen him or one of his Assassins and most people believed that he was a figure in Saracen folklore and that the stories about him may have had their origin in some far less picturesque tyrant who had terrorised the land long ago. Certainly very few people actually believed that if they could search Lebanon thoroughly they would come across the Old Man, his tribesmen who murdered for pleasure, his turreted castle, or his fabulous pleasure gardens, comparable with Paradise, where lovely, scented, jewelled houris wandered amongst the fountains and the flowers.

But it was interesting to talk about him, idly, speculatively, as the feasters were doing now.

Suddenly Raife of Clermont laid down his knife, leaned forward, and spoke. Except in moments of excitement, he usually took pains to mask the certain shrillness of his voice and spoke with a deliberate gruffness. Now his words reached even the far side of the circle of tables, though he looked only at Richard.

"Would it surprise you very much if I told you that I have seen the Old Man and his establishment?"

There was the expected murmur of surprise, interest, and

251

disbelief, out of which Philip of France's precise "Indeed, yes, it would both surprise and amuse me," sounded very clearly.

"Then I will tell you," said Raife, casting Philip a glance of cold dislike and then looking back at Richard. "I went once with my—with the Sultan when he visited him. It was a very secret visit, and he chose to take me to attend him rather than a native because he trusted my discretion." A peculiar look, half smile, half sneer, flitted across his tanned face for a second. "There is a castle and there are domes and floors of silver, just as they say—or rather more fantastic than they say. The castle stands on a ledge of rock, surrounded by the gardens, of which, again, the stories are rather understatements than exaggerations. At the edge of the garden the mountain drops down to a ravine so deep that it looks like the edge of the world. One day as we walked there the Old Man said in an idly curious way to my—to the Sultan, 'Now you are no mean ruler, would any of *your* people jump over that edge if you gave the word? Willingly, joyfully, I mean.' The Sultan looked at me and I felt the sweat break out. Not that I would have jumped, of course, but—well, they hold life cheap, and until you have seen——" He faltered and then went on, holding now the fascinated attention of the whole company: " 'Mine would,' the Old Man said. And he said something and made a sign, and I swear, my lords and gentles all, I swear by Holy Cross that six men, sprung as it were from nowhere, came running and with jubilant cries— indeed, there was no mistaking—with jubilant cries they threw themselves into the abyss. 'You see,' said the Old Man, turning away as calmly as though he were leaving a supper table, 'they know that by obeying me they go straight to Paradise.' And it is in that belief, of course, that they go forth to do these almost ritualistic murders at a word from him."

They paid him the tribute that all storytellers crave, the breathless attention, the hush of appreciation. Then Philip of France leaned forward and spoke.

In these last days, with little to do save watch and listen, I had realised that the King of France bore one of those almost involuntary grudges against Raife of Clermont, akin to a man's hatred of blue eyes because once a blue-eyed girl jilted him, or a housewife's distrust of all red-haired men because a red-haired pedlar once sold her a bad comb. Philip could never look at Raife without remembering that the surrender of Acre had been made to Richard alone. Richard's fussing over Raife and Raife's obvious deference to

252

Richard had, for Philip, a hateful significance. When Richard had eventually taken Raife along to Philip's tent and exhibited him as the first rescued prisoner and told his story, Philip had been incredulous—or chose to seem so—until given proof.

Now he was asking again for proof.

And of course, though we did not know it at the moment, those of us who were Richard's friends should have been grateful that Philip did not let this moment pass in easy acceptance of a dramatic story, but leaned forward and said most courteously:

"Sir Raife, did you really *see* this, or are you repeating—in good faith, I am sure—a story told you? I ask because your story is so very true to the pattern of the legend, and also because since my arrival I have gone to some pains to make inquiries about this mysterious old man, and they have all led me to the conclusion that he is a mythical personage."

Raife's dark face went darker.

"That, sire, is tantamount to calling me a liar. I tell you I saw him."

"I would not deny," Philip said with patient civility, "that you saw a tribal chieftain and were impressed by his eccentricity. But what—as an impartial and curious inquirer—I must ask is this. Is there really one who calls himself the Old Man of the Mountain, who has the——"

"But hasn't he just told us——" Richard began.

A smooth, velvety voice, the voice of Conrad, Marquis of Montferrat, broke in:

"One moment, my lord of England! My lord of France, when you were seeking information about this mythical personage you should have applied to me. I could have told you that he does indubitably exist. I know. I had a letter from him."

The centre of attention shifted.

"Signed?" Philip asked.

"A letter, written with some substance resembling tar with an implement like a pig's foot on a sheet of white silk—but in tolerable Latin withal. And signed, 'The Old Man of the Mountain.' Why is that so unbelievable, Philip? You sign yourself 'Philip, King of France.' He's an old man and he rules in the mountains, and when he takes his pig's foot in hand that is how he signs himself."

"But I was given to understand," Philip said stubbornly, "that no such person exists—that he is akin to the fairies and hobgoblins of the West."

"Oh well," Conrad said pleasantly, "if you insist, I have received a letter from a fairy. And a sizable cake, too. Quite solid and about so big." He cupped his hands together.

"My lord—*he* sent you a cake?" Raife of Clermont asked, forgetting to control his voice and letting it ring out thin and shrill.

Conrad of Montferrat nodded and smiled at him. Then to the company he said, "Some time ago, in Tyre, I had reason to hang two of his Assassins. At least perhaps 'reason' is an exaggeration. They were there, they were involved in a street brawl, and if they didn't deserve hanging, then they'd probably deserved it in the past or would have shortly had they stayed alive. I hanged them. The Old Man sent me a very insolent letter demanding some ridiculous *quid pro quo*. Naturally I ignored it. So the other day he sent me a cake. It was found by my bed in the morning, and my servants almost died of terror—rightly, for it proved them negligent. But apparently it is his amiable habit to send out cakes as a sign and a warning. The cake by your bed means the Old Man of the Mountain is after you! I believe it is a fact, Philip, that men have died of fright upon receiving one of his cakes."

"It is tantamount to a death sentence," Raife said solemnly. "You should look to yourself, my lord."

"I do," the marquis said cheerfully, "and I spoke severely to my fellows. 'Do you realise,' I said, 'that whoever put this cake by my bed could have stabbed me as I slept?' "

"For them that would have been too simple, too easy. They send the warning so that you may be alert and watchful and thus be worthy of their skill," Raife said.

"But what proof have you, apart from the superstitious suppositions of your servants—all natives—that the cake was actually sent by this personage?" Philip asked.

"Dear man, none! And when a tile slips from a roof as I pass and splits my skull or a fruit seller whips out a dagger as I chaffer with him and stabs me to the heart, there will still be no proof. Look, Philip, if his existence and his methods were susceptible of proof we would not be sitting here talking of him now. It is the mystery that gives him such power."

"But don't you spend your days and nights in terror?" asked Leopold of Austria, releasing his niece's plump hand and speaking for the first time.

"No. I've lived here long enough to be of one mind with the Saracens over that, at least. Death comes when it comes.

Court him too soon, and he will evade you; avoid him after he has marked you, and you waste your effort."

"And there, Conrad, I agree with you," Richard said.

My lady, with her nice and accurate judgment of how far a subject should be pursued and when abandoned, then turned and signalled to me to play. The Old Man of the Mountain, with his letters on silk and his cakes and his threats, was relegated to Limbo. Philip, who from the first had doubted his existence, was perhaps justified in his later scepticism, but Leopold at least should have remembered that he had asked that question about terror by day and night.

VIII

The guests rose to take their leave and go to their own places, and the King of England, after courteously seeing them on their way, turned back to his wife, his bride of three days and nights, and scrupulously civil, saying that he had much to do and must be afoot early in the morning, kissed her hands and took leave of her.

To say that everyone who remained in the banqueting room was astonished would be to emulate those musicians who deliberately mute their music in order to make people listen. He had married, cut short his honeymoon, been separated for many days and nights from his bride, and was now reunited. He had been triumphant, Acre had fallen, and now in this palace in the centre of the city his bride awaited him. And with a kissing of hands he prepared to leave her.

Her face looked to me like a sweet sun-warmed white rose overtaken by a sudden frost. Not pitiable, for to be pitiable is to make some appeal, conscious or unconscious, to those who have it in their power to help you, and she made none. Tragic, rather, for tragedy is battling with fate and being defeated. And I have no doubt Richard thought that she was content with the arrangement! And probably everyone else— except, perhaps, Anna Apieta—recovering from their astonishment, went on to think that she was cold and hard and impervious.

I have heard it said that she was stupid, but that is not true. A stupid woman at that moment would have betrayed herself, probably begged him to stay, provoking him to embarrassed evasion and her suite to sniggering mirth. Berengaria merely bade him good night with that gentle dignity and air of unawareness which were amongst her greatest charms—and which were to be her only defence, poor thing.

But I had seen her face and judged Richard guilty of deliberate cruelty, the one unforgivable sin, and I thought: May I be damned if I go with you again and act as your lackey and nurse and secretary and musician! Why should I spend my time in your company, you brute?

So I watched him go and then went out to the kitchen quarters and renewed my acquaintance with the pages and cooks and scullions, whom I had not seen since the days in Cyprus, and tasted for the first time some Palestinian wine known as the Blood of Judas. The wine had a legend attached to it. They say that after Judas hanged himself in the potter's field somebody planted the ground with vines which, in the press, yielded a vintage of a kind never yet known to man. It was a dark red wine, very sweet while it was on the tongue, but leaving behind it an astringency and a faint bitterness. It was reckoned to be both preventive and curative for stone in the kidneys, and to this reason was ascribed the fact that vines from that field had been transplanted to other places where their peculiarities and virtues had been reproduced. The wine was not a very popular drink except with those who were concerned with the state of their kidneys and those who drank in search of oblivion rather than good cheer. And it so happened that Berengaria's chief steward was one of the former and had laid in a large quantity as soon as he heard of its virtues. So it was handy and we drank it; and presently I, at least, was very drunk. A comfortable haze was settling between my inward sight and the memory of her stricken face, and it was well worth the dryness of my mouth, which felt as though I had been eating sloes from the hedges, and I was looking about for some place to sleep when a page came calling, "Is Blondel here? Has anyone seen the lute player?" Several helpful hands pointed me out, several willing heads nodded in my direction, and the boy came close and said, "The Queen, my mistress, is calling for you."

I had been sitting on a bench and leaning back against a wall and had not realised, until I stood up, how helpless my legs were.

"I can't come into her presence in this state," I said. "I'm drunk as a tinker's bitch. Go back and say that you failed to find me. Or tell her the truth. Small matter. Trot along."

He stood and goggled at me, mumbling some protest.

"Go on," I said roughly, "or do you want some help from behind?"

256

I remembered that last time I had had to do with him I had helped him—stupid homesick young creature—to write a letter to his mother. He probably remembered it also. He gave me a look and turned and fled. And I sat there and mused how low I had fallen; so befuddled that when my lady sent for me I was not fit to stand before her, so befuddled that *I* was threatening young pages with kicks from the rear.

For that kind of self-hatred there is but one cure—more of the Blood of Judas. Oh, apt name! Some poet christened that wine, and rightly all wines should bear it. The traitor's label. Thinking that thought, I gathered to myself another brimming jug and went and sat down in my corner. The kind haze gathered again and began to blot out this last iniquity. And then there was a disturbance. Pages, servingmen, scullions, cooks, stewards shuffled and stirred, and I lifted my eyes, where the drunken slumber weighed heavily, and looked up and saw Anna Apieta standing in the doorway.

For the feast she had worn a scarlet dress, but now that was discarded and she was clad only in a grey undergarment with a shawl clutched round her shoulders. As soon as she saw me she stood still, lifted her hand, and beckoned me. And because she should not have been there, because she was not properly clothed, I rose at once, staggered to the doorway and joined her, and turned, kicking the door closed. We stood in a dark passage lighted by a single candle sconce.

"You must come," she said in her direct way. "The King sent over to know if you were here, and the Queen wishes you to go to him at once. But first she must see you. She is quite frantic. Can you understand what I am saying, Blondel? I can see you are completely flown, but can you understand?"

"I understand," I said truthfully. "Understanding is easy; standing is more difficult, if you will forgive the play on words."

She laughed, quite unshocked, and asked in a conspiratorial voice, "What shall we do? What can we do? She has set her mind on seeing you." She tapped her little fingers on the wall against which I was leaning. "You must *try*, Blondel. Go and walk briskly three times round the courtyard, and breathe deeply and pour cold water on your head. I'll wait here."

I went out, dipped up a bucket of water, poured it on my head, drank a quart, and was immediately sick and imagined that I felt better. Twice during this procedure I measured my length on the ground, and when I got back to the passage where Anna waited she dusted me off in no very gentle manner, looking at me sharply while her hands dealt the brushing. Then she ran her fingers lightly down my arms, from shoulder to wrist, in a soothing gesture that was almost a caress and said, "You look very well—considering. Now pull yourself together; we must hurry."

"I'm not going back to wait upon His Majesty of England, if that is what Her Majesty plans," I said.

"Don't be silly," she said. "Why not?"

"Ah, I have my reasons," I said darkly.

"Well," she said, "don't imagine that you are coming back to *this* household. She never wholly forgave you that remark about the collar——" She was making that remark sharply and then broke off, remembering, no doubt, as I was, her own extraordinary behaviour on that occasion. There was an awkward little pause.

"I'm not bound to either of them," I said truculently. "There are other households in the world. Or I could go back to the road."

"Very true," she agreed, "but let me tell you this: If your reason for leaving Richard is the one which I suspect, by refusing to go back you make yourself as bad as he is!"

I took several steps, thinking that out.

"And what do you know about my reason?"

"I didn't say 'know,' I said 'suspect.' And if you weren't so extremely drunk you'd see that if a man kicks a dog in the stomach the way to show your disapproval is not to turn round and kick the same dog under the chin. Here we are!" With that she opened a door and pushed me briskly into a small lighted room where Berengaria sat on a stool while Joanna of Sicily brushed her hair. There I was in her presence, with that sharp, shrewd sentence about kicking the kicked dog still sounding in my ears and the old question about the extent of Anna Apieta's knowledge rearing its familiar head.

Both my lady and Joanna of Sicily had been crying. Joanna, who cried easily and in the ordinary woman's way, had red eyes and a swollen nose and had just reached the snuffling stage of recovery. Berengaria's face showed no betraying sign, but there were dark patches on the bosom of her blue gown and at the edges of her long sleeves.

"Oh, there you are, Blondel," she said. "We have been concerned about you. His Majesty sent back to know if you were here, and at first we thought you were lost, and then that lying little page said you were drunken, rolling in the kitchen." She came a step nearer to me and looked at me with the eyes which some people thought so expressionless but which I found eloquent always. "Are you drunk, Blondel? Is that why you did not go back to camp?"

"I'm tired of the camp," I said. But even to myself the words rang false.

"I wonder," she said. "Blondel, has he chided you? His temper is touchy, I am told." ("I am told," she said, speaking of the husband, the stranger.) "But you know, Blondel, I feel bound to say that sometimes you can be very exasperating." She softened that statement with a smile, rather wavering and uncertain. "What happened?" she asked in the voice of one who coaxes a confession from a child.

Could I say: He left you, he stabbed you to the heart, made you cry; I hate the sight of him? Could I?

"Nothing happened," I said. "I went out through the kitchen and found several old friends whom I had not seen since we were in Cyprus, and we celebrated our reunion a little too well. And I am tired of the camp. Truth to tell, madam, I have little stomach for war, and when——"

"Stop," she said. "Prevarication leads nowhere. You refuse to be honest with me, but I will be honest with you. Blondel, I want you to go straight back to the camp and stay there. I know you live—as he does—in great discomfort, and there is danger and you see horrid sights. But please go back. When he was ill, Blondel, your letters saved me from going distracted. No message from any courtier—no, not from the King of France himself—could have brought me such comfort."

She began to pace about the room, taking long jerky strides and working her hands together. "They all hate him," she said. Joanna muttered something and she rounded on her. "Why shouldn't I say it? Blondel can be trusted—he wouldn't tattle—and, for that matter, I'd say this in the open any day. They hate him; they're jealous. Did you mark Philip tonight, doing his utmost to provoke, to whip up his temper so that he can turn round and find an excuse for his own perfidy? Blondel, if you can imagine what it is like to be a woman, to know these things and yet to be locked away, shut out. Did you hear him tonight? When he leaves Acre we are to stay here. There will be weeks, months of waiting and not knowing the truth about anything. That is not to be borne." She stopped in her pacing, close to me, and laid her hand on my sleeve. "Do you realise," she said violently, "that when he was ill they said he was dead? If I had not had your letter, Blondel——"

"Dear Berengaria," Joanna said, putting an arm about her

and beginning to cry again, "you must not excite yourself. You will make yourself ill. And it is to Richard that you should say——"

"Joanna, just for once let me have my say. Blondel, listen. Before ever you came to Pamplona I dreamed about you. Yes, that is true. I never told anyone save Anna, and I told her that first day when you came and played. Do you remember? I dreamed I was in an oubliette and you got me out. When you came back from England I thought that dream was broken, fulfilled, done with, and I almost let Anna carry you off to Apieta—but I dreamed the same dream again, and that was a warning. I dared not let you go. And now you see. When he moves out towards Jerusalem and I am left here, that is my oubliette. Only you can help me because you are the only person I trust to keep watch and tell me the truth. Blondel, if my brother Sancho had come it would have been different. As it is, there is only you. Do, please, I beg of you, go with him, stick close to him, keep watch and ward over him, and from time to time, as chance offers, let me know how he fares."

I stood there and looked at her, and she looked back at me pleadingly. Not for me to hurt her, who had been so much hurt already.

"If it would make you happy," I said at last.

"It would make me more comfortable in my mind." She sat down suddenly on the stool and clasped her hands in her lap. "At supper when the marquis was speaking of careless servants—did you hear? I thought that you—you sleep in his tent. Pages and servants are careless and open to bribery, but you ... Not that you shall lack reward, Blondel. I promise you. When we go home from this crusade I'll give you whatever you ask, anything you desire." She leaned forward and pointed one hand at me, palm upwards. "There! That is what I mean, Blondel, when I say that you can be exasperating. I ask you a great favour, I open my heart to you, I even tell you about my dream. Then when I promise you a reward you put on a mocking, scorning look as though you didn't believe a word I was saying. Why do you look like that? Don't you believe that if you do this for me I'll give you anything you ask?"

"Oh yes," I said. "Of course I believe it." And I wasn't looking mocking or scornful at you, only at my thoughts; at the great discrepancy between what I desire and what you could give me.

"And you will go back and stay?"

"I will go back and stay," I said.

"And keep watch and ward?"

"Yes."

"Then God bless and keep you, Blondel."

IX

The King had missed me so soon because he wanted to entrust me with a task, an interesting one and to my taste—the making of the preparations for the reception of the three thousand Christian prisoners who were expected within a fortnight.

Acre yielded up fourteen Christians in all, Raife of Clermont and thirteen others. Four of these had been captive for a long time, nine taken recently. Richard had had the outwardly reasonable notion of letting them help me to make arrangements for the reception of the others, but the plan did not work well. The ordinary man who has known neither captivity nor liberation may imagine that these fourteen men with a shared experience would make a closely knit, intensely friendly group. But that was not so. Raife had been chosen as interpreter at the surrender, and Richard, on the impulse of the moment, had taken him into his tent, taken him to his table, and introduced him into the highest company of the crusaders. He had been, for a few days, a rarity. The other thirteen, coming in later, housed in a tent together, and regarded with less astonishment or curiosity, resented their more ordinary treatment. They vied with one another in the comparison of hardships endured, experiences sustained, in the demand for luxuries, most of them unobtainable, and in their jealousy of Raife.

I chose a palace, larger than the one which housed the women, and set it out, so far as possible with the means at my command, like a castle in the West. We made stools and tables and beds of ordinary Christian height from the floor; we put spits in the kitchen. We sent out petitions throughout the whole camp asking for contributions of spare clothing and equipment. By the end of ten days we had so arranged it that every returned prisoner, though he might not be fitted out completely, could at least feel his welcome and have enough to inform him that he was home at last and amongst his friends.

Some of the gifts were rather touching. A man from Suffolk, an archer, arrived one evening with a smallish bundle wrapped in canvas. He spoke English, and that in a dialect which two of the returned English prisoners failed to understand. But at last we found one who understood him, and this was the theme of his speech.

"Years ago I was fighting with his late Majesty in France and had the mischance to be wounded. Twelve days I lay a-raving and a-starving, and then I come to and all I wanted was a bit of Suffolk ham, and there wasn't a bit to be got anywhere, naturally. So this time, before I set out from home my owd mother, she cured a ham for me, killing the pig special, and she say to me, 'Johnny, my boy,' she say, 'keep hold of this against the time when you want it most particular.' But now I've sawn him in half, and if so be there's a Suffolk man amongst them chaps that's coming in, do you give him this, for to a Suffolk man there's nowt like a bit of Suffolk-cured ham, as I can give my word for. But if so be there ain't no Suffolk man, do you be so good as to give it back to me. For I shall need it myself before this is over, and if any but a Suffolk man et it my owd mother would never forgive me."

Unwrapping the canvas, he revealed a half ham, black as pitch on the outside, browny-pink within, and the whole as hard as a stone. I set it carefully on a shelf in the storeroom, and later on I took great pains to search through the whole of the army and to give that Suffolk archer back his treasure.

For no prisoner came in.

Why, I never knew, nor, I think, did anyone else. Saladin had agreed to the exchange, and it seemed to me that the garrison of three thousand men from Acre would be of more value to him than a similar number of Christian prisoners scattered throughout his domain, many of them old and decrepit, all of them unwilling. Moreover, Saladin had proved himself and was to prove himself again and again a chivalrous enemy, a scrupulous keeper of rules and treaties. Nevertheless, the stipulated fortnight passed and neither prisoners nor excuses arrived, and Richard began to worry the matter over in his mind. After a few days he sent messengers in search of Saladin, but they returned with the news that the camp in the hills was deserted and had been for some days; there was a rumour that Saladin had gone to Damascus, another that he had gone south. Richard chose to believe the latter and lashed himself into a rage.

"Very clever!" he exclaimed. "He knows that these prisoners are a clog on my leg; I can neither feed and transport them when I leave nor afford men to stand guard over them, so he thinks I shall sit here playing watchdog while he looks to his defences in the south. Little he knows! I give him three more days. . . ."

In Palestine in summer there are two lovely hours in the day, one just after sunrise, one just before sunset. In the morning the sky is the colour of a hyacinth, the sun is pleasantly warm, and everything is drenched and sparkling with dew. In the evening, after the heavy, sultry heat of the day, a little breeze springs up, the cool shadows lengthen, the earth shakes itself and smiles.

In the lovely morning hour of the day after the expiration of Richard's last time limit, 2,844 Saracen prisoners were mustered in the enclosure in front of their place of captivity, gravely giving thanks to Allah because they thought that the exchange had been made and the day of delivery had come. And in the lovely evening hour of that day they all lay dead in their blood on that field. No, I lie when I say all, for towards the end of the day the swordsmen whom Richard had picked to be executioners had grown weary, hasty, careless, and had stabbed and clubbed their victims instead of cleanly striking off their heads as he had ordered. So here and there a wounded man moaned and cried, and here and there amongst the mounded dead one yet living stirred, so that the satiated vultures rose, flapped heavily, and then settled again to the feast.

And Richard Plantagenet, looking across that scene of horror, said, "Now I can begin my march on Jerusalem."

On the great and dreadful Day of Judgment that sentence will be heard again, quoted, either as accusation or exoneration. And the Judge on that day will be impartial, disinterested, just. We none of us were, so our verdicts are warped and invalid.

The great mass of opinion in the camp was that Richard had acted sensibly and expediently. "We are here to kill Saracens, and if three thousand of them can be wiped out in a day without loss of a single Christian life, that is all to the good," summed up the attitude of the ordinary soldier on crusade. Those who most loudly professed their horror of the act all too often revealed during their denunciations that it was not the mass murder but the man who ordered it whom they detested. "We always said he was bloodthirsty and treacherous, and this proves it," was what they said. But it should be remembered that the massacre lasted for a whole day and that no effective steps were taken to stop it. The grumblers let him deal with the prisoners as they had let him take Acre—singlehanded. If Philip of France had actually felt that day as later he said he felt—that Richard was a bloody-minded homicide, crazed by his lust to kill—surely on that day he should have done something to restrain him. Richard always swore that he informed him overnight of his intention and that Philip said, "Those who take prisoners are responsible for them." That sounds like Philip; "responsible," used thus, has a delicate ambiguity which a more subtle man than Richard might have noted and paused over. Richard simply took it as a recognition of his authority in the matter; a justifiable assumption, since Philip spent that whole day on a picnic in the foothills where the weather was cooler and the view more pleasing.

My own feelings about the massacre I dare hardly examine. I was shocked and horrified, but then I was a novice to the art of war, and any sort of killing, even in the heat of battle, shocked and horrified me, and if I am honest with myself I am compelled to admit that if Richard had been a kind and loving husband to Berengaria I should have accepted more readily the three facts to his credit which even those who hate him must admit. He had waited a long time and made an effort to make Saladin keep his bargain; the problem of the prisoners was a real and pressing one; the method of execution was the swiftest and most merciful one known.

And now that I have seen so many die of slow disease, of wounds which will not heal, of starvation and thirst, I sometimes ask myself whether there are not worse ways of dying than to come out into the sunshine, happy in the belief that you are to be free, and meet the sharp swift edge of a sword. Even the untimeliness of death—for many of those men were in their prime—was no sorrow to them. It was the will of Allah that they should die that day, and they accepted their fate with Eastern imperturbability.

But I was young then, and I was shocked, and it was a long time before I could look on Richard with anything but abhorrent hatred.

x

With the prisoners disposed of and a garrison installed in Acre, Richard made ready for the long march to the south.

Amongst the things taken when Acre was captured was a bundle of maps which were not only superb examples of draughtsmanship but miracles of accuracy compared with those formerly in the crusaders' possession. Richard, with a perspicacity which proved that, inactive as his imagination could be at some points, there were others where it was lively and keen, had suspected these maps at first. "They may have been left there in order to mislead us." So he had taken one of the maps of a surrounding district and with Raife of Clermont, who had firsthand knowledge of the terrain, had ridden out and spent a day checking the pictured detail with the actual, visible scene. He returned, satisfied, and set me to work copying certain of the maps so that each commander might have his own. "As a compliment, Blondel, and a precaution in case any should have the misfortune to be separated from the main body."

Raife, who had some skill in his fingers, helped make the copies, and we amused ourselves by copying the scrolls and what he called "arabesques" which decorated the borders of the originals. The followers of Mahomet, for some inscrutable reason, took literally the injunction laid down in the first commandment, "Thou shalt not make unto thee any graven image, nor the likeness of anything that is in heaven above, or in the earth beneath, or that is in the water under the earth." So there were no birds or flowers or leaves in their borders, merely flowing curves, angles, triangles—but pleasing and decorative.

As a matter of frank confession I will say that Raife, who had experience in the manner, did the arabesques better than I did, so I conceived the pretty fancy of reserving one corner of each map and there drawing and colouring the standard and insignia of the commander for whom it was destined.

I was actually at work on a sultry evening finishing off the corner where the lilies of France bloomed on the map intended for His Majesty of France. Raife was putting arabesques round another, and Richard, brooding over the original, was counting wells and streams and endeavoring to arrange so that each day's march would end near fresh water.

"It cannot be contrived," he said at last, laying down the map and pushing back his sweat-soaked hair with his hand.

Without pausing in his work Raife of Clermont said, "The route was planned for the spice caravans to Egypt, sire. All camels. And spices are not bulky. Those camels move swiftly, and if they fail occasionally to rest by water, it does not matter."

"Well, there was a fund," said Richard with a grin, "for

265

providing camel transport. I spent it on mules. Camels carry, they don't haul—at least I never saw one harnessed. Did you? And anyway, where, at this hour, would I muster a sufficiency of camels for our baggage? We must arrange to carry some water. Casks for the beasts, and—Raife!"

"Sire?"

"Stop scribbling. Go take ten men and gather together every wineskin and waterskin in Acre. And what about new ones? Wait, write out an order, address it to the governor, and I'll sign it. Tell him to slaughter every goat and lamb he can lay hands on, salt the flesh—Rolf the Dispenser can see to that for him; take Rolf with you—and have the hides made into waterskins with all possible speed. I want as many men as possible to carry one—— Oh, what have we here?"

Four French nobles, dressed in their best clothes, stood hesitant in the doorway. Guillaume of Pontigny—who vied with the Count of Algenais for the title of "Oldest Crusader," for their birthdays fell on the same day, stood a little ahead of the others and carried a little silver casket in his hands.

Richard, with a quickly suppressed sigh of impatience, stood up. He had cast off all but his shirt and drawers, and they were soiled and sweat-stained. The thick black ink which the Arabs used, which Conrad of Montferrat had likened to tar, had, although it was impervious to cold water, a tendency to smear and melt when touched by sweaty hands, and the map Richard had been handling had been heavily lettered on its underside. He had brushed his soiled hands over his clothes and his face, and in contrast with the neat clean Frenchmen with their freshly oiled hair and beards he looked dirty and bedraggled.

"Come in, my lords, and be welcome. And forgive my attire. Had I known of your visit I would have been more fitly arrayed." Then his cheerful, boyish grin lit his face. "I stand before you as I stood at my crowning." He pushed back his hair again, sullying his face anew and, turning, gave orders for seats to be brought forward and wine served.

Not one of the French lords spoke a word. They advanced solemnly and in silence to the trestle table, and my lord Pontigny, when he reached it, looked at the maps that were spread there and quickly looked away, and quickly set down— as though it were burning his fingers—the silver casket he carried.

Richard, made uneasy by the silence and by the manner of the lords' approach, which in truth very nearly resembled the

266

conduct of mummers at a funeral, said in a voice that rang out very loud and boisterous:

"What is this, my lord Pontigny? You bring me a gift? From my brother of France. Well, by the glory of God, I have one for him too. A lantern to light him on his way to Jerusalem." He reached over and took up the map I had been making.

Old Guillaume Pontigny raised his eyes, looked at the map, looked into Richard's face, and then, turning his head away, lifted his arm and brushed his face with his sleeve. He was weeping.

"In God's name," Richard shouted, "what ails you, my lord?" He dropped the map and came round from behind the table and would have set his hand on Pontigny's shoulder, but the old man took a hasty step backwards and jerked out, in a voice thickened with tears:

"My lord, we were sent to tell you, the King, our master, is going home."

"Home?" As he repeated the word in a stupefied voice Richard's face went crimson and then, just as suddenly, deathly pale. He sucked in his cheeks and bit hard on their inner sides, released them, and drew in a great breath through his mouth.

Then he said quietly, "Raife, go do as I bade you. My lords, pray be seated." He sat down himself.

"You have come to tell me that Philip of France is abandoning the crusade?"

"My lord, he is going home. He is a sick man. He has ailed constantly since he landed, and he feels that on the march he would be a hindrance."

"I was sick a while back," Richard said in that same quiet voice. "No tears were shed for me. Why do you weep, Guillaume?"

Pontigny did not answer. One of the others said:

"Our master lacks the vigour that is your good portion, my lord."

"True. The same might be said of thousands of others. However, my lords, I can see that he sent you an errand little to your taste; we will say no more about it." He reached out his arm and lifted the silver casket and threw open its lid. His fingers fumbled and brought out a crucifix slung on a thin gold chain. He gave it his meticulous attention, as though he had never seen such an object or even anything remotely like it in all his life before. Then he laid it down on the map that lay in front of him, bent his head, and stared, and looked up.

"Many men," he said, "would take that for an omen. It fell squarely on Jerusalem. My lords, carry my greetings and my thanks to my brother of France and tell him that I will carry his emblem until I can lay it to rest in Christ's tomb."

Something like awe checked the tears in old Pontigny's eyes.

"Sire, all the French are not retiring. Five thousand men remain."

"Under the command of my lord of Burgundy," Richard said; not as a question, but in the voice of one completing the recitative of a lay.

Pontigny nodded.

What a pity, I reflected. For Hugh, Duke of Burgundy, had a sharp wit and a talent for parodying songs. Immediately after the taking of Acre, when a new song about Richard's prowess had been on every tongue, he had amused Philip's supper table by a version in which every compliment had been twisted into an insult. "Where he strikes, death follows," can be easily made into amusement for the silly if "strikes" is replaced by a simple word for a physical action which even kings must perform. The crude parody appealed to the primitive sense of humour of the very men who had earnestly sung the original song and was soon to be heard all over the camp. Richard listened, laughed, and retaliated in kind. It was all very silly and childish, but it showed how the land lay. Better for everyone, I thought, if Hugh of Burgundy had gone home with his master.

Richard, however, merely said, "Burgundy is a good soldier." And when the deputation had taken their leave he leaned over my shoulder and said, "Wash out the lilies of France and paint in Burgundy's sign," in a voice which seemed to deny that the change had any significance.

The reluctant admiration with which I was becoming familiar moved in me. I could have taken the hand which he had laid on my shoulder and kissed it and choked out some words of reverence. But, as always, something withheld me.

Later in the evening I heard Hubert Walter, discussing the matter, say: "You take this very lightly, my lord."

"How would you wish me to take it? It is to his everlasting disgrace, Walter, not mine. And truth to tell, I can bear Philip's disgrace with equanimity!"

And yet, with the King of France's going something was broken and something was ended. He and Richard had taken the Cross and made their vows together, and however much and however bitterly they had quarrelled amongst themselves, they had always stood together as joint leaders of Christendom against Islam. Now there was not even the pretence at unity.

There is always a moment at the merriest, most blazing feast when the candle in the windiest corner gutters and fails. The others burn brightly, a new one is lighted, but there has been that little patch of gloom, that momentary reminder of the engulfing night.

XI

We left Acre at the beginning of July and reached Arsouf in the second week of September, and those ten weeks, though they were marked by no major battle, constituted, I think, a test of endurance unmatched in the whole crusade. The well-beloved song, "When Richard Marched through Holy Land," always rouses rancour in me because although it takes count of the Saracens—indeed, I think, exaggerates their part in the story—it ignores the other, more insidious enemies: the midday heat blazing down on breastplate and helm, dazzling the eye, drying the throat; the sudden, astonishing chill which comes with darkness, turning the clammy sweat-soaked clothes into cold shrouds and waking a need for blankets which no man, however determined, however foresighted, could have carried through the hot day; the flies, the perpetual torture of the swarming flies, bluely iridescent, bloated ghouls that moved as we moved, lighting now on the steaming mule dung and then on the piece of bread you stuffed into your mouth—and often accompanying it to its destination so that the squeamish, feeling the living, wriggling thing in their mouths, spat out food and fly and the stouter fellows said, "All grist to this mill," and swallowed both.

There was the dust too. Mounted men in armour rode in the van, in a long protective column on the inland side of the toiling foot soldiers, and at the rear. If you had stood on one side to watch this army pass you would have seen with some clarity the first dozen knights and then a long grey-brown, earth-hugging cloud through which a multitude of ghosts moved. All but that first dozen or so lived, day after day, with dust in their nostrils, dust in their eyes, dust filming and roughening their skins, gritting and souring their mouths. I never turned in my saddle and looked backwards without thinking of the "pillar of cloud" which by day had guided the Israelites across this very land, nor without wondering wheth-

269

er it had indeed a supernatural origin or whether it had been mere dust kicked up by the heels of Moses and Aaron and the dozen favoured ones who walked ahead. So blasphemous a thought would at one time have set me crossing myself contritely, but not now!

I can speak of the dust—and certain other torments—without indulging in self-pity, for I moved "with Richard through Holy Land" more easily and more comfortably than almost any other man. I was mounted but not armoured. I rode as lightly as the Saracens who kept pace with us through the hills on the landward side and swooped down every now and then to make little harrying raids.

I rode the grey horse, Lyard, to begin with. And I rode near Richard in the van, where the dust was thin and bearable. But after a day or two Richard said to me civilly—indeed, almost apologetically:

"Blondel, I wish you would change mounts with Raife of Clermont. He is heavier than you are; his mare falls behind every day towards the end. And he knows the country; he is useful to me. Moreover, though lately unpractised, he is a knight and bears arms. I would he were better mounted."

Very sound arguments. They would have sounded better in my ears, however, if Raife of Clermont had not sought me out at our first halting place, expressed great admiration for Lyard, and asked me where I had obtained such a steed. His envy was as obvious as Mount Carmel.

Neither Richard, who had given, nor Raife, who envied me the grey horse could know that every time I saw or touched Lyard an old, unhappy memory woke and stabbed me and that the exchange was welcome. My common sense told me the change was reasonable, yet something in me—pride? the feeling of having been outwitted?—*something* made me resentful.

"Sire," I said coolly, "Lyard was, and is, yours to give."

Richard looked at me hard for a moment without speaking. Then he said with an underlying savagery in his voice, "You don't understand."

"Oh yes," I said, "the useful, arms-bearing man should have the better horse. Anyone could see that."

(Even if he goes sneaking round, asking for favours, saying, "After all, I *was* a prisoner all the best years of my life!") I did not mention that I had got myself a sword and that Godfrey of Angers was schooling me in its use and said that my father and my abbot had been wrong in their judgment of my wrist. A born sword wrist, he called it,

270

naturally flexible and capable of becoming strong with practice. Riding in the van with Richard, armed with sword and dagger, I had been prepared to be at least independent, self-defensive, nobody's responsibility. But now, relegated to the plodding brown mare which had been Raife's mount and which was, in truth, incapable of keeping pace with Flavel, I fell back and generally rode with one of the few other mounted, non-armoured men. Sir Escel, the physician.

One morning as we rode through the burning heat and the stifling dust he began to talk about a fact he had just dredged up from the vast uncertain seas of old sailors' lore—the fact that sores which stubbornly resisted all other treatment often healed under the application of a mouldy ship's biscuit.*

"Now that sounds like a superstition, does it not?" he asked. "But I have proved its worth. The biscuit must be mouldy, and the more mouldy it is, the quicker it works. Why that should be passes my understanding. What are ships' biscuits made of, would you know?"

"Dead men's bones and mud," I said.

He laughed. "No, seriously. There's nothing in them but flour and water, is there? Dried out, baked hard. And, but for the omission of yeast, similar to bread. The virtues of a bread poultice are well known, but that is mainly because the bread retains the heat long enough to reduce the inflammation. And yet a mouldy ship's biscuit will heal a sore which a bread poultice leaves untouched." He pondered and then reached out his hand to a great sack strapped to the back of his saddle. "I have a supply here; I keep them damp, hoping to make them mouldy. The trouble is that in this heat they will dry out so quickly." He pondered again. "Isn't it fortunate that His Majesty found me this horse? I should find it almost impossible to *carry* this sack. Strange to think that I made a little model which kills men, ergo the King mounts me, ergo I can carry a sackful of healing. If only I can keep it damp." He turned in his saddle and felt the sack. "As I thought," he muttered. He took his waterskin from the front of his saddle, untied the string which closed the neck of the sack, and poured all the water over the biscuits within. I could hear the little snappings and hissings as the dry hot biscuits drank in the water. I hoped that on the midday halt we should find water near. That didn't always happen.

"It is possible, you know," he said when he had closed the

*Penicillin, recognised eight centuries later, is a mould. N.L.

271

sack, "that this apparently inanimate mould has a life of its own. If you leave a mouldy biscuit long enough it is consumed, becomes a mass of soft fluff. Is it feasible, do you think, that the mould is vigorous and voracious and *eats away* the sore as it eats away the biscuit?" He looked at me sideways, a little shamefaced. "It's very unorthodox to talk of an inanimate thing having life. I should be in bad odour if it were known; it does savour of heresy, doesn't it? But frankly, that is the only explanation that occurs to me."

"Rotten cheese is alive," I said, trying to be helpful.

"Umm"—he nodded—"even on the Pope's own plate! And if rotten cheese can develop an undeniable life of its own, why not a rotten biscuit? Thank you, Blondel. That was an argument which I had not thought of. You see, I wanted—after one or two further confirmatory experiments—to send news of this discovery back to my colleagues in Valladolid. Sores—not sand sores, but other kinds—are very prevalent there, especially amongst the poor and especially in summer. I would like them to know that a mouldy ship's biscuit——
On the other hand, I have no wish to lay myself open to charges of superstition or heresy. We doctors, you know, work between the flesh and the devil, while the churchmen stand between the flesh and God. Dear me, what am I saying?"

"A very profound truth, I suspect," I said. And at that moment a man, labouring in the dust, clutched my stirrup and said:

"The King is asking for you. He sent me back to find you."

He spoke gruffly—rudely, in fact—but, looking down at his dusty, sweat-streaked face, I could feel no resentment. He had come back on foot and would have to hurry to regain his place. He had a right to be sour. And I had noticed lately that many men looked at me a little askance. I rode, they walked. They fought, I played a lute and wrote letters. . . .

Blind, blind innocent fool that I was.

I hurriedly detached my waterskin and held it towards Escel. "If we find water by midday," I said, "pour this into your sack of mystery. If not, drink it. I'll come back for the skin." Then I turned to the fellow who had been sent to fetch me.

"Hop up behind me," I said, "and I'll ride you back to your place in the column."

He gave me a queer look.

"No, thanks," he said, "I don't want my mates laughing at me."

Perhaps he would have lost dignity, bumping along on a pillion like a market woman behind a farmer.

"You ride, then," I said after a glance towards the head of the column, shrouded in dust and probably by this time a mile ahead, for as the day passed the column stretched out. Poor man, he'd had to cover the same mile three times on my account. "The horse is meek as a sheep," I said, "and I'll ride behind you."

"And His Majesty'd ride me all right," he retorted, and some genuine consternation showed on his face. But he said less gruffly, "No, you get along fast as you can. I'm a man. I can walk."

Later I understood the significance of that encounter. At that moment I merely thought: Very well then, walk if you prefer it. I pulled my mount out to the left and, making what speed I could over the bad road, pushed forward and fell in in my usual place, just behind Richard. He beckoned me forward and eased his horse over so that I could ride beside him.

"Where have you been?"

"Back with Escel, my lord. Talking to him."

"What about?"

"Mouldy ships' biscuits."

"There's no need for that," he said sharply, casting me a cross glance. "The march has taken longer than it should, and they harry us so that we can't live off the country as we might do. But I was prepared for that, and if anybody has to eat mouldy ships' biscuits there's something very wrong somewhere."

"He isn't eating them," I said, and I would have gone on to tell him about Escel's experiments, for that was the kind of conversation in which he delighted, and we might have gone on for an hour worrying out the possibilities of mould on ships' biscuits. Then I could like him; then I was at ease with him, could see him in a form that was acceptable to me. But he cut me short.

"Just ahead," he said, "there's a narrow defile, and Sir Raife, who rode out scouting, says that it is ambushed. There may be some real fighting for a change. Now listen. The safest place for you is with the baggage wagons. They're well defended. So pull out now and wait for them. When they stop, dismount and stand between a wagon and your horse.

273

Then nothing much can happen to you. Keep your head down."

He might have been speaking to his grandmother.

"Sire," I said gently, "you forget. You left your womenfolk in Acre!"

There was silence that had the same taste as the silence with which he had received my remark about Lyard being his to give. Then he asked sharply:

"Have you any weapon?"

"Sword and dagger," I said, not without pride.

"Look to yourself, then! God keep you!" He turned as far as his mail allowed, raised an arm, and with a shout, "*A moi!*" set spurs to Flavel. The armed and mounted men thundered past and into the defile.

It is a fact, and I challenge anyone to refute it, nobody who has ever taken part in a battle can describe it satisfactorily. If a man could sit suspended between earth and heaven and be endowed with a hundred eyes, he might afterwards give an account of the pattern, the movements; but his account would lack the noise, the confusion of reality. By the same token the single-minded, single-sighted man who is down in that noise and confusion can only tell you what happened to himself.

I found myself between the charging knights and a group of archers and I remember thinking: This is the worst place of all for me; I shall get a Christian arrow in my back. And with that I saw a slim brown man on a slim brown horse making straight for me. He had one of the curved Saracen swords, called scimitars, in his hand, and I could see that in a flash of time it was coming down to slice through my neck just where it joined my shoulders. So I raised my sword, clumsily, desperately, I thought, in a way that was at odds with all Godfrey's teaching. And I was surprised to feel the jolt which shook my whole arm, surprised to see the slim brown hand, still clutching the scimitar, fall off, severed. Just before they reached the ground the fingers of the hand relaxed and released the scimitar. Blood from the Saracen's wrist spouted out over me.

So lucky a stroke would, I suppose, have made a soldier of me if anything could have. It just made me sick. I saw that hand, so complete and ordinary-looking, falling through the air in that fantastic fashion; and I leaned forward on the brown mare's neck and was sicker than I have ever been in my life. My whole stomach turned inside out and fell back like an empty sack. I could hear the arrows hissing over me,

274

but I felt too ill to feel fear. Then, quite suddenly, while my eyes were still misted with the water of sickness, I saw another brown man lying on his back on the ground with blood pouring from a wound in his head. He had a dagger in his hand, though, and he was just about to stab up and strike the brown mare between the forelegs. I gulped in a chestful of something that seemed more like thick flannel than air, lifted my sword again, and set it, point downward, on his neck. And I pressed, felt the sickening crunch as the blade went through flesh and bone, but saw with vast satisfaction the hand which held the knife fall limp and harmless. Two, I thought, two.

And with that the battle was over.

The dust cleared, and there were a few horses without riders, a few men in armour on the ground side by side with some white-turbaned bodies. And there was Richard on a wildly prancing Flavel. The edge of his great axe was bloody.

> When Richard marched through Holy Land
> The infidel dared bid him stand,
> But with his great axe, fearless, he
> Did cut his way to Bethany.

Every time I hear that example of the minnesingers' art of simplification I think: Yes, if the crusade has been just a long series of battles, small, like the one at this ambushed pass, great, like the Battle of Arsouf, Richard would have cut his way. But there were so many opponents against which even that great axe was impotent, worthless as a reed.

Sunstroke was one: the old biblical "destruction that wasteth at noonday." We bound our heads, Saracen-fashion, with old clouts, bits of linen, pieces ripped from our garments—even the handsome helms were so covered—but every day men would stagger out of line or drop as they marched, with swollen, plum-coloured faces which all too often changed suddenly to the shrunken pallor of the dead. Often the men who walked beside the stricken ones would step out of line, too, and with the precious scanty supply of water they carried and sometimes with the incongruously pretty little fans they had picked up in Acre, they would attempt to revive their comrades. As they did so, as the column passed on, two or three of the Saracens who hung on our flanks as wolves might hang about a flock of sheep would swoop down from the hills; arrows or the light lances which they flung with such deadly precision would whir through the air, and the sound man would fall beside his friend. Few of those who stepped out of line ever joined it again, and finally Richard gave stringent orders that no man must step aside to help another. It was a ruthless, logical order, not invariably obeyed, and it resulted in Escel's demand that as the stores carried by the pack animals and the baggage wagons were lessened by consumption the transport should be used for slightly sun-struck men who had a chance of recovery. But that led to trouble, too, for it was difficult even for the physicians to decide in a moment whether a case was slight or likely to be fatal.

We suffered, too, from myriad fevers. There was the one which attacked almost everybody soon after his arrival in the Holy Land and then recurred in a mild, nagging way at shortish intervals. Richard suffered from that himself, and it was that which had sent Philip of France home. It meant that a man sat his horse or was helped along in a daze of pain and fever for a day, sweated profusely during the night, and rose, weak but on the way to recovery, next morning. But there was another more virulent kind which twice went through our ranks like fire through a dried cornfield and struck so many men into unconscious stupor or raving lunacy that movement was impossible. We all camped until it was over, the recently recovered staggering about, tending the lately stricken.

And there was the one most horrid ailment which was with us all the time. The polite, physicianly name for it was "water in the bowels"—the ranks had many other words for it. It was painful, weakening, and disgusting, and in extreme cases as fatal as sunstroke or the virulent fever. It became so prevalent and so many men were pounced on by the Saracens during their necessary fallings out—and it could make twenty or thirty fallings out imperative for one man in one day—that Richard commissioned a band of horsemen to ride ten arrow lengths behind the main body in order to cover the sufferers. Our invisible attendants soon learned that it was not safe to venture forth to shoot or cast at the cursing, squatting crusaders as it had been at the sun-struck and their friendly helpers.

There were, too, always with us the sores which made such demand upon Escel's supply of mouldy biscuits. Either the heat or the dust seemed to prevent the natural tendency of the skin to heal; a sore would be as small as a seed of corn today, tomorrow the size of a groat, and on the third day as large as the palm of one's hand. Then the centre of it would suppurate and grow hollow, as though the sound flesh beneath were being consumed. After that, unless the blue-green biscuit worked its magic, there was small hope.

Still we pressed on, and though it was a sadly weakened, much-winnowed force which approached Arsouf, it was yet an impressive one. Once indeed Richard did say, "There was a time in Messina when I thought I had too many men. May God forgive me that thought and forget it."

XII

At Arsouf, which stands guard across the road leading to Jerusalem and Jaffa, the Saracens did not wait to be attacked. A great army of them met us, and simultaneously a second force bore down on our left flank and a third closed in behind. It was plain from the first that this would be a day for killing or being killed. I determined not to be sick and not to be sentimental. As it transpired, I was given no chance to test these resolutions. I am a little sorry, especially now that I come to write this history, that I saw nothing of the Battle of Arsouf. It was one, if not the greatest, of Richard's victories and the one where he struck such terror into the Saracens that afterwards they spoke of him as Christians speak of the devil.

For one fantastic moment I thought my experience at the pass skirmish was to be repeated. Having no armour save a short, sleeveless jerkin of leather sewn over with flat metal rings which the friend of a sun-struck yeoman, having no need of it himself, had sold me for four aurei (there was a flourishing market in such things), I was not set in the front with the fully armed knights for the forward charge but put on the defensive as cover for the baggage and the sick; an honourable if not glorious task which I shared with sundry fully armoured men who had lost their horses and had not been able to replace them, a few fully armed mounted men who had been lightly wounded in the previous small battle, and one or two very young knights who, for lack of experience, might have been more hindrance than help in the charge.

If that first charge had been successful we should never, in our position, have seen action at all. But the Saracens met Richard's onslaught with equal fury, and at once they and the crusaders were mixed, infiltrating one another's lines and fighting small singlehanded engagements all over the place. A

Saracen, this time a very stout, heavy man, holding his scimitar in exactly the same fashion as the man whose hand I had sliced off, bore down on me and I tried to repeat my slicing action, sweating and wildly praying for a similar result. But he swerved, my sword whistled ineffectively through the air, and before I could raise it again the scimitar struck me just where the sleeveless jerkin ended. My shirt sleeve and a great flap of flesh from the thick part of my arm fell over and hung to my elbow, and the blood came pouring down to my fingertips. I felt no pain at all. I felt nothing save surprise—and, in a second, pleasure, when I saw the sword of one of the young knights pass with a beautiful thrust clean through the body of the man who had struck me.

How long I should have sat there staring I do not know, but all at once the knees of my brown mare buckled, and as she fell I shot forward over her head. And there I stood for a moment after I had disentangled myself and scrambled to my feet. I was angry, not because my arm had been sliced, but because my brown mare had been slain. After this, I thought, I'll kill and kill and kill. . . .

But there was no sword in my hand, and when I bethought myself of my dagger and moved to draw it from my belt, there was no power in my arm. The noise of the battle seemed to recede, and everything I looked at ran away from me into blackness.

Then there was pain. Someone was slowly and deliberately slicing into my arm. I moved it and the pain struck sharper. Then I lifted my left hand to defend myself and struck my hand against something very hard and yelled out and opened my eyes.

I was lying on my back with my head and shoulders under a baggage wagon, wedged tightly between two other wounded men, for since shade was so rare and precious every inch had been used. My arm had been tightly tied up with a strip of canvas and hurt excruciatingly, and I was so thirsty that the longing to drink was an added agony. Turning my head this way and that, however, I very soon perceived that I had reason to be thankful. The man on my left had been pierced clean through the jaw by an arrow, and the lower part of his face was a horrible mess of torn flesh, splintered bone, and broken teeth; the one on my right had been spitted by a lance through his belly—but he was dead and his misery ended. The smell of blood, of dust, and of dust soaked in blood hung on the air.

I turned my head back so that I was looking up at the floor of the wagon, lay still for a moment, and then carefully raised my head to peer out under the wagon's edge. My head felt enormous, the size of a barrel, with a loose mangonel stone smashing about in it; my neck felt long and overpliable, like a piece of thread. But I looked out long enough to see that the sky was a lake of rose colour with islands floating in it, some dusky-gold, some the purple of the grape. Sunset, I thought, letting my head fall back on the blood-soaked dust. And quiet. There was no noise of battle; just the ordinary sound of the camp and the groaning of men in pain. The day was over, and so was the battle.

And oh, if someone would only bring along a drink of water, however dirty, stinking, or full of little dark wriggling things. I shut my eyes and thought about water; of buckets coming up out of deep wells, spilling silver drops; of raindrops dancing into muddy puddles; of ditches brimming when the snow melted.

Presently from a great distance I heard my name spoken. I opened my eyes and saw Escel's face, unstable and wavering as a weed under water.

"Water," I said.

"They're bringing it." He crouched down, and I could see him more clearly: his face drawn with weariness and whiter than the tabs on his collar, his hands under the rolled-back sleeves as red as a butcher's. "I'll loosen your bandage," he said. "I had to tie you tightly, you were bleeding like a stuck pig. Luckily I soon reached you." I saw him glance across me to the man who lay on my right.

"It hurts," I said.

"I know," he said quite gently, but in a voice that was empty of pity because pity is expendable and too many demands had been made on his that day. As he loosened the bandage I felt a slight relief, quickly forgotten in the maddening throb and tingle with which the numbed limb came to life again.

"You'll mend," he said. "It was the best kind of wound, a good clean cut. Here is the water. . . ."

He straightened himself and sighed like a tired horse and moved on. In his place was a water carrier with a full skin and a little cup. He began to pour and some water spilled over and I cried out. Never again, I thought, should I see a drop of water wasted without protest.

When I had drunk I said, "What of the battle?"

279

"Oh, we won. We've taken Arsouf." The water carrier moved on to my neighbour with the shattered jaw.

"Water?" he asked; and then when the man did not answer he stirred him, not roughly but callously, with his foot.

"Do you want water now? It'll be gone in a minute."

Did he? Behind those mangled lips and broken teeth and splintered jaw, did there rage a thirst as urgent as mine had been? Could he hear the torturing question, and the threat? And have to lie there, powerless to answer, unable to drink?

"Wait, wait," I said. "Couldn't you pour a little—just a drop—into where—— Perhaps he might swallow a drop."

"Waste of water," he said quite cheerfully. "He's past it!"

But it might be you in similar case tomorrow, I thought, and I suddenly remembered a conversation I had once had with Anna Apieta on the subject of pity—how far is it tainted by fear for ourselves?

Then I thought: And this is only one dreadfully wounded man whom I can see. There may be others, worse.

I cried a little then, lying on my back so the welling tears ran down the sides of my head and into my ears. And then I was glad of the pain in my arm. I have something to bear too, I thought, and was crazily glad and relieved, leaning back on my own pain for comfort from the pain of all the others.

Presently I was conscious of a smell of boiled mutton mingling with and then overpowering all the other smells. I opened my eyes again and saw two men, one carrying a great steaming bucket, the other a ladle and a number of bowls.

"Who's for mutton stew, fresh mutton stew?" cried the man with the bucket.

"Dead," said the one with the bowls, peering at my right-hand neighbour and moving on to peer at me. "The next is all right. Hi, boy, want some fresh mutton stew? Put you on your legs in no time."

"No, thank you," I said, and ridiculous fresh tears came into my eyes as I thought how welcome, how wonderful, fresh mutton stew would have been last night; to me with an unsickened stomach, to the man on my right who would never enjoy anything again, to the man on my left who last night had had his teeth and his lips and his tongue as God made them.

"Now, now," said a cheerful voice away to my right and beyond the wheel of the wagon, "never say no. Soldier's first rule. You should sample this stew. Fresh mutton it is, though

I had doubts when I first heard them crying it. Yon Richard of England should give it out—every wounded man gets fresh mutton broth. Do more good, that would, than the four aurei he gives for bravery. What's the use of four aurei in this Godforsaken country now he's even forbidden the women to come along? But a basin of good mutton stew, now that is something that any man'd take a risk for." There were noises of the stew being enjoyed. "What's more, though none of those doctors would believe it, a good mutton stew'd cure all those ——ing sores!"

I lifted my head and through the gathering twilight saw a Flemish archer propped against the rim of the wagon wheel, with one bandaged leg sticking out stiffly, one arm hanging limp. Between his sound leg, which was drawn close to his body, and his stomach there rested a bowl of stew into which he was digging with his sound hand.

Two wounds. And still cheerful, still hungry. I was filled with admiration. And since I knew that the sores worried Escel more than anything, more than the fever and the water in the bowels, which he could accept as unavoidable, I thought I would attempt to ignore my own pain—and all the others'—in the quest for information.

"What makes you say that mutton stew would cure sores?" I asked, and put my head down again.

"I once saw it do it. Wait while I drink off this liquor and I'll tell you. I was at the siege of Therpont. That's a long time ago and forgotten now. Fifty weeks we were shut up there, well provisioned, beef in cask, salt fish, ham in plenty. We could have held out three months more if we hadn't been relieved. But we were rotten with sores; maybe they weren't as festering as they are in this country, but bad enough, and many tall fellows died of nothing else. Well, one day right up to the town walls there came a little goat girl with a flock of about fifteen head. Part of the old fosse was green over with grass, and maybe she thought she was safe, or maybe the goats strayed and she followed them. Somebody looked down and saw this young female in her red skirt and said, 'How about a little raid?' They made a quick sally and brought her in. With the goats. What happened to the girl I needn't tell you. The goats went into the pot because, as you know, though goats will eat most anything in nature, they don't take kindly to salt herring. Into the pot they went, and the old duke being a just man, every man Jack got his share. And in two days the sores were healing up like clean wounds. Nobody seemed to notice except me, but then I'm a noticing

281

man; noticed you didn't take stew, didn't I? And when I mentioned it they laughed me to scorn and called me Goat-gut. All the same, I know what I know."

"Well, that's very interesting," I said. "And it could be proved or disproved. Go on, tell me more things you have seen and noticed. When I'm listening to you my arm hurts less."

"Bless you, I could talk all through the night telling you tales you wouldn't believe, tales that'd set your hair on end. But in half an hour from now it'll be ——ing cold. Too cold to sleep. So I'm going now. Once I am asleep I am asleep, and nothing but a good kick in the arse'll wake me, so I'm going while it's warm enough. If you take my advice, you'll do the same."

I heard him arranging himself, grunting with pain as he moved. An old campaigner, the stuff of which armies are made, brave, unself-pitying, taking the good with the bad, the rough with the smooth. And what did they get out of it? I asked myself. Every village had its old soldier, one-legged, one armed, one-eyed, cobbling or carpentering a little, begging a little, stealing when a chance offered. And they counted themselves lucky. Thousands of others were dead in their prime, brave, cheerful, unquestioning men. Was it worth it? I asked myself. Was anything—from a little disputed throne up to the Sepulchre of Christ itself—worth the toll of death and pain that was being exacted in this one place on this one night?

And then the cold came and the pain increased. The man with the smashed jaw suddenly made a noise like a rapidly boiling pot, and the smell of fresh blood tainted the air anew. And here I lie, I thought, between two dead men.

Then the thought which had not come to me before came at last. Why do I lie here? I asked myself. I have the use of my legs. I edged myself out from under the wagon, clutched the side of it with my sound hand, and pulled myself upright. The great stone inside my head smashed to and fro and made me sick and dizzy and my knees turned to melted wax. My fingers melted too. They released their hold on the wagon side and I sank down again, close to the Flemish archer, who was now sound asleep. Flat on my back again, I felt better; the thunder of my heart, the smashing loose thing in my head quietened. The moon came up, a great bronze-gold plate in a dark velvet sky. I was thirsty again. And cold, colder than I had ever been in my life. I edged myself close to the archer and lay there entertaining a thought, a crystal-clear and rock-sound thought which in after days I tried in vain to recapture. It was very foolish, I reflected, for men to make themselves miserable about their loving or their sinning when all that was needed for happiness was freedom from pain and a modicum of comfort. I remembered all the hours when I had lain in my bed, warm and easy, fretting myself about my love and my conscience. Now, if only the pain in my arm would ease, if I could have a drink of water, if I could be covered warm, no thought of Berengaria, no thought of the damage my new mangonel had wrought, no thought of the men I had killed would hold me back from peace.

Finally, then, nothing mattered save physical well-being. Could that be true?

The moon changed from bronze-gold to silver. Here and there amongst the wounded a man stirred and moaned—suffering pain and thirst and cold, like me. But on the whole the night was quiet.

When I saw at some distance two tall figures moving, stooping, peering, and moving on again, I hoped that they were water carriers, but they progressed too swiftly. Just before they reached the wagon near which I lay they parted; one came on, became recognisable. Raife of Clermont, with a bloodied clout of white linen covering his ear and one side of his head.

He stooped and peered, recognised me and said, "Ah," straightened himself and called softly, "Here, sire."

"You're hurt too," I mumbled.

"Nicked on the ear. What happened to you?"

"My arm——"

"Arm," he repeated, and though he had no time to say more, the single word asked why, then, had I not walked on my sound legs and saved him the trouble of searching for me? But by that time the King, moving swiftly now, had come round the wagon and was bending over me.

"We've been looking for you. Are you sorely hurt?"

"Only my arm," I said, suddenly and unaccountably ashamed. "But I couldn't walk; I did try. I fell down——" Through my chattering teeth my voice came peevish, childish, complaining.

He bent lower and put his arms about me.

"You'll be all right now," he said soothingly. "Put your sound arm round my neck."

He straightened up, lifting me as easily as though I were a child. A voice from under the wagon said, "I want some water."

"You shall have it, my good fellow," said Richard cheerily. "Raife, go rouse those idle louts; I've said a thousand times they were to go round every hour after a battle. I'll have them flogged in the morning. . . . Blondel, you're as cold as a corpse; I can feel the chill of you through my jerkin."

"They're all just as cold," I said, speaking grudgingly because I had been sought for, found, and was being carried to shelter.

"They shall be comforted," he said. "We took Arsouf and the town is full of blankets. I'll get you settled and then——"

XIII

We lay at Arsouf for some time while the wounded mended or died and the dead were buried. Day after day the committal words were spoken and the bugles sounded, "Dowse lights and all to bed," over men for whom sun and candle would never shine again.

Richard, whom victory had made magnanimous, had wanted the Saracen dead buried with ceremony. But Hubert Walter had said:

"Then, sire, you must find someone else to speak the words. How can I or my like commend to the keeping of God the Father of Christ those who spit on Holy Cross and reverence the camel driver?"

"They fought so resolutely," Richard said with regret. But he deferred to Walter and contented himself with orders that the Saracen dead should be carried to an appointed place and little flags of truce erected so that those who wished might come and take the bodies for burial. Yet the garrison at Acre had fought resolutely, and they had been slaughtered like sheep and left to the vultures. It was, like so many things about Richard Plantagenet, incomprehensible.

From Arsouf to Jaffa and from Jaffa to Ascalon I footed it like many others whose mounts had been killed. The Saracens attacked the horses from deliberate policy, knowing that they could not be replaced in that unfriendly country, and it was now a common thing to see knights bribing the wagon drivers to carry their armour for them, while they, dressed in their soft leather under-jerkins, trudged along near at hand, ready at a second's notice to be harnessed into their mail. Or one would see yeomen or arbalesters marching along, taking turns at carrying some pieces of armour in return for a small coin or a small luxury. Fortunately the weather had changed with the coming of autumn and there were cool days when walking was pleasant; men were no longer stricken down by the sun and there were fewer cases of the virulent fever, though the sufferers from the one known as "hot-and-cold" or "double devil" still had their recurrent "bad days."

My arm healed badly—as did so many wounds that there was some justification for the vulgar belief that many Saracen weapons were dipped in poison. To the tips of my fingers my arm swelled and stiffened and, fearing that I might lose the use of it altogether, I spent every spare moment I could in practising writing and later, when the right hand could just hold the lute, playing with my left hand. At first the process was so slow and clumsy, the results so disastrous, that I often despaired; then one day skill seemed to come suddenly. I was until lately completely ambidextrous, which to a penman is a great blessing, for when one hand tires the quill can be moved to the other and the work can go on without respite.

On account of my wound I took no part in the Battle of Jaffa. I did see it, and I did see the happening which, though—or perhaps because—it has been remembered in the minstrels' tales, is doubted, called fantastic or legendary by sober men.

Richard, on the day before this battle, had had one of his "bad days" and had been able to eat nothing and had been tremulous as a poplar leaf when they harnessed him. But he fought like a fiend all day, dashing about the field, always with an eye to the spot where the fight was hottest, always with an eye to the most formidable opponent. In one encounter he was struck heavily on the helm and reeled in his saddle, recovered and dealt a blow that felled the Saracen, and, turning Flavel's head, rode straight at another—an emir by his dress—who was bearing down on him. A Christian knight who had seen Richard take that mighty blow and reel called as he passed, "How fare you, my lord?"

"I'm hungry," Richard said, and charged on.

The emir, with superb horsemanship, swerved and circled—all Saracens, unless they chose to ride straight at their object, could be as elusive as wasps—and called out in Latin, understandable but of a kind which would have brought Father Simplon's rod into action:

"Hungry, great lord? Draw off, then, and eat."

Richard, suspecting—as he explained later—an infidel trick, yelled back:

"Eat? When the battle is joined?"

The emir, still circling like a wasp, shouted:

"Battle is better with full belly."

"Draw off first, then," retorted Richard. And the emir, never ceasing to circle but now controlling his horse by his knees, raised his right arm high above his head while with his left hand he took a little silver whistle from his girdle and blew a long shrill blast. Immediately every Saracen turned his horse and galloped away to a little eminence which edged the field and there sat on their alert, quivering, rapidly breathing steeds while the Christian knights, puzzled by the manoeuvre, looked stupid for a moment and then turned to Richard for guidance.

"We're going to eat," Richard bellowed. "And I have nothing."

That was where William the Fowler gained his place in song and story. Opening his wallet, he ran forward and presented his King with something which he had doubtless been preserving against the day when he should need it. Like my Suffolk archer's piece of ham, it was a highly individual comestible, a round dark object wrapped in bladder.

"A real black pudding, my lord King."

(I took pains later to investigate this matter. William the Fowler hailed from Bakewell, from that part of England which still, in secret, held apart and called itself Northumbria after the ancient kingdom of that name. And there they make "black puddings" of congealed pig's blood and meal enclosed in a bladder for better keeping. "I'd carried that one for eighteen months," he said when I asked him about it, "and if anybody'd told me I'd give it to any but a Bakewell man I'd have struck him down. But the best man deserves the best, see?")

Richard looked at that black pudding and set his teeth into it. The Saracen emir looked at it, too, and as though it had waked his own appetite, he wheeled round and rode back to his own company. After a little time another Saracen, of lesser rank, rode out and offered to Richard of England a platter of dried figs, sweet dates, and little cakes, with a flagon of the curious effervescent drink, sherbet, which the strict followers of Allah and Mahomet use in place of the wine which is forbidden them.

"Tell your man with the whistle to signal when he is

ready," Richard said. "And take him this with my good greetings." He sliced off a piece of the black pudding.

I didn't know—nobody near at hand except William the Fowler knew at that moment that the black pudding was made of pig's blood, and probably he did not know that to the Saracens pigs were beasts of the utmost uncleanliness. So I doubt whether anyone but I—and I only afterwards in retrospect—enjoyed the sight of a Saracen emir eating a black pudding and pretending to like it.

The emir rode forward presently and asked, "Belly full?"

"Belly full, thank you, and hungry now for battle," Richard replied.

The emir, without moving from Richard, blew another blast on his whistle, and the Saracens charged down the little slope, each taking, so far as was possible to judge, the station where he had been before. And the battle went on. The emir who had sent the figs and the dates and in return had eaten the black pudding succeeded, before the day was over, in slashing Flavel's neck so that he died and Richard joined the great company of the dismounted.

That is a true story. Many men sing of it, few believe it. But I saw it happen. They say that the Saracen emir was Saladin himself. I have no proof of that. Just as Christians look out for and think they see Satan everywhere, as the Saracens tell tales of Richard's queer appearances and disappearances, so the crusaders were always seeing Saladin—in the old water carrier, the dirty drug pedlar, the one lonely horseman scouting against the sky line.

I have no proof. But I did see Richard sit out between the Christian and Saracen lines, eating a black pudding given him by a Northumbrian and fruit and cakes contributed by the Saracens. I can only tell what I saw.

XIV

Much against Richard's will we moved from Jaffa, not direct to Jerusalem, but by a detour through Ascalon.

The whole story of the crusade is the story of the relationship between Richard and his allies, and much is made of the quarrels and jealousies between them. It is only just, therefore, to recount that in this instance he endeavoured to please them. He wanted only to move forward to Jerusalem, and after the Battle of Jaffa he was ready to do so. They wanted to take Ascalon and fortify it so that it might stand guardian on their southern flank. I was so often in his tent, practising my left-handed writing; I was so often called to take down note of this or that, that I should be as well informed as any save the participants of the argument, but I must confess that the motive of Leopold of Austria, Hugh of Burgundy, the Grand Masters of the Templars and the Hospitallers eludes me, unless it can be taken for what it seems—an attempt to delay the taking of Jerusalem. Why Ascalon must be taken and fortified—and not Gaza—I never could see, and neither could Richard. But they urged it, and they were four to one and he gave in. (Conrad of Montferrat had been obliged to go back to Tyre after the Battle of Arsouf. Civil—or should one say internecine?—strife had broken out in that city, and since it, with Acre, formed the crusaders' link with the West, trouble there could not be ignored. I was present when Richard took leave of him, and there was no hint of any ill feeling on either side; and I must admit that often during the later discussions and arguments I, at least, wished that the marquis had been with us. His smooth voice, his good spirits, his cheerful carelessness would have eased many encounters. But he had gone and, as Richard admitted, the rest were four against one.)

So we moved on to Ascalon. The Saracens had abandoned the town just before our arrival, but they had destroyed it. The humble clay houses had been left entire, but the walls and the towers had been reduced to heaps of rubble. Not a grain of corn, not a mat or a blanket which might have been useful to us was left in the whole town, and no living creature moved in it. Men who had been looking forward to loot and rape fell into a mood of disgusted disappointment; and it would have been easy enough for Richard to say, Here is the town which *you* said threatened our southern flank!

But he said nothing. He set to work to make Ascalon what his allies desired it to be, a strong Christian fortress. We camped amidst the ruins, and every day small mounted forces of known good fighters set out on raids into the surrounding countryside, charged to bring in horses, donkeys, grain, dried fruit, anything which would be of use; and the rest of the army, even the bladesmiths, blacksmiths, cooks, and storekeepers, were set to work rebuilding the walls, much shortened, and four towers.

Richard, whose nature and talents inclined him to join the raiding parties, every day saw them off and turned back to labour with pick and shovel. Many knights and nobles followed his example, turning the labour into a joke, laughingly comparing the blisters on their hands, the stiffness of their muscles.

"I reckoned myself a strong man," said the old Count of Algenais, "but now I know that every grovelling peasant on my demesne is my master."

But the armed man's prejudice against menial labour was not to be overcome in a day, and though Richard's digging and delving inspired those who liked and trusted or even unwillingly admired him, it evoked in others distaste and scorn. The Austrian knights particularly held themselves aloof and sometimes made jeering remarks as they passed. Finally Richard issued an order that every able-bodied man should take turns at the labour. That brought several waverers to stone-laying, but the Austrians said, "We follow the archduke *on* the field and *off* it."

We could well do without the unwilling Austrian labour, but their attitude affected others. Why should any French or Burgundian knight soil his hands building a fortress which would defend the frivolous Austrians as well as the industrious Franks? And the question, once asked, spread in all directions. Why should archers lay down their bows, engineers abandon their arbalests and mangonels if certain knights retained the privileges of their caste?

One evening Richard came in, dirty, sweat-soaked, and exhausted.

"If Leopold would come down only for an hour, if he would lay a single stone, his men would follow and this ridiculous situation would mend. Hugh of Burgundy called off all his men today, and it was as much as I could do to hold my own to work! True, the Austrians will always ride on the raids, but the others would like to take their turn at that. And why not?"

He washed his hands and sluiced his face.

"Blondel, have I a clean shirt? I'm going to make a formal call on Austria. By God's eyes, I'll even take him a present. Where is that scimitar I had from the emir who fed me at Jaffa?"

It was the only concrete evidence of his many triumphs in battle, that weapon with the long curved blade so tempered that it would cut through a floating feather. The blade was of finest Damascus steel, and the hilt of pale Kubistan gold, curiously and beautifully wrought. Its beauty was wasted on Richard, but he cherished it for the sake of the way in which he had won it. After he had eaten in the middle of the Battle of Jaffa he had joined battle with the emir again, and they had fought for an hour—wasp and bull.

By the end of that time they had both tried every feint and trick of skill they knew, and it was plain that only sheer exhaustion or some chance bit of luck, good or bad, would give either the victory. Richard with his heavy armour and strong right arm and swift eye could always divert the blows of that flashing scimitar; the emir, light and mobile, could never be smashed or run through. The action was as pretty as fighting can ever be—none the less so because both were in deadly earnest; and men on both sides who felt momentarily safe enough to do so watched it as though it were taking place in a tourney. At the end of the hour the emir, wheeling away for the last time, shouted in his faulty Latin, "We waste blows which, dealt elsewhere, might decide the day. And your horse is wounded. We will meet again."

That was Richard's first intimation that Flavel's failing paces had been due to anything more than weariness. He dismounted, clumsy in his armour, to investigate the damage, and the emir rode off, twirling his scimitar, which suddenly left his hand, shot in a flashing arc through the air, and landed almost at Richard's feet. Accident? Gesture? No one could say.

Richard had cherished that scimitar, practised with it indefatigably, shrewdly assessed its qualities and faults as a fighting weapon.

But he took it out now, breathed on the curved blade, polished it on his sleeve, and went off to present it to Leopold of Austria.

He was gone only a short time, and he came back with a look on his face which I had never seen there before and never saw again. He was ghastly pale, and his prominent blue eyes were large and bright with the threat of tears.

Raife of Clermont was in the tent, and so was Hubert Walter, who had come in and elected to await his lord's return. Richard walked in, sat down on the end of his bed, and put his face in his hands.

"I hit him," he said. "Well may you gape! I have struck the Archduke of Austria as though he were a villein!"

Hubert Walter's broad red face lost a little of its colour, and in the hush that followed Richard's announcement Raife of Clermont's harsh intake of breath was audible. But neither spoke immediately. I saw Walter hesitate, reflect, and realise that no expression of dismay would be either serviceable or welcome. He said at last, with a kind of ponderous lightness:

"Only one buffet, sire? Surely he deserved more!"

Without lifting his head Richard said, "He leaves tomorrow. And his men with him."

Hubert Walter sat down a little abruptly on a stool, planted his knees wide, and laid his work-blistered hands squarely upon them.

"My lord," he said in a voice that was at once incredulous and reasonable, as though it were Richard himself who planned some unfeasible action, "do you mean to say that *now*, with Jerusalem within striking distance, in our very grip, you might almost say, he goes home because of one blow struck in anger?"

Richard raised his haggard face.

"No, Walter. The blow is the excuse, not the reason; the last twist on the pulley that sets the stone flying. He goes home because men get wounded—they do, you know, in battle! And they get fever, and sores, and water in the bowel. And he goes home because Philip of France went long since and because Conrad of Montferrat had business in Tyre and has not returned. Also, there is sometimes a shortage of food and eke of water. And why? These things happen, Walter, because I am not fit to lead an army. Nobody has confidence in me any more. I am mad; I have not even a horse; I work with my hands like a serf. How can any man trust me? Oh, it all came out. He has a thousand reasons and he gave me them down to the last one. Most generously he forgave me the buffet! That in itself, he said, was a sign that I was overwrought and beside myself." He brought out the final words with fine irony, but I saw his great shoulders shake, and he lifted his hands and pushed back his hair with a gesture which, if not distracted, approached that state. "Am I mad, Walter, Raife, Blondel? You are near me; you should know! Am I overwrought, beside myself, and incapable of leading an army?"

"Sire," Walter said, "go out and ask that question of your English archers! For myself I am a plain man and can only say that, churchman though I be, you are the leader whom I would follow to the gate of hell and beyond! Because, lacking a horse, you pressed on; because, lacking labour, you toiled like a serf for the liberation of the holy places. And, my lord, God Almighty, if He is worth His salt, looks on you as I do."

Hubert Walter, Bishop of Salisbury, was a man of level mind, of integrity of spirit, and in control of his tongue. From him such impassioned speech was a tribute indeed.

Richard said almost apologetically, "He provoked me, you

291

know. I went and suggested civilly—I swear by Holy Cross, civilly—that he should pretend, only *pretend*, to take turn at the work so that his lily-handed knights should pretend, too, and the malcontent Burgundians have their answer. And do you know what he said to me? With a jibing grin on his face he said it: 'I am not the son of a mason or carpenter.' As though I were! And you, and Algenais, all the true men who have sweated. Before I could think or had time to swallow my gorge my hand went out and I struck him." He moved his right hand and looked at it and then dropped it with the other between his knees, and they hung there, looking oddly clumsy, helpless, and pathetic. "I'm not clever enough with words," he said. "There are many things I could have said, sharp, punishing things more hurtful than any blow. But I haven't the skill. Leopold and Philip could always taunt me; they've made me writhe many a time. Tonight I struck back—a clumsy riposte—with the only means I had, and tomorrow he goes home with the best of excuses."

"Tomorrow he may repent his decision," Hubert Walter said, but there was no conviction in his voice.

"It was not a decision," Richard said. "He seized an excuse. In the last issue men do what they want to do. Philip wanted to go home, his illness excused him; Conrad wanted to go home, business called him to Tyre and kept him there, mark you. Leopold wants to go home, but he needed an excuse acceptable to Christendom, and now he has it. He will go."

"When Christendom knows the truth, my lord——"

"How can it?" Richard interrupted. "How can anyone who stayed at home understand? Leopold will go back and ask, How can anyone work with a crazy man who demands that nobles dig and delve and strikes them when they demur? Christendom will side with him to a man."

It was not the first time that I had been struck by the acute awareness of Christendom which Richard Plantagenet suffered. In many ways the least imaginative, certainly the least self-critical, of men, he had always a nagging sense of being watched, judged, praised, or blamed by a vast vague mass of opinion. This flaw in his otherwise impenetrable self-assurance interested me; it hinted at the need which every human being feels for some standard of judgement overruling his own. We say of a brave man, "He fears neither God nor man," and so far as that can be true of any, I judge it to be true of Richard; but he did fear the adverse opinion of Christendom—a body made up of many members, any one of whom, as an individual, he heartily despised. I have noticed several similar cases of men appointing their own arbiters, stout fierce fellows who live by the light of some woman's judgement—wife, mother, mistress—not merely by reason of love but because they respect her opinion and fear her censure. And such wear a yoke heavier, I think, than do men who defer to God or Holy Church, whose rules of conduct are laid down clearly and whose judgement is given in advance.

When Richard said, "Christendom will side with him to a man," although he exaggerated a little, he showed great prescience. Leopold did go home and did give his reason almost in the very words Richard had used. And his letter of explanation to the Pope—of which I have seen an accurate fair copy—reads like the letter of a man who has by good luck escaped from a Gadara where the most raving lunatic of all had been put in charge.

Richard put his head into his hands again, and Hubert Walter sat silent, watching him, trying to think of some comfortable thing to say. I could have whispered him the words or, for that matter, have said them myself, but I felt that they would have more weight if spoken by a fighting man. And in a moment Raife of Clermont said them. "My lord, when you have taken Jerusalem, Christendom will have nothing but scorn for the men who went home."

I couldn't have worded it better myself; no man could. He had made mention of the two things which really mattered to Richard, the taking of Jerusalem—with a "when," not an "if"—and the good verdict of Christendom. And certainly Richard lifted his head and straightened his shoulders, but for once the old fiery enthusiasm failed to take possession of him. He said sombrely:

"I was counting on the Austrians. They suffered less at Jaffa than we did and lost fewer horses. And they have better health——" He stared at Hubert Walter, frowning. "It is in my mind, Walter, that those sausages they carry and depend on so completely are a more healthful food than our own salt beef. They have fewer sores—Escel would bear me out there; he has noticed it too—and since all other conditions are for them the same as for us, even to the drinking water, I do wonder about those sausages. Did you ever note them, Walter? I once gave an Austrian footman an aurei for one. I had it somewhere in my gear." He got up, moving more slowly than usual, less resiliently, and turned towards the heap of his possessions.

"I know it. I'll find it," I said. He looked at me gratefully and sat down again. I disinterred the object which, in his opinion, kept the Austrians healthy: a fat reddish sausage about the length of a man's arm from elbow to fingertip and about as thick as the thickest part of his forearm. Solid as wood, enclosed in a tough skin, that sausage had travelled in a bag of shirts and shoes since Richard had bought it in Arsouf, and now it emerged in its pristine state; even the end where he had cut it in order to taste and examine it was neither rotted nor moulded.

"Now look at that," Richard said. "Absolutely indestructible. Compare it with our salt beef and pork. We've covered the casks with sacks and kept them wet to prevent warping, but they've warped and the meat has rotted. Leopold's men carry a bunch of these at their saddleside or slung on their backs. They hack off a slice with their swords and they're fed and they don't get sores! Why should that be?"

"How should I know? I'm not a physician," Walter said.

"All this talk of eating reminds me that I have had nothing since morning," Richard said. "Let's sample Leopold's sausage." He took his knife, cut four slices, and handed them about.

It was very hard, hard as the oldest cask beef, but neither tough nor stringy; it had a pleasant savoury flavour and, for army rations, one superlative virtue. It was very filling.

"Give me beef, however rotten," said Hubert Walter, staunchly insular. "There is virtue in beef too. By the quantity and quality of their beef the men of Kent deem their rations good or bad—and I have yet to see better fighting men!"

Raife of Clermont gave his little deceptively tittering laugh.

"Oh, you English! I remember one of you, Martin the Bowyer, who was taken soon after I was. The Emir of Famia had him for slave, and once when they were hunting together—Martin bearing the gear and bursting his chest running alongside—he saved his master's life when the mountain lion they were hunting leapt up to the horse's haunches and clawed the emir's back. Martin dropped everything and shot a true arrow. The emir was—not unnaturally—pleased and promised Martin a stewardship and gave a feast to celebrate his escape and Martin's promotion. And at the feast he took up and presented to Martin the choicest tidbit from the dish. Can you guess, sire, what it was? A sheep's eye, most highly esteemed! Martin, stout fellow as he was, turned pale when he recognised it, lifted it on the point of his knife, and cast it to the dogs. The emir was deeply offended; Martin did not get his stewardship—but he did get a beating!"

"Poor man," Walter said. "I feel for him."

Richard, though he had listened to the story with his eyes on Raife's face, made no comment but now interrupted:

"Blondel, go and find Escel. Here, give him my purse. He has tended all sick impartially and is in good odour with the Austrians. Tell him to move about amongst the purveyors and storekeepers and baggagemen and buy every one of these"—he tapped the sausage—"that they can be persuaded to part with. They're going home—they'll be in reckless mood—and if they sell too much and starve before they take ship at Acre, so much the better. And you, my lord of Salisbury, go back to your men of Kent, pick out thirty or forty sensible, trustworthy fellows, and tell them to move amongst the Austrians as they pack their gear and to buy or beg the sausages. Raife, do you the same with the Christian prisoners. If we can't take the Austrians with us to Jerusalem we'll take their sausages, and if they save us a sore or two that'll be the Austrian contribution to *this* crusade!"

He spoke the words with irony, with defiance, but the wild, overdriven look was back in his prominent eyes, and all the lines in his face were harsh. I remembered with a little pang the first time I had heard him mention the word "Jerusalem," the passion and beauty of his own song, "Jerusalem, on Thy Green Hill." It seemed a far call from that glowing enthusiasm to this sour, disillusioned plotting for sausages.

Bound on our curious looting errand, the three of us were near the tent door when one of the guards burst in, crying with more excitement than formality, "My liege, my lord, the old infidel has sent you a horse!"

Hubert Walter, who was somewhat of a disciplinarian, said sternly, "That, my man, is no way to enter your King's presence. Before you stand guard again I will give you a lesson in manners!"

The man who knew Walter's method of teaching blanched a little and stammered. Richard's voice from the far end of the tent said:

"Leave be, my lord. He is excited; and if his news is true, I shall be excited too. Did you say 'horse,' fellow?"

"My lord King, a horse, a most beautiful horse."

Richard moved to the door; his step was still heavier and slower than even physical exhaustion could make it, but the expression of his face had already changed; the planes had shifted and lifted and the lines softened into interest. We stood aside to allow him to pass and then followed him out.

The open square before the tent was torchlit, and in the glare we could see the lovely horse, pale cream in colour, with long mane and tail of slightly darker shade. It had the narrow head, the slender lines, the alert but not nervous look of the Arab breed at its best. A woven rug, silky and pliable as velvet, lay under its saddle, and the saddle itself and the bridle and reins were of scarlet leather studded with silver, which caught and reflected the torchlight—as did the horse's hooves, polished into the brightness of black steel. Stretching upward to hold the bridle was a child or a dwarf with a dark monkeyish face. He was fantastically dressed in long baggy trousers of deep orange colour, a short blue jacket, and a yellow turban in which a long peacock's feather nodded.

At the sight of Richard he said, "Melech-Ric?" and drew from his sash a letter.

"There may be some trick," Hubert Walter said hastily, and reached out to take it. Most crusaders believed that the Saracens were skilful and subtle poisoners; even the opium eaters were inclined to attribute the drug's good effects to itself and its bad to some adulteration added by the pedlars.

The small dark creature snatched back the letter and said again, "Melech-Ric."

"Here," Richard said, and held out his hand. "Good my lord, would anybody poison a letter with the whole saddle to work on?"

He broke the sealed string which bound the letter and spread the page.

"Is it Arabic, my lord?" Raife of Clermont asked.

"Answer yourself," Richard said, handing it to him. He himself stepped forward and laid a hand on the smooth satin neck of the horse. The animal turned its head and looked at him; a little shiver rippled through the shiny body, but it stood still.

"I make nothing of this," Raife said, puzzled. "My lord of Salisbury, do you?"

Hubert Walter took it, stared, scowled.

"It could be Latin," he said suspiciously, "but such Latin as I have no knowledge of."

"Now let Blondel draw his bow," said Richard, turning back to us but keeping his hand on the horse's neck.

With a grunt Walter handed me the letter, and for a

296

moment I stared blankly at the wild-looking jumble of black scrawl. What had Conrad of Montferrat once said? "Written with some substance resembling tar with an instrument like a pig's foot." Never was description more apt. But he had added, "In tolerable Latin, withal." That was true too. This letter had been written by a Saracen scribe taking down the dictation of one who had rather less Latin, I thought, than the marquis's correspondent. I thought of Gorbalze and Father Simplon's little rod! But it was readable, once one made allowances for the script and the faults of grammar. A little proud of my understanding, I read aloud:

"Good friend and preordained enemy, it has come to my ears that you go on foot. When outside Jerusalem we meet for the end, I would that you be mounted. Therefore, accept in good spirit this horse, not heavy enough but the best obtainable, swift and meek.

"Salal-al-Din"

"May God and Jesus Christ and Allah and Mahomet look kindly on him for this," Richard said solemnly.

"Remember, sire, what you yourself said about the saddle," said Hubert Walter gruffly.

"And you remember what I have said so often and in good faith, Walter. Nothing can touch me until I have taken Jerusalem."

This time the word rang out with the old jubilant assurance. Lithely, lightly, he set foot in the stirrup and vaulted into the red saddle. The little dark imp jumped briskly aside, and the lovely horse stood poised for movement, awaiting the controlling touch. Before he gave it Richard turned to us and spoke. "A sign from heaven," he said. "So good an enemy deserves the best fight I can give him. I will go and apologise—on my knees, if need be—to the archduke and beg him to reconsider his decision. Wait here until I return."

In no account of that famous quarrel can I find any reference to this apology. Leopold denied that it was ever made. It suited his case better to say that Richard struck him and stalked away. But the Bishop of Salisbury, the knight, Raife of Clermont, and I, Blondel the lute player, know that Richard went forth to apologise and returned, saying, "I wasted my errand. I offered him that he should ride in the van and set his standard first in Jerusalem when it was taken. All to no avail. And it would be better that those who remain should not know that. Let us see them depart light of heart, as though their going mattered nothing. You three go now and look to the sausages."

Despite his failure, his mood was now cheerful and resolute, rooted, I think, in an ease of conscience. It occurred to me to wonder whether he reflected, as I had, that that promise about setting of standards in Jerusalem could only remind Leopold of the tearing down at Acre. Such considerateness was months too late. And a scrap of gossip which I gleaned from a French harpist from whom I bought six sausages later that evening, and who had been in or near Leopold's tent when Richard returned, was very illuminating.

"You ride this evening," Leopold had said in the course of the interview.

"On a horse sent me by Saladin's self," Richard had replied, pleased and anxious, by confiding, to please.

"A pretty present," Leopold had commented, and dropped the subject. But later, when Richard had left, denied and repulsed, the archduke had said to Hugh of Burgundy:

"Look to yourself, my lord Duke. For I leave you with a man who loves his enemies better than his friends. And when the time comes to make treaty with the enemy, it is the Plantagenet's friends who will suffer."

How far that drop of poison in Burgundy's ear influenced his future actions none can say. I have my own opinion.

xv

Early next morning the Austrians began to move away. Richard in his soiled, sweat-stained clothes went back to the building of Ascalon fortress, noisy, overenergetic, singing and cracking jokes as he worked. The stolid English and most of his own Aquitainians worked as usual. But soon after midday he gave proof that he was not the simple blustering fool of whom so many songs tell. He had posted a page to watch Leopold's headquarters, and presently the page came and whispered. And Richard, all dusty and dishevelled, stopped work and shouted:

"My lads, the Archduke of Austria is about to set forth. We must send him off in proper style. No time for finery! We'll give him a workman's farewell. Come on, pick and shovel, present!"

He marched out, bearing his own shovel—clownish, filthy—and the workmen followed him, lining up alongside the road

Leopold must take. He began to sing, no serious or inspired song, but the ribald, popular ditties which had built themselves up, phrase by phrase, cadence by cadence, in the mouths of unskilled versifiers and unskilled songsters all the way from Acre; soldiers' homemade marching songs. "I had a little Saladin, I fed it on raw pig," and "Jaffa grows great oranges as great as my two——," and other such. And the men sang lustily, concealing their wonder that their homespun stuff should be familiar to their King. But when Leopold finally emerged Richard held up his hand for silence and slowly, along both the long-extended lines, quietness came. When the archduke was level with him Richard lifted his voice and the words rang out like a trumpet call:

"We wish you safe journey! You should have it, for the road back is clear and the Saracens lie that way!" He flung his arm out in the direction of Jerusalem.

Leopold rode on, unhearing, unseeing, unheeding, as a man of stone; but the performance was not designed for his benefit. It attained its own purpose: the common man went back to his labour without suffering the sense of being deserted; and after five days Richard, who had never in his heart set much store by Ascalon, very shrewdly left it, hastily garrisoned and with the mortar still wet in its walls, and moved on to Bethany. This village with its sacred associations—for in Bethany our Lord raised Lazarus from the dead and restored him to his sorrowing sisters—was to be our last resting place; from it the final assault on Jerusalem was to be made.

I am, I think, as little given to superstition as any man, but it seemed to me then, and still seems as I look back across the years, that a blessing rested upon that short time between the Austrians' departure and the day in Bethany when Richard called all his commanders together to issue his final orders. During those few weeks there was a sense of unity throughout the whole company, a crusading spirit, a feeling of high endeavour. In many men the awareness of dedication, frayed and worn thin by delays and doubts and constant concern with petty mundane matters, sprang up again, renewed and vital. And in no man more than in Richard, who now, for the first time, found himself in undisputed control of a united force. With Leopold's going the rallying point of opposition and criticism seemed to have been removed, and even Hugh of Burgundy, who had been disputatious and lukewarm before, now treated Richard with friendly respect, took his orders without question, and carried them out energetically. Despite our lessened numbers and sad lack of horses we were, in spirit at least, a more formidable army when we set up headquarters in Bethany than at any time since our landing.

Richard knew it. He said once to me, "We have been winnowed out; the husks have flown and the good grain remains." It was rare for him to speak in metaphors, though he used them well in his songs. Rarer still for him to mention the past, as he did now. "It reminds me," he said. "I once had a chaplain who knew many stories, and one day he told me about a commander who was about to take a city and had too large, too fainthearted an army, so he set them a test—something to do with how they drank from a running stream." He frowned in an effort to remember. "No matter! The point of the story was this—those who failed the test were sent home, and with the small army the man took the city. So, pray God, may it be with us."

With a little shiver—apprehension, superstition, romantic appreciation—running over my shoulders I said, "Sire, the man was Gideon, the town he took was Jericho, a stone's throw to the north, and it might well be that the stream where he tested his army is that which runs here below us."

"Say you so?" he asked, and looked thoughtful for a moment.

I remembered Gideon again when it came to the matter of sending out spies, not mere scouting knights as hitherto, but serious, well-disguised spies.

The idea was Raife's. "I'll go," he said. "I know the language and all the small things by which another might betray himself. With a donkey and a pannier of stuff to sell I wager I could get into the city itself."

"Mummery," Richard said in the harsh voice with which he did occasionally address his favourite. To him, the knight of Western chivalry, such procedure smacked of trickery.

But Raife persisted. "Send out your scouts with a fanfare of trumpets to announce them if you choose, but let me go in my own fashion."

They argued for some time; Raife reminded Richard of the number of Saracen spies that had been taken in our various camps, and Richard reminded Raife of what treatment had been meted out to them.

"I shall not be taken," Raife said. "And if I were, remember, sire, my late master, the Emir of Damascus, was one of the two who rode safe out of Acre. I have it in mind that an appeal to him would not be disregarded!"

This speech, for some reason hidden from me at the time, made Richard very angry. His face turned purple and the whites of his eyes shone red; in a voice vibrant with fury he forbade Raife to set foot outside the camp. Yet overnight, in some interview at which I was not present, Raife persuaded him and gained permission to go so long as he did not go alone. He chose another man who had been a prisoner for a long time to accompany him, and they set off so well disguised that on the edge of our camp a guard arrested them and, disregarding their protests, called for his commander, saying, "Here's two Saracens with a crafty brand-new story."

There was no building to do in Bethany, and I wondered that Richard did not himself ride out to look on the defences of the threatened city. The more so when the mounted knights who went scouting came back with sorry-sounding tales. They said that not only did the city appear to be heavily armed and defended but that all round it lay a wide belt of fortifications. The Saracens had dug trenches and ditches, planted them with pointed stakes, arrows, and lances, and covered them with turf and small bushes. A full mile from the city two of our knights had fallen into one of these traps: one, with his horse, had been killed; the other escaped to take his place with the unmounted men. "It looked like a meadow," the scout who reported said, "green grass and those little pink flowers like pigs' snouts just coming into bud. We saw a camel train coming in from Jericho, and guides ran out from the city to lead them through. Evidently they have dug such traps on all sides."

"While we, to make our flank safe for Leopold's satisfaction, wasted time at Ascalon," Richard said bitterly.

Every scout brought in a similar tale. One reckoned that thirty thousand men were in camp outside the city itself, between the walls and the outer fortifications.

"Thirty thousand," Richard said incredulously, "more than Saladin commands when all are mustered."

But the old Count of Algenais, whom Richard trusted completely, broke in: "Sire, not Christendom only has united for this battle; Moslems, too, have come in from the four quarters of the earth. Seljuks, Armenians, Kurds, my lord, Egyptians and night-black men from the outer lands. As Christ has called up His crusaders, so the devil has gathered his own! But when did God value an easy victory?"

After some days Raife of Clermont came in. He bore out every ill report that we had heard and added his own. Every store and granary in Jerusalem, he said, was stuffed to bursting; thousands of sheep and goats were penned between the ruins of Solomon's great temple and the viaduct the Romans had made; soil had been carried in and spread thick upon every flat roof so that in time of siege the gardens thus contrived could grow vegetables and corn. The curious rock dwellings, caves, where the poor of Jerusalem had lived in time past, dwellings cut into the rock and reached only by flights of steps, had all been emptied, and mangonels, flame throwers, and arbalests had been set on their terraces, with the men who worked them snugly housed in the rock behind.

Raife said all this and then with immense self-satisfaction went on: "But ill news is not all I have brought back. Wait a moment, my lord." He stepped briskly out and returned bearing in his hand the piece of soiled and tattered canvas which, being a Christian and a merciful man, he had laid across his donkey's back before fixing the panniers. The canvas was deep buff in colour, and one had to look very closely to see upon that dark rough surface the lines and dots and blobs of darker brown which to any but the keenest eye would look like dirt on dirt.

"Now I must explain this," he said. And then, with his finger on a blob, he lifted his head, looked Richard straight in the face, and said with his tittering laugh, "This is my blood which was shed for you." Richard gaped at him. "Well," Raife said, "a donkey-driving huckster couldn't produce quill and inkhorn, but why shouldn't he wipe his bloody thumb on his donkey's saddle cloth? And wipe I did, to good purpose!" His strange high laugh rang out again. "The trouble was to keep this wound open. These accursed shoes blistered my heel and that wound will not mend, but my thumb—twenty times a day I must break it open and squeeze! But look, sire, I have here, accurate and marked, all the safe approaches on the south and west sides of the city. These lines are the trenches and ditches of which you have heard. The other marks are reminders of objects from which I took my reckoning. Thumb again, top joint fifty paces. For instance, this spot tells me of an old olive tree, and see, half the length of the top joint of my thumb—that is, twenty-five paces away from it on either side—these ditches begin. So for a width of fifty paces after the tree is cut down there is solid ground for your horsemen. I can translate every mark on this cloth and map out our safe passage."

302

And well might he look so pleased with himself, I thought. And well might Richard put his arms about him and kiss him warmly.

Who, at such a moment, could have caught and been concerned over that casual reference to a blistered heel?

We settled down together, Raife and I, to make the information on the dirty canvas into intelligible maps. We worked hard because Richard deemed it imperative to move before the information it brought us was outmoded by alteration. By evening we had them finished and clear, with a hand's span as the unit of measurement for fifty paces instead of a thumb joint and with separate maps for the south and west. And then Richard went—in the very civil way which he now used towards his fellow commanders—to request the presence of Hugh, Duke of Burgundy, and the two Grand Masters, one of the Templars and one of the Hospitallers, of Hubert Walter, of the Count of Algenais and one or two others, in his tent for a final conference. He himself put on a clean shirt and tunic and the plain circlet that served him as a crown; and he ordered candles and torches and good wine, thin wafers flavoured with precious ginger, sweetmeats of pounded almonds, figs, pressed dates, and oranges. Raife, with the precious maps rolled up and ready for presentation, went and sat amongst the company. I stole out. During the day a courier had arrived, bringing letters from Acre, and there was a letter for me. Not from my lady, but from Anna Apieta. Busy with the maps, I had had no time to attend it; and now by torchlight, squatting by the guards' brazier—for the spring evenings were still cold—I read it.

Dear Anna! Forgive me if that offends you; none shall see this history but you, who ordered it, and I expect and intend that when you read it I shall have toppled, drunk, into my grave. So what matter? Dear, dear Anna Apieta, that was the letter in which you told me that every one of my letters had reached *her* and saved her from distress. After Arsouf, after Jaffa, I had sent back my reports, hoping that they might outrun the racing rumours. And they had. And you told me. I was very grateful to you.

But that letter, reaching me across all the dusty miles, penned probably in a room where Berengaria breathed and moved in her beauty, had an unsettling effect on me. I looked over the past with all its misty memories, the present with its strangeness and uncertainty, the future, which, if it existed at all, was blank and hopeless. And it was odd to think that only

303

a little while ago I had been quite busily and happily engrossed in making maps. And of course for the wretch on the rack nothing much has altered; a handle has been given a slight twist. That is all.

I sought my solace where I knew it was to be found, and presently, through the pleasant gathering haze of not feeling, not caring, I became distantly aware of commotion in the space outside Richard's tent. His guests were leaving. The light glinted on Hugh of Burgundy's plum-coloured mantle, on the Grand Master of the Templars' long white cloak. I got up and moved forward. Richard was used to me by this time and seemed not to care whether I entered his presence drunk or sober.

I saw old Algenais's face, grey and hard as stone, with slow difficult tears creeping along its furrows; I saw Hubert Walter's, dusky purple and twisted with rage. Then I saw Richard's, and his was the face of a man who has been dealt a mortal wound too deep for agony, who realises his stricken state and waits, feeling nothing save, perhaps, a mild surprise that the blow should have fallen in such a way, at such a moment, and with such finality.

The Count of Algenais put out his hand and laid it on Richard's arm and said shakily, "My lord, would that I could find words to comfort you."

Just so might one man speak to another whose wound is plainly beyond comfort or aid.

"All that was to be said has been said," Richard replied dully. He moved clumsily past the table where the candles were guttering amongst the wine cups and the sweetmeat dishes and the maps which we had made and cast himself upon his bed. As his head touched the pillow the gold circlet tilted, stood on its rim for a second, and then rolled to the floor and lay on the bare stamped earth. Hubert Walter stooped and lifted it. Holding it between his hands as though it were a symbol in some ritual, he said harshly:

"The curses have yet to be spoken. 'Whom thou blesseth, he shall be blessed, and he whom thou curseth, he shall indeed be cursed.' Almighty God, by Whose word and power such charge was laid upon me, Walter of Salisbury, on the day of my appointment, bring now Thy judgment to bear upon Philip, King of France, and the henchman that does his bidding, Hugh, Duke of Burgundy. Together they have conspired to turn back at the moment when all true men would move together to liberate the holy places where Thy Son, Jesus Christ our Lord, worked His miracles and shed His holy blood. Almighty God, let the curse of all traitors lie upon them forever. Afflict them, I beseech Thee, in mind, body, and estate; let their flesh rot, their vitals wither, their wives be unfaithful, their daughters turn harlot, and their sons work rebellion. Let sickness and poverty come upon them and the Father of Lies take them into his keeping both in this world and in the world hereafter so that they tread the lowest pavement of hell through all eternity." He paused and breathed deeply, and some of the purple colour left his face. "In the name of the Father, the Son, and the Holy Ghost. Amen."

Richard neither moved nor spoke, but Algenais and Raife said, "Amen," and my slow, wine-bemused assent added itself afterwards.

There was a slight awkward pause after that. Algenais and Walter stood and looked at their King; Raife stared at the painstaking maps, whirled about suddenly, and went and flung himself down by Richard's couch, clutching at his knees.

"My lord," he said, forgetting to keep his voice low and screeching out like an hysterical woman, "let us go on! All the lukewarm, the cowards, and the traitors have gone now, and only the best remain. You shall lead them to victory."

"With the Saracens twenty to our one, Raife? And virtually no horses! Should I lead those who do trust me to certain death? Whose cause would that serve save that of my declared enemies?"

"That," said Algenais heavily, "is wisely spoken, sire. With you and the flower of England and Aquitaine mown down outside Jerusalem, Philip would be all-powerful in the West."

"And your brother John—" began Walter eagerly. It was as though seeing through Philip's putative schemes comforted them a little for being victims of his perfidy.

"My brother John was not born to take kingdoms," Richard said. "Nor is this the time. Leave me, trusty Algenais, good Walter; go to your beds. I shall have my bearings again by morning."

"Time brings solace," Walter said, as though he stood in a house of bereavement.

"And vengeance," muttered Algenais softly.

They took their leave.

Raife, still crouched by the bed, lifted his head.

"Sire, if it were just a matter of horses—I could steal them. They are so tame, the Arab horses, that they are never picketed but wander at will amongst the tents. They come at

305

a call and follow like sheep. I know the calls. I could steal ten a night and lead them to you. Fool that I am," he said wildly, "not to have thought of that before!"

"Listen," said Richard, harshness invading the dullness of his voice. "Walter is faithful and ardent and knows his English well; Algenais is a true man; Robico of Bohemia is under vow never to take meat, wine, or women while the Saracens hold Jerusalem; the Templar, monk as he is, is a brave man. But tonight when Burgundy had spoken they were all of one mind. *This* crusade is over!"

Raife went to his bed, and I heard him sobbing. I thought of his lost youth, plundered manhood, his hunger for vengeance that must go unassuaged. Presently he slept, sobbing himself into quietude like a child. How many times had he done that?

I lay still in my corner, thinking this and that. There had been the courier that day from Acre, and I wondered whether it were by his means that Philip had sent his orders; whether the long arm of the friend turned enemy had reached out from Paris to snatch away all hope of victory in the very hour of its possible attainment. Or had Philip, when he left, charged Burgundy to proceed up to the final throw and then withdraw. Who could know? Would anyone ever know? And what now? When Richard had found his bearings in the morning, what would they be and where would they lead him? Back to the land he ruled, to the woman who loved him? Would he turn and seek compensation for thwarted ambition in the small sweetnesses of ordinary existence and live to say one day, "When I was on crusade ..." or "I remember once in Palestine ..."

I knew that he was wakeful. Now and again he sighed and the bed creaked as he turned restlessly on it. Only once, and that for no more than an hour—though that was long enough for me to commit myself—had he seemed a hero, a little more than human to me; I did not love him as Raife did, nor wholeheartedly admire and revere him as did Walter and Algenais. His behaviour to Berengaria always, in every issue, lay between us. But over this barrier I saw him more clearly perhaps than those whose emotions were free to run forward; and I could guess as shrewdly as anyone what his thoughts and feelings were in this hour of travail. Even that blessed sense of unity and peace which had lain over us all for the last weeks had its own bitterness to contribute to this moment. Without any sense of blasphemy I thought: Just so the triumphant procession on Palm Sunday was followed by the lonely agony in Gethsemane. (Anna, the wine fumes were still in my brain. It was merely an idle thought. Richard Plantagenet never seemed Christlike to me.)

But Richard did not watch alone or agonise without pity. Presently I fumbled under my pillow. And I said softly, "Sire, you are awake, I know. Do you wish to sleep?"

There was no answer for a little time. Then he said, just as softly, "I've gone back step by step, Blondel, reckoning every mistake, every misguided action, and every unwise word. Do you know when this crusade was lost? You were there, you saw it happen! I was turned back from Jerusalem that night in London, in William's Tower!"

"No," I said soothingly. "That is a night thought, sire. They are always feasible in the night, and always hurtful. But in the morning we perceive their fallacy."

"This is true. If I had married the French princess Philip would have stayed by my side. And Leopold. Is that too deep for you? Isaac of Cyprus wouldn't accept my bride because he had wanted her for himself. If I had married Alys, not Berengaria, I should not have attacked Cyprus and disinherited that little fat girl who is Leopold's niece! The greatest joke and the sourest that God ever played on any man, my boy! Save for my mother, who once beat me for discourtesy when I was almost full grown and thought myself almighty, I never cared a fig for any woman; they mean nothing to me at all—and yet two women have brought me down."

Too simple, of course, to be taken as fact; it ignored too many things which had contributed to this situation, but it was feasible and it was hurtful—it was a night thought! I knew the kind. But it was new for Richard Plantagenet to lie awake in the night and look backwards, he who had always cast his spent days behind him as soldiers throw orange peel, who had always pressed forward to the glittering future which had proved to be a mirage.

There was nothing I could say. Except, "If you would sleep, sire, I have here the means to make you."

It was the kindest thing I could do for him who had, whatever his faults, been invariably kind and indulgent to me. I offered him a night of sleep, of strange and beautiful dreams, which, unlike the ordinary ones, bore no relationship to waking life but took the dreamer into places and amongst creatures which had no like on this earth. Waking, of course, would be horrible, but then tomorrow would in any case be a hard day for him, and it might even be helpful to have something else to blame.

307

"You're a goodhearted boy, Blondel, but I don't want your drugs. What has happened has happened and must be borne. You go to sleep."

I remembered that Christ in the hour of His agony had turned His head away from the hyssop and myrrh on the merciful sponge.

I swallowed a pill myself and slept.

XVI

That is my account of the crusade which Anna Apieta bade me write, saying, "Write what you saw and what you know, Blondel." The Third Crusade ended that night in Bethany; and by rights I should end my account with this final falling away of an ally and the abandonment of the war.

But I am going to write on a little for my own diversion and my own satisfaction. So many writers, both priestly and secular, have moistened their quills in order to record their own opinions and guesses concerning what happened next that it will amuse me to set down what I saw and what I know of what happened when the crusade was over. Philip the Penman, writing seven years ago in his cloister at Rheims, expressed himself thus: "The time between Richard Plantagenet's sailing from Acre and his appearance in Vienna is a time shrouded in mystery. Some stories assert that he was at that time accompanied by a lute player, a person represented by some writers as a servant of faithful devotion, by others as the traitor who gave him over to his enemies. The most reliable authorities now agree, however, that this lute player was a mythical character, having no existence outside the minnesingers' imaginations."

So much for "the most reliable authorities"; so much for Philip the Penman.

In that early spring of the year the crusade was over, but there was fighting still to do. The Saracens closed in and besieged the garrison we had left at Jaffa, and when Richard reached that town there was a hard and successful battle, in which he fought with all his old vigour and daring and skill, as though he enjoyed a brief resurrection of the spirit. Resurrection is, I think, an apt word, for, save at such moments, the man who rode back from Bethany to Acre was a dead man. He ate food when it was served to him, but it had neither taste nor nourishment in it; he shovelled it into his mouth, and it might have been chopped hay. He grew thin and gaunt. He lost what little care he had ever had in his appearance, never combed his hair or his beard, would never have changed his shirt save for the fact that I occasionally handed him a clean one. He no longer rode in the van, and he had given his cream-coloured horse to Raife of Clermont, who was suffering from the festered blister on his heel. His leg was now grotesquely swollen, and Richard had said, "Ride the Arab; its smooth pace will jolt you less," and had himself ridden the lame and stumbling steed which Raife had acquired after Lyard had been killed.

The lame horse had been glad to accommodate its pace to that of the men on foot—the vast majority now—but the Arab would grow restive and occasionally Raife, grimacing with pain from his poisoned leg, would give him his head and let him gallop on a detour.

From one such he returned on the morning when the retreating rabble which had been an army wound its way around the south of a line of low hills which divided it from the city which it had marched out to take, Jerusalem.

"Sire," Raife said in the tender voice which we all used towards Richard now, "you have never looked on Jerusalem. Take this horse and ride to the top of that hill and you will see it shining in the sun."

Richard turned on him a face as bleak and stripped as a winter countryside.

"Those who are not worthy to take it are not worthy to look on it," he said.

But for Hubert Walter, to whom discipline was, as it were, a self-contained virtue, something to be cherished for itself alone, the retreating army would have been more demoralised than it was. As it was, it was bad enough. Until we came to Jaffa, which the Saracens had retaken. There Richard fought like an inspired fiend—trying, I thought, to get himself killed.

Then when the terms of the treaty with Saladin were under discussion he came to life again. Jaffa and Acre must be left in Christian hands. Saladin fought hard for Acre—it was the key to Palestine—but Richard held firmly to his demand. "I may not be able to take Jerusalem with the force at my command, but I can and will hold Acre till Judgment Day." And with that in mind he roused himself, reissued, too late, his orders against women camp followers, drinking, quarrelling, fouling camp, opium taking, waste, and general disorderliness.

Saladin capitulated over the question of Acre, and the treaty was drawn up for peace for three years, three months, and other threes down to three seconds. And there was a hint there that one day, in some computable and not far distant time, hostilities might be renewed. That one day, with new allies or no allies, Richard would take the van again and the standard of England would open its folds anew to the eastern sun. But he said nothing, hinted at nothing. With something that had been an army, had degenerated into a rabble, had been half reclaimed and was now mainly a mass of men eager for home, he came back into Acre, camped, and began to make arrangements for the embarkation.

There was now no shadow of excuse for his avoidance of the palace as a place of residence, but his tent and his bed were set up as usual near Hubert Walter's; and the common soldiers, noticing this, amused themselves for a whole day with ribald comment about what *they* would be doing in the circumstances. Not that they were now suffering from lack of women, for Richard in his new mood seemed not to notice that many of his orders had fallen into desuetude; and although he had fought in the old fashion at Jaffa, after its retaking that town had been the scene of loot and rapine on an unprecedented scale, unchecked and unreproved. This was no longer a disciplined crusading army; it was a mob of defeated soldiers on their way home, not averse to a little fighting now and then, but unamenable to the former strict rule.

Many Saracen women, especially of the poorer sort, who had lost their husbands and their homes, followed the retreating Christian army to Acre, and when the embarkation began there were some pitiful scenes. Women whose future obviously held nothing but starvation and degradation clung to their temporary protectors and begged to be taken aboard; and although many men took the parting as lightly as they had taken the women, there were others who felt the wrench sharply. Maybe to the end of their days, lying beside their sturdy-bodied, stolid Flemish and French and English peasant wives, they remembered and dreamed of the small, honey-coloured, doe-eyed women with the downpouring black hair and pleasantly flattering Eastern subservience to the male; women who could never nag or scold because they knew so few foreign words. And doubtless the memories grew more enchanting as the men exaggerated the exotic charm of their temporary mistresses and forgot the drabber aspects.

Indeed, one or two knights with money enough to bribe, or craft enough to outwit, or power enough to ignore the shipmasters, did smuggle women aboard; and that, too, was food for speculation. Did they live, these women, and give birth to little half-breeds fairer than their mothers, darker than their fathers; or did they pine and die in the stern cold castles of the bleak North and West? How were they explained? How comforted?

The King of England, for whom the loveliest and most lovable woman in the world waited, sent her a courteous message announcing his safe return, and then on the third day another, equally courteous, saying that if it were agreeable to her he would sup with her that evening. The page came back with a letter, a single sentence, but written by her own hand: "My lord, I live for that hour."

"Now, Blondel," Richard said, "hunt out our best clothes and tie a ribbon or a bunch of flowers on that lute of yours. And if you can think up a *pretty* story, relevant, but fit for women's ears—" He broke off, and that bitter, beaten look of dead defeatedness washed over his face again. It was more painful to watch than physical torture. Not thus had he meant to return to her.

I managed to wrench my mind away from my own comparatively petty problem.

"Her Majesty will have little thought or time to spare for any story or for music. You have returned safe and sound, sire, and that will suffice to make her very happy."

"Where other people have spit in their mouths, Blondel, you have the sweetest oil of almonds. Would all were like you!"

"Now *my* tongue," said Raife from his bed in the corner, "drips bitter aloes—but it says the same thing. The Queen has long forgotten that there is such a place as Jerusalem; and if Blondel, telling his story, mentions Jaffa, she will think: Oh yes, Jaffa, where the oranges grow! That is the great virtue of women—the blind capacity to comfort. God made them soft and smooth and silly—buffers—like chamois jerkins."

There was a moment of silence after that, during which we all three pursued our own thoughts. Then Richard said:

"Of the Queen, yes, you both speak true—and of my sister. But there's that little crooked one—Anna. I shall read Jerusalem writ large in her eyes. With understanding and pity. ... Raife, God boggled with some of us, did He not? Anna isn't soft or smooth or silly."

"Then let Blondel give her a really vivid account of water in the bowels," Raife said. "That'll take her mind off the subject."

There was, of course, every excuse for him. The blister on his heel had never mended. Escel had tried not only the mouldy biscuits but every known and reputed remedy: poultices of herbs and of bread, salt packs, dressings hot and cold, applications of tar, oil, various wines, crushed figs, which the Saracens swore by, and even, at last, not without protest, warm cow dung, which rumour said was used most successfully in India. Nothing availed; the heel had rotted. Escel had cut away the putrefying flesh, scraped the softened bone. Raife had suffered great torment, but he bore it all with sour patience, with furious resolution. Midway between Jaffa and Acre he had been forced to abandon even the smooth-paced Arab and take to a hastily rigged litter, and now he lay abed, lame to helplessness, racked with pain, but indomitable and still in full possession of his sharp wits.

Thinking of his state, I thought I saw a loophole for escape. It was more than a year since I had looked upon my lady, and the absence, combined with the comfort of the wine-bibbing, had brought me a kind of peace. But I knew how precarious a peace it was. It had been shattered by the mere prospect of seeing her.

"If you can dispense with my services," I said, "I will stay here and keep Raife company."

"But I counted on you—to help entertain them. A song or two and a story . . . God's wounds, Blondel, it's a twelve month since I saw them—and nothing but failure to report. Raife, we'll be gone little more than an hour, and you won't be alone. Sibald will come and play chess with you if you wish."

"Thank you, no. My sufferings are sufficient. I shall lie here and think of you. But I pray you, give me no thought."

"You see?" Richard said, turning to me.

The year's passing seemed to have touched them very lightly if at all. Anna's sharp little face looked a trifle sharper and smaller, and the Lady Joanna's hair seemed slightly less bright, but Berengaria was so exactly as I remembered her that it might have been an hour instead of a year since I had taken leave of her.

Her greeting, cooler and more careless than ever, for she had eyes for no one but Richard, made mock of the tumult of emotion within me, a mockery which my own mind

312

shared. I stepped into the background of this tender scene of reunion thinking about the threefold nature of man: body, mind, and spirit. Body knew its lusts; mind ridiculed the whole situation; spirit, on its knees, worshipped the beauty, the sheer loveliness that was akin to the perfection of a flower or a sunset.

The women had somehow, with feminine skill, made a fine meal. Food was now scarce and poor everywhere. The natural resources of the country were exhausted, and when the army had turned back from Jerusalem the majority of the supply ships had held off.

"This smells good," Richard said as a dish of young goat cooked with herbs came to the table. "Here, Blondel, no ceremony, sit in by me. ...." He made room for me beside him. The Duchess of Avosola, who had been seated by him, made herself small. Hot-faced, awkward, hating him for his tactlessness, I sat down. Standing back, holding my lute and waiting, I had at least the right to a minstrel's place; here, squeezed in, defying all order, I was like a pet dog. But he meant it kindly, and after months of hard living—I had not even smelt fresh meat since the day when I had been wounded—I tackled the food resolutely, determined to enjoy it.

So long as we were at table the subject of the crusade was avoided so scrupulously that it shrieked aloud through the very omission. The ladies talked gaily about future plans, the joy of going home, making it sound as though we had all come to Palestine on a visit which for some reason had proved more dull and disappointing than had been expected. It was lovely to be going home.

I could feel a growing restlessness in Richard, and a glance at his face told me that it wore its bleak, winter look. Once he mentioned abruptly that next day or the one following he expected to go to Damascus for the signing of the treaty. The word "treaty" dropped into the bubbling conversation like a stone. But the ladies cheerfully ignored it and began to chatter about Damascus. The buildings in Damascus were famous, were they not? The Cathedral of St. John was said to be wonderful. ... I saw Berengaria glance at Joanna, who, like a puppet whose string has been tugged, leaned forward and asked:

"Richard, couldn't you take us; not all of us, of course, just Berengaria and me?"

"Quite impossible," he said shortly. "It's a long way and a bad road. The dust alone would—— Besides, we can hardly mount those who are bound to go." He turned to me and

313

muttered, "Get up and play now; I've had enough of this babble."

Before I had half finished the first song I saw another glance exchanged; this time it was Joanna who looked significantly at Berengaria, who turned towards Richard and said with rather more directness than she ordinarily employed with him:

"My lord, will you withdraw with us? Joanna has something of importance to talk over with you."

Something of warmth and interest came into his face, and he looked along the table and smiled.

"Here, Raymond, come and plead your own cause."

Count Egidio rose, looking a little confused. Joanna went rosy-red.

"For my part," Richard said with sudden heartiness, "I have quarrels enough of my own. The feud 'twixt my mother and your sire, Raymond, means nothing to me."

The four went into an inner room. Richard had said enough to indicate that his consent to the betrothal would be easily won. A fresh babble of talk broke out about the table. A voice at my elbow said:

"Finish that song and then come out on the balcony. They are not listening. . . ."

I looked down and met Anna's sweet yet derisive little smile. She hobbled away, and I brought the song to an end prematurely and joined her in the far corner of the balcony where she stood, leaning her elbows on the marble balustrade and staring up at the star-filled sky.

"Well," she said without turning her head, "and how are things with you, Blondel?"

"Much as they were, my lady. And with you?"

"Precisely as they were," she said, and laughed. "I notice that you still play left-handedly."

"Yes. The wound healed, but the strength hasn't returned to my arm yet." I did what I did a dozen or more times a day—whenever I thought of it, in fact—lifted my arm to shoulder level, bent the elbow, stretched it, flexed and unflexed my fingers. Anna half turned and, as I let my arm fall again, caught the ends of my fingers in her little palm.

"So cold," she said, "on such a warm night. Is the other hand——" She touched that, too, and, finding it warm, withdrew her hold. "Was it properly attended?"

"Oh yes, by Escel himself. It is doing well; I should exercise it more." Moving it, talking of it reminded me that it was heavy and limp and weak. I detached my fingers from hers and thrust my hand into the front of my jerkin; there, released from its own weight and warmed by my body heat, I could carry it and forget it.

"You trained your left very quickly and well. After each letter you wrote I tried to write with *my* left, just for curiosity, you know. My letters were quite illegible." There was a small pause.

"The King has taken his failure hard," she said. "I suppose it is true, what they are saying, that the French deserted on the very eve of the assault?"

I told her briefly as much as I knew of the affair.

"So it's over. All the sweating and straining, the hope and—all the dead men. What are you going to do now, Blondel? Have you any plans?"

"None very sure. It would sound silly, ridiculously self-important, to say that I should stay with the King as long as he wanted me—and yet—well, Raife of Clermont and I were there when it happened and he seems to rely—I mean to be more at ease with us at this moment than with anyone else except the Bishop of Salisbury, and of course he doesn't attend him."

"We expected Raife of Clermont to supper." The remark followed smoothly on the mention of his name, yet I was left with the feeling that she had abruptly changed the subject.

"I doubt if he will ever sup out again," I said. "He's very brave and resolute, but he's more gravely ill than he admits, even to himself. Escel says he will die."

"Then the King will be lonelier than ever, and more——" She broke off. "It's selfish of me, but at this rate I shall never get my house built."

"You still cherish that dream?"

"Why not? It is a comparatively harmless ambition."

"And still want me to help with the building?" She nodded.

"Many men could do it as well," I pointed out. "Nevertheless, this present state of things will end soon. When we leave Acre the King will cast all this behind him and will take up his ordinary life again. He'll have no need for me then."

"And you will come and help me build? Is that a promise, Blondel?"

"A vow."

"Well, when this Raife of Clermont dies—if he dies—don't go trying to take his place, making yourself indispensable. . . ." There was a note in her voice that I remembered from the old days, sharp, dictatorial.

"I could never do that," I said. "Raife has qualities that I lack." I was prepared at that moment to give her a eulogistic and perhaps fundamentally untrue account of Raife's qualities, for the threat of imminent death had cast its peculiar light upon him, diminishing his faults and enhancing his virtues. But even as I thought of that it occurred to me that really every one of us was going to die and that we should all of us, always, regard one another in that light. And before I could speak Joanna and Egidio, with their hands linked and a halo of happiness about them, stepped from the inner room on to the balcony; and almost immediately Richard was calling for me and saying that it was time we returned.

One can never experience exactly the same emotion twice over. Rather more than a year ago when Richard had left his wife in the same sudden, cold, heartless fashion I had been angry, shocked, disgusted. Tonight, as he hurried me through the dark, saying that he had given his consent to his sister's betrothal and that he hoped this time she would be very happy; saying that he wondered whether the message from Saladin had arrived and if they would ride to Damascus next day; saying he wondered how Raife was now, I found myself trying in vain to muster up those old feelings. I succeeded only in feeling sorry for him with the pity that one would feel for a bilious man at a feast, a cripple on the march, a blind man standing in the sunset glow.

Saladin had sent word. The leaders of the crusade were to set out next day. And Raife of Clermont had fallen into the comatose state which Escel had predicted as inevitable.

In the morning, when he was ready to leave, Richard committed Raife to my care.

"Look after him, Blondel. If he wakes and wants anything, get it, whatever it is. And have a priest ready." He drew on his gloves and stood scowling. "When the time comes—hold his hands; they say that eases the passing. I must go, you know. The others are so anxious to get home they'd sign away Acre if I weren't there. I must go." He gnawed his gloved thumb, staring down into Raife's blank, fever-flushed face, and then turned abruptly away.

Raife died next day at sunset. Escel had been in and warned me that he was dying and I had sent for a priest, who had gone, I thought, to fanatical lengths to rouse him and make him aware of his condition. But the slappings and shakings and douchings with cold water had failed, and at last the sad, beautiful rite was performed and I was alone beside the bed.

The camp was very quiet. All the commanders, accompanied by as many men as they could mount, had gone to Damascus and the ordinary men had drifted into Acre or down to the harbour, now crowded with ships awaiting the great burst of embarkation. In particular our tent was deserted since pages and servingmen alike were anxious to avoid the place where a man lay dying.

It was a stifling hot evening, full of dusty purple light; the stench of the rotting flesh and the sound of Raife's heavy snoring breath filled the tent. I should, sober, have felt very melancholy; but I had taken the precaution of laying in a full wineskin of the Blood of Judas. A year of wine-bibbing had changed me from the novice who reeled and retched and fell on his face into one of those deceptively sober-seeming drinkers who with wine in them can do most things they can do empty, and some things better. I was quite drunk, quite numbed of mind when the sound of Raife's breathing changed, but I was alert and far more calm than I might have been sober.

He had been breathing as though his open, cracked-lipped mouth had been gulping in thick broth instead of air; the noise ceased suddenly and I went towards him. He opened his eyes and looked at me with recognition.

"Blondel?"

"Yes, Raife."

"It's—very dark."

"It is evening. Shall I make a light?"

"No. Where is the King?"

"He was obliged to go to Damascus. Saladin sent word that he was ready to sign the treaty."

"I know. Acre . . . he must have Acre. He means to come back alone to take Jerusalem. I shan't be there."

However honest one is, one feels it incumbent to refute such a statement and I gave the traditional answer:

"Come, man, be of good cheer; the war can't be resumed for three years, and you—"

"You know where I shall be, Blondel. Get me some water and then listen to me carefully. I have something to say to you."

I went to the waterpot which stood, covered with a wet cloth, outside the tent door. At some distance, out of sight, several horses were moving rapidly and in rhythm. For a moment I hoped that something unforeseen had brought Richard back to hold Raife's hands himself, but the clatter came no nearer.

317

I turned back to the bed. A change had come over Raife; he had shrunken into the pillows and lay with his eyes closed again, looking very small and pitiable.

"Here is the water," I said, and put the cup to his mouth.

He turned his head a little aside. "Later," he said. "Listen, the King is a great man—and great men have faults in proportion. Little men shoudn't judge. Do you understand me? You must be tolerant—and kind." He opened his eyes and stared at me, and I was reminded of the look Father Simplon would turn upon a boy temporarily stupid-seeming though usually of good understanding. Boy, make an effort, understand this, you must, you shall understand! The compelling, would-be eloquent stare bored into my eyes for a moment and then clouded over. I said hastily, "Yes, Raife. I understand. I will."

But he was not satisfied. His cracked, darkened lips moved again, but no sound came. Then he struggled feebly in an attempt to rise, and I slipped my arm behind his shoulders and lifted him a little from the pillows, at the same time putting my head close to his.

"I can't get—any air," he whispered. Then there were some other words which I could not catch. I loosed my right hand from its resting place and reached for his; he took it and for a second it seemed as though he were trying by the clasp of his fingers to communicate, to pour something from his mind to mine before death severed all the threads and sealed away all his knowledge forever.

"Yes," I said loudly. "I know. I understand. I'll see to it. I promise."

He gasped and shuddered. His hands fell away from mine and I knew that I held a dead man.

I laid him down gently, closed his eyes, and folded his arms across his breast. Sober, I should have wept a little, prayed a little, indulged in some sombre thoughts. As it was, I fumbled my way through the dusky purple twilight towards my wineskin, thinking wryly that I had done more than fulfil my orders to hold his hands. I had held him in my arm and sped him with a lie. I knew, I understood nothing of what he had tried, too late, to tell me.

XVII

Next morning while I was making arrangements for the funeral I heard the explanation of the sound of horses which I had heard overnight. Conrad, Marquis of Montferrat, had been murdered as he rode along a street in Tyre, and his widow, acting, she said, on his instructions, had come to put herself under Richard's protection. Despite this fact, by afternoon the whole camp was humming with the rumour that the assassin who struck the blow had been hired by the King of England.

Men seemed to find that very easy to believe. "No more than the deserter deserved," they said. Or, "God help Burgundy, then, riding alongside him to Damascus." Nobody stopped to ask why, of all the deserters, Conrad should be singled out. Philip of France was safe in Paris, Leopold of Austria in Vienna; no far-reaching vengeance had overtaken them. Nobody remembered Conrad's feud with the Old Man of the Mountain or the little threatening cake. Richard's enemies gladly seized upon this further evidence of his bloody-mindedness, and his friends almost as openly rejoiced that the taking of vengeance had begun, and so successfully.

A few Burgundians hurried off towards Damascus in order to warn their duke. The English and Aquitainians veered like weathercocks and expressed bald-headed belief in Richard's innocence and hurried off to prevent the carrying of the calumnious story. They overtook the Burgundians at Chorazin, and there the last blows of the doomed campaign were dealt, in the deadliest, bloodiest battle of all, a battle never mentioned by the minstrels, fought to the death among men with the Cross on their shoulders. The vultures did well out of that rumour. They were still busy when Alberic of Saxham and I reached Chorazin.

Alberic of Saxham had landed at Acre at noon of the third day after Raife's death. He had asked to be directed to the King of England's tent and, following his instructions, had duly arrived there to find me, its sole occupant, sleeping through the noonday heat. He shook me roughly, demanding to know where he could find the King, and I told him what anyone else could have told him, that the King was in Damascus.

"And where be the Bishop of Salisbury?"

"With the King," I said.

"And which way do this Damascus be?" he asked.

By that time I was fully awake and staring. I saw a squat, dishevelled little man, his hair and beard stiff and encrusted with salt, his face scorched and peeling with sunburn. He looked, he spoke, he stood and moved like a pedlar, a tinker, or a smith, but he was attended and accoutred like a nobleman, and he bore credentials and a letter for Richard from no less a person than the Queen Mother. He showed me the letter. "Urgent," he said. "I promised to carry it faster than ever a letter had ever been carried before, and so far as I can make out I have made the journey in ten days less than ever it was done before. So now if you'd be so good as to point out the general direction and tell me where I can hire some horses I'll be gone."

I made a sudden and, as it proved, momentous decision.

"If you like," I said, "I will ride with you and show you the way. I've never been to Damascus, but I've mapped it often enough to know. And I doubt very much if we shall find horses." Richard and the other lords had taken the pick of the mounts in camp, the Burgundian knights had taken sixty more, and the following force had actually ridden out knowing themselves outnumbered but with every horse that could be mustered. "We might get mules," I said.

"All's one to me." He turned his shaggy head and looked contemptuously at his little train, two squires and four pages.

"Let you and me go by ourselves, young man," he said. "They're all bone-weary; there's been times when, what with their being sick and being tired and always wanting regular food, I've been ashamed they should bear my coat of arms." That made me look a little curiously at the sign emblazoned on the pages' bright orange backs; it showed a bulging pedlar's pack bristling with knights' lances, very original and peculiar.

"I'll go and hire the mules," I said, "while you take some refreshment. But—I shall need some money."

"I don't need no refreshment, no more than I carry with me. Young man, I'm ready to move."

A very precipitate little man, most suitable messenger between Plantagenet mother and son.

Within half an hour, mounted on mules, we were trotting along the road to Damascus.

I was very glad to get out of Acre. Ever since Raife's death, with no bounden duty to hold me in the camp, I had been subject to temptation to go into town, to stroll past the white palace, to linger and stare at its doorways, its open, vine-shrouded verandahs. Now and again the temptation would assume a very reasonable face and I would think that I ought to visit the Lady Anna, who had always written to me kindly and faithfully. Fortified by much wine, my determination had held for three days, but they had been long days. And when Conrad's widow had come riding in haste from Tyre in order to obey the Marquis's last wish and to put herself under Richard's protection, and every idle curious man in the camp had gone to stare at the palace in the hope of catching a glimpse of her, I had almost gone too; it would have been so easy to stand in the packed, anonymous crowd. . . .

Now I was safe, with the mule's nimble hooves putting distance between me and the source of temptation. And presently something almost forgotten began to nag at my mind, a welcome distraction. We were on the road to Damascus; the road to Damascus. Why had that such a familiar and significant sound? I picked over the thought. It was the road to Emmaus where the risen Christ had walked with two of his disciples all through the day and their eyes were holden so that they did not recognise him. Emmaus, not Damascus. And yet the road to Damascus seemed to mean something more than a mere matter of direction.

Alberic of Saxham rode thoughtfully, too, and I was a little startled when he said abruptly:

"I must be getting old; there's things I disremember."

"I'm flogging my mind at this moment to remember something," I said. "With me I'm afraid drunkenness, not age, is to blame."

"No, you're still young, ain't you, despite all that white hair? That's what's bothering—— By God's footstool!" he said, and slapped his thigh so that his mule, out of hard experience of threatening noises, leapt forward frantically. And I thought, Light has broken for him! Which thought immediately prodded my memory, and I knew what had been nagging in me. It was on this road, the road to Damascus, that St. Paul had been blinded by a great light and known conversion. It might have been, I thought with a little chill and thrill of the blood, this identical spot.

When my mule caught up with Alberic's I thought he looked at me very queerly, but he said nothing.

Outside Chorazin the darkness which here, even in summer, came suddenly fell on us and we halted as soon as we found water. The Lord of Saxham shared with me the bread and cheese he carried in his pouch, chiding me for lack of foresight in coming on a journey without provisions. "Never count on nothing that ain't in your very hand; that's my motto," he said.

"If you substituted 'pack' for 'hand' and put it into Latin," I said, "it would go well with your coat of arms." I spoke jestingly, but he took it seriously.

"So it would. That'd look well and do credit to an unlettered man like me. I'll get it set out."

"I'll set it out now," I said, and amused myself for the last moment or two before sleep came by shaping and reshaping the motto. When I had reduced it to "Count only certainties" I was content and slept.

Next morning in Chorazin we managed to buy flat meal cakes and fresh fruit and I said, "Certainties are good, but sometimes the unexpected has more flavour."

He laughed, only half in agreement. "Unexpected. That's me with Saxham Manor, and carrying messages for royalty. And along of you, of all people." He gave me another queer look.

So, talking of this and that, we jogged along and presently saw in the distance a haze of sun-gilded dust. The leaders of the dead crusade were returning to Acre.

They made a splendid sight in the clear hot sunshine, for they had put on all their finery for their visit to Saladin, and as they bore down upon us they looked like a glittering, many-coloured wave coming up to engulf us. And we, to them, looked like two shabby travellers, mule-mounted, blocking the way. True, Alberic of Saxham had clothes which, closely inspected, hinted at rank, but they were soiled and dusty and creased from being slept in, and I was exactly as I had risen from half-drunken stupor the previous noonday, save that I had wound a length of cloth about my head to shield it from the sun.

One or two of the young attendant knights rode straight at us, shouting and indicating by gestures that we should make way for our betters. But Alberic pulled his mule broadside across the narrow way and raised his arm, and then his by no means negligible voice, and announced that he had a letter for His Majesty of England. The first riders of the cavalcade parted company and edged their horses past us, and then there was Richard, surly and grim-faced, staring down as he reined in and asked, "Who called for me?" And a man in full armour—I never saw his face or knew his name—pushed his horse forward, saying, "Beware, sire. Remember what I told you." But by that time Richard had recognised me. His face lightened.

"Why, Blondel," he said, "did you also come to bring me warning?"

Before I could speak Alberic of Saxham said in his blunt way:

"No, my liege, he came to show me the way. I bring you a

322

letter from your mother." Most oddly his voice reduced everything to bare essentials; Eleanor's long lineage, great heritage, two kingdoms, and all the rest were eclipsed by the fact that at one time she had, in the common way of females, conceived and borne a son. "Your mother" said all that. And he dug in his pouch and produced the letter which was, I saw with all a scribe's horror, no little soiled by its close contact with the cheese.

Richard took off his pearl-encrusted gloves and carefully with a movement of his finger waved on those whom his halting had checked. As Hubert Walter drew level, he called to him, "Walter, news from England." And my lord of Salisbury reined in, and the man in armour pulled his horse into line on Richard's other side.

Richard took off his pearl-encrusted gloves and carefully broke the seal of the letter, peeled off its outer covering with the greasy marks on it, and read—dourly at first, frowning, biting his lip. Then suddenly he laughed as he had not laughed since that evening in Bethany.

"Read that, Walter! My little brother is so anxious to take up my leavings that he even proposes to marry the French princess!"

Hubert Walter, for all his soldierly demeanour, was a scholar. His eyes ran over the letter quickly.

"My lord," he said as he reached the end, "this is grave news indeed." He lifted his eyes and looked at his master, his stunned look shot through with commiseration.

"Grave news," Richard agreed. But nobody but a fool could help seeing that the news had already restored and reinvigorated him.

"Most fortunately," said Walter, pursuing the obvious line of thought, "we are about to go home." He looked at Richard again and then quickly away. I saw the white shadow of fury creep about his lips. "I never coveted the papal throne till this moment," he said vehemently; "I'd like to excommunicate them both!"

Richard gave his great hearty barking laugh again.

"That would hurt Philip! Not John—he excommunicated himself years ago. But never mind." The laughter left his face. He brooded, urged his horse forward, and rode for a while in silence. "Listen, Walter," he said at last, "since the moment I landed and Baldwin died you have been my right hand, my right eye. On all matters save the most trivial we have been in accord. Do you now as I bid you without question or argument. Embark all the men and every bit of gear that can possibly be carried, and bring them to Dover. Give my Queen and my sister again into Stephen de Turnham's charge. Garrison Acre, and on your way home call in on Guy of Cyprus. Talk to him, tell him everything, make him feel that though he may *seem* abandoned, a last outpost—you know, Walter, brace him, link him with Acre and the pilgrim road. And, Walter, Jonathan of Adana owes me forty crowns which I lent him at Jaffa. Collect that, and then pay Algenais what I borrowed from him." He smiled, lifting his face and blinking the dust out of his eyes. "I can think of nothing else to bother you with, Walter, my good friend. If I could make you Pope, by Christ's Cross, I would, but I do here and now appoint you in Baldwin's place. My lord of Canterbury, will you graciously perform the petty duties I am compelled to leave to your care?"

He had spoken the last sentences very disarmingly, showing, for a man of his kind, surprising sensitiveness to the fact that his hearer might think he was asking a heavy service but offering a substantial reward. That was, indeed, a fact, but he had most astonishingly been first to realise it and had cloaked it with a lightness which none but a churl would have disregarded.

Hubert Walter said, "And you were the man who disapproved of knighting men on the battlefield! Hadn't you best keep your bishopric until the errands are done, sire? And in the meantime, where do you intend to be yourself?"

"In England," Richard replied. "I'm going to surprise them. I can't, in the circumstances, go as I'd like, by sea to Marseilles and through France—they know that. They'll imagine me buffeting round the coast of Spain and through Biscay Bay, and I shall be upon them weeks before they expect me! I shall go by ship to Trieste and overland through Augsburg and Mainz and so down the Rhine. The shortest road and the quickest."

He spoke and looked as though he were well pleased with this plan, a little like a juggler who has performed a difficult-seeming trick with skill and success. His glance at Hubert Walter invited his approval. None came, and the bishop's highly coloured, hard-textured face took on a look as near horror as possible.

"You must be sun-struck!" he said roughly. "Or have you got—unbeknownst to me—on such new good terms with the Archduke of Austria as will make you welcome in his domain and in the Emperor's?"

"I'm not looking for a welcome. Nor will they be looking

for me. I'll go as a pilgrim, or a merchant. . . ." He turned his head to where I rode a little too close to his horse's flank, held there by curiosity. Expecting, deserving rebuke, I drew off a little, but he beckoned me and grinned the old boyish grin which I had not seen for many a day. "I'll take Blondel. We'll be strolling players, maybe. And that reminds me, Walter, I shall want all the money you can lay hands on."

"You won't get a penny," said Walter, his voice and manner too grimly concerned to be lacking in respect; indeed, making respect seem a trivial thing. "Nor," he went on, plainly using the argument as he forged it, "will you rush off on such a wildcat scheme, leaving me responsible for the army's safe return and making it look as though I had connived at your mad idea. I'm not going back to England to face the charge of being the biggest Judas of the lot and encouraging you to walk into enemy country."

Richard threw him a sidelong, very foxy look. Quite jovially he said, "It's a sound plan. But tell me, Walter, if I adhere to it, what will you do?"

Walter was not deceived by the jovial tone; his face, as he turned it towards his master, was the face of a man defying a known peril. The flesh of his firm red cheeks twitched, but he eyed Richard with a steady, level stare and then said:

"I should put you under restraint, my lord. There are still five or six sound men in Acre and even more who, if not ardent in the crusade, are neither dupes nor rogues. And rather than see you walk into that viper's nest, we would restrain you as a person no longer responsible for his actions. After all, sire, if you were mad with fever it would be our duty to prevent you from doing yourself a fatal injury—and this plan of yours is as mad as anything a fever-crazed brain could suggest."

I waited for the roaring rage—thereby proving that, though I thought I knew Richard well, I still had much to learn.

"In short," he said, "in your opinion my plan is suicidal and you would hold me back from it as you would from any other form of that sin?"

"That was exactly my meaning," Walter said. He was not lulled by his master's apparent reasonableness; his cheeks twitched more violently and the colour had drained out of them, leaving them pale and hard with a red streak here and there, like suet, horrible.

"Your wimple's all crooked, old woman," Richard said, and cackled with laughter. Then with disconcerting abruptness his voice and manner changed. In a quiet deadly way he began to recount the names of all those who had failed him, the number of times he had been thwarted since he had set foot in Palestine. Listening, I realised that nothing, not the smallest thing, had escaped his notice during the past year. Little incidents, chance words of which at the time he had appeared to take no notice or had smiled over—every one had been marked and remembered and added to the great burden of bitterness which lay on his heart. His powers of observation and of memory outdistanced mine by twice as much as mine outdistanced those of the dullest footman in all that army. I was amazed. The sour account of motives misinterpreted, orders misunderstood or disobeyed, insults, slights, outright treachery lasted for some minutes; then he ended it with the words: "And now that my brother and my one-time ally are conspiring together to take my kingdom, you, my lord of Salisbury, who once declared that you would follow me to hell, threaten to treat me as a madman because I make a plan to circumvent them quickly!"

Walter was unshaken. "My lord," he said, "if so it seems to you, so it must. And you *are* a madman if you can't see that if you set foot in Austria or Germany, alone and unattended, your brother John stands a good chance to take your kingdom, not by force, by inheritance."

We rode for a while in silence. Then Richard said, "You are doubtless right, Walter. I have noticed that, save in the heat of battle, you err on the side of overcaution, but your judgement is sound. I will go by the long sea road."

The suety look on Walter's face vanished, engulfed by a flush of triumphant relief. Richard's voice had sounded surly and grudging, but I noticed that he did not wear the furious thwarted look which I had seen on these occasions when he had been compelled to give way to another's judgement. Innocently I attributed this to the fact that Hubert Walter was the one man of whose integrity and good will he was, at heart, utterly certain. And I was glad, because I was in agreement with every word my lord of Salisbury had uttered.

XVIII

Of that last busy, crowded hour in Acre I remember only certain isolated moments.

One was when Richard walked into his tent and looked towards the place where Raife's bed had been. The corner

326

was empty now, for I had cleared away every reminder of him. I had even rolled up and stored out of sight the maps he had helped to make. Yet he was there, an all but tangible presence at that moment.

"Was it easy?" Richard asked.

"Very easy."

"Yes, they say death deals gently with those life has used hard. God rest him in peace." Under the hot canvas the silence gathered, positive, pulsating. Then Richard broke into the old shouting, bustling energy; admirable order weaving its pattern through apparent chaos; one clear mind directing a great mindless activity.

Another memorable moment was that when those few who had been informed of his imminent departure came to take leave of him. Long ago I had seen the first candle gutter and die with Philip's departure; I had seen in Bethany the crusade's requiem. I had imagined that with the treaty of Damascus even the ghost had been laid. But I was wrong. The stricken, poisoned, ailing spirit of the Third Crusade woke and stirred and bled and suffered once more, and then died forever as men crowded about Richard to touch, to kiss his hand and take leave of him.

They were not all his friends; they were not by any means all ardent crusaders, but they were all touched, all illumined by this last dying light. It was the gleam that cries, tragic, irreconcilable, out of each day's sunset. It was the end.

The mind of man is a thing of infinite mystery. There I was, huddled in the tent corner, very thoroughly drunk, thinking of the evening when he had sung about Jerusalem and the evening cry had broken on my ears for the first time and I had given him my idea for the mangonel; thinking of the first gloom and the gathering gloom and the night in Bethany when we had all said, "*This* crusade is over."

But I was, with all this in one part of my mind, very calmly and very neatly writing letters. One to Anna Apieta, explaining how, what with nursing Raife and going towards Damascus as guide to Alberic of Saxham, I had had no time to visit the palace. The other was to my lady to let her know that I was still fulfilling her bidding and was leaving with the King and would, to the best of my ability, take care of him. They both sounded, when I read them over, cold, stilted, and impersonal.

I was writing them when Richard put his hand on my shoulder and said, "I am going now to take leave of the ladies. Will you come with me or meet me at the harbour in half an hour?" And again my mind split asunder—one half clamouring that I must see her, just for one moment, for one last time; the other half stubborn and cold as clay, repeating the arguments for holding apart.

"I shall be at the harbour," I said.

"The ship is the *St. Josef*."

"I know," I said. "I shall be there."

I folded and sealed my letters. I gave them and my last gold coin to the page I trusted. Then I walked down to the harbour. The crusade, the Holy Land, my lady, all left behind; an episode, an experience ended. So we press on into the eventual, the inevitable dark, with the frail barrier of days between us and the grave lessened by one. . . .

When Richard joined me his mood was cheerful; his thoughts all centred on the journey; his interest engaged by the ship, the speed she could make, the signs of the weather. When we had been aboard for an hour he broke to me the news that we were not, after all, bound for the long voyage by sea but heading north for Armenia and the old overland road by which so many crusaders and pilgrims had travelled in the past.

I realised then that part of his cheerfulness was due to the fact that he had outwitted Hubert Walter, that faithful friend and servant who would sooner have called him mad and put him in chains than see him set out on such a dangerous venture.

XIX

This sudden departure from Palestine and the secret change of route are responsible for the mystery, the confusion, and the contradictory stories which surround this period of Richard Plantagenet's career. Two years later at the Diet of Hagenau, when his enemies were pressing and his friends refuting the accusation of his culpability in Conrad of Montferrat's murder, a great deal was made of the fact that he had left Palestine at a moment's notice, and without ceremony. "He so feared," said one witness, "the vengeance of the marquis's family and friends that he dared not remain so long as to see his own Queen safely embarked." And there is no doubt that such a statement did carry weight with ordinary level-headed, conventional-minded men, to whom the idea of rushing across half the world, unarmed, unattended, in an

328

attempt to save a throne from two well-established enemies, did seem too fantastic for credence. Fortunately there was Hubert Walter's evidence of Eleanor's letter having been delivered and of Richard's having gone, unarmed and alone, to the women's palace, where Conrad's wife had taken shelter with the Queen of England and where nigh on two hundred of Conrad's adherents who had escorted her were installed.

These facts, having been dealt with in the open court, have found their way into the records of the historians. The minstrels, deeming them dull, generally omit them from the songs and stories. They concern themselves more closely with what they call Richard's disappearance. And almost invariably they sing of shipwreck. That is understandable. Richard left Acre with the professed intention of taking ship for England. Hubert Walter and every one of those nobles who had taken leave of him on that sad afternoon (and who could deny that there was any deliberate "secrecy" about that hasty departure) understood that he was bound for one of his own Cinque Ports. Then he disappeared and was next heard of in the middle of Europe. Why? The simple answer—he was shipwrecked. For a long time—until, in fact, I was in a position to do so—nobody save the master and crew of the *St. Josef,* who seemed never to have been heard of again, was capable of contradicting this story, and by that time the songs, spreading from mouth to mouth, had sped the tale of a shipwreck beyond easy recall. So to this day they sing, "Alas, off Istria's rocky coast, a fearful storm did rise . . ."

Actually we sailed through the placid golden October weather of Seleucia, where we bought two horses and a supply of food and rode off without delay.

It was a curious and in many ways a pleasant interlude. For me travel always brings a kind of suspension of thought and feeling. I can move, a detached, rootless creature without past or future, living as I am inclined to think the only really happy people always do, in and for the immediate moment. I had learned that when I was on the road with Stefan, and again on the roads in the Holy Land. Only when I am still do my thoughts overtake me, and when they become too unbearable my immediate impulse is to run away. So, but for one thing, this could have been an almost perfect journey.

The country was wild and lonely but very beautiful, and those few people with whom we came in contact as we bought food for ourselves and our horses were not unfriendly. There had been hostility in the past, but the traffic between the West and the Holy Land had been heavy enough in the last two generations for the natives to learn that a dead robbed pilgrim or a murdered stripped crusader gives only brief profit, deters other travellers, and sometimes invites sharp retaliation. Better to smile and sell at vast prices.

I cannot, for the life of me, understand why I have this pricking necessity to tell the truth. It does no good, serves no purpose. I could so easily say: And so we rode from Seleucia in Armenia to Eedburg in Austria. I could describe the good sunny weather, the way we halted at night and hobbled the horses, ate our supper, and rolled in our cloaks to sleep, to wake, refreshed and ravenous, and so on again. I could speak of the castles that crowned the heights and overlooked the road; some of them ruined, abandoned relics of other crusades—all that and more I could tell.

But all this record has been made truthfully, and I have set down everything as it appeared to me at the time. If I slur now or evade, this last portion, which I wrote for my own satisfaction, will fit on the rest as ill as an unmatching patch on a coat. And since it explains so many things, truth here is necessary as well as expedient.

Here, then, it is. On the second night out from Seleucia I learned exactly what it was that Raife of Clermont had tried to tell me on his deathbed, and I knew exactly why Richard Plantagenet had no love for or need of his wife.

I swear I did not know until then.

When Anna Apieta set me to write the story of this crusade I knew that in common justice what I learned at the end must not influence the beginning, and I have been meticulous to set down everything as it appeared to me, in my innocence, at the time when it happened. Now I look back, scrutinising what I have written, and hope that I have been just. It seems to me now, of course, incredible that I could have been so blind and stupid, especially over the matter of Raife of Clermont; but I honestly thought that Richard favoured him first out of pity for his long captivity and then because he was useful and a good knight; and when the grey horse was transferred to Raife I saw no more significance in the transfer than I had in the original gift. I have tried, as I wrote, to re-enter that state of blind ignorance. I have tried to be fair. But is fairness in recounting enough? How about fairness of thought? Now, in these quiet years, when the shock and revulsion of that moment seem as far removed from me as the mood of fury in which I struck down the

330

Saracen horseman, I ask myself: Was he to blame because he had an inclination towards men rather than towards women? Surely no man would choose it any more than he would choose to be deformed, or cowardly, or diseased. . . .

It is very easy to condemn: it is indeed wiser and safer to condemn. One's own immunity from taint is better established by loud protestations of horror and disgust than by speculation or attempts to understand.

What does puzzle me about it all is the inescapable sense of shame which attends even the thought of the subject. It is, we say, "against nature"—but then so are so many things: patricide, matricide, infanticide—yet the mention of them brings no blush to the cheek. True, it is sterile, it defies God's order to "be fruitful and multiply," but the same is true of all monastic and conventual vows which are considered most honourable. It is not forbidden in the Ten Commandments; nor does it take rank with the seven deadly sins. Yet in all but its addicts it violates some deep instinct and starts a recoil which even pity, even curiosity cannot mitigate. Not that the addicts escape shame. The difficulty of approach, the constant danger of rebuff, the constant risk of mockery are all pregnant with shame. So different from the normal procedure; for even at that low level where the coupling of man and woman is free and easy and not a matter of family or social procedure a girl can rebuff a man and he can laugh and say, "She would have none of me," and be lowered neither in his own esteem nor in that of his small world. And the way to a girl's bed is usually so well posted with familiar signs, with soft or provocative glances, sweet words or kind gestures, that none but a man set on folly need err therein. But this outlaw path is necessarily blind and leads to scenes like the one I shared, fantastic to partake in, most horrible to remember.

When everything had been made plain between us, I—for some quite inexplicable reason—was afflicted by a sense of guilt. I began to remember with painful clarity all the times when he had been kind to me and had shown me favour or indulgence. I was conscious, as it were, of a burden of undischarged debt; and that in turn made me angry. I owed him nothing, I told myself savagely. If he had all along been mistaken in me, that was his affair, and why should I, on this score at least utterly innocent, feel guilty? But it would not be so summarily dismissed. The feeling of having failed him nagged at me, and I kept remembering Raife's last words. And then my mind took the most perverse turn of all and I

331

began to reckon his many virtues, his great courage, his justice, his attention to detail, his lively mind, his fortitude in adversity; even the fact that he was, when he chose, a minstrel without peer leapt up to give me a sharp stab. I had always preserved a sense of proportion in my attitude towards him, had never fallen into the state of hero worship as so many diverse kinds of men had done. In the great days of his triumphs and resounding exploits some corner of my mind had stayed sour. Now in the days of his failure, with his fatal weakness exposed, my cursed minnesinger's art set to work on him and I saw him as a great man, a hero—rebuffed by a sniffling, prudish little lute player.

I could not explain why I felt guilty towards him, but one evening, lying on the verge of sleep and thinking over the matter, I did understand with a shock of surprise why it was that I could now admire him without reserve. It was very simple. I was no longer jealous of him. As simple as that. In the eyes of the world he was Berengaria's husband, but she could never belong to him as a woman should belong to a man. He was no more capable of enjoying her than I was. Therefore, my body could forgive him, and my mind, following suit, could admit that he was the best knight, the most inspired commander, the grandest minstrel of his day.

Whereupon my sick sense of guilt swelled larger.

We rode on together. There was now a coolness, a consciousness of the unspoken thing between us, and our eyes were reluctant to meet. Three days' ride out from Seleucia I choked out an inquiry whether he would prefer to ride on alone.

He said, "Bless you, boy, no!" And it occurred to me that perhaps this uncomfortable situation was not unfamiliar to him. Well past his thirtieth year, he might have met many similar rebuffs.

We reached Styria, and there the good weather broke and a furious, bone-searching wind from the north blew rain and sleet in our faces. We were obliged to abandon our habit of sleeping in any handy sheltered place and take to lying at inns, always filthily dirty and exorbitant in their charges. Retiring became a matter of embarrassment to me; so often there was only one bed and so seldom a third traveller. Perhaps Richard guessed; he always made a great show of tiredness, stretching and yawning and declaring that he should sleep as soon as his head touched the pillow. And one day as we talked on the road—for we did still talk, quite avidly at times—out of a conversation, I think about army discipline, the word "rape" cropped up.

"With that," Richard said with complete calmness, "I have naturally no sympathy at all. Even along my own line I consider reciprocity to some degree desirable." And he looked me in the face and laughed. So set your mind on that score, boy, the look said. I felt silly and shamed.

I was shamed again, and perhaps with better reason, outside Graz. Richard grumbled blasphemously about the weather but said it was healthier than the heat of Palestine and seemed immune to it, but I developed the worst cold I have ever had. My bones ached, my nose and eyes dripped rheumily, my head ached, and great hammers beat in my ears. Dreading his sympathy more than his scorn, I made as little of my affliction as possible, but he noticed and at the first inn we reached after midafternoon he said, "We'll stay here. What you need is a brick to your feet and some mulled wine."

There was a hind in the yard, and we left the horses to his care; usually I saw them safely stabled and fed. Richard himself mulled the wine while the woman of the house heated the brick.

In the morning I was much better, but our horses had vanished. Whether they had been stolen or whether, as the innkeeper protested in dumb show, insecurely stabled and had wandered, no one could say with any surety. The stable was certainly nothing more than a piece of thatch supported by two posts, and I should have hobbled the horses before leaving them there. On the other hand, horses tend to huddle into any shelter.

Richard was furious but restrained himself from violence because of the unwisdom of drawing too much attention to himself. The landlord, with wide gestures, invited him to search the whole village, which he did, very thoroughly, anxious to find, if not our horses, some horses capable of carrying us on the next stage of our journey. But there was not a horse in the whole village. Four draught oxen, six cows, and an incredibly agéd donkey which worked a water wheel were all the livestock, Richard reported. And, "Shall I buy the donkey?" he asked. "It could carry you today, I *think*."

I protested that I could walk. The landlord, putting himself into the attitude of a child riding a hobbyhorse, bobbed up and down and said, "Eedburg. Eedburg." We understood that to mean that at Eedburg we should find horses. A very precise and accurate piece of information it was, too; what he did not convey to us in mime was that Eedburg was seventy-five miles distant.

At Eedburg there were horses—we saw six in a field—and the rain clouds lifted to let through the sun, and the road forked. Three good things. We had been alert for the fork in the road, for the road which ran westwards to Augsburg and the Rhine; and now here it was. Eedburg lay in the fork with an inn of some size and substance lying at the point of the V, and on the far side of the right-hand road, which led to Vienna, there was a field with six horses in it. A wall of roughly piled stones separated the field from the road, and we leaned on it for a moment, looking at the horses. Then Richard straightened himself, set his hand under my arm, and propelled me towards the inn. He called for mulled wine and, when it came, lifted his cup and said, "You have walked valiantly."

Then he said, "If horses are as rare as they seem hereabouts we shall need money." And he opened the plain leather pouch which hung at his plain leather belt and began to count out his coins. Then, sweeping them together, he said:

"Losing the horses and having to walk has delayed us somewhat. Passages down the Rhine will cost money, and by that time news may have leaked. We might need money in a hurry. Better be prepared. I have two salable things—" He broke off and smiled at me. "You don't carry a secret hoard, by any chance?" I confessed my complete dearth of money.

"I have these," he said, flattening his gloves out on the dirty table, "and my belt." His hand went to his waist, where under the leather belt, under his tunic, lay the embroidered belt which Berengaria had worked for him during the long time of waiting. It was made of blue velvet, stiffened with a length of woven horsehair, and lined with soft leather. The embroidery was done in gold and silver thread, and a pattern of pearls and sapphires was worked all round it. I remembered how she had brooded over the design, how diligently she had stitched, how she had overlooked the craftsman who pierced the needle holes in the stones and finally sacrificed her diamond brooch to make the clasp. It would be a pity, I thought, to sell it before the need for money was more urgent.

"This is a small place," I said. "The belt would not fetch its price here."

"The gloves, then," he said, and looked at them with affection and regret. I looked, too, and realised that, once fine, they were now shabby from long wear. Made of tough goatskin, well cut, firmly sewn, they were still shapely and whole, but the palms were scored and scruffed, and in several places on the pearl-embroidered backs threads had worn through so that pearls had been lost and the pattern broken. Struck by the same thought, Richard took out his knife and carefully severed some of the loose-hanging threads.

"My one finery," he said. "It goes against the grain to part with them." And again his hand went to his waist. Remembering the considerable amount of gold still in his pouch, and bearing in mind that his notions about money, especially where his personal expenditure was concerned, were warped by a panic niggardliness, I asked, "Is it necessary to sell them *now?* In such a small town, and while you still have money?"

"I look ahead. This is no time to be sentimental," he said.

"Then I will go out and sell them," I offered, laying my hands hastily on the gloves. "You might be noticed."

The market place lay a little back from the Vienna road. I tried first a booth where decorative trinkets were for sale, and a gnomelike little man, as soon as he saw that I was anxious to sell, not to buy, waved his arms and drove me off with what sounded like curses, as though I were a straying bullock. On the other side of the open square I found a booth where leather articles are displayed. There a more agreeable man took the gloves, turned them about, nodding his head over the pearls, shaking it over the worn palms and the places where the threads had given way.

As he hesitated a man, plainly a citizen of some substance and importance, crossed the square and approached the booth. He was a short, thickset man, dressed in velvet, and he was followed by three little dogs, the like of which I had never seen before. Their bodies were half as long again as those of ordinary dogs, their legs very short, the front ones bowed. They had flap ears, bright intelligent eyes, and their hides were so smooth and sleek and shining that they, too, seemed velvet-clad. Fantastic as unicorns.

The booth owner, with a significant glance at me, laid down the gloves and turned his attention to the newcomer. The little dogs surged about me, and I bent over them as they scrabbled at my hose with their overlarge blunt paws. When I straightened myself again the owner of the dogs had Richard's gloves in hand and was studying them with every sign of approval. He and the booth holder were conversing in their own language, and though I understood no word I gathered that he had come in search of just such gloves. Finally he opened his pouch, took out two gold pieces, held

335

them up inquiringly, and then laid them on the edge of the booth. It was twice as much as any reasonable person could have hoped to make from the sale, and I was delighted, but hesitant. The man who lived by making and selling leather goods should, I felt, have a picking. But the dog owner turned and strutted away across the square, and the booth owner lifted his shoulders, spread his hands, and smiled. I took up the coins, thanked him, and made my way back to the tavern. At the door I became aware that one of the little dogs had followed me. I bent over, touched the velvet head, where the skin was all puckered into wrinkles of bewilderment or concentration, and said, "Go home. Go back to your master," and waved my hand in a gesture of dismissal. Then I went in.

"Well?" Richard asked.

"I sold them. And very well. They chanced to fit a passing citizen with a full purse." Rather proudly I laid the two gold pieces on the table.

"I don't need them now. Perhaps it would be as well if you carried them, Blondel," Richard said. "I thought just now, when you said you had nothing, what would have happened if some ill chance had parted us?"

"I have my lute. I can always sing for my supper."

"True. Nevertheless, pouch the glove money and hold it against our need. I'll go now and bargain for the horses."

"I'll go," I said. For throughout all this journey I had never been quite easy in my mind when we were stationary and people were able to look at him closely. Everywhere I looked for the flicker of wonder, of recognition. His looks were so remarkable, his fame so widespread, and old soldiers were everywhere. "I am, you must admit, a shrewd bargainer," I said, "and I do know a good horse when I see one."

"And you are blue with cold," Richard said. It may have been true; it was a sunny day, but a biting wind was blowing and I had shuddered as I stood waiting by the booth. "You stay here by the fire and finish the wine. I'll bring up the horses and whistle."

I gave way to temptation. Ever since I had set foot on the *St. Josef* I had been a little more sober than I liked to be. It was not that Richard would have minded, but he was, on the whole, a very abstemious man himself, and I could not with any seemliness outdrink him. So now, like a wallowing hog, I turned firewards and guzzled.

Once I heard the sound of hooves, but certainly no whistle; and though I hastily set down my cup, gathered my cloak round me, and made for the door, whoever had ridden by had disappeared by the time I had rounded the inn and looked first along one road and then the other. Anxiety began to gnaw at me. I reminded myself that Richard was a hard bargainer and that time always seems long when one is waiting. I went back to the fire, kicked a dry log into a blaze, and thought that I would not begin to worry until it was consumed. It blazed, it became a hollow red shell, it fell apart into pinkish dust. Then I got up and went out, straight to the field where we had seen the horses. There were now five in the field, their tails and manes streaming out on the wind.

A few of those to whom I have told my story seemed inclined to blame me for not making more fervent and thorough inquiries at this point. But even as I plodded through the sticky mud towards the house which stood at the far end of the field where the horses grazed, something which in the circumstances wore every aspect of truth bore down on me. The King had decided to travel on alone.

I could give myself several good reasons for his action.

I was now little but an embarrassment to him; it was my cold in the head which had made him curtail a journey and lose our horses; he believed that he was short of money.

And besides reasons there was, I thought, evidence. Insisting on leaving me at the inn while he went to do the bargaining; insisting that I keep the glove money because he had been wondering what I should do if we were parted . . . It all fitted in.

The door of the house was open when I arrived at it, and the man who sold horses and a woman whom I took to be his wife were standing together, heads bent, over a table. I saw them clearly as I lifted my hand and knocked at the door. The man turned about swiftly, defensively, placing himself before the woman, who fumbled on the table. I heard the clink of coins even as the man asked in his own tongue, which his expression made quite understandable, what the devil I wanted. I knew all about peasants and their secret hoards and I guessed that Richard had given a good price for the horse and that they were adding it to their savings and that their embarrassed, furtive looks were due to my having disturbed them. Face to face with the man who stood in the doorway as though keeping guard, I was aware of the curse of Babel. He could understand nothing. I pointed to the horses, held up one finger, patted my pouch, measured Rich-

337

ard's height on the doorpost, sketched an imaginary beard, all the time asking, "Man? Horse?" in French, German, Latin, and English because we had, along the road, found many natives who could at least recognise single words used by crusaders and pilgrims. This clown recognised none, did not even understand gestures. He just stared at me and looked at once surly and frightened.

Then the woman, who by this time had put away her hoard and recovered her composure, moved forward. She laid a rough brown hand on her man's shoulder and twisted him out of the doorway. I noticed her eyes, bright and brown as a bird's, intent on me as I went through all the gestures again. She took a second to consider and then, pulling herself up, she adopted a haughty look, touched a great beard, drew out her eyebrows, lifted her arm, measuring a giant's height on the wall, waved towards the horses, and held up all the fingers and the thumb of her left hand, the thumb of her right. Yes, six; did I understand there had been six horses? Then all tucked away save the first finger of her left hand, which she tapped with a finger of her right. See? One sold. Sold to a tall man with a great beard and bushy eyebrows. And to make everything plain she stepped out into the mud and pointed first towards the road to Vienna and vigorously shook her head, then to the road towards the Rhine and nodded with the same vigour.

And the bright brown eyes slid round towards her husband: you see, I understand, I could answer him. The clown's face was, after all, capable of some other expression besides surly fear; he looked at her now with admiration, not unmingled with doubt.

I smiled my thanks at her; she smiled back. Then, as though aware that she was wasting precious time, she stepped back briskly into the house and slammed the door.

I am not the first man to have been outwitted by a woman. But was I too easily deceived, too ready to receive proof of what I already felt to be true? It is so easy to be wise afterwards. Then it all seemed clear and logical. Richard had tired of our uneasy association; he thought that he would travel more swiftly and more cheaply alone. So he had left me enough money and gone on, fooling me as much as he had fooled Hubert Walter.

Five

Anna's House of Stone

Anna Apieta continues and closes the story.

WHEN THE LAST OF THE MASONS AND CARPENTERS had shouldered their tools and gone away, whistling, they left a great quiet and a feeling of finality.

Now that every stone was in place I could walk round and see, in its entirety, the house that I had built. I pretended that I was a stranger seeing the place for the first time; and when I had proceeded from the entrance gate with its neat porter's lodge, inwards until I stood in the garden which, backed by the birchwood and lovingly tended for the last five years, had an air of greater maturity than its age warranted, I stood and laughed aloud, so loud that the doves flew up and fluttered in fright.

This, I thought, is my house, my house of stone. And I remembered an old Navarrese saying, "Be careful what you set your heart on; you may get it!"

Always, ever since I was a young girl and realised the limitations and the possibilities of my condition, I had planned to build myself a house with a glass window and a garden and no awkward stairs. Then later I had planned that Blondel should be the architect and that he should live under my roof.

Well, there the house stood, the low sprawling roof shining in the June sunlight, and here was the garden, with little apples just forming on the trees and a pink rosebush in bloom and a clump of white lilies in bud and the lavender hedge growing spiky with flowers. And I knew just where I could find Blondel. Allowing for the errors inherent in every translation, this house, a translation from dream to actuality, might be regarded as the thing upon which I had set my heart.

I had meant to build a small cosy house in Apieta, and instead I had built a large and imposing house in Aquitaine. That was all. I had come nearer than most people ever do to attaining a heart's desire.

Nevertheless, there was something in my laughter that frightened the doves.

I remember exactly the moment when I abandoned my plan for building my house in Apieta. It was just after the hasty visit which Richard Plantagenet paid Berengaria in order to inform her that he was leaving for England within an hour and that she and her women were to return to Aquitaine under the care of Sir Stephen.

By this time it was plain to everyone, even to Joanna of Sicily, who was much torn between her sisterly loyalty and her fondness for her sister-in-law, that this marriage was a hopeless failure. Richard had given up all pretence of behaving like a husband. There had been three nights immediately after the wedding when they had retired together like any other married couple and been bedded. What happened then? Berengaria gave no clue; in her the dignity of the bride had never broken down into the half-obscene, half-lyrical confidences of the young wife. When Richard left Cyprus in haste for Acre she seemed to accept his reason; and when in Acre he camped with his men she accepted that too. It seemed not to occur to her that almost every other man in the crusading army could spare an hour now and then for his lusting, if not for his loving, and when finally Richard started his march to Jerusalem she was mainly concerned for his personal safety and took great comfort from the fact that Blondel was going with him.

We waited in Acre for more than twelve months in a state of infinite boredom. I lightened mine by studying Arabic, tutored by an old man who had been a prisoner in Saracen hands ever since Eleanor's crusade. Even with that as a hobby, and maintaining my custom of going out and about freely, just as I chose, I almost went mad with the heat and the monotony and the enclosed, dull, futile manner of life, and how the other women bore it I do not know. Blondel sent letters with all possible regularity; Berengaria seized on them, read them, and left me to write the replies. When the news—I thought it dreadful, heartbreaking, and yet dramatic —of the crusade's failure arrived, Berengaria said, "Then Richard will soon return."

Richard returned, but not to Berengaria's bed; he camped again amongst his men and paid her only a formal visit. I believe that during that visit and up to the moment when he left, hope had run high in her. She looked so beautiful, with that something of warmth and liveliness in her loveliness which only appeared when he was there.

But he left, with the courteous—and in other circumstances feasible—excuse that he had a good deal to see to before he left next morning for Damascus. When he had gone Berengaria retired and bolted the door against us.

Joanna, Pila, and I sat on the verandah as the sun went down and the breeze sprang up and the pleasantest hour in all the Eastern day arrived. Pila snatched up her embroidery and went on stabbing away with her needle long after it was too dark for her to see where she was placing the stitches. She had a bursting, choking look, and but for the way her eyes shone and the fury with which she plied her needle, I should have thought that she was struggling against the more violent and audible form of indigestion. Joanna, who was in love with Count Raymond Egidio, had learned a little earlier in the evening that Richard had given consent to the marriage; and she leaned on the marble rail that ran round the verandah and drifted away into a sweet lovesick dream. I sat and thought my own thoughts, about Blondel and Apieta. More stars pricked out one by one.

Finally Pila drove in her needle, folded her work as though crushing some obnoxious insect in its folds, and burst out:

"He may be your brother and I have no wish to hurt your feelings, but I think his conduct is infamous! Disgusting and infamous! What right has he, or any man, to shame a woman so, make her a laughingstock in front of the whole army?"

The word "brother," I was glad to think, absolved me from any need to consider myself addressed, so I sat quietly. I knew what I had heard, I knew what men were saying, but then my manner of life exposed me to street gossip. How much Pila had heard, or Joanna, I had no notion. The subject had never been opened amongst us, and I wondered what form this present conversation would take.

"You mean Richard and Berengaria," said Joanna, coming out of her dream. "Yes, it's such a pity, isn't it? They should have been so happy."

"A pity!" exclaimed Pila. "It's a crying scandal. He out there sleeping with his men, and she here, eating her heart out. Is that, I ask you, a marriage? It should be annulled. I shall tell her so. His Holiness is well known to be lenient in such cases."

"But—but Richard hasn't *done* anything. At least not *so* dreadful," Joanna faltered, rather unwillingly taking up the cudgels.

Pila let out one of those squeals of laughter which are the very voice of obscenity. It would have enlightened any but the most extremely innocent.

"Hasn't *done* anything," she repeated mockingly. "Isn't that what I'm complaining about? Isn't that why she, poor dear, is crying there within at this minute?"

"I know. I am sorry. But there isn't anything we can do, is there? I mean if she can't persuade—" I could sense rather than see the blush on Joanna's cheeks. She was older than I by some years, she had been married and widowed, but she

342

had retained a virginal mind, and the new courtship had made her even more like a girl.

She hasn't heard anything, I thought. Or, if she has, the meaning has escaped her. I made myself ready to deal with Pila.

"I never expected Richard to make a very *good* husband," Joanna went on in a gently worried voice. "He never cared much for women. He was one they never had to worry about in *that* way. My brother Harry had got him a bastard before he was fifteen, and Geoffrey seemed always to be falling in love with married women whose husbands resented it—but Richard never seemed to notice. Of course he's always been busy fighting and building and thinking about Jerusalem; and always with men. ...." She paused as Pila laughed again. "I can't see what is so funny, Pila. It's extremely sad never to have had time to take notice of women and to fall in love."

"Oh, it's *sad*, but it's also——"

"Pila!" I said sharply. She understood. "Sympathy with the Queen might be better expressed by the making of a cool sherbet drink than in futile discussion," I finished.

"I'll make it. I'll go. She'll be more likely to open to me," said Joanna, snatching at the opportunity of getting back to her dream.

"You know then. You've heard," Pila said eagerly while the curtains behind us still stirred from Joanna's passing.

"Long ago. But they don't know. And they are not to be told."

"Not to be told?" she said in a loud voice, jumping to her feet and coming to stand in front of me. "They should be told. Not that that mealymouthed little fool would understand, but Berengaria would. She isn't a fool—not deep down inside. She'd understand and then she could begin to get rid of him. I'm going to tell her myself. I won't see her crying her eyes out for a——!"

I could see that Pila was affected by the deep, very real disgust which some women do feel for this form of perversion. It makes them want to stamp on, to hurt the participators. Quite understandable; it threatens something that women stand for. It cuts out, disowns, disinherits them. And there is more to it than that. Women are fertile, this thing is sterile; they were put into opposition at the first moment of creation.

Easy for me, of course, to take an impartial, academic view.

I remembered that and said quite gently:

343

"Pila, I don't want Berengaria to know *now*. They've never had much chance. Now that the war is over, things will sort themselves out. Tomorrow he goes to Damascus to sign this treaty. Then he will come back and they will go on together to Europe. Let her hope, let her cry. Eventually he will either have to live with her as a man should live with his wife or admit—— It may come right. I wouldn't have a hasty word spoken even though you mean well, I know. But if you let so much as a hint drop, or a laugh in the wrong moment, Pila, I shall be very much annoyed."

"Oh," she said in a nasty voice, gladly bending her bow of spite in my direction. "And if *you* were annoyed it would be a grave pity, wouldn't it?"

"It would," I said quite lightly. "Because I should then make it my business to see that you didn't get the pension Father promised you."

"You couldn't——" she spluttered when she had dragged in her breath. "You wouldn't——"

"Try me," I said.

We waited again, and after a few days Richard came back from Damascus, dashed into the palace as a man might dash into a tavern, and was gone, taking ship to England, where affairs had reached a crisis which even the She-wolf couldn't handle. We women were to return to Europe under the care of Sir Stephen de Turnham.

They say that rats know instinctively when a ship is about to sink and go swarming away. Maybe there is always one rat who finds that the lines are cut, the anchor raised, and the shore already receding when he comes to make his escape. I was that rat.

Joanna Plantagenet wept at taking leave of her brother, and wept anew as she faced Berengaria, saying, "I shall stay with you until I marry, but now that Richard has given his consent, I might marry soon. Dear, dear Berengaria, I shall hate to leave you, but I must. . . ."

Berengaria kissed her. "Dear Joanna, we shall be together until we land. And I hope you will be very, very happy."

Carmelita, Duchess of Avosola, who had never been much more than a decoration to our household until she fell victim to the prevalent fever, was out of bed that day and came tottering out to the verandah to enjoy the evening air.

"So we are going home at last," she said. "God be praised. Sometimes I thought we should linger here until death released us. Now I can go home and look after my naughty Pepita." Her daughter Pepita had married a cousin of the brotherless, heirless King of Castile. "Three times while I have stayed here," said the duchess, raising three slim, fever-bleached fingers in the air and then dropping them languidly to her lap, "has she miscarried. She is sad beyond words. And worse, her husband grows impatient. I shall go home and see what she does wrong. Maybe she still takes little dogs in her lap, or goes hunting, or eats the flesh of cow or ewe or doe. Who can tell? I spoke my warnings before I left and I have written repeatedly, but she is so careless. She does not heed. However, now that I can go home———"

"Dear Carmelita," Berengaria said, "I am sure that with your wise guidance your daughter will bear a son, who, God willing, will rule Castile."

What an apt, gracious, knowledgeable little speech, I thought. Yet I swear that in ordinary circumstances one might have discussed Castile, its King, his cousins, and the order of succession for an hour in Berengaria's presence without rousing a flicker of interest or eliciting an intelligible word.

Pila said, "So we're going home. I hope that means to Pamplona."

"Aquitaine."

Pila went momentarily crazy. "Aquitaine?" she squealed. "You mean we wait again in Aquitaine? While he goes prancing off to England, Scotland, Brittany? And we wait, you wait, as we waited in Marseilles, in Brindisi, in Messina, in Cyprus, and here—here in Acre, over a year! I'll not do it," she said. "I'm going home, home to Navarre. And you'll come with me, and tell your father. We'll get a divorce. I'll help you. I'll write. I'll go with you to His Holiness if need be. We'll get a divorce."

"A divorce?" Berengaria spoke the word as though it were some new thing she had never heard of. "You seem to be beside yourself, Pila. If a little waiting—in the most comfortable circumstances, I would remind you—is so obnoxious to you, the last thing you should call yourself is lady in waiting. You have my leave to retire."

That was royally spoken. Pila went out, as Joanna and Carmelita had done, throwing me a dark look as she went.

And there were Berengaria and I alone together.

I had no wish to go to Aquitaine. I wanted to go to Apieta and build myself a little stone house with a glass window and a garden. I wanted Blondel to come with me, to plan the house and oversee the building and then settle down to overlook my small estate, share my books, make music for me, marry some plump pleasant girl, and have some children to whom I could be godmother.

I had kept myself informed of his whereabouts. I knew that he had not accompanied Richard to Damascus but had stayed to tend Raife of Clermont—the man whose name cropped up in all the stories about Richard; and I meant to sit down that very evening and write him a letter. I took great comfort from the knowledge that this time he had not hung about our household. I'd sent him to England, he'd come back; I'd taken him to Apieta, but no, he must go with her on crusade; I'd so contrived that she "gave" him to Richard, and now he'd been away for a year or more and hadn't even attempted to see her. He was cured. Now we could go to Apieta and begin our orderly, pleasant, permanent life.

Pila slammed the door behind her, and I drew a deep breath, making ready to be the last rat.

Berengaria stood very straight and still in the middle of the floor. I was a little sorry that I had allowed all the others to speak first, very conscious of being the last, most heartless deserter.

In what seemed to be one unbroken movement Berengaria took the veil from her head, ripped it into shreds, overturned a marble urn of lilies and kicked and stamped the flowers into a mash, and banged her head four times against the wall, so violently that she broke the skin on her temple and dribbles of blood ran down to fall plop-plop on her shoulder. And all over in a moment.

I was on my feet; I had seized her arm and hung on it with all my weight, swinging her away from the wall. But I was too late, and it was a gesture rather than an action.

"It's all right, Anna. I had to. I had to hurt somebody." She stood and shuddered, and the blood fell, plop-plop. I hauled her towards a chair and pushed her down into it.

"It's all right," she said again. "I just could not restrain myself another minute. Ever since Richard told me I've been holding myself down." I was relieved to hear her speaking coherently, and relieved that she was not crying.

"Mop your head," I said, handing her a piece of soft old linen. "You're ruining your gown. And I cannot bear the sight of blood dripping."

She mopped obediently and looked at the stained cloth in a

346

surprised way. "I'm sorry," she said, "I didn't know. I didn't know I'd broken it; it felt as hard as a pomander ball! Well, at least I managed to control myself until we were alone, though how I did it I do not know. Richard talking his hypocritical rubbish and then all these women showing what they think. I know what they think, Anna. That my days as Queen of England are numbered. Pila thinks I shall divorce him; Carmelita thinks he will divorce me; Joanna thinks I shall end in a nunnery. They'll see! I shall be Richard's wife and Queen of England so long as we both live. My heart is broken, but I won't be shamed in the eyes of the world as well." She jumped from the chair and began walking in swift uneven strides about the room, swooping round like a swallow whenever the wall barred her way. "That was what made me so furious with him. He doesn't even bother to preserve a decent face on things. I begged him. 'Let me come with you,' I said, 'I could be ready within a quarter of an hour.' How much better it would have *looked*, Anna. All his sweet pious talk about danger and discomfort; he wishes me to be safe and comfortable. God's eyes! How could any privation hurt me as much as being left here, knowing the talk, the filthy jokes that are going round? Oh, I could have smashed *his* head against the wall! I had much ado not to do it!"

"Mop your head," I said. I looked back to other evenings, other rooms, remembering how she had paced other floors, crying that just to be with him, to see him, would be enough; she would polish his mail, groom his horse, just to be with him. And this scene was in no way a denial or contradiction of the others. She was quite consistent. She would have done and borne anything for the man who treated her as his wife, however badly, as a husband, he had used her. What had happened was the very worst thing, the most tragic thing. And quite unpredictable. We hadn't known——

And how much, I wondered, did she know now?

As though the unspoken question had reached her, she swooped round, bearing down on me, and asked quite quietly, without anger or excitement, "You know what Richard is, Anna? Or are you as ignorant as the rest and think that Lydia has supplanted me?"

"I know it is wrong about Lydia," I replied cautiously. It was difficult to believe that she knew. She had never gone out alone, always with Joanna, who was clearly innocent as the day—and that so rarely—and I could not remember a single time when she had received a visitor or a messenger alone.

"About Raife of Clermont?"

A sick feeling moved in my stomach and rose to my throat. It was one thing to accept a situation of this sort, to gobble it up, as it were, in a vague general interest in the curious ways of the world; but it was another to sit there and look at the beautiful woman whom any man might have loved and admit, acknowledge, that a handsome young virile man had turned from her embrace to that of a man.

"Yes," I said unhappily. "I had heard about him. I didn't know you had. But since you *do* know and realise what Richard is and are annoyed because he doesn't even trouble to pretend, you know, Berengaria, there is a good deal to be said for Pila's suggestion. In the circumstances a divorce would be easily obtained. You're what? Twenty-two. But you are as lovely as ever, lovely as any girl of fifteen. Think of Joanna—as old and widowed and quite infatuated with Egidio. *You* would have a dozen suitors."

"I know," she said surprisingly. "I have thought of that quite seriously and often since I learned. But there's something twisted in *me* too, Anna. You know, you've heard me say it a hundred times, no man ever even interested me until I saw Richard. And no other man ever *would*. In the circumstances that may sound ridiculous, but I know it is true. If it had been Tancred's niece or Lydia or this Montferrat woman, I would have fought, Anna. I'd have torn out her hair, scratched out her eyes, made her so hideous that no man could look at her without horror—but this thing! It can't be fought because it is something in Richard. And besides, no woman could, in the full face of the world, openly declare her rivalry with some snivelling little page boy!"

She had always been a woman of few words. Now and again, certainly, when jerked out of apathy, she had made a sharp comment, a shrewd observation. But on the whole she had been inarticulate rather than eloquent. Now the sentences followed one another, lucid, reasoned, strangely perceptive.

"What then," I asked, "do you propose to do?"

"Fool them," she said, swooping round again. "Fool everybody. Do you remember that night?" She put a finger to the jewelled collar that covered the scar on her throat. "Father was peeling an apple and he said to me, 'This is no more than a passing fancy, sweetheart, and we all outlive our fancies.' I thought, I'll show you whether this is a passing fancy or not—and I snatched at the knife. Now they are saying, 'Richard Plantagenet is a——'" She used the coarse word

348

which Pila had spat out earlier, but calmly, without passion. "And I will show them too. I will never admit—— Look, Anna, you are a woman of property. Now suppose one day you saw a necklace in the goldsmith's booth—great sapphires, say, set in chased silver—and you wanted it more than you ever wanted anything in all your life. You went out and sold all you possessed and then hadn't the full price, but must lie, steal, cheat to get the remainder. And at last you held it in your hand, your own at last, your very, very own. And realised in that same moment that what you had taken for sapphires were chips of Venetian glass, bits of a broken goblet, and the setting wasn't silver but Cornish tin, the whole thing valueless. When you'd given your all and the whole world knew what you had given and how much you had wanted the trumpery toy. What would you do, Anna? Yell to heaven that you had been cheated, that you were a poor deluded fool? Or would you fasten it about your neck and say: This is just what I wanted and it pleases me well? Which, Anna, which?"

I don't know, I thought. (I can't answer. I never got what I wanted; I just want to take Blondel and build a house in Apieta—and now ... There wouldn't be even old Mathilde to tend her when I left. She had died soon after we arrived in Acre. But she'll get some more women. And she isn't as helpless as she seems; she's proud and tough and I admire her. And you aren't bound to look after people you admire. I will go now and write to Blondel.)

"God save you, Anna," Berengaria said as I did not answer. "You are a woman and kin to me. The same blood runs in our veins. You know that you would never admit your folly. As I never will. Let them talk, let them whisper, let them guess. There are as many stories about women as of the other sort—and nobody *knows.* I shall always follow him wherever he goes and wear my glass-and-tin necklace so proudly that those who most suspect will be most fooled."

"I think that perhaps you are wise. If you are quite certain that all that is left for you is a long pretence, a masquerade."

"And you, Anna. I am most particularly fortunate in having you, with whom I need not pretend. Ever since Richard left, while all the others were making their speeches, I kept thinking: Presently Anna and I will be left and then I can let go. . . ."

But I am not going to be with you long. Isn't it just my cursed luck to have leave-taking made so difficult? However, it can't be helped. I must say it.

349

I had actually opened my mouth. But her back was towards me again and her voice went on:

"After all, Raife of Clermont is dead, and as soon as we get to Aquitaine I shall take steps to deal with Blondel."

"With Blondel? What in the world has Blondel to do with all this?"

She turned. "Didn't you know? Now that Raife of Clermont is dead, it—is—Blondel."

"You haven't any right to say that! Sheer, malicious, filthy gossip!"

"But, Anna, Richard told me himself. He has taken Blondel with him. I could have gone with him; I would have been ready in ten minutes. That was what made me so very angry. No, he was going alone with Blondel. Doesn't that speak for itself? Anna! Are you going to be sick? God in heaven, I thought you knew. I thought you understood what we were talking about——"

I knew that, whatever I looked like, I couldn't look as sick as I felt. Afterwards I thought how silly it was of me to be so shocked, so immeasurably surprised. It was such a likely development. But I had never given it a moment's thought. And I was the one who had schemed to get the boy out of the bower and into the camp!

"We let him go. We sent him," I said.

"Most fortunately. Blondel is discreet. He won't flaunt his position and draw attention by demanding advantages— unless he has changed completely. And it looks far more decent for a man to go about with a lute player who has his music to commend him than to be fussing over Raife of Clermont, who was neither knight nor menial. I was much relieved. This could look like an innocent situation, and I shall make it my business to make it appear so. Even those who aren't deluded shall be puzzled."

She lifted her chin. I thought of Father's expression, "an iron mule." Once she had set her mind on marrying Richard, and despite the apparent impossibility of the attainment, she had had her way; now, just as stubbornly, she had set her mind upon a certain course of behaviour. She would carry that to the end too. One could not but admire.

Then I thought of the old Pyrenean proverb, "God lays His burdens on the strong backs." There was a grain of truth there. Almost any other woman would now have been weeping and wailing, wallowing in self-pity, inviting the pity of others—and the scorn and the ridicule which so often accompany pity.

I knew that she was far braver than I. She looked things in the face. I was already seeking refuge in evasion. I'm not going to believe it about Blondel, I thought. I won't believe it. He wouldn't have written all those letters in that level-headed way, tempering his admiration with criticism, his praise with humour, if this thing had been true.

One fact, however, I had to face, and immediately. Blondel wouldn't be coming with me to Apieta. It would be too painful just now to proceed there alone, and I didn't wish to go back to Pamplona. I might as well go on towards Aquitaine.

II

It was arranged that we should land at Naples, proceed overland to Rome, and thence be escorted by Young Sancho to Rouen or Poitou. We arrived in Rome first and settled down to wait, and I can imagine no more fascinating place in which to spend a time of waiting than this great busy splendid modern papal city which was built on, and of, and amongst the ruins of a city which had been the centre of the world before ever London or Paris or Pamplona were named.

Now more than ever I was seeking escape from uncomfortable thoughts by taking interest in things outside myself, in books and people and gossip, in minstrels' songs and in strange places. Rome suited me perfectly, and I embarked upon a round of eager sightseeing. After the cramped, confined life on shipboard the liberty was a blessed relief, and every day I hobbled about until I was so tired that I fell asleep as soon as I lay down on my bed. I even ventured into the catacombs, those awesome underground places where, in the early days of Holy Church, the first Christians in Rome assembled in secret to celebrate Mass and to bury their dead according to Christian ritual.

Occasionally Berengaria and Joanna came with me, but they only enjoyed looking at the shops; they soon grew tired and petulant. Things which I found most interesting they deemed dull and made dull too. They were with me on the day when I finally found Paul's Cross.

St. Paul the Apostle is not a popular saint. Few churches and hardly any boy babies are named for him. And in Rome, where he lived so long in prison and was martyred, his memory is almost completely eclipsed by that of St. Peter, the Church's founder and the Pope's especial patron. One might almost think—so little is Paul regarded—that some strange rivalry between the two great Apostles had survived the centuries. However, patient questioning, made easy by the fact that Latin is understood in Rome, though the language of the common people is a very debased form of it, led me at last to my goal. And Berengaria and Joanna were with me when at last I stood in a small dusty square, surrounded by squalid houses and little shops, and looked at the humble stone cross which marked the spot where Paul had met his martyr's death. It stood in the square, unprotected; bits of rubbish had blown and come to rest against its base; and even as we looked towards it a mangy mongrel dog ran up and lifted his hind leg against it.

"Well," Berengaria said, "I can't think why on earth you dragged us here, Anna. There's nothing to see——"

Oh dear. Saul of Tarsus, the persecutor, whom God wanted, who was struck down on the road to Damascus and rose up blind but converted, who regained his sight and went out to preach the Gospel to the Gentiles. Paul, the scholar, who could meet and defeat in argument the great sages of that time. Paul, who made that proud, astonishing statement, "I am a Roman citizen," and stood by his rights and demanded that the Emperor should judge him here in this very city. Paul, who said, "I die daily." His adventurous, cantankerous, unsentimental spirit had been set free on the very spot where the little dog had lifted his leg.

But there was nothing to see!

I was relieved when, dawdling back through the street of shops, we found a mercer's and a roll of yellow silk.

"Richard did give his consent," Joanna said; "it wouldn't be premature to start on my wedding gown, would it?"

After that they were busy stitching and embroidering and I was free. Often I went out for the whole day, buying food when I was hungry, sitting down when I was tired.

The shops alone in this city had an infinite fascination; there was nothing that could not be found in them, for they catered to visitors from the very ends of the earth, pilgrims and men of all nations who came on business with His Holiness. I never tried to buy an elephant in Rome, but I am quite sure that if I had attempted to do so it would have been produced either immediately or within the shortest possible time.

One day just before sunset I was on my way home, loitering through a street where there were many shops, reluctant to go back and engage in female chatter and discuss whether the embroidery should be repeated on the sleeves of the gown or confined to the hem of the skirt. I paused by the window of a goldsmith's shop. At home in Pamplona no goldsmith would have displayed his wares; you knew where he lived and if you wanted anything of him you went in at the door, made known your requirements, and were shown what he had—which was very little, since there most things were made to order. But here in Rome the goldsmith, like everyone else, was set upon tempting the passer-by. And very cunningly too. There was the open window in the wall and, jutting out into the street, there was a stout iron railing, studded with sharp spikes as a pomander ball is studded with cloves. Within the window was a sloping table covered with velvet just the colour of the night sky, and scattered upon the dark blue surface, like stars upon the night, were the lovely things which were for sale.

Certainly no thought of purchase was in my mind. I never carried more money on these expeditions than would buy me a bite of food, a sup to drink, and I certainly had all the jewels I needed; but I halted by the window, fascinated by the display and the cunning way in which it was protected.

Jewels made for ears, necks, fingers. What a rich city this is, I thought, that one shopkeeper should set out such a display of wealth each morning and shutter it to safety each evening. And an emerald, I thought ... Not as fine as mine, of course, but very fine, green in the fading light, and how that ruby glows, blood-red, answering the sunset; oh, lovely, lovely! Then, like a hound that has just scented its quarry, I stood still and stiffened.

In the centre of the blue velvet lay the belt which Berengaria had made for Richard while she was waiting for him to marry her. I recognised every stitch of it, every single jewel. And I remembered how oddly touched he had seemed when she gave it to him—surprised, a little embarrassed, but pleased, saying that he now had two treasures—with a glance at his gloves.

What was that belt doing here?

I hobbled into the shop, which was just like a cage. An old man, rather finely dressed, rose up behind a line of iron bars and opened a grille. I mustered my Latin and my cunning and said that I was interested in the belt in the window. He said perhaps I would like to look at it more closely. Indeed, I said, I should. He laid it in my hands with a remark about the fineness of the sapphires and the beautiful diamond buckle, showing me how it fastened. And I remembered how I had been the one to suggest that fastening; it had been made from one of Berengaria's brooches.

I tried to find out where the belt had come from. Quite frankly, so far as I could see, the old man said that he had bought it at a sale of precious things last month in the market. Objects of value came in from many places and were sold, auctioned. It was an expensive way of buying things because each purchase was taxed—oh, very heavily. It was like buying slaves; public auction was much the worst way! But just occasionally there were things of such value and beauty that one could not resist . . .

Undeterred, I pressed on with my questions. I said that I wanted the belt for a cousin come back from crusade. I said I would have liked a belt of Eastern workmanship—for the sake of association. Oh, this belt, he said, was not of Eastern origin—anyone experienced could tell that at a glance; besides, nowadays, with the crusade ended, so much Eastern stuff was coming in—flooding the market, in fact—that it was always auctioned separately, on different days. This belt's origin? A little difficult to say. Stones were cut in much the same fashion the world over, but the holes which had been made in the sapphires were rather roughly bored—country work, he would surmise—and the pattern of the embroidery showed Moorish influence, Spanish perhaps. Had a Spaniard then put it into the auction sale? Ah, but who could say! Any vendor with a thing of value could put it into the sale and collect what it fetched—minus charges for the sale and minus the tax—oh yes, vendors also paid tax, wasn't it iniquitous? Tax on the seller, tax on the buyer, and then people wondered that things were so expensive!

Propped against the little open grille, I talked, I should think, for half an hour, asking, probing, seeking one enlightening word, one thread of a clue as to how Richard Plantagenet's belt should now be on sale in Rome. But I gained nothing. And presently the gathering dusk and the scent of food cooking in some fastness behind the shop reminded the old man that business was business. About the belt now?

I would buy it, I said. I had not my purse with me, but I would come back first thing in the morning and complete the purchase.

With that the haze of academic interest lifted; he looked through his grille and saw a plainly dressed hunchbacked woman who had wasted his time. His manner cooled. He was not angered; he was saddened. I knew as I left his shop that he never expected to see me again. So doubtless he was pleasantly surprised when next morning, early, with gold in my purse, I went back and bought the belt.

When it was in my hands I did not know what to do. I didn't even know at that moment why I had bought it. Richard Plantagenet had most curious ideas about money and possessions; it was quite possible that he had sold the belt long ago in order to buy some baggage mules or some casks of beef. Or it could have been stolen from him. Taken from his dead body . . .

And Blondel?

I went back to where Berengaria and Joanna were bent over the embroidery; they had decided without my help that it should be applied to the sleeves as well. And I talked about embroidery until I had drawn the conversation round to the belt.

"He always wore it," Berengaria said. "Even on that last day when he was trying to look like an ordinary poor traveller he had it under his leather one, under his tunic."

"Oh!" I said. "Did you see it?"

"Yes, he showed me. He opened his tunic and said, 'You see, I wear your gift,' and there it was."

Was that true? Or said for the benefit of Joanna and Egidio, who were there at the time?

And suppose I produced the belt now! I could just imagine the tears and confusion, the *pointless* fuss.

I said nothing. I left them to their embroidery and I went back to the shop, where I said that I should like to see the auction; where was it held and on what day? Having bought the belt, I was restored in the old man's esteem, allowed my little peculiarities. There were sales every day. He directed me carefully to the place where they were held.

In the old days, in that bygone time which is only recoverable by an effort of the imagination, it had been an amphitheatre. The tiers of seats—were they of stone or marble? Marble, I think; I imagine them white and cold. I imagine people taking cushions or spreading their cloaks—they were all gone now. But there was the circular slope running down to an open space. Gladiators wrestling, fighting with spears— "The Christians to the lions!" I could see it all as I stumbled down the broken steps that led from the street to the lower level where the auctions were in full swing.

Here again everything was on sale: slaves, donkeys, bales of silk and linen, spices, vegetables, fruit, sheep and oxen, little monkeys, hounds, dogs for petting, hides, corn, everything in the world. The noise was deafening but there was a certain order in the crowd. Few people were there merely to watch; most had business and knew exactly where and what their business was. Without much difficulty I found the place where a swarthy young man was auctioning small and precious things. A broken column stood behind him and beyond that an arched opening filled with rubbish. My shopkeeper had mentioned an old pillar and I knew I had found my objective, but even then I looked beyond to the blocked archway and thought about gladiators and lions.

I stood and watched until the young man had finished his sale; today he had little to sell and the bidding was slow and apathetic. Then a man in papal livery came forward with an abacus and a slave accountant. Taxes, I thought. Finally I stepped forward and said, "I wonder if you could tell me something." He reverted to the jocular manner in which he had been cheering and jeering the crowd, a manner which had vanished completely while he dealt with the tax gatherer.

"I could tell you anything *you're* likely to need to know, lady," he said. And his eye swept over me, not unkindly, but with a look I knew and was resigned to because, after all, if I had been straight and comely I shouldn't have been able to walk about in strange cities—in any city—alone, free as a bird.

"Then tell me, if you can, where this came from," I said, and I shook the belt out of the piece of linen in which the shopkeeper had wrapped it.

"That's very easy," said the young man cheerfully. And then, swift and definite as the drawing of a curtain, I saw doubt and suspicion blot out the shallow, vulgar good humour of his gaze. "I sold it here last month to Emilio, the goldsmith," he said, as though continuing with his sentence.

"Yes," I said, "I know. I bought it at his shop this morning. But we had an argument about its origin. It's silly," I said, "but I do like to *prove* my point. It's beautiful, of course, and I don't grudge what I paid for it—but you couldn't call it Eastern work, could you?"

"If Emilio said that was Eastern work he must be in his dotage! Here, let's have another look." He took the belt from me and put up quite a little show of esoteric judgement, cracking his thumbnail against the sapphires, breathing on the gold and silver thread, and then rubbing it with his finger.

"Vienna," he said pontifically. "That's where that came from, if you really want to know."

"Oh," I said, taking back the belt and assuming an air of

356

bright interest. "How interesting. How clever of you to be able to tell so quickly! How did you know?"

"Just part of the job," he replied airily, but flattered all the same. "Why, just the way those holes are bored shows me they were done in Vienna."

There must be some reason, I thought, why, out of all the towns in the world where the belt was *not* made, he should have picked on Vienna; something other than the way those holes were bored had led him to that conclusion. But I still hesitated to ask the point-blank question because that might put him on his guard and defeat my object; a thing of such value might have been stolen.

"I've never been in Rome before," I said conversationally, "and of all the things I have seen, this market, full of things drawn from the four corners of the earth, has impressed me most, I think. Imagine this"—I touched the belt—"coming all the way from Vienna!"

"That's nothing," he said. "Why, the man who brought that in for me to sell had been farther afield than Vienna. He'll buy anything, anything salable, but mainly he trades in furs. Last month he'd just got back from a place called Minsk away up near Lithuania, and a lovely lot of furs he had for sale, besides several things like that belt that he'd picked up in a casual way from Vienna and Innsbruck and Padua on his way home."

"Oh," I said, "Lithuania—why, that's the very edge of the world! Holy Mother! How I would like to see a man who has been such a journey. Is he in the market now, do you think?"

The auctioneer laughed. "You're a funny lady, you are!" he said. "Fancy wanting to see a man because he'd been to Lithuania! I'm downright sorry I can't point him out to you; he'd laugh! And he'd tell you some tall tales about bears and wolves and frosts hard enough to crack great branches off trees. What a pity his tongue and your ears can't get together! But he's off again into the wild lands. He's an afflicted man—itching palms and itching feet—that's what he suffers from!" He laughed heartily at his joke and elaborated it. "His palms itch for money and his feet itch for strange roads. This time—so he said—he was going to push farther than Lithuania, going on to Russia, where furs are better and cheaper, he reckoned. He won't be back here till next year, if he ever gets back."

"Oh dear," I said, and there was no need to put false regret into my voice. I had been working towards this moment ever since I came into the market, and now I was but

357

little better off. "Still," I said more brightly, "I might be here next year too. I shall look out for him, and with more interest than ever if he has been to *Russia* and got back alive. What is he like? And what is his name?"

"You'd know him if you saw him, lady; he's short, kind of bent over; he's——" The young man looked at me and broke off. "But as strong as two men and active as a flea," he went on, a little embarrassed. "His name, if I remember rightly, is Peter. But we call him nicknames; for one thing, he squints."

Peter the Hunchback; Peter Squint-eye. I saw him very clearly. I saw him plodding away on his road to Russia, bearing the information I needed, carelessly, unwittingly, uselessly locked in his brain.

"Well, good-bye," I said. "This has been a most interesting conversation. And this belt, I must remember, came from Vienna."

"That is so, lady. Peter picked it up in Vienna—besides, I recognise the workmanship."

And so, to my sorrow, do I, I thought as I turned away.

Before supper that evening I found myself alone with Count Egidio and Sir Stephen. I had spent the day pulled this way and that by indecisive thoughts. Berengaria had certainly said that Richard had worn the belt when he left Acre to take ship for England, but she had set herself a course of intentional deception, and it was just possible that she had lied. The belt might have been sold even in Cyprus. I knew Richard to be quite capable of taking it and expressing his gratitude even as he assessed it in terms of money. It might have reached Vienna and come on to Rome in the legitimate way of trade and I might be making a coil about nothing.

Then I would remember that Blondel had been with Richard. And with that the belt, on sale in Rome, would assume a dark and dreadful significance. Might there be some reason why I had walked in that street, paused by that window? Might there even be some hint of guidance in the fact that I found the two men alone?

I said, "I would like to show you something—but if the women or anyone else comes in don't let them see, and contrive to talk of some other matter. Look, I found this in a shop—and I have made quite certain that it is Richard's."

I shook the belt out before their eyes, and some part of my mind, the part which had accused me of being fanciful, romantic, over-dramatic, overconcerned, was quite satisfied. If I had shaken a live and venomous snake in their faces they—being brave knights—would have blanched less.

"Great God!" Egidio said. "What did I tell you?"

From sentences cut short, from single words, I gathered that for the last month or more there had been anxiety about Richard's well-being. Ships which had left Acre several days later than the *St. Josef* had arrived in Dover, in Sandwich, in Romney. The word "shipwreck" was beginning to be handed about, cautiously, as though it were a red-hot chestnut by a winter fire.

"But this belt," I said, "shows no sign of having been in salt water. Look, the soft chamois leather she lined it with is smooth and supple. Salt water would have hardened and wrinkled it."

"That is very true," said Sir Stephen, testing the leather between his finger and thumb.

"The Queen says," I ventured, "that he was wearing it when he left Acre—not that I have mentioned my purchase to her or to Joanna."

"That was wise," Egidio said.

"And so far as it was possible to make certain, I did make certain that the belt came from Vienna."

"And that," said Sir Stephen, "opens up other possibilities than shipwreck—dear God!"

"Leopold?"

Sir Stephen nodded. "I will take the belt to Rouen," he said.

Mindful of my private doubt, and meticulous because Blondel was concerned, I said:

"Of course the Queen may have been mistaken. You will understand that I hesitated to question her too closely. All this may mean nothing—if she were mistaken—Richard may have sold the belt long before he left Acre."

"I believe he did once say that he would sell London if he could find a buyer," Egidio said. "But the belt his wife gave him ..."

"Could you make sure, Lady Anna? Positively sure that this belt was about his body when he set sail?" Sir Stephen asked.

"I could try," I said with a certain distaste for the task, but remembering that where Richard was there Blondel was likely to be.

"You look tired," I said to Joanna, "and you are to hunt with the count in the morning. You go to bed, I will do the hair brushing."

And presently, in the old, familiar intimacy, I said:

"You carry the pretence well, Berengaria. I thought that your asseveration that he was wearing your belt was quite a masterly, artistic touch."

"Dear Anna," she said, "you credit me unduly. That was true. He was wearing the belt and he did mention it when he left."

Then it wasn't shipwreck that had overtaken them.

III

The days that followed were full of confusion and speculation and restlessness. Sir Stephen took the belt and rode away to Rouen. He, Count Egidio, and I had agreed to say nothing to Richard's wife and sister about my find until it had been inspected and discussed at headquarters, and the secret was kept well until Young Sancho, for whom we had tarried at Rome, arrived at last. Partly he came to welcome Berengaria and escort her on the last stage of her journey to Aquitaine, and partly to make his peace with Count Egidio, with whom he had a feud of long standing. Since the marriage of Egidio and Joanna would bring the two young men into a relationship made closer by the affection which existed between Joanna and Berengaria, it seemed advisable that they should come to terms. But Sancho came bearing not only the traditional olive branch but news from the outer world, gossip and chatter which Egidio and I had taken some pains to exclude from the bower, and within five minutes of his arrival he had blurted out what, I suppose, all Christendom knew by that time—that Richard's ship was long overdue and that there was a grave fear that he had been shipwrecked.

Joanna wept desolately. Although in a moment of fury she had confessed a lifelong jealousy of her brothers—it was in Sicily during a quarrel with Eleanor that she had accused her mother of caring only for her sons—she had plainly been devoted to Harry, the "Young King," as they called him, to Geoffrey of Brittany, and to Richard; and when Harry and Geoffrey were dead she had concentrated upon Richard all the force of her sisterly affection. She had admired him so much; even her jealousy of him had its roots in admiring envy; she had taken such pride in his exploits, shared his disappointment over the failure to take Jerusalem. She was all woman, gentle, easily moved to tears, interested only in

360

her small personal life, but she was a Plantagenet woman, and Richard fitted exactly the pattern of manhood to which she would have conformed had she been a boy.

"Now they are all gone, all my brothers. John is not my brother—he was a changeling even in his cradle. All my handsome, brave, merry brothers gone!"

Berengaria wept too, shedding her tears beautifully. I knew, as no one else did, that the full flower of her passion for Richard had withered and shrivelled in the cold winter of disillusionment; that the sapphires and the silver had proved to be glass chips and tin. But death—or even the rumour of death—bestows a kind of sanctity, spreads glamour. The dead man's faults fade away, his virtues increase and shine, and the widow of even a bad man will forget the long unkindness and remember the single amiability, the one charitable word. It is true of dead women too. Father, when he set the lovely memorial altar in place, wasn't commemorating the mad creature who had sprung at him and clawed him with her nails. Life may or may not bring disillusionment; death most certainly brings illusion. So Berengaria wept—not for the man who had left her for Raife of Clermont, but for the redheaded knight whom she had looked upon from the ladies' gallery at Pamplona; and her sorrow was genuine enough.

Sister and wife could weep, and I envied them. I couldn't very well sit down and cry about a lute player who had shared the King's fate, whatever that was. I did not, even then, wholly believe the shipwreck story; that belt had never been in salt water. But I realised the shakiness of the evidence. Richard might have sold, lost, been robbed of the belt long before the waters closed over him.

And there were times, too, when I thought: If Blondel were dead I must have known. I wouldn't have uttered such a word to anyone in the world. But I could not forget a day and a night in Acre when I could neither eat nor sleep; when for me the sun was clouded as though a dust storm raged. Nothing had happened; there was no thing, however small, to which I could point and say, That is the cause of my misery! But I was sunk in misery. Blondel's next letter, clumsily writ with his left hand, told us that he had been wounded on such-and-such a day, and reckoning back, I knew that that day of clouded horror had been the one when he had been smitten. He couldn't be dead and I not know.

Aloud, of course, I could only mention the belt which had not been in the sea. And having mentioned it, I must tell the story of its finding and go on, picking over the evidence and meekly accepting rebukes for my secretiveness until I was almost crazed.

Then Berengaria said that we could not stay in Rome any longer. We must move nearer the centre of things. So we packed and proceeded to Le Mans in Maine, where Sir Stephen, his errand in Rouen completed, had found us comfortable accommodation on his way back. There Young Sancho left us, and there we settled down, well within range of every story concerning Richard's fate which rumour chose to spread.

They were so varied and so colourful, those stories, that if I had not been concerned for Blondel nor felt pitiful towards Joanna and Berengaria, I should have taken delight in them. Richard, they said, had never taken ship from Acre at all; he had turned back to Damascus and joined Saladin, and together they were setting out to repeat Alexander the Great's conquest of India. All along Richard had preferred Saladin to any of his Christian allies, hadn't he? And hadn't Saladin sent him presents?

Richard had joined the Templars. Some obscure shipmaster had come forward with a story of carrying a mysterious passenger, "taller than ordinary and of overbearing manner," to Malta. And Richard, whoever else he had insulted during the campaign, had always treated the Grand Master of the Knights Templars with deference, hadn't he? And hadn't he always been a monk at heart? Look at his behaviour to his wife; when she was within a stone's throw he had held off, celibate, in his tent.

Richard had been seen in England; in Sherwood, where an outlaw named Robin Hood held sway. An archer who had lost his right arm at Acre and returned home and joined the outlaws because he was starving and was the kind of person to whom Hood's charity extended had seen and recognised him. And wasn't that reasonable? The outlaws were the body who defied Count John, Longchamp, and Geoffrey of York alike. With their help Richard intended to retake his kingdom.

Richard was in Normandy. A milkmaid in Caen had looked up from her milking and seen a tall stranger with a red-gold beard who had begged a drink of milk. She had given him not only the milk—he had a compelling eye, she said—but the manchet of bread and the onion which comprised her noonday piece. He had promised her a manor in return and said, "England was once conquered from Normandy, and by God's eyes, she shall be retaken therefrom." Wasn't that a feasible story? Wasn't that just how Richard would speak?

People who too readily believed each story did so, I thought, because they didn't make allowances for the enormous upspringing, overwhelming power of imagination in common, downtrodden people. Every one of these stories originated at a low level, from people who had held their hands to a candle and *imagined* themselves warm, had chawed a bacon rind and crust and *imagined* a feast. I had walked amongst and talked to the poor in Pamplona, in Sicily, Messina, Acre, and Rome, and I *knew* why the poor are given to easy credulity, gossip, and superstition. If poor people ever looked things straight in the face they would cut their throats from sheer despair; they don't; they pretend, they decorate, they imagine, they believe. They make the best Christians simply *because* they believe. And they believe because they must. The shipmaster who landed a man who didn't tell his business, the archer who saw a recruit to the outlaws, the milkmaid who gave a stranger a drink of milk— they chose to believe that they saw Richard. And if the thought of the world had tended towards the second coming of Christ instead of towards the mysterious whereabouts of Richard Plantagenet, what they saw would have been a divine being with a halo, not a mere king.

But to whom, now that Blondel had gone, could I say such things? He would have understood, would have delighted in the flight of fancy, but now I was surrounded by the realists, the flat-footed seekers after fact, the most easily deceived of all men.

So I held my tongue, only repeating what I knew and pursuing my own worrying—what had happened to Blondel?— until the situation took another turn.

It began with a young groom scrambling up outside our window and thrusting his tousled head through the aperture and shouting excitedly. "My lady, they're saying in the town that the King has been found."

"Where? Where?" we cried, for as often as the stories had come in, as often as they had been disproved, hope, in the absence of any certainty as to Richard's fate, had lingered, though it weakened with every passing day. The young groom had nothing to add to his announcement. "Run and find out," Berengaria said, "and come back as soon as you hear anything more."

Nothing fresh was learned all that day. I went out myself

363

and listened and gossiped and asked questions. The King was found, thanks be to God! And that was all anyone knew.

"Count Raymond will be back this evening, straight from Rouen," Joanna reminded us.

The betrothed couple were passing through a trying period. The marriage had been more or less arranged between themselves, and with Richard's careless consent, before we had left Acre. But though Richard, who loved his sister in his way and could forgive anything in a good crusader—which Egidio was—had overlooked the fact, his mother, Eleanor of Aquitaine, and the count's father, lord of Toulouse, were bitter enemies. Eleanor actually had a claim of some validity to the count's territory and had more than once made attempts to take possession of it. Joanna, backed by Richard's consent to the marriage, could have ignored her mother's feelings in the matter, but that was not her way. She wanted everything to be amicable and pleasant. She had written to her mother from Acre and again, several times, from Rome. Eleanor, desperately trying to hold England for Richard, desperately disappointed by the crusade's failure, was in a chastened mood, in no mind to take another fight in hand. She would, she wrote back, give her consent to the marriage; she would even, not renounce her claim to the lands, but pass them on to her daughter (a typically Eleanor Aquitainian arrangement!), provided that she approved of the young man himself. Egidio would have gone to London. He would have gone to Baghdad—barefoot, if needful—so much in love was he; but Eleanor repudiated that notion. Presently, she wrote, she would be in Rouen, Richard would be in Rouen, and the whole family could gather and discuss this matter. Then there came the news of Richard's disappearance, and Joanna herself thrust away all idea of the wedding. This was no time for such thoughts. Egidio agreed. But time passed; what would have been the period of mourning, had we been quite certain of Richard's death, ended. Egidio stayed with us, and Berengaria and I were as tactful as possible, humouring the lovers, leaving them often alone. But it was an irksome situation. Then Eleanor—now more than ever distraught by the way affairs were going—did arrive in Rouen, and there was a suggestion that we should all move on to that city. It came to nothing. Rouen was very crowded; emissaries, ambassadors must be accommodated; we were well placed in Le Mans, were we not?

"And it would hurt her," Joanna said, "to see me, her

useless daughter, safe and sound, while Richard——" She burst into her ready tears.

But Egidio had grown impatient. By this time the stories had come in, dozens of conflicting tales, credited and then proved false, and one day he had said, "We have our lives to live, when all is said and done." So he had dressed himself in his best, chosen his retainers, kissed Joanna heartily, and ridden off to Rouen to seek Eleanor's approval. "And if she doesn't like me I shall merely regret her bad taste in men and come back and marry you out of hand," he had said cheerfully.

The news of Richard's new appearance reached Le Mans just at the moment when Egidio was expected back. Between the two excitements Joanna was almost demented.

Egidio was late in returning, so we dismissed everybody and sat up by ourselves, with food waiting on the side table and the necessities for mulled wine ready to hand, for the night was very chilly.

When at last he arrived his ordinarily pleasant face was set in sulky lines and he had, I think, been drinking. His manner, as we all rushed forward clamouring for news, was at odds with his usual courtesy. Pushing us aside, he strode to the fire and held out his stiff hands, then swung round.

"So the tale has travelled this far."

"Just the bare news," Joanna said. "We were hoping——"

"Your mother," he burst out angrily, "couldn't spare a moment even to *see* me. She was closeted all day, writing letters to the Pope!" A fine contempt flavoured the last words. At that moment he was a rather pampered small boy whom some adult, busy with some ridiculous adult concern, had brushed aside.

"Oh dear," said Joanna, tactfully pretending to a disappointment which at the moment she could not feel because her mind was engaged with the other subject. "Still, oh, my lord, if this good news is true, we can have Richard at our wedding, and that would be more than we dared hope. Tell us, is it true?"

"My honey-sweet love," the count said, snatching up the cold fowl from the side table and pulling off a leg, which he proceeded to gnaw and champ as he talked. "How could it be true? There was the shipmaster, wasn't there, who saw the King of Malta, and the archer who recognized him in Sherwood Forest, and the milkmaid to whom he spoke in Caen? This time it is a lute player who 'lost' his master outside Vienna, couldn't look for him thoroughly because he was ill, and then thought he'd better plod back to Rouen and just mention the matter——"

"Oh!" I exclaimed. "Then it could be true. There was a lute player—and the belt was found in Vienna."

"There you are," the count said, pointing the chicken bone at me accusingly. "It's the credulity of people that encourages these tales." He was so angry because Eleanor had failed to give him her attention that he chose to overlook the fact that it was he who had brought home for us the stories about Malta and Sherwood and half a dozen more, and had shared our excitement and speculations. This new story had rendered his errand vain, therefore he would have none of it. "Consider, Lady Anna, the things which make this story unbelievable. In the first place, the young man asserts that he set out with Richard to travel overland. Now everyone knows—and the Bishop of Salisbury gives his oath—that Richard embarked for a sea voyage from Acre to Dover. The minstrel, like all the rest of them, is inspired by a crazy desire for notice; and of course, being a professional spinner of tales, he embroiders his with several pleasing little touches which were lacking in the others. 'I lost him at Eedburg near Vienna.' How, can you tell me, does one 'lose' a man the size of Richard Plantagenet? Not in a fight, not from sickness, oh no, just lost like a pin in the grass." He threw the chicken bone into the fire. "What I detest and deplore about these tales," he said more gravely, "is their effect on people to whom Richard was dear." His eyes travelled from Joanna to Berengaria. "They keep open a wound that should have been healing now. Richard, God rest his soul in peace, was shipwrecked and drowned; he should be mourned and Masses said for his soul and——"

And forgotten! I thought. The broken threads knitted up again into the implacable pattern of life, and young men who wanted to marry young women should be properly received and listened to. I looked at Berengaria; after all, we were talking of her husband, of the man she had desperately loved once, even though . . .

She was breathing pantingly; I could see her breast palpitating unevenly under her bodice.

"If Blondel says he lost Richard near Vienna, Richard was lost near Vienna, Count Egidio," she gasped out. "I know Blondel went with him from Acre, and I have known Blondel very well for a long time and never known him to tell a lie. Or seek notice. He went with Richard to Jerusalem, and every courier that came back brought us letters—as Anna can testify—precise and honest and never once concerned with his own exploits. What is more, he promised me long ago that he would take care of Richard for me; and if he 'lost' him we can be quite certain that some kind of treachery was at work." Apart from a slight breathlessness, her voice was controlled, and when she moved from us towards the side table where the cold viands stood, she moved so smoothly and quietly that I imagined she was about to offer Egidio more to eat or help herself to wine. Instead she picked up the big silver bell which we used to summon the pages and shook it so vigorously that the sound pealed through the whole house.

"I'm going to Rouen," she said, setting the bell down. "If many people think as you do, Count Egidio—and I have no doubt they will, after so many false stories—I must go and do my utmost to prove to them that this one is true. And I must see Blondel and hear the whole story from his own lips."

"I will come with you," I cried, for she had spoken the very words I had in mind.

"I shall ride hard," she said warningly.

"And I."

Joanna stood looking from one to the other of us.

"I can't stay here alone. Had I—shall I——" She looked at the count. She did not wish to leave him; on the other hand, he had only just come back and could hardly be expected to ride out again that night.

"Count Egidio will escort us, of course," Berengaria said sweetly, and I swear even I could not tell whether she spoke in innocence or guile. "It is the King's business we ride on." She turned to the sleepy page who, smoothing his tousled hair, appeared in the doorway, and gave him his orders. Daughter of a long line of kings, wife to a king, at that moment she was fit mate for a king; magnificently wearing the ornament of glass and tin as though it were priceless.

IV

I was shocked by the change in Eleanor. Often enough in Pamplona, Brindisi, and in Messina I had been astonished by the way in which she had retained not only her vitality of body, her vigour of mind, but her looks. She had come out to Navarre straight from sixteen years' retirement, virtual imprisonment in Winchester, and sometimes it seemed to me that those sixteen years had been a preservative like the wax a good housewife rubs into eggshells to keep them fresh through the winter. She had emerged with energy unimpaired, wits undimmed, and the looks of a much younger woman. Now she looked her full age and more. Her handsome, firmly fleshed face had shrunken and in shrinking had fallen into heavy harassed lines; the colour had gone from it and here and there, around her mouth, in the hollow temples and eye sockets, an ugly brown pigmentation spread a stain. Her plentiful hair was now completely white and seemed too heavy, too lifeless to be manageable, and she had contracted a nervous habit of pushing her hands through it.

But the old fire still burned undiminished.

Despite all the hard pressure to which Berengaria had subjected us, the journey from Le Mans to Rouen had taken almost three days; by the time we arrived the new story was seven or eight days old, and Eleanor had not been idle. Letters to the Pope, letters to the Emperor, Henry the Stern, letters to Leopold of Austria were speeding on their way.

Before we had laid aside our mire-encrusted cloaks or warmed our hands Eleanor was telling us of the steps she had taken towards Richard's release. They included one of the true, typical Aquitainian touches, the kind of crafty opportunism which in the past had gained Eleanor her name, the "She-wolf."

"I told Leopold quite frankly that if he gave me his aid now I would give him my granddaughter, my namesake, Eleanor, whom they call the Pearl of Brittany, to be his wife. In Acre he often spoke of her to me; he saw her once in Bruges, and when he talked the lust showed in his eyes. And I told him plainly then that I had lived long enough to realise the folly—and the wrong—of these forced, arranged matches. I said that I should always support the little wench's own choice—within the right degrees. He used to squirm at that, knowing full well that no girl with good sight and the freedom to choose would choose to marry him! But all that is altered now, and if he will exert himself—he has great influence on the Emperor—I am prepared to sacrifice the girl. She is young; she will outlive him with any luck, and then—like you, Joanna—she can marry the man she favours."

Joanna, who had married the man her father had chosen for her, and Berengaria, who had been prepared to die rather than marry Isaac of Cyprus, were both, now that they knew

368

that Eleanor had accepted Blondel's story and taken action, prepared to be diverted by this mention of matrimonial arrangements. Dropping their mired cloaks, kicking off their wet shoes, they pressed about the fire, asking questions about the Pearl of Brittany, calculating the force of the bribe Eleanor had offered.

"But of what value," I felt myself bound to ask, "is a bribe to the archduke when we do not even know *where* Richard is being held? Suppose he is out of Leopold's jurisdiction or the Emperor's? There are a number of German princes, and all, I understand, very independent and absolute in their own domains."

"That," said Eleanor, swinging round to face me, "is the heart of the matter. We don't know. We know that he disappeared at Eedburg, a little place near Vienna; but who took him, and why, and where he is now, there is no telling." She pushed her hands through her hair. "It is the uncertainty ... And Richard in prison would fret like an eagle caged. Still, the Pope, if he will act—*all* Christendom minds him; and Leopold, well bribed, could act if he held him or if he knew that the Emperor did. What more could I do?"

I did not say it, but I remembered what I had once heard, that many German princes gave only lip service to the Pope. Half of them weren't even Christian, though they chose to be regarded, for mundane reasons, as part of Christendom. The vast, loosely knit body over which Henry the Stern held nominal sway and which was called the Empire, was composed of some very old, varying elements. More than a thousand years had passed since Attila and his Huns had swept over Europe; they had been fought, defeated, absorbed, and forgotten; in places, save for the wanton destruction they had wrought, they had left little mark. But in parts of what they called the Empire the Huns had remained, a hard core of alien culture: immensely brave, unconquerably tribal, curiously indulgent to women, children, horses, and hounds, merciless to their enemies, and given to the worship of strange gods. There was a place called Gastein, for example, where they worshiped the "spirit" of a great waterfall which came tumbling down from the mountains through a narrow gorge. And every Midsummer Day a young girl, the prettiest unpockmarked virgin in the district, was thrown into its boiling torrent; and for the next twelve months her family was honoured, regarded as holy, so materially favoured that there was a great deal of competition when it came to selecting the victim. The Pope wouldn't approve of that! And a papal letter, sent to such a community, wouldn't have much effect. Nor in the province of Tulzburg, where a curious form of cannibalism still survived and one ate with great ceremony certain bits of the body of a dead enemy who had showed courage, in the belief that thus his courage entered into one.

Odds and scraps of knowledge which I had harboured in my mind as a needlewoman stores bits in her rag bag. They couldn't be mentioned in the presence of Richard's wife, mother, sister. But I could, and I did, say, "I think the first thing to do is to find out, if possible, exactly where in the Empire he is held."

"But how?" Eleanor asked, pushing at her hair again. "That is why I offered Leopold a bribe—so that there should be one person in power anxious to find him, if possible, and let us know the truth; for it is all too evident that both John and the King of France will find it to their advantage to keep him hidden and locked up until he dies. Unless Leopold swallows the bait, how should we ever know?"

She looked so wild-eyed that I hastened to say comforting things. And saying them, I waited to hear Berengaria mention Blondel, ask to see him, listen to his story. But she seemed to be content now that she knew that Eleanor had believed him and taken action, and she and Joanna, with their feet to the fire, completely relaxed after the long hard ride, drifted off into a conversation mainly concerned with the value of Pearl of Brittany as a bribe and the chances of Leopold's rising to the bait. They remembered and commented upon his susceptibility to Princess Lydia and from that passed on to a discussion of exactly what the forbidden degrees of relationship were and how far the Pope was empowered to overrule them; and they tried to remember whether ever, in history, uncle and niece had been legally married. It was a true-to-pattern waiting women's conversation, the kind of thing which Berengaria ordinarily avoided with great fastidiousness but which she could tolerate from Joanna. It made me so furious that I longed to knock their heads together. But it went on, and in the end I was forced to say:

"And the boy who brought back this story, where is he, madam? I should be interested to hear his account."

"He should be in Canterbury now," Eleanor said. "I sent him to tell his story to Hubert Walter after the clerks had taken it down for me to copy in my letters. You see, Anna, there was always the fact that the story Blondel told was in direct contradiction to all that Walter has been asserting all this time, and I did think that it would be both test and proof of the boy's veracity if he could face the bishop himself. It's all very difficult to explain now," she said, and her hands went to her hair in that distracted gesture. "I believed the boy implicitly. . . . I had reason to believe that when Richard left Palestine he would—well, take *some* companion, inconspicuous, useful, agreeable. And Blondel had been with him throughout the whole campaign. What more natural, eh?" The straight stare of her pale eyes, paler than ever ,in their dark sockets, was frank, but defiantly frank. I thought: She knows, and what a thing for a mother to know! But I still was not convinced that Blondel—— "I believed him implicitly," she repeated, "but I felt that if I wrote to Hubert Walter and said, 'A minstrel, a lute player, has come in with such-and-such a story,' the man would tend to disregard it. There have been so many stories. And I felt that the boy, if there were a flaw in his tale, would have hesitated to face Walter with it. Walter knew him and——"

And what you *think* is his history, I added. Aloud I said, "You are a very clever woman, madam." And I meant it from my heart.

"Women are not meant to be clever," she said harshly, and her eyes turned eloquently towards the fire, where Berengaria and Joanna chatted. "Men hate clever women—and so does God, Anna Apieta. And I recognise His hatred, and I think that makes Him angrier than ever. How can I believe that God is my friend when things go the way they do? Of my four beautiful boys—for even John is beautiful and could charm a bird from a tree if he so wished—two remain. Richard lies in some unknown dungeon, and John depopulates his brother's kingdom with fire and sword. Truly, nothing I care for flourishes and nothing I have a hand in prospers."

She looked towards the fire, towards Berengaria again, and then went on in a harsh voice: "When I left Messina I went to save England from Longchamp. I so reduced, so harried him that in the end he tried to skulk out of Dover disguised as a woman, and the fishwives set about him and tumbled him—a fitting exit. Now, I thought, I can deal with John, the wind-bladder. But what happened? To spite me, Philip of France must turn back from the crusade and come home to bolster and stiffen John so that he could defy me. My doomed, fatal luck renewed! And now," she said, thrusting her hands through her hair, "there is this business of Richard. I *know*, I know in my heart that if I handle it I damn it, but/

371

who is to deal with it if I fold my hands? I am his mother.
. . ."

I looked back over as much of her life story as had come to my knowledge, either directly or in song and story, and truly it seemed that her luck had never been good; she was clever and she was wily, yet failure had been her lot. And the task which confronted her now was a formidable one indeed.

All at once I felt sorry for her and found it in my heart to forgive her for the looks of scorn and disgust and sheer physical repulsion which she had turned on me in the time we had spent together. I answered her as cheerily and hearteningly as I could. I could always be kind to the afflicted.

v

And in the days that followed they were all afflicted.

His Holiness sent back nonsensical, soothing letters, maddening in their futility. Anyone capable—as Eleanor was, as I was—of dissociating the man from the office was bound to see that they were the letters of a weak, vacillating, bewildered man who meant well but had no idea of how to put his good intentions into action.

The Emperor wrote most friendly and heartening letters. For the perusal of fools! When he knew, when he was certain, when his cousin of England had been found—but the Empire was so wide, there were so many Prince Electors, and it would of course be fatal to show a suspicion that could not be verified. . . .

Leopold wrote characteristically. Richard, he said, was not within his jurisdiction or he would have released him and taken Eleanor of Brittany to wife. "He insulted me many times, he tore down my flag, I have little reason to love him. But if I knew where he lay at this moment I would gladly exchange that information for the promise of your granddaughter's hand."

None of them said, Why ask me? Didn't Richard Plantagenet drown, and am I the custodian of drowned dead men?

I pointed that fact out to Eleanor. She agreed that it was significant and added:

"There is a note of regret in the archduke's communication. He wishes he had the information—he wishes he still had Richard in his hand. And there is a note in the Emperor's letter—when . . . when . . . He is bidding for time, time to see which way the cat jumps. If John and Philip get control of England, Richard will never see the light of day again; if they fail, the Emperor will *find* him quite suddenly. I see through it! But, Anna, what can I do?" Her face was twisted with agony. "What can I do more than I have done?"

It was painful to watch her, to listen to her. And there was Berengaria, neither maid nor wife nor widow, stupid, perhaps, in bemoaning the ardent redheaded lover who had never existed save in her imagination, but horribly, shrewdly stating a truth when she said:

"Of all men on earth, Richard is least able to bear imprisonment. He'll die or go mad. And he was such a good fighter; he deserved to die in the open."

And there was Joanna, weeping and weeping.

The weather without was cold and pitiless; day dawned late and it was dark again soon after noon, and the castle in which we lodged was the coldest and most comfortless place on earth. Snow blew in at the windows and sometimes lay all day unmelted on the floor, where the rushes shifted and swayed in the draught.

Pamplona lay low, sheltered from the cold north wind by the mountains, and what winter we had there had been brief, exhilarating, never losing its novelty because it was so soon over. And our bower had been cosy with its shuttered windows and its great hearth. (These northern castles seemed to me to be fitted neither for hot weather nor for cold.) On the higher slopes of the mountains to the north of Pamplona snow often fell and lay for three or four weeks, and the frost forbade the growing of peaches except in sheltered places; and there, in winter, the peasants wore coats of sheepskin, loose and baggy enough to be worn over ordinary garments, and with the fleece turned inwards. And they had some manner of dressing the sheepskin which made it supple, so that men could work and move easily while wearing such coats, women could spin in them and children play. They were called "grotis."

One day Berengaria, shivering and blue as we huddled over a fire which seemed to give out no heat, said, "I envy the peasants at home their grotis." And I turned aside and sat down and wrote a letter to Father, asking him to send four grotis with all possible speed. I thought as I wrote the letter that the winter would be over by the time they arrived, and the summer, just as ill prepared for, would be upon us; but writing the letter was something to do, and the grotis would keep, I thought.

Six weeks later they arrived, and it was March and colder than ever. In every room the rushes had blown into heaps in the far corner, snow was heaped inside every window, and icicles hung from the walls. We had muffled ourselves in every garment we possessed, and still our teeth chattered.

Father had sent the very best; the skins were soft as silk and beautifully embroidered in coloured wools, dyed with saffron and onion and elderberry juice. Each groti had loops of wool along one edge of its front and carved peach stones or acorns or bored pebbles to serve as buttons. I slipped my arms into the first one that I took from the bundle, and a comforting warmth enveloped me. I forced the taut woolen loops over the acorns and was enclosed, invulnerable.

Then I shook the other three free of their canvas wrapping and went to the cold, smoke-darkened room where Berengaria and Joanna spent most of their time, and threw a green-and-blue embroidered groti over Berengaria's shoulders and said, "Here's what you wished for!" and a pink-and-purple one I bundled into Joanna's lap, saying, "This will keep you warm." The third one, orange and yellow in colour, I carried on towards the specially cold, most dreadfully draughty little room where Eleanor Aquitaine wrote her letters, interviewed her visitors, and walked up and down, tearing her hair.

Outside the heavy iron-studded door—for the northern castles, if unfitted for comfortable living, were so constructed that each separate compartment could, if need be, withstand a siege—I listened, not wanting to disturb a serious interview. There was no sound of voices, so I knocked, and she called, "Come in." I meant to go and lay the groti across her shoulders, to surprise her with its comforting warmth, and so I edged through the door, opening the coat as I moved, and holding it high, shoulder level for her, eye level for me. I knew so well where she sat with her back to the door. So I walked in, the groti spread before me, and planted it on her shoulders and said, "Madame, a little present from Navarre," dropped the groti and my hands and, with vision thus unimpeded, saw Blondel.

I heard myself say, "Blondel," in a strangled voice, as though someone had me by the throat. He came and went on his knee and kissed my hand, and I put my other hand on his shoulder. I heard him say, "I thought you were in Le Mans." And I said, "I thought you were in Canterbury."

"He brought me this letter from the archbishop," said Eleanor. She was holding it at arm's length away from her eyes, as old people do. "No other message?" she asked.

Blondel straightened himself and went and stood by the

corner of the table and answered her, and I looked at him and saw him clearly for the first time and was smitten with a curious wonder that I had so instantly recognised him. Once in Pamplona, in bleak revealing light, I had seen him as he would look when he was old—or so I had thought; but what I had seen then had been the young suffering boy's face grown old and worn by years. The face I now stared at across the corner of the table was entirely different. It was a dark, sardonic mask. It bore little trace of the frank, boyish beauty which I had so loved.

I suppose I would have gone on staring for an hour, but Eleanor, with a great sigh, laid down the letter and became aware for the first time of the groti which I had laid across her shoulders.

"What is this?" she asked.

"A groti," I said, speaking as though out of sleep. "A thing peasants at home wear in cold weather. Father sent one for each of us."

Blondel moved and lifted the coat, holding it open so that she could slip her arms into it. She sat for a moment hugging the warmth to her. Then her face contracted in a spasm of misery and two of the scanty, slow, difficult tears of old age gathered in her eyes and crawled down over her furrowed face. She put up her hands to hide them.

"Richard . . ." she said in a broken, terribly bitter voice. "I never go to my warm bed, or hold my hands to the fire, or eat a good dish without thinking—some cold dungeon, couched on damp stone, empty-bellied, even galled by chains. Oh God!" she cried, and dropped her wild-haired head to the edge of the table while her shoulders under the incongruously gay orange-and-yellow-embroidered groti shook with her sobs.

"All Walter can say is that he regrets that he did not put him under restraint as he threatened. . . . By the same token I might say that I regret I did not smother him in his cradle! Dear God, what is there to do that I have not done? Holy Mother, you had a son—but He did ride in triumph into Jerusalem and He hung on the Cross in pain for only three hours. . . ."

Over the bowed head I looked at Blondel and he looked at Eleanor—through the mask. It was exactly how at the Christmas revels people hold up the most grotesque and unlikely masks and look through the eye slits with their own eyes. The sweetly curved, sensitive, easily troubled mouth had hidden itself behind one that was hard, ironic, easily amused, most of all self-amused; but the eyes, I now realised, were the eyes of the boy who long ago in the market place at Pamplona had looked at me and then at the dancing bear with precisely the same expressing of pity. Presently Eleanor lifted her head and said resolutely:

"I must not lose heart. Hubert Walter at least seems to have control of England, and when Philip sees that England is not going to drop into John's hand like a ripe plum he may change his tactics. For I think he knows. And so does the Emperor—and Leopold. Is it possible that Richard, who even if he weren't King of England would from his size and looks alone be a man to mark, could lie hidden anywhere for a year and no word, no rumour go round?" She paused. "Of course dungeons are deep and dark; and every little castle, even if it has no well and depends upon the ditch for drinking water, would have a dungeon. And Germany must be full of such little castles. I suppose it *is* possible that nobody knows." She brooded and then, as though talking to herself, went on: "I wonder, has the Pope pressed *hard* enough on Philip? There's a monkish streak there. I'll write to the Pope again. He must make Philip see."

There are times when a desperate hopefulness is far more touching than despair. The Pope had rebuffed her, kindly but certainly, again and again in the last months; but she was going on, tackling him anew, vainly seeking a hold like a toothless old bulldog baiting a particularly lively bull.

Pity for her made me say, "I think His Holiness has done all that he intends to do, madam; whether it was all he could do or somewhat less is not for me to say. Whatever the secret of Richard's whereabouts is, it has been kept well these many months, and secrets are seldom discovered by point-blank attacks. I can remember a very similar case. Have you ever thought of pursuing *private* inquiries in Germany? Matching secrecy with secrecy?"

"Spies? Yes, Anna, four I despatched myself, and Hubert Walter sent some of his own. Of my four, two have not returned, one whom I regarded with a degree of affection died at Württemberg, and of the other I know nothing. But the others all say the same thing: The Empire is so vast and the medley of languages makes inquiry impossible. Poor Alberic of Saxham, God rest his soul, set off with a simple but not despicable idea of hawking ready-made shoes, several pairs in varying sizes, and one pair enormous. As you know, Richard has the largest feet in the world. He thought Richard might need shoes. Anyway, he said that wherever those shoes

376

were sold he would nose about like a hound until he found the feet that wore them. It was a chance. It would have given a clue—perhaps. But as I say, he died at Württemberg, crafty to the end, for he got a message back to me in a manner it would take too long to explain now. He had not sold the shoes. And it may be, of course, that Richard is dead. They may all be telling the truth. But I think I should know. That may sound strange to you, Anna, but then you are not——"

"A mother," I finished for her.

"And for that mercy," she said with sudden violence, "you should thank God, fasting!" She reached out and drew her quill and her inkhorn towards her. "I must waste no more time in talk. Anna, would you mind carrying a message for me? Find Sir Amyas and tell him I want him to set out for Rome immediately, now, as soon as I have written this."

I turned to the door and there looked back at Blondel. He stood by the end of the table, his face inscrutable, looking down at her. The scratch of a furiously driven quill began to fill the room. I put my hand to the latch of the door. The room was cold enough, but as I opened the door a furious gust of even colder wind swept in. It seemed to rouse them both. Blondel looked towards the door like someone waking from sleep; Eleanor halted the quill long enough to say, "Thank you for bringing the letter so swiftly, Blondel. You may go."

"Is the—Queen here too?" he asked as he joined me outside.

"Yes."

"And similarly distraught?"

"She is very anxious. And sad. I think she, more than Eleanor, is inclined to believe that he is dead."

That was true. Berengaria's thoughts tended more and more to dwell on the handsome knight who was dead than on the man who might be suffering captivity. From every point of view such thoughts were easier to bear. If Richard had been lost in Messina, in Cyprus, or in Palestine immediately after the fall of Acre it would have been a different story. Then I believe she would have gone on foot, beating on every castle gate in Europe. But Richard himself had forced her into a passive position, made it clear that she had little to hope for from him, wherever he was. In fact, she had served a long, hard apprenticeship in the arts of waiting and resignation and seemed able now to practise them with ease.

"It would be better if he were," Blondel said harshly, and

then added—but the break had been perceptible, "Captivity to a man of his kind must be the worst form of torture. And the uncertainty is torment to those who care for him. My lady, will you lend me four crowns?"

"It is a deal of money," I said thriftily. But I smiled, pleased because it was to me he had turned.

"I'll use it to good purpose."

"What purpose?"

"In the first place, I need a new lute."

"Oh," I said, "what happened to your own?"

"I sold it. I kept it almost to the end. It earned my bread. But when I was so near the border that I knew I shouldn't starve before I found someone to whom to tell my story, I sold it and hired a horse."

"Ever since I heard you had returned I have been longing to hear the whole story. Oh, Blondel, there is so much for you to tell me; all about——"

"I will tell you everything another time. Stories to entertain you till the end of time—in return for four crowns now."

"A lute won't cost even half of one," I said.

He laughed—and his laugh had altered; I had so often striven to make him laugh in the old days, to enjoy the gay, wholehearted, boyish sound of mirth.

"All women are alike," he said. "I've noticed it a hundred times. A man will toss you what he can afford, and if half an hour later you're drunk in a ditch it's all one to him; but if a woman reluctantly hands you a penny it's, 'Now don't go spending it in the tavern, young man; what you want is a new pair of shoes!' Can't you lend me four crowns and ask no questions?"

Again I was aware how much he had altered. In the old days he would have blushed, been hesitant and diffident if he had had to borrow. Now he was wheedling; his voice had almost the professional beggar's seductiveness, but defiant and mocking too.

I had my purse and my money in it because here in our temporary room I had no lockfast place. I took out four crowns and laid them in his palm and closed his fingers over them. And in an effort to match my manner to his, I said:

"Now don't go spending it in a tavern, young man. What you need is a new tunic." And that was all too true. The one he wore was shabby and had been patched and the patch had broken away, and it was soiled and crumpled too. Staring at it—at first in mockery and then in earnest—I recognised it as

378

the one Berengaria had provided for him to wear in England all those years ago. And he had grown—I saw that with a curious, weakening clutch at my heart. He was no stouter, but his shoulders had widened and his arms lengthened. He'd gone here and there, always on somebody else's business— and nobody had thought to give him new clothes. My throat swelled and ached with love. My dear one, to whom I would have given everything in the world that I could lay hands on! I suddenly spoke from my heart.

"Look," I said, "when will you have done with all this chasing hither and thither? I still long to go to Apieta and build that house. Let's leave the kings and queens and the knights and the bishops and the castles—this is a chess game and we're just the pawns, and I for one am sick of being a pawn! Let's hop down from the board and go about our own business."

"I have just this one more thing to do. Then I swear, my lady, nothing in the world shall stand between me and building that house—if you still want it."

"And what is this one thing?" I was willing then to brush anything aside. To walk out of the door and start for Apieta that very afternoon.

"All right," he said. "If you promise not to say a word to anyone. I wouldn't for all the world raise a false hope, but there is just one thing that I, and I alone, can do. And you, Anna Apieta, put the idea into my head." He told me what he meant to do.

I shrugged myself out of my groti.

"You must have this," I said. "I can easily get another. And of course you need more money. Fool to be setting off with four crowns on such an errand!" I opened my purse and was emptying it into his when the door of the Queen Mother's room opened and the powerful old voice shouted into the gathering gloom, "Amyas!"

"God speed you," I said. "Have a care to yourself. And come straight back to me."

VI

Eleanor Aquitaine was no fool. When seven months later Blondel came back and said, "I have found him. He is in a castle called Tenebreuse at Drurenberg, which is in Austria but not strictly in the archduke's jurisdiction," she had wit enough and cunning enough not to begin screaming to the

379

world that Richard had been found by a lute player who had spent seven months on foot in the Empire, sedulously playing by every castle wall, every tower, every prison, the first verse of a song which he and Richard had composed in Sicily, waiting to be answered, plodding on, disappointed, and finally almost despairing until the dramatic moment when, as the first verse, "Sing of my mail," died into silence, another voice took up the strain and the words, "Sing of my sword," told Blondel that his quest had ended.

No, that was a fantastic story, more fitted for legend than legal evidence; and Eleanor, taking up her squeaking quill, merely wrote letters which began, "I have incontrovertible evidence that Richard of England is held in durance in the Castle Tenebreuse at Drurenberg." And in writing to Leopold of Austria she had guile enough to add that he would be "astonished and concerned" to know this fact.

"Incontrovertible evidence"—that phrase combined with Leopold's guilty conscience and his desire for the young Eleanor to spur him to action. It took His Holiness by the elbow and said, "Now, now—no more vacillation is possible!" It frightened the Emperor, who had always said, "When we have proof . . . When we know . . ." Most guilty persons will confess if somebody looks them straight in the eye and says, "I have incontrovertible evidence."

And such a burst of confession, of hand washing, of dragging out the other person's dirty linen began in Europe at this time that it would take three good scribes a lifetime to give the details.

Amidst all this bustle Blondel was completely overlooked and forgotten, save by Eleanor, who gave him a hundred marks—with many an inward groan, I am certain, for already the word "ransom" was being bandied about.

I never understood that ransom. Richard was not a prisoner of war. He was a returned crusader inoffensively making his way home through the country of a man who, however bitterly offended he may have been personally, was at peace with England and the rest of Richard's domains. He was thrown into a dungeon, with no reason given, nor any trial, and his whereabouts kept so secret that those most eager for his release were helpless. And when at last his enemies were forced into the open and that farcical trial was held at Hagenau, he was acquitted of every charge.

One would have thought that if any money were concerned it would have been a large sum paid to Richard as indemnity for fourteen months' reasonless imprisonment.

However, the fact was that Richard hadn't a single strong friend, not an ally nor a relative capable of saying to the Emperor, "Set him free or I will come and make you." Every really important man—with the possible exception of the Grand Master of the Templars, who had fought with Richard on crusade, hated him like poison and would have been delighted to see him hanged. Philip of France, who had left Palestine with the promise that he would do nothing to hurt Richard's interests while he remained to fight, had broken that promise a dozen times and was hand in glove with John, the would-be usurper. England was divided and weak. So when all the commotion died down, when charges and countercharges had been made and refuted, when Philip and Leopold had tried to justify their conduct by accusing Richard of the murder of Conrad of Montferrat—who had laughingly mentioned his own death sentence at a supper table, within arm's reach of me—then it was that the Emperor, with unequalled audacity, declared that Richard could go free on the payment of one hundred and fifty thousand marks. And nobody uttered so much as a formal protest. There was just the old white-haired, wild-eyed woman saying, "It must be found!" and Hubert Walter, sorely anxious as to what had been taking place in England while he was at Hagenau, saying, "Madam, I doubt if at this moment there is so much—God help us, half so much—money in all England."

I think that when Henry the Stern set the ransom at this impossible sum he had done so after a pretty shrewd assessment of the resources of England and Aquitaine and reckoned that the money would never be paid and Richard would languish on in prison for the rest of his days. But, like most of his kind, Henry underrated the ordinary common people. To them Richard Plantagenet was a hero, whatever he might seem to his peers; and for every commander who cherished a grudge on account of a brusque word, an uncivil criticism, or a countermanded order there were fifty lowly archers who remembered that Richard, even at his busiest, had always found time to see that their food was as edible, their quarters as comfortable as his own. And for all the masses who had never been to war with him, he represented something not quite ordinary, something larger and more colourful than life. They were proud of him, they owned him; their King had been the greatest leader, the best fighter, the one who struck fear into the Saracens; and of course he would have taken Jerusalem if he'd been given half a chance. Also—and this should not have been overlooked—Richard had been for a long time absent from his domains; that made it very easy for men who felt themselves wronged and downtrodden to say, "Things wouldn't be like this if the King was here." The rulers who were there were, like all rulers, unjust, extortionate, cruel; the ruler who was absent was just and mild and humane, as well as being a popular hero.

The scribes and the clerks who deal with such matters reckoned that when all the demands were met every one of Richard's subjects had been stripped of one fourth of his possessions and most had paid the dues gladly, without complaint or protest. Even the religious houses, exempt from secular exactions and rather given in such circumstances to plead, "This is not *our* treasure, but God's; touch it at your peril!" opened their secret stores and contributed heavily. In Aquitaine every sheep was sheared to the hide; and it was quite a common thing to hear a man crying in the market that half the price this cow made or a third of the sum this horse fetched was going to be given towards "the great ransom of our liege lord, now held in durance vilè by the Emperor." The word "German" came into popular abusive use, just as "Assassin" had been in Palestine. It was synonymous with everything that was treacherous and disgusting or, running down-scale, bothersome or awkward. "My German old pot sprang a leak this morning and put my fire out," I once heard a woman say to another.

While all this was going on in the outer world Berengaria and I were back in Le Mans, precariously and uncomfortably housed in a corner of the bishop's house. Less than a week after Blondel had set out on his secret errand Eleanor had found time to cast her eye over Egidio and give her consent to the marriage. So Joanna had left us, and we had been very tactfully and considerately but firmly pushed out of the castle at Rouen. Even the few mean rooms we had occupied were needed for the accommodation of the visitors who perpetually arrived to discuss business with Eleanor, with Walter of Rheims, with Hubert Walter when he could spare time to come to Rouen. There wasn't room for two redundant women.

Eleanor was now the kingpin, the moving spirit, and Eleanor was no longer comfortable in the presence of her daughter-in-law. I could understand her feelings perfectly. She was the alchemist whose experiment in gold making has failed and who wishes to wash all his unsuccessful ingredients into the gutter. She had hoped that the marriage would be successful, that an heir would be bred, that the wife—so lovely and so lovable—would work the miracle of conversion. From the moment when she had set eyes on Berengaria until the day she left Messina, Eleanor, the least meek of women, the least tolerant, had gone out of her way to be pleasant and agreeable to her son's bride. But the miracle had not happened, and when they met again Berengaria roused in Eleanor nothing but a distaste and a memory of failure. Berengaria was Queen of England, the legal, impeccably behaved, unchallengeable consort; it was impossible to ignore her; but the sight of her, the mere mention of her name reduced Richard from the status of favourite son, great crusader, most famous knight, wronged King to that of plain bad husband. And that Eleanor resented. And now and again while we were in Rouen some overpunctilious messenger or ambassador would seek audience of Berengaria, who was, after all, Queen of England until Richard's death was an acknowledged fact; and every time that happened Eleanor was irritated.

So we went back to Le Mans and did our waiting there.

When the ransom was being raised Berengaria gave many of her jewels and extracted one hundred marks from Father. That was the last of her requests he ever acceded to, for he died, dear man, shortly afterwards.

The news that the ransom had been raised in full was announced one Sunday morning in church, and there were great rejoicings.

"So now he will soon be home," Berengaria said; and although they were almost the same words in which she had received news that the crusading army had turned back from Jerusalem, her voice, her manner of speaking revealed to me that her mood was no longer one of purely pleasurable anticipation. Doubt and something like dismay tinged it. While Richard was lost and while he was imprisoned her pretence had been very easy to maintain; now, very soon, he would be back, unwilling or unable to share the pretence, exposing her to fresh humiliation.

But even to me she did not admit her doubt, her mixture of feelings. With that dogged courage of hers she went about making her small, pathetic preparations to receive him, ordering a new gown, new shoes; saying, "When Richard comes . . ."; asking anxiously, "Have I changed? Do I look older?"

There are days in early autumn when the trees stand, still green but touched with gold, warily waiting for what the day

383

brings; sunshine, then they take on their ripe summer look and no leaf falls; but if rain comes and wind, how they despair, strip off each yellow-touched leaf and, shivering, moan against the winter.

Berengaria was like a tree at such an indecisive season.

Eleanor's behaviour was the first cold blast. With the ransom money and an impressive train she left for Mentz, where she was to meet the Emperor and reclaim her son. She left without a word either of information or invitation to Berengaria and was indeed three days gone before we heard of it. She had, it is true, matters of great urgency and weight on her mind and she had long ago dismissed Berengaria as a person of no importance, but the callousness of her behaviour was nonetheless inexcusable.

Berengaria wept and threw herself about the room, crying:

"She should have taken me! Who should be there if not his wife? What will people think and say? How can I preserve even the pretence that all is well when his mother treats me like an old castoff clout?"

There was no answer to that.

"What have I done," she demanded, "that this should happen to me? I loved him with all my heart. I meant to be a good wife. And even now I ask so little—just to be saved from being a laughingstock for the whole world. Now when the eyes of all Christendom are turned towards Mentz and everyone of any importance in his kingdom is there to give him welcome, I am left behind. What have I done to be treated so shamefully?"

There was no answer to that, either.

The wretched day stretched endless, but at last she was exhausted and allowed me to put her to bed with a cup of wine into which I had slipped a drop or two of old Mathilde's medicine. She cried on for a while and then slept.

I was exhausted, too, and I did not fall asleep so soon, so in the morning I slept on and was awakened by her shaking me.

"Wake up, Anna. We're going back to Rouen today. He must go there; it is his capital as well as his favourite town. And I shall be there when he arrives. I won't be overlooked and forgotten again. I'll show that old she-cat who is Queen of England!"

Leaning over me in the half-light of early morning, she looked strange, I thought, but my eyes were still full of sleep and I reflected that the emotions of the previous day were calculated to leave some mark. When the sun rose, however, and my fully wakened eyes looked at her in the bright light, I saw that the change in her was greater than I had thought; it was extraordinary, a little frightening.

In Acre I had often noticed the thing which had so impressed our grandfather—the curious invulnerable tranquility in the eyes of the Saracen women. All but the very humblest—and some even of them—had had in infancy the same small operation which Ahbeg had performed upon Berengaria; consequently you might see a young Saracen woman clutching a dead child to her breast, rocking to and fro in a transport of misery and shedding tears from eyes as calm and untroubled as pansy flowers. But somewhere in the course of a lifetime a change must take place, for every old Saracen woman had eyes in which all the sorrowful wisdom in the world seemed to dwell. It was as though, I thought, all the expression of emotion which in youth was held back by the artificial barrier had suddenly come flooding in and taken possession.

Exactly the same thing had happened to Berengaria. Her eyes were still as blue and as beautiful as ever, but they were vulnerable. They reflected her feelings as other women's eyes did. The thought occurred to me that now she would find pretence less easy. Even her eyes had turned traitor.

Rouen was very empty and quiet; as Berengaria had said, everyone of importance had gone to meet the King. Almost alone save for servants, we settled down in the castle for another period of tedious waiting, and when at last our backwater peace was broken it was in the worst possible manner.

Richard had gone straight from Mentz to Amsterdam and there taken ship for England. They said that he was preceded by a terse warning message sent by Philip of France to John, "Take care, the devil is loose!"

So far as I was concerned the devil was loose that day in our apartment. I was mortally afraid that she would do herself an injury; she was so uncontrolled and I was neither heavy nor nimble enough to restrain her for long. "Don't, don't!" I would cry as she beat her hands on the stone of the wall; and I would hold her by the arm and be flung off as though I were a lap dog. After some hours, bruised and shaken and very near hysteria myself, I was thinking that I must slink away and seek help. She was mad, and mad people must be restrained; one could understand the provocation and pity the sufferer, but one couldn't go on this way.

And then, as though conscious of my thought, she stopped in the middle of a screaming tirade and said:

"Unless I take care I shall end like my mother. Anna, I will be calm. I'm sorry, Anna. I won't be driven crazy. I will be calm." She came over and knelt beside me and put her head in my lap and burst into a storm of ordinary tears, the kind you administer to with little comforting pats and cluckings. Then she began to say things which, I suppose, had I been a woman of another sort, I should have found subtly flattering: "You're all I have, Anna, my only friend, the only one who knows and understands everything. You'll stay with me, won't you? You won't leave me. You're all I have. . . ."

But I could look down the long vista of days of being indispensable, of being bored and bonded; and I made as few promises as were compatible with the desire to comfort.

VII

My instinct had warned me rightly. I can still remember the very flavour of the time that followed. She shrank from all company but mine, so it seemed heartless to go out on my little expeditions and equally heartless to drag her with me. She had an idea that everyone looked at her with scorn or pity.

In the long evenings, evenings which would have sped lightly if I had been able to read undisturbed and unconscience-stricken, I was aware of her all the time. A sigh, a restless movement, and I felt bound to lay aside my book and suggest some occupation. I tried to teach her chess, a game in which I took some pleasure, but although she tried she was so forgetful, so sweetly inattentive, that I found myself wanting to scream and throw the chessmen at her. I tried "nobbin," a very exciting, very old English card game which I had learned in Acre. Unless you gambled on it, however, it was merely dull, and since she couldn't or wouldn't attend to that either, I invariably won and was embarrassed.

She was so pathetically sweet and amiable, so anxious to please me if only I would put down my book.

"Nobbin? Oh yes, Anna. Now tonight I'll bet a mark on 'Jack's Astray.' " But with every card for the wanted hand save one in her possession, she would lose interest, let it pass, let it lie on the table under her nose. And I would win. There was no thrill, no pleasure, no interest in it for me.

386

Bored, bored, bored. Sometimes I wondered whether it was possible to die of boredom.

I made an infinite number of suggestions. I pointed out that a queen of England should be properly attended; some gay, accomplished waiting ladies would enliven our lives.

"Yes, I suppose so. But, Anna, I don't want anyone but you. They would giggle and talk and make mock of me behind my back. You understand; with you I don't have to pretend or explain. Think how glad we were to be rid of Pila."

I suggested that we go back to Navarre—just for a visit, I said craftily. If we did that Father would surely guess, and some action might be taken with or without Berengaria's consent. And at least there would be Father and Young Sancho to talk to. In Pamplona, too, in her own home, I should be justified in leaving her for short periods. Oh, how I longed to walk out, to stand and stare, to listen to gossip at street corners and in front of booths.

"But to go back to Navarre would be to admit failure. No married woman goes home to her father unless——"

"Just for a visit," I argued.

"Father would know. He would laugh at me and be sorry for me and most likely start something that would let all the world know."

Most of our conversations came to such dead ends. Yet she was eager to talk. "Talk to me, Anna. Tell me something." And I would rack my brain for some fresh sturdy subject which would not, after two sentences, dwindle and fail in the arid soil of our lack of common interest.

Finally in despair I started her on a piece of tapestry. For short periods she would stitch away fairly content while I read. Then I would join her, set myself some impossible target of achievement, and stitch away madly; and at least while we were both working, held together by our work, we could communicate in short disconnected sentences.

The wretched tapestry grew apace. And one evening I said idly, "What are we going to do with this when it is finished? It is too large for this room. Or for any in our apartment at Le Mans. We should have thought of that."

"I have thought of it, Anna. Not in connection with the tapestry—with us. One day if this state of things continues I think we should have an establishment of our own, don't you agree?"

"I always meant to have a house of my own," I said, and halted my needle. Here was a safe and fruitful subject. I began to tell her about the house I planned. The one spacious room with a glass window; the garden for herbs and flowers; the shelf for my books; the table where I could write; the candle sconce by the bed; the absence of troublesome stairs. It was so real to me that I could see it, could smell it as I talked.

"It was to have been in Apieta, and you wanted Blondel to help you with it," she said in a remembering voice and looking at me with great sorrowful eyes. "And I wouldn't let him go!" She dropped her needle, pushed the tapestry from her lap, and began to stride up and down the room. "I've been paid out for that bit of selfishness, Anna, and for being so superstitious about my dream. Not that that was all wrong—the oubliette part was true enough; I'm in it now, God pity me! Pushed away, forgotten, and all alone except for you, Anna. That's irony, isn't it? How you must want to laugh sometimes! Do you remember that evening just before we left Pamplona, when we quarrelled over Blondel? And you said, 'Must you always have your way?' My way! Think of that now, Anna, and laugh."

"There's nothing to laugh at," I said as soothingly as possible, trying to forestall the tears and the hysteria which seemed to threaten. "Come along and sit down and tell me what to do next."

She took no notice. "Look, Anna, I have no right to keep you here, spoiling all your plans and making you miserable. You go back to Apieta and build your house and live in it and be happy. Take Blondel with you—he's no use to me any more. I'm not sure that I should ever be comfortable in his presence again."

"Easy enough to say 'Take Blondel,' " I said, speaking as lightly as I could. "I haven't the slightest knowledge of his whereabouts even. He took his news straight to Rouen, and I believe Eleanor sent him on to England, and after that——" I spread my hands.

"He went to Mentz, I suspect, to share in the triumphal procession. Eleanor on one hand, Blondel on the other! 'But Your Majesty, didn't you once in an absent-minded moment marry a wife?' 'Oh yes, I forgot, I seem to have mislaid her somewhere!' Isn't that a *pretty* situation?"

I heard the hysteria mounting in her voice again.

"You know, I still don't believe it." I hastened to say the first thing that came into my mind in an effort to fix her attention.

"I should have thought this last dramatic piece of service would have proved it beyond all doubt."

"It doesn't. I don't believe that Blondel went to look for Richard because he was—infatuated with him. He did it because he was sorry for Eleanor. I know just when the idea was put into his mind. *I* put it there, I think, telling Eleanor that secret spying often found the answer which eluded direct questioning. If he had been—well, let's use frank words—in love with Richard, the idea would have occurred to him and not waited to be engendered by Eleanor's tears and a word from me. I don't believe Blondel was ever anything but Richard's minstrel."

"You are vehement," she said, turning and pausing to stare at me.

Be careful, I admonished myself; don't betray anything at this late hour.

"Am I? Maybe. But it seems to me that a thing of that kind is so easily said about a young man in Blondel's position who happens to come into contact with a man of Richard's sort, and it isn't a suspicion that should be *lightly* entertained."

"Not that it makes any difference to me *who* it is. But why don't you believe that Blondel——"

"I don't know," I said rather feebly; "I just don't. He isn't like that."

"Would anyone think, to look at Richard?" she interrupted bitterly.

"The only thing I really have to go upon," I said, "is the way he wrote about Raife of Clermont and about Richard. And then he nursed Raife while Richard was in Damascus. It just doesn't leave the impression——"

"No, I always understood that these cases were riddled with jealousy. What I do not understand, Anna, and I wonder whether you do——"

Well, at least that got us through one more evening. Bedtime arrived unexpectedly, and as I disrobed I thought it was typical of our whole odd relationship that our first really serious, almost impersonal discussion should be on such a subject!

A day or two later she startled me by saying, "Anna, I've been thinking about you and your house. Could we, perhaps, build one together? The way we live now is very undignified, to say the least. And the building would be interesting."

"Do you mean you would come to Apieta?"

389

Once or twice in the old days I had thought that, when Young Sancho married, if I had a house I might be expected to share it with Berengaria if she were still unwed—and the prospect had seemed to me most uninviting; but she had changed, and circumstances had changed, and I had changed. Now I seemed doomed to share her life, and better at Apieta than anywhere else. Just the idea of going home, of having a place of my own, made my heart leap. Then, as I said the word "Apieta," it fell again like stone. Blondel should have come to Apieta with me. We had indeed once gone there together and talked about where we would build. Just for one moment my old resentment against Berengaria blazed up again. She should not have dragged him on crusade with her and so compelled me to follow. We'd have been happy and snugly ensconced by this time, and she would have been no worse off. Maybe God would have been kinder to her if she had been kinder to me. But that thought lasted only until I could recognise it and smother it.

"Apieta?" she said blankly. "Why, no, Anna. That would be as bad as going back to Father. I must stay here in Aquitaine. But I don't see why we shouldn't build a house here and be comfortable. We could have some little dogs, or perhaps a monkey, in a place of our own. And doves, Anna—a lot of white doves; they look so pretty and make such a pleasant sound on a summer's day. And I think I should like to work in the herb garden. Do let's do it, Anna."

She looked at me and enthusiasm glowed on her face—perhaps for the first time. It had always been so expressionless until the change came, and since then it had generally worn a look of sorrow, discontent, disillusion.

L'Espan owes its existence to that look on her face. I simply had not the heart to wipe it out.

"Building costs money," I said cautiously. "Labour in a place like this would be very expensive. In Apieta every peasant owes me about two years' labour in days I have not used. Here we must hire it all. And with all this castle building going on, stone and timber will be costly too. But," I said, seeing the light die out of her face, "that could be managed."

"I'll ask Father," she said eagerly.

"He'll scarcely have recovered from your last demands," I said; "we'll leave him until we reach the end of my resources." As I spoke I realised that I sounded as though I were already committed to the scheme. "Anyway, it will do no harm to talk about it."

Happy to turn my back on that miserable tapestry, I got out my quill and my ink and started to draw. "This will be the solar, with the window facing south, one door giving inwards and one opening on the garden. That will be draughty in winter. We'll have a little porch—perhaps if we had some plants which needed shelter from the frost we could put them there for the winter and see a green leaf while all the trees outside are bare." I scratched away, happily busy.

Berengaria reached for the tapestry, unfolded it, threaded the needle that she had left empty overnight, and began to stitch. "We shall need this and several like it, Anna, if our walls are to be well hung." And I thought: Yes, we could be comfortable. Happiness cannot be commanded or bought, but comfort can be. A place of one's own; small, often valueless possessions which one has chosen because they give one pleasure to see or to hold or to touch; just salvage, perhaps out of the shipwreck of one's great bright fleet of dreams and plans, but better than nothing.

And, I thought, I can leave her with the tapestry! I can say that we need yards and yards of tapestry, that we need curtains, thickly embroidered, cushions for settles and stools. Her task. Mine to see that foundations are well dug, stones squarely cut and soundly mortared, water divined by somebody with a gift and a forked hazel twig and a good well dug. I shall be occupied all day. There will be stonemasons and carpenters to talk to, orders to give, problems to solve.

Already they were arising. Could I afford two glass windows? One for the solar and one for my own chamber, which, I thought, must be my own, my very own, to serve as sleeping apartment and living room when I wanted to be by myself. And how did one arrange in a small house of this sort, of a sort never planned or built before, that food reached the table hot enough to be palatable, when it had been cooked in a place far enough away for the odours of cooking to be bearable? In castles and large houses that problem was easily solved by having the dining hall immediately above the kitchens. But the house I planned wouldn't have any stairs at all. I wanted a house where I could move about all on one level.

"Oh dear," I said at last. "I can plan in my mind, but to draw it defeats me. I wish Blondel were here."

I laid down my quill and Berengaria stilled her needle. I repented those words as soon as I had uttered them. If I

391

were now chained to Berengaria, perhaps it was better that he should stay away from me.

"Now where should we build?" Berengaria asked with that air of deliberate bright interest which she now brought to any subject which she thought to my taste.

"That depends," I said. "Do you wish to stay in Rouen?"

"Oh no. So long as I am in Aquitaine and at hand if ever he does come, or if he should send for me. As a town I think Le Mans is preferable, don't you? And the country around is far prettier."

Once more I was struck by her curious awareness of things one would have sworn had escaped her notice. Le Mans was much the pleasanter town, smaller, friendlier; and the country—though how she could know that I could not guess—was infinitely more beautiful than the flat expanse around Rouen.

"The prettiest place near Le Mans is L'Espan," I said. "It lies between the birch forest and the river."

"L'Espan let it be," she agreed.

With that my mind drew back a little.

"It all needs more thought," I said.

"Well, it's nice to have something to think about, isn't it?"

I agreed heartily.

Two things influenced my thinking. First came the news that Father was dead. Grief drew us, his children, close together, mingling our tears. And when I thought, as I did, very poignantly of all that he had done for me, his unwanted, ugly bastard—and a daughter to boot—I was stricken with the sentimental fancy, common to those recently bereaved, that I could pay back some of his kindness by being increasingly kind and faithful to Berengaria, who had been his favourite. For a night or two after the news came I would hear myself sobbing into my pillow and promising that I would look after her and make her as happy as possible. I was clear-minded enough to see that this was a means of self-comfort, but the promises were genuine enough. At other times I had some outlandish notions which would have called my orthodoxy seriously to question had I ever revealed them. I felt that Father wouldn't linger in purgatory but would go straight to the company of saints and angels and that, looking down from heaven, he would see the plight in which his lovely, petted little girl found herself and would refuse to be happy in heaven while she was so miserable on earth, would solicit, demand a miracle on her behalf. And even though he had been a little careless about attending church, he had fought valiantly against the Moors in Sicily—some saint might listen and work a very small miracle and make Richard send for his wife.

What happened was quite otherwise. The next news we had of Richard informed us that he had moved against the rebels who had taken refuge in Nottingham Castle and had been successful in reducing them. John at the last took refuge behind Eleanor's skirts and, led by her hand, came into the presence of the brother he had betrayed and tried to supplant. I could imagine Eleanor's state of mind: Of all my beautiful boys, only two remain, and it is for me, their mother, to make peace between them. Sentimentalism is apparently an ailment from which all human beings suffer sooner or later. She had avoided it in her youth, and it had overtaken her in her dotage.

Richard said, "I forgive you, John, and I wish I could as easily forget your offence as you will my pardon."

I could have warmed towards him for that speech, so nicely turned, generous, witty, and shrewd; but the tale reached us together with the information that he was being crowned afresh at Westminster to wash out the stain and shame of his imprisonment.

He could so easily have sent for Berengaria to share that coronation; he could have washed out deeper stains, darker shames. But he did not.

Berengaria received this new rebuff quietly. But it was a buffet on a bruise, and my heart ached for her. When next she spoke of L'Espan I was only too glad to humour her.

VIII

We went back to the cramped lodgings at the end of the bishop's house and began riding out in the brightening spring days to choose the place where our house should stand. We set our hearts on a site that lay on a gentle slope with the birch forest running down towards it and the shining Loire at its feet; the hill and the forest protected it from the north wind and the small but very substantial castle of Sir Godric L'Espan stood guard over the valley. In less than a fortnight the tentative, vague idea had hardened into a determination. Whatever the cost, it was well worth it to have something to talk about, some common interest; and Berengaria, riding out in the air, sitting on a stump to eat a snack at noonday, looked healthier and happier than she had since the day when we set out from Pamplona. Women really did need something to take their minds off themselves and their men, I decided; and perhaps that was why God gave so many of them so many children.

Deciding the site was interesting and easy. Getting possession of it was very difficult. All the land for miles around belonged to Sir Godric, and he was unwilling to sell an inch of it, particularly to Berengaria. He was a coarse, jovial, illiterate man, but very shrewd. Manifestly there was something queer—to his thinking—in a queen running helter-skelter about the countryside trying to buy land on which to build a house. Rightly speaking, every castle and every manor house and every bit of land belonged to her—or at least to the King—and if she couldn't find a suitable place of residence ready made for her, well, that was a pity and His Majesty should do something about it. He, Godric, wasn't going to encourage any such runagate scheme and find himself in trouble. Asked directly what trouble he imagined could result from such action, he had no answer; it was just that the scheme was unheard of and he didn't want to have anything to do with it.

"Well," I asked at last, "what about me? Am I allowed to buy a patch of land and build *myself* a house?"

That he said was a little more canny but still outrageous. He wasn't in favour of the idea at all. Pressed, he promised to think about it.

A fortnight passed, and then one morning I received a present of venison from Sir Godric—just a quarter of venison with a formal message and no word about the land. I took that as a sign of a negative decision and said to Berengaria, "This is asking for bread and receiving a stone—but reversed. I think we must abandon the idea of L'Espan."

Two days later, before we had had time to settle on an alternative plan, Sir Godric called on us. At least the page announced that he was waiting without and asking to see me. Berengaria cried:

"He has come to say yes. Bring him to me at once."

"Look," I said, "if the frailest chance remains, the less you enter into it, the better. And if he has come to say no it will embarrass him less to say it to me. You stay here."

I went out to the odd little chamber which served us as anteroom, sent the pages skipping, and prepared to listen to what Godric had to say. He appeared to be very ill at ease, fidgeting about with a little switch he had in his hand and now and again striking himself quite a sizable blow, either on the hand or the leg.

"I've been thinking about this business. I can see no real reason why *you* shouldn't build there, Your Grace, but the terms of the bargain I wish to make may not be acceptable to you."

An attempt to raise the price.

"Oh," I said noncommittally. "And what are your terms, Sir Godric?"

"I suppose you have heard the news. The King has declared war on the King of France and has called for all true men. I shall keep Easter in Normandy, Your Grace."

"Oh," I said again, and added the polite word, "I hope it will be a short campaign and successful."

"If God so wills it." Then with a change of voice, "My brother-in-law is taking charge of my castle and my estate—and my family; he was wounded at Jaffa and never fully mended. He will not ride out again."

"A convenient arrangement," I said. He was not a man to waste words, and doubtless these irrelevancies were going to knit into some pattern presently. I waited.

"I should leave with an easier mind if you and I could come to some arrangement, Your Grace."

"And we should reach such an arrangement more speedily if you would tell me what you have in mind," I said a trifle sharply.

He struck himself two stinging blows.

"It is about my sister and her daughter," he said with the air of someone about to ford an unfamiliar stream. "To put it plainly, there are too many bitches in my kennel. Giselda's husband died of fever at Acre and Châteauroux passed to her nephew, so she came to make her home with me. Unfortunately my lady and she cannot agree on so small a matter as to whether a fire needs another log or not. That is very truth." He paused and looked at me, begging me to believe this seemingly incredible statement which I, who had lived with so many women, could believe only too easily. "I might perhaps leave them to their quarrels—but there is that poor child. You have seen my niece Jehane?" I had, once. A born idiot, all drooling mouth and eyes like a frog's.

"A mother," said Godric miserably, "has feelings no other can share, and when my lady—patience exhausted, as is understandable—whips Jehane, my sister is moved to retaliate. Last Thursday sennight they inflicted really grievous wounds on one another. I, of course," he said with some pride, "can see both sides of the matter and I can control them. But my brother-in-law, being my lady's blood brother and very like her in temper, will certainly side with her. And when I was a little boy"—he raised his head suddenly and spoke more freely, moved by a memory—"when I was a little boy I had no mother, and my father was a man of great ferocity. Giselda, my sister—she was two years older, big and strong even then, and of intrepid courage—would spring to my defence like a cat with kittens. One does not forget these things, Lady Anna. And now when Giselda defends Jehane, yea, even though it be against my own lady wife, I think: Even so did she defend *me* in days past! I shall not be happy in Normandy at the war if I think that Jehane is being whipped and put in the dungeons and my sister helpless. . . ."

He looked at me, and his eyes, which were ordinarily shrewd and bright—I had thought when we were bargaining that they were very like the eyes of a rat in a tallow barrel—were eloquent and clouded with misery. And appealing—as even a rat's eyes can be when it finds itself trapped. But what was I supposed to say or do to deliver him? Enlightenment soon came.

"I will give you the land," he said quickly. "I will send up every serf at my command to clear and level the place. I will hire skilled workmen from Le Mans. And when you are housed there I will see that milk and eggs and flesh and fowl are sent regularly—if only you will invite Giselda and Jehane to live with you. Giselda is a skilled housewife—the best I know, though I dare not say so at home; she can brew and bake, make soap and candles; she can spin and weave and embroider and can play many games and knows many songs and stories by rote. And the child is *not* vicious. Ugly and stupid, yes, and of course she kicks and bites when she is beaten; but, treated kindly, she is like a dog, a lame-brained but faithful dog. She knows me, she knows I am her friend, and she brings me my boots; nobody at L'Espan dares touch my boots if she is free. You know, Your Grace, there is a saying, 'God makes the rules, the Pope makes the dispensations, but the Devil makes the children.' I think of that whenever I look on that child. Giselda's husband was her cousin—he was her half brother, too, when the whole truth was told—but as I said, my father was a man of great ferocity. We couldn't—— So there they are. A horse lame beyond cure or a hound toothless with age one can dispatch in the name of mercy, but an unwanted woman and an idiot child are not so easily disposed of."

"There are nunneries."

"That is true. With rules which the little one could never mind. Or if it is an easy place, like Angers, then it is no better than a whore house. And at Blois the abbess is the woman who wanted to marry, who *should* have married Châteauroux; she would persecute Giselda. Oh, I should be so much happier about them, so much easier in my mind if you——"

"Why not build them a house yourself?"

His florid face went quite pale.

"With room to spare at the castle—for there is room; it is not a question of room—why, my lady would—— No, that would be the worst thing. . . ."

I allowed my mind one moment's diversion. I had seen Godric's wife. She was half his size and certainly no more than a third of his weight; her face was the colour of a candle and as flat as a dish. And he was obviously terrified of her. How did some women manage to attain such ascendancy?

"But if I could say," he went on doggedly, "that you—and Her Majesty, of course"—he skirted that uncomfortable patch of ground quickly—"had invited Giselda, I could say it was because of her housekeeping." And thereby, I thought, score a final triumph in a war of attrition that has gone on ever since Giselda came to the castle and said, "I always hang a hare four days, or stuff a duck this way, or bleach linen thus . . ." Oh, I could see it all. And that drooling idiot face.

Yet I was sorry for him. Stripped of his possessions, he was just a simplehearted, kind man; he remembered a past kindness, was torn between two loyalties. And he was going to a war whose causes concerned him very little. There would be arrows to pierce his eyes and jaw and vitals; axes to mutilate his limbs; the many sicknesses which most sedulously waited upon every army ready to lay him low.

So I answered him kindly—far more kindly than he had answered me when I first sought a favour of him.

"You realize that in this matter I am not sole arbiter? But the Queen and I will talk the matter over. This very evening. I will let you know."

To my astonishment Berengaria took kindly to the idea of housing Giselda and her idiot child.

"When we have a house we shall need some kind of chatelaine," she said.

"There's the idiot, remember," I pointed out ruthlessly. Ugly as she was, I could regard the little girl without much repugnance, but I preferred to voice myself, beforehand, the complaint which might so easily be made by Berengaria too late.

"We could arrange not to see her very often. We should have our own apartments."

We talked the matter over for the whole of an evening.

"And suppose, Anna—this is just supposing—but suppose at some time Richard did wake up to a sense of duty and wish to install me, say, in London, and you did not wish to accompany me. It would be nice for you not to be alone."

"If that should happen—and if you wish it, Berengaria, God grant you your wish—I shouldn't stay, either alone or with Godric's castaways, in L'Espan." I almost added that I should be off to Apieta like an arrow from a bow, but I feared to evoke her self-reproachful mood.

As it was, she looked stricken and began, "Oh, Anna, I've——"

I forestalled that by blurting out immediately another thought which had struck me suddenly:

"Truth to tell, this might be from that point of view a good arrangement. We have all the amusement and interest of building without the responsibility of full ownership; and if we ever did want to leave we could simply leave it to Giselda. Godric merely looks for an excuse to get his sister out of his wife's clutches and safely installed. He wouldn't mind whether we were there or not."

"And I would like the house to be at L'Espan."

Born of pity and boredom, L'Espan was nurtured on pity, expediency, and obstinacy.

I saw Sir Godric again, and we were very frank with each another.

"Now," I said when I had told him that we considered the proposition favourable, "whose house is this to be? For me it is an experiment; I've always wanted to build a house, and this is a trial of my skill. To the Queen it is an amusement, a change from tapestry work; to your sister it is a place of refuge. But since you would not sell the land, it remains in a sense your property. Suppose, then, I wish to sink a well or even make a fountain, are you likely to say, 'Not there, here!' Or will your sister wish to put a sage bed where I desire a lavender hedge? Because, if so, I warn you, my interest would very quickly wither. My first plan has been so twisted out of shape that already I regard it coldly. It is better," I said, "to speak bluntly now."

"It must be your house," he said quite solemnly. "If Giselda guessed that I had done this for her she would fling the fact into my lady's face, as urchins fling mud—not," he added hastily, "that Giselda is ill-natured, but she has suffered much." His eyes suddenly admitted a twinkle that I found endearing. "Suffering sweetens the natures of saints, Your Grace, at least so we are told, but for the rest of us——"

And I reeled back as though from a blow, struck by the thought that Berengaria had been sweetened by suffering. It was terribly true.

Suppose I had been present at the making of a saint!

What rubbish! I thought, and braced myself to talk stern business with Sir Godric.

IX

Blondel came back when the site had been cleared and levelled, the foundations laid, and the walls reared to about the height of my girdle.

It had been a beautiful early spring day. Under the birch trees at L'Espan the dog violets and the primroses had woven a carpet lovelier than any from Ispahan. I had had what for me was a happy day. I had ridden out to the site, eaten my noonday piece sitting on a stump in the sun, and listened to the overseer's story of his son, the clever little boy who had wormed his way into the choir school at Le Mans, taken priest's orders, been appointed secretary to the Bishop of Nantes. A pleasant story, humble love and earnest prayers culminating in worldly success. "And never forgetful of his parents," the old man said. And I had said, "I can see where he gets his brains, the way in which you managed ..." I flattered him shamelessly.

On the whole, a very pleasant day.

Berengaria had stayed at home. It was no good; the workpeople just couldn't accept and ignore the Queen. They stopped work to stare at her. They were horrified if it looked likely that she would soil her shoes. She had thrown her whole heart and mind for the moment into the matter of building, and one day, with my roughly drawn plan in her hand, she had halted by a fellow as he dug and said, "And this is to be *my* room?" in a tone of bright interest. And he had gone distraught and tried to kiss her feet and

said that no room was good enough and that by rights ...
Oh, on and on he went, carried away, earnestly and well-meaningly saying terrible things. Me, after a brief spell of curiosity, astonishment, and faint disapproval, they could accept as in the end everybody accepted me; shapeless, sexless, I could hobble and stumble where I pleased. Now and again a man would halt his pick or shovel and reach out a rough kind hand to help me over a difficult place, but here, as in Pamplona, in Acre, in Rome, my affliction made me free.

It also made me very tired. Jogging home, I thought I would have my supper brought to my bed, and I would have a candle and lie and read a book which the bishop in his kindness had lent me yesterday. And I would be spared the effort of making conversation with Berengaria. From that my mind slid off to contemplate the future. I had by this time seen and talked to Godric's sister, Giselda, and found her a sensible, accomplished creature, suffering from cramp of mind and body, like a big dog chained to too small a kennel. You could almost see her shake and stretch herself. You could see, too, that she was all ready to adore Berengaria, to wait upon her hand and foot, to pamper every whim. I could imagine them working endless tapestries together, Giselda trying on Berengaria all her dainty little dishes, her nourishing possets, her well-regarded recipes.

I should be free again if things worked out well. Free. And lonely. What of that? Loneliness was freedom's other face. In all my life I had only seen one person with whom I wanted to share it, and even that mild wanting had brought a forecast of the weight of the chains.

I dismounted and stumbled stiffly into our living apartment; and there, in a room where the candles were brighter than usual and the newly lighted fire clearer, was Blondel sitting close to Berengaria, busy with what she would once have called "a mess of scribble." She looked up and said:

"Anna, Blondel has solved the kitchen problem. We have to dig as though we were making a dungeon, but a wider hole so that light and air can get in from the empty space in front. Show her, Blondel, show her what you have devised. ..."

Over the neatly drawn sketch of an underground kitchen with an underground forecourt outside its door, Blondel's eyes met mine. Loneliness receded before that look. So, more reluctantly, did freedom.

As soon as the roof was on and the well dug we moved out to L'Espan and busied ourselves with being busy. Keep busy, keep talking, don't think. When I look back on those years I can hear the busy voices.

Let us pave a path so that we can walk to the wood dry-shod; let us build a dovecote; let us try Giselda's cowslip wine; let us start a new tapestry; how much better Jehane looks now that she is happy; what amusing stories Giselda tells; here is a new book, a new song, fresh news of the war; have you tried this game; have you eaten this dish; have you tasted Giselda's blackberry wine; look at these primroses, so early; look at these bluebells, like a stretch of sky fallen under the birches; look at the bees in that lavender bush; look at that rose, how late. Christmastide, Easter, Whitsun, Lammas, Michaelmas again, my, my, how time flies; how time flies when you are busy! And who so busy as the figures on Grandfather's Greek vase, forever chasing round and round, forever calling: Have you seen the robin's nest, have you heard the cuckoo? Listen, that's the nightingale; look, the swallows are mustering.

If you stop, if you are silent for one moment, you will hear the questions that cannot be answered; you will hear your own heart going thud-thud on its steady march to the grave; you will hear time slipping away on the fleet-footed seasons; you will see Berengaria fading because there is no nourishment in resignation; see Blondel fuddled with wine whenever he is not busy. You will even see your small comfortable house becoming a caricature of itself, a refuge for unwanted women, and yourself a kind of unfrocked abbess.

Better not to stop, not to listen, not to look except at the birds and the flowers. Go on being busy.

Shall we take in the Lady of Tinchebrai? Hers is a sorrowful story, and somehow it does Berengaria good to hear of other women's sorry fates. Let us take in the Lady of Tinchebrai and also that strange Englishwoman, Huldah. Aren't these windflowers lovely? So graceful. Jehane fed the birds this morning; yes indeed, she did and she said "pretty," not quite clearly, perhaps, still it shows that there is *some* understanding. Isn't Giselda's pickled pork the best you ever tasted? So Philip has suffered two reverses, one at Fretéval and one at Gisors—perhaps it would be as well not to say too much about that. It *reminds!* Blondel, you drink too much; no, I have never seen you drunk since that night in Acre, but all the same, you drink too much. Let us make a seat under this tree; let us have a bed of marjoram; let us make lavender bags for the linen chest; let us be busy, busy, busy . . .

XI

In all this time Berengaria had received but one crumb of notice from Richard. He made over to her the dues from the tin mines in Cornwall and Devon.

"Pensioned off like an old lackey," she said.

But the apparent finality of that gesture was misleading. Before we could say, "Michaelmas again, how the year flies," Richard, after the victories of Fretéval and Gisors and the mighty exertion of building his new castle, Gaillard, took a day off for hunting.

In the forest which he had chosen for his sport there lived a wild-eyed hairy hermit who, just when the chase was in full pelt, leapt out from his cave or his hollow tree and seized Richard's horse by the bridle and burst into a wild jeremiad. Despite the two recent victories, he screamed, Richard's campaign would come to nothing unless he took heed, mended his ways, and returned to his good and virtuous wife. Richard, they said, laughed and tried to push the hermit aside. The old man fell back but still held onto the bridle so that the horse stumbled and then reared, and Richard, unprepared, was struck on the mouth by the metal trappings between the horse's ears. "And you will sicken and die untimely," cried the hermit, releasing his hold and rolling away into the underbrush.

Within a week Richard sickened. In Palestine he had, like almost all crusaders, fallen victim to that recurrent fever which never completely relaxed its hold, the fever which meant a day of aches and pains, a day of sweating and shivering, a day of weakness—the routine illness which many returned crusaders casually referred to as "my three bad days." But three days passed, seven, ten. Doctors gathered like vultures, but not one could alleviate or even name his ailment.

The cavalcade, sent to fetch the queen to the bedside of her husband, arrived at L'Espan at four o'clock on a beautiful summer's morning. At that hour the birds wake and greet the first light of dawn and go to sleep again, and at L'Espan I

402

always woke and heard them. On this morning through the bird noises I heard the creak of leather, the clatter of hooves, the voices of men, subdued yet urgent in the enormous silence of the dawn. I was the one to wake her and say, "He has sent for you."

The moment had come. In Pamplona, in Brindisi, in Messina, in Cyprus, in Acre, in Le Mans, in Rouen, and in L'Espan she had waited, been desperate, impatient, angry, resigned, proud, defiant, patient. Now the moment had come.

By six o'clock, with the sun rising on a dew-drenched, flower-hung, bird-enchanted world, she had gone, so happy, so entirely fulfilled and justified, that it was awesome.

"Well," I said, turning back into the house, ignoring the gibbering Jehane, who hung upon my arm, and speaking to Blondel, who walked on my other side, "They say in Navarre, 'You come at last to the place where your heart is.' God send her a good arrival."

"You do," he said, "if you set your heart in a possible place. *He* would have looked like that if he had ever entered Jerusalem."

" 'Rusalem," said the idiot, who was given to such senseless, broken repetitions.

XII

There were now seven women—eight, if one reckons Jehane—living under L'Espan's sprawling roof, and building was still going forward. There were times when I looked at the place, or merely thought about it as I lay on my bed, and felt like someone who mounts a gentle old palfrey in order to ride a mile and is no sooner in the saddle than the mount is transformed into a rearing, half-broken stallion which takes the bit between its teeth and gallops for twenty miles over hill, over dale in quite a different direction.

Perhaps in quiet intervals between battles Sir Godric boasted about the clever arrangement he had made for his sister; or perhaps his lady talked of the way in which she had been relieved of the burden of her sister-in-law; or perhaps Giselda's friends rejoiced over her happy fate. I only know that somehow or other the idea that L'Espan was a place for unwanted women spread all over Maine, and we were overwhelmed by pitiable requests.

The fate which had made me physically so pitiable and in almost every other way so very enviable had also made me

403

prone to something which at its best was the virtue of compassion, at its worst the deadly sin of pride. I had never deluded myself about my motives, not even in the far-back days when I fed the beggars in Pamplona. I knew why I was sorry for the afflicted, and I knew how I felt when I could render aid. There, but for my better fortune, go I, I would think, recognising the taint; and see, I am as I am, but just look what I can do, I would think.

And all these women appealed both to my pity and my arrogance. Not because they were misshapen, not because they were invariably poor, but because they had never had a place, or, having had one, lost it, in a world, in a framework of society which pairs off men and women and decrees that without a man a woman is little more than a piece of rubbish, while at the same time nature and war and morality issue their entirely conflicting decrees, that more infant girls survive and that women outlive men, that men shall be killed and women spared, that no man can have more than one wife. God, I often thought, either didn't intend every woman to have a husband, or He was no believer in monogamy. Sometimes it seemed to me that the Saracen way, where a man could have as many wives as he could support, was more merciful, and the Jewish way, where widows were regarded as a family responsibility, was more moral than the Christian way, which perpetually forced two groups of women, the unmarried and the widowed, onto the rubbish heap.

It was not, as most pitiable situations are, the result of poverty; poor women can work and, married or single, can enjoy the fruits of their labour. In every case where we were asked to house, to invite, to shelter a woman there was some man—brother, father, son, nephew—willing to make a monetary contribution; he just wanted to get rid of the woman—of a sister because he was about to get married, of a mother because she quarrelled with the wife about the children, of the daughter because she would never find a husband now and it was a man's duty to see his daughter settled. Space and security were what was lacking. One woman—she was Thérèse, sister to the Count of Thouars—arrived at L'Espan with a wooden casket of jewels worth nine hundred marks under one arm and a small wheezy dog under the other. "These were my mother's and are rightly mine," she said, giving me the box, "and if I can stay here instead of going to Blois, where dogs are forbidden, I'll give them up gladly. The stones will glitter for anyone; my little dog knows me and loves me."

Oh, the thwarted affection in that speech! And the misplaced trust, I thought. What was to prevent my taking her jewels and turning her into the woods?

They were all very trustful and, the unmarried ones especially, most significantly ignorant of money, hardly knowing a mark from a groat. They had never had any of their own to handle.

Berengaria, who had once lived in a world of her own, remote and unassailable, now that that world had crumbled and rotted, was inclined to take an almost frenzied interest in anything which would keep her mind off Richard and her own peculiar situation. And the women offered more distraction than the birds and the bees, the butterflies, the flowers.

I was naturally vulnerable to appeals to my pity and pride. Blondel was more often sober when there was work on hand.

So the young L'Espan drew further nourishment from a queen's despair and a drunkard's drunkenness.

But that grain of mustard seed in the Bible story, which grew until it sheltered all the birds of the air—we are not told through what richly rotten, what chance-dunged soil it spread its roots.

I found myself entangled with the complicated, fascinating, and sometimes distracting question of finances.

Often—but even more frequently after Berengaria had gone—I would stop the busy, busy, busy, look, see, notice, taste, listen roundabout, and think about Apieta. Suppose I left this house of mine, which was not and never had been and could never be *my* house. What would happen to them all?

I began very seriously to turn my mind to the problems of finance and administration through that summer after Berengaria joined Richard. And I received help from an unexpected quarter; from none other than Blanche. If anyone had ever told me that I should seek advice and get it from that silly, vacillating girl who had tried for years to flirt with men *and* with Holy Church, I should have laughed and dubbed him fool. But so it was.

Blanche had married quite suddenly and, considering her age, quite well. And she seemed likely to make Thibaut of Champagne a good wife. But she had not, after some months of marriage, quickened, and early in the spring she decided to make a pilgrimage to the shrine of St. Petronella at Le Mans. St. Petronella was a virgin, but she had the reputation for curing sterility, and there was a deep groove worn by the feet of anxious childless women about her resting place, and at all seasons of the year there were little posies on her tomb, many anonymous, but many others labelled, "With gratitude for Geoffrey," "Because of Guillaume," "St. Petronella sent John to me." (Presumably some girls forced open the stubborn wombs, but they were regarded more as a promise than an achievement, I suppose; and although often when we were living at Le Mans I went and looked at these tributes, I saw only once a posy labelled, "Thank you, dear saint, for Mary Petronella." My heart had warmed to that mother!)

Blanche, partly because she was now in a family mood, partly out of curiosity about Berengaria, and partly for convenience's sake, came and lodged at L'Espan. And when we had discussed her marriage and the mystery of Richard's behaviour towards Berengaria—she had no idea of the truth and said, "But I never expected her marriage to be very successful; she never seemed to me to be more than half alive," which I countered by saying that Berengaria had greatly altered, which was true, and I had confessed my ignorance of the latest developments, for though Berengaria in that rapturous dawn had hugged and kissed me and promised to write, she had never done so—then we began to talk about L'Espan. And Blanche, who had spent years in nunneries, never blinded or bound by vows, always free to observe, told me everything she knew of conventual administration. No Jewish usurer could have bettered her account for conciseness and shrewdness—or for cynicism.

"Abbesses are never chosen for their holiness! Holy Church selects leaders just as any other army would. Command goes to the competent, the vigorous, the clever. No abbess I ever knew would have been a monk if she had been a man—she would have been a soldier or a cardinal or an outlaw. You would have made a good abbess," she said. "And after all, L'Espan is a nunnery in all but intent."

"I would hesitate to make such a claim," I said, laughing, "what with dogs and cats and monkeys and idiots and Camille's illegitimate child."

"And the abbess's pet lute player!"

"Architect and foreman builder," I amended—not too quickly. "Anyway, I never had any ambition to be an abbess, and if you call me that I shall withhold my good wish for you."

"And what is that?"

"Why, that St. Petronella will send you a fine big boy, of course."

I wanted to divert her attention, and little did I think that I was idly pronouncing her death sentence.

XIII

Busy again, but without the fever, the need to distract. Vaguely, without urgency, preparing for the time when I should go to Apieta, leaving L'Espan self-governing, self-supporting. A busy, happy autumn. With books and music and human interests and impersonal problems and Blondel for company.

He drank, but that I could understand. Out of the dark forest we all endeavour to find a path—your way is not my way; each must find his own—and though it grieved me to see his eyes grow bleary and his face puffy, and to notice the increasing slovenliness of his dress and bearing, that was better than seeing him unhappy. He was never unpleasant or noisy in his cups, and never sodden to insensibility; many of our most interesting and animated conversations took place after the flagon was empty. And though I knew why he drank so much, knew by name and from shared experience the pain that he thus alleviated and forgot for a while, there was a reason which could be announced to the whole world. His arm, though the wound had healed, was still troublesome; it ached before rain or when he was tired; in the morning it hung heavy and weak. And it was growing small, shrivelling like a blighted branch on a tree. Fortunately during the time when it was first disabled he had begun to train his left hand and could now write and play his lute equally well with either.

It sounds, perhaps, a curious ménage in which to find happiness. But those months at L'Espan have a light on them, the light which makes me imagine, as I look back on them, that the weather was always fair, the sun always shining.

Then Berengaria's letter came.

I have often noticed a special pathos about the writing of those who can only just master a pen or of those who, even if they are more skilled, dislike writing and seldom practise the art. The pen is a great diviner in the hands of novices. Practised writers can hide behind fine phrases, telling figures of speech; but the others—maybe it is a compensation—they

407

write the really heart-wringing phrases, just as they make the most eloquent omissions.

"I wish you were here, Anna, so that I could talk to you."

We had spent long-stretched, endless hours together with nothing to say to each another, but I knew what she meant by that.

"The King got better very soon and has since been busy. Once in a battle the French broke through and the fighting was so close I could see—like a tournament, but horrible because men were killed and I feared he might be. It was two days before I knew." That told me a good deal.

"I have several ladies now. It is fashionable to take amusement in talking English; even those of Aquitaine are beginning to gabble it. They would have me learn, but as you know, I am not quick to learn. And Richard does not use it, though he can understand it." If he had spoken it she would have given it all her attention and mastered it as swiftly as any of the gabbling women who no doubt used the strange tongue to exclude her.

"There is talk that we might spend Christmas at Le Mans. I heard of Blanche's visit. Arthur of Brittany was to have come to Richard, but his mother Constance forbade it and Richard was angry."

Most informative! The marriage was now sufficiently mended for Berengaria to be thinking about a child and from that to jump to young Arthur, Richard's nephew and heir presumptive. I'd warrant that at Christmas she would be following in Blanche's steps to St. Petronella's tomb.

The letter ended with the warmly expressed hope that, wherever they spent Christmas, I should join them. I would learn English, I thought, and sit deceitfully amongst her women.

The idea pleased me, and the study enlivened the autumn and made another link of interest between me and Blondel; he knew a little and wished to learn too.

Amongst the women who had come to take shelter at L'Espan was a battered, gaunt old woman named Huldah, who boasted that she was English not only by nationality and rearing but by blood. Her great-grandfather, she said, had been one of Harold's thanes and had died in that group of the faithful who at the end of the long day had lain about the last "King of the English" on Senlac Field. His widow, already the mother of a girl baby, had later married a Norman lord, and she had started a course of craft and guile which had, for well over a hundred years, kept one strain in the family pure and unsullied by Norman blood.

"My mother told me when I was eight," the old woman said, "I was *her* Saxon child; she had bedded with a hind while the man who thought he was my father was fighting the Scots for Stephen. If you look at me you can see the peasant blood in my face—but it was Saxon blood and to my mother more precious than that of Norman kings. She told me the whole story, and I realised then, child as I was, why I had always seemed to be her favourite. She promised me that if she could contrive it she would find me an English husband, for the English, mind you, were coming into their own again and there were noblemen of pure blood here and there to be found. In return she made me promise that if her schemes went astray I would bear one child of Saxon blood and to that child confide the secret of its heritage and exact the same promise. After that," said the old woman with a sigh, "I bore my knowledge and my responsibility as though it were the Holy Grail. But my mother died when I was ten and still unbetrothed. I was very plain, as you see, and no one had taken a fancy to my hind's face, and there were ten of us, for my mother had done her duty to her husband too; therefore our dowries were not tempting. But I was witty, and to my cost; one evening when Francis of Arcachon supped at our table I made him laugh. He was a dour man who suffered much from his stomach, and laughter was precious to him because so rare. In the morning he asked my father for my hand. My father was so pleased and flattered, and when I ventured to protest he beat me black and blue. So married I was and to Arcachon I came, where I never had sight or smell of a Saxon man. So in me the carefully cherished line ends. I bore four half-breeds who have inherited as half-breeds do, the worst of both stocks, and that is why I am here. If I had been fortunate enough to get myself one Saxon child, that child would have been dutiful and I should not, in old age, have found myself dependent upon charity."

"Hardly that," I protested. "When your son made—the arrangement—he turned over to L'Espan the revenue of the mill at Le Bocage and all the fishing rights in the river between St. Laurens and Villenau——" And a fine peck of trouble I have had over their administration, I thought to myself.

"It is, nevertheless, charity," said the old woman with great dignity and great venom. "Because it was for you to say yes or no when my horrid little half-breed asked whether you would take in his addlebrained old mother."

It occurred to me that perhaps she had always regarded her half-Norman offspring as horrid little half-breeds, treated them as such, and that was why not one of the four now had much filial affection for her. If she had succeeded in bearing a pure Saxon child she would probably have lavished all her love on it and thus insured against an unwanted old age. But it was almost half a century too late to point this out to her. And she was very pleased and proud to teach us English.

"If you live long enough, as you well may," she said, "you will be glad. Every day this tongue, once so despised and neglected, is being spoken more and more. I am too old, I shall not see it, but the day will come when English will be heard in Westminster; and it will cross the sea, too, and be heard in Rouen and in Paris and in Rome."

I left her her illusions and merely said that I had already heard it in Acre.

So all that autumn Blondel and I learned English together. He had the start of me because during his stay in London he had begun to learn and had added considerably to his vocabulary, at least while he was with the army. But once my competitive spirit was roused, I made great headway and my grammar, Huldah said, was sounder than his.

"You *must* not think," she said fiercely, "that because in English a table is not *she* and a piece of butter *he,* as in your ridiculous French; or because in English the word is 'tree' whether we say 'that tree,' 'under a tree,' 'the tree is green,' or 'oh, tree, how lovely you are'—therefore English has no grammar, no rules. It has. Of course," she added, "it is because English is not concerned with the non-existent sex of tables and calls a tree a tree in all circumstances that it will in time become the language of the civilised world."

Blondel looked at me; I looked at him. No muscle in our faces moved. We saved that joke for private enjoyment later.

XIV

Berengaria's wish to spend Christmas at Le Mans was granted. The whole court—or at least a company as nearly resembling a court as Richard was capable of tolerating—came south on the twentieth of December and took up residence in a grim grey castle which stood guard on the road to Orléans. I jointed them there two days later.

Blondel stayed at L'Espan, busy, busy, busy, planning all manner of merry diversions for the revels there.

Berengaria greeted me with the warmest affection and herself showed me to the little room which she had chosen and had made ready for me at the foot of one of the towers.

"We wanted somewhere where we could be alone sometimes, so I said that you hated stairs. Even more, you would hate being bedded with all those giggling women. They're all detestable, Anna. No nice woman stays in this household longer than a month; they make some excuse and go."

I turned myself about and took a good searching look at her. She looked as much, and as little, like herself as she would if the Twelve Days of Christmas had already started and she were taking part in the revels under the Lord of Misrule. Her hair, which she had always worn simply dressed, in plaits before her marriage and in a great shining knot at the back of her head after, was now most elaborately contrived into two twisted horns on either side of her head. Behind the horns, covering the back of her skull, was a little close-fitting cap of gold filigree work studded with jewels; and floating from the lower edge of the cap, just covering her neck and touching her shoulders, was a piece of gauze, a shrunken kind of veil, weighted at its edge with more jewels. Her gown was of velvet, the colour of a ripe plum, cut very low and so tight that little gussets had to be inset to accommodate her breasts, and even then it was so close-fitting that the nipples were plainly outlined. Below the narrow, tightly laced waist the skirt of the gown flared out a little and then tightened, so that at the knee, in order to allow for walking, it had to be slit, revealing a petticoat of pink silk embroidered all over with little flowers of plum colour and leaves of bright green. The sleeves of the gown were skintight to the wrist, where they widened and fell away in a kind of fantastic open cuff which, when she lowered her arms, reached to the hem of her skirt, and the cuffs were lined with the same embroidered stuff as the petticoat. Her shoes of purple velvet had long pointed toes. All very grand and very beautiful and very newfangled, but not, I thought, very dignified or modest, or like Berengaria.

There I checked myself sharply. I had been buried in the country, immured at L'Espan, wearing, if truth be told, the same dresses with which I had set out from Pamplona and seeing women dressed in similar ancient style. For me even mentally to issue judgment on this fine apparel would be as

411

silly and futile as that old priest ignorantly fulminating against the laced gown he had never seen.

"You look more beautiful than ever," I said.

"It profits me nothing."

"Oh dear," I said, "I rather hoped that things were well with you." Not quite true; her letter had informed me otherwise, and that was why I was here and not making evergreen wreaths to hang in the dining hall at L'Espan.

"Tonight," she said, "after supper, when they are having music and jugglers and tumblers—will you come with me, Anna, to the cathedral? St. Petronella—you know . . ."

"Willingly." I suppose my doubt sounded in my voice or peeped from my eyes. You look more beautiful than ever; it profits me nothing; will you come to St. Petronella's shrine? A link broken somewhere.

"It may sound crazy—perhaps I am crazed—God knows I have had enough to make me. But, Anna, I did think that if St. Petronella had the power they ascribe to her and was kind—I mean if she wanted to give me a baby—— Of course I shouldn't say this to you, but you are so understanding about everything even though—— And to whom else could I say it? To have a baby, you know, you have to have a husband first. And if St. Petronella really does give babies, then it is obvious—— Blanche is with child, did you know?"

The cold rigour that always assails me when I hear of miracles or ghosts or other things which reason cannot explain away shook me.

Say coincidence or simply determination on the woman's part, and where were you then? Doubt the power of the saints and you proceed to doubt the power of God. Deny that little Guillaume, little Geoffrey, little John, little Mary Petronella owed their existence to some particular intervention and you committed yourself to unplumbed depths of heresy.

But believe it—and Berengaria's words were entirely, utterly reasonable.

"Does he bed with you?" I asked, putting bluntly the question which had always been at the back of my mind.

"When there is no excuse that he can give his own conscience, Anna, which means when he is not in camp, not on a journey, he comes to my bed." A hot wave of colour rose from the edge of the low-necked gown and poured over her face. "Let us not talk about it. Come with me this evening. We'll slip away quietly. Oh, Anna, it is so comforting to have you here. . . ."

The cathedral was deserted when we reached it; the quiet and the cold reminded me of my visit to the cathedral at Pamplona, when I had knelt and prayed my desperate prayers—prayers which had been answered; that no one could deny! But perhaps one should be rather more careful about one's prayers. Tonight I let her go alone into the little side chapel where St. Petronella lay, and stayed myself in the darkened nave and confined myself to ritual prayers, parrot-like, with the simple addition, "God make her happy!"

Time passed slowly in the dark, in the cold, in the incense-laden air. I mustn't be impatient; mustn't imagine that an hour has passed, mustn't think of the cold. "God make her happy." Time tames us all, supples us, makes us gracefully accept the crumbs and avert our eyes from the laden table where other men feast. Blondel plans little rooms and fuddles himself with wine; I busy myself with fishing rights, mill dues, toll fees, take pleasure in his company and in the happiness of the women I harbour. But she has nothing, no resources. God make her happy in the only way in which she can be made happy.

At last I was sure that an hour must have passed, even making allowances for the fact that kneeling is painful for me and that when one is cold and uncomfortable every moment seems endless. Presently I was aware of a dim figure moving about the altar; the light there brightened as the candles were renewed. It must be drawing near midnight. I rose to my feet, rubbed my hands together, and then chafed my knees, which were numbed from the cold stone.

Then I heard a voice, Berengaria's voice, in the side chapel. It was too far away for me to hear what she said, but there was a note of agitation and alarm. Possibly the priest who had renewed the altar candles had gone into the side chapel and startled her, and although she was the bravest woman I knew about darkness, sudden noises, mice, and what Blanco called "haunts," nevertheless, in this great silent church, at such an hour, and in the deadly cold which I at least always found lowering to the spirits, it was possible that even she was frightened. I began to hobble rapidly towards the entrance of the chapel, and as I did so I heard her voice again. It said, "Come back—come back. I haven't made you understand. If you understood you would forgive me. ..." No other voice answered.

By that time I had reached the opening in the screen of stonework and could see into the chapel, which was, in comparison with the dark body of the church, quite well

413

illumined. I could even see the bunch of late frost-bitten roses and the posy of holly berries stripped of their leaves and surrounded by a frill of white lace which lay on the flat tomb. There was nobody there save Berengaria, who stood rigid, staring at the wall and stretching out one hand in the gesture of one who would detain a passer-by. I called her name softly. She turned, looked at me blankly, and drew a deep breath. Then she said, "Anna," and very slowly she came towards me, walking as I imagined a sleepwalker does, though I had never seen a sleepwalker. I put my hand on her arm and could feel that she was shuddering violently.

"Anna," she said again before I could speak.

"I heard you talking," I said, a little shaken by her manner, by the memory of the tone of her voice, by the lateness, the darkness, the strangeness, the more than winter cold.

"I tried to explain," she said, as though she were refuting an accusation. "If she had just let me explain, but she wouldn't listen. She walked away with her jaw stuck out and her head in the air and just didn't give me time to explain. I was so overwhelmed at first, Anna, I couldn't find words; then when I recovered myself she'd gone. . . ."

She spoke a little more loudly than people usually speak in churches, and the sound of her voice stirred something, not an echo, but a curious vibration, in the great building.

Almost completely unnerved, I said, "What are you talking about? You were alone in there." Then I guessed. Greatly relieved, I said, "You fell asleep and were dreaming. Talking in your sleep. Come on. It's late and horribly cold. Let's get home."

I pulled at her arm, and she moved obediently. We came out through the great door, through the porch and into the frosty starlit night. There, in front of the cathedral, she halted, shook her head and like someone suddenly awake, and said:

"I was not asleep, Anna. I saw her as plainly as I see you now. She is a short woman, thickset, with a brown peasant's face and a scar puckering one eyebrow. I was kneeling there praying, and then she was there, and I thought how quietly she must have come in, and then I looked at her shabby old brown cloak and hood and thought how strange and rather pleasant it was that this poor woman and I should be there at the same moment, asking the same favour. And then I thought that I mustn't let anything distract me from my intention and started to pray again. And then—in a gruff angry voice she began to rail at me, and I realised——"

She shuddered, and that superstitious chill ran over my flesh again. And yet I was not convinced.

For credulity is a very variable thing. Ever since I could read I had been stuffing myself with stories of the lives and miracles of the saints. Most penmen were monks, so quite naturally most of the books they produced were of a religious nature, and though I was light-minded enough to prefer secular literature when I could get it, it was hard to come by, so I was by this time immensely familiar with stories of saints who had seen visions, of saints who had appeared in visions. And if I had read in a book that on a certain December night St. Petronella had appeared to a would-be mother in the cathedral in Le Mans, I should have found no difficulty in believing it and should have read on, untroubled by doubt, to learn what the saint had done or said.

But to read a thing in a book and to have it told you by somebody whom you have just seen eating supper, somebody you know well, somebody you suspect of having taken a little nap, are two very different things—which is, I suppose, why all saints and mystics seem to suffer from the cynicism of their family circle.

However, despite my doubt, I was curious, so I said, "Why was she angry? And what did she say?"

"She was angry because she saw through me—that I wasn't just asking for the sake of the baby. She said, 'How much farther will you carry this mummery? Do you think to deceive the very saints? Am I God, to put fruit into a virgin womb?' I knew then, Anna, that it wasn't just the peasant woman gone crazy—because in all the world only Richard and I know—even you, Anna, didn't know that I was still——
And then she railed at me like a virago for being what she called sly and deceitful. She cursed me too. And then vanished before I could explain and justify myself. You see, I was startled and taken aback; it was—unearthly. But I was recovering myself, and if she had given me a chance I would have answered her and told her that I had a case; that I did really want a baby, too, and that it was important because of the succession."

Yes, I thought, that was Berengaria! What she had believed to be an unearthly vision had taken her by surprise, had shaken her by a sudden assault; but in a moment her brave blood had been roused and she had cried, "Come back . . . If you understood you would forgive me!" If St. Petronella of Talmont had remained embodied for just another moment, Berengaria of Navarre would have been prepared to answer her attack.

"The curses," Berengaria said, "were quite horrible!"

"Dear Berengaria," I ventured again, "take no heed. I still think you were dreaming. Think—all these things were in your mind and in your thoughts when you knelt down to pray. Saints in genuine visions—I've read of hundreds—always tell the human beings who see them something new, something revealing, something they couldn't have got out of their own minds, asleep or awake. Do you see what I mean? There is nothing here that you didn't know or couldn't have thought of yourself—even the curses. You probably did feel a little guilty about asking for a baby when you only wanted it as a means to an end. You fell asleep for a moment as you prayed and had one of those short vivid dreams that often come when one sleeps in unlikely places—and your own little guilty feeling suggested the curses."

"I wish I could believe that," she said slowly, slackening her step. "But, Anna, it isn't quite true. You see, she did say something which I swear I should never have thought of in a hundred years. In the middle of her tirade she broke off and laughed, such a coarse, nasty laugh, Anna—I'll warrant that when she was alive plain Petronella of Talmont, she was a fishwife! She said, 'No woman ever knelt there,' and she pointed to her tomb, 'and asked for a baby in vain. I'm proud of my power and my reputation, and for my own sake, not for yours—you who, having deceived the world, thought to deceive heaven, too, and get your own way willy-nilly—I'll give you a piece of advice. You'll never get a baby out of Richard, but if you could contrive to deceive him too ... You've got a pretty face and there are many tall knights around you, are there not?' Anna, quite apart from the thought, which you *know* couldn't have come out of my mind, those words convinced me that she was real. She was very plain, and when she said that about the pretty face her voice was the voice of a jealous woman. And 'many tall knights around you'—she said that as though she were the one who sat out at the revels and watched somebody prettier surrounded. Oh dear, perhaps I shouldn't have said that; she may be listening and angrier than ever."

"Rubbish," I said. Then I gave my mind to the problem whether this might genuinely rank as a revelation. I had said that St. Petronella had said nothing which could not have been in Berengaria's mind. She had countered that statement. But could it still be true? For there are things that we think, things we admit to our minds, and there are other things, unadmitted, which burrow about in our minds and stay hidden even from ourselves. Was this suggestion actually St. Petronella's or something which Berengaria, set to deceive the world, had once thought of? A vague idea which had crawled in and burrowed and then, in favourable circumstances, crept up to the surface as earthworms creep up after a warm rain?

"Tell me," I said, "did you ever read anything about St. Petronella?"

"Anna, you know I never read! All I knew was that she had a reputation for making babies. I didn't even know that until Blanche told me."

When I found an opportunity to read a life of St. Petronella I learned that she had spent her youth in Talmont gutting herring and salting them and packing them in barrels. I also learned that one day a woman who worked alongside her, exasperated during an altercation, had attacked her with a knife. Only the direct intervention of God, so the book said, had saved the saint from losing an eye; as it was, she carried the scar to her grave. The account of her virtues—which were many—mentioned "an honest bluntness of speech," a "distaste for deceit in any form."

With that I was driven to wonder. Also, thinking it over, all in all, I found that I had a good deal of fellow feeling with the woman who had set about St. Petronella with the gutting knife!

xv

So far as anyone could see that was a very merry Christmas. Berengaria's new ladies were a gay, lively crowd, and the nobles and knights matched them. Even Richard threw himself into the revels with good heart. He had changed very little, despite the years, despite his cruel disappointment over Jerusalem, despite his long imprisonment. He was still incomparably the handsomest man in Christendom, still capable, at the age of forty, of developing the boisterous high spirit of a boy. Or he could be subtly witty, bluntly outspoken, immensely considerate, inexcusably rude, in turn. Under the topsy-turvy custom of the Twelve Day revels, Eddi, the castle jester, was appointed Lord of Misrule and his word was law. (The custom had, I believe, in years gone by led to confusion, chaos, and even bloodshed; but nowadays the Lords of

417

Misrule knew to a nicety how far they were supposed to go, and unpleasant incidents were very rare.) Richard was appointed Court Minstrel, and when he took lute in hand and played and sang—sometimes sweet tuneful romantic songs, sometimes impromptu witty variations—I think every woman in the hall fell in love with him. Except me, and even I found myself thinking how attractive he was and what a pity—and so on.

By this time the rumours about him had spread far and wide; one or two bishops had felt it their duty to speak to him bluntly about his behaviour, and bishops inspired by a sense of duty are seldom very discreet. Hugh of Lincoln had once accosted him at Mass, caught him by the sleeve, and delivered a straightforward lecture on his various sins which was heard by everyone present in the church. Admittedly Hugh had a quarrel with Richard concerning a fur cloak, but the lecture was not about the sin of covetousness.

However, there was always something about Richard Plantagenet, especially when he was present in the flesh, which seemed to give the lie to the rumour. Since Raife of Clermont had died long ago in Acre nobody had actually been named as his successor in Richard's affection. And he now lived with the Queen, didn't he? Childless—yes, but then that was usually the woman's fault, and some women were childless. The rumours were eagerly spread, seized on, believed, and then—like an appetising but indigestible dish— they tended to be vomited up. Men found it difficult to attribute such a vice to a man who was so brave, so virile, so noisy, so capable, so altogether what a man should be. And every woman, every single woman who ever came within range of him, felt that if she had been Berengaria she would have found it very easy to make him an ardent lover, a glad father of great boys with red-gold hair and prominent blue eyes.

I know this was so, for I spent all that Christmas listening to women talk, often openly, often in a language they thought I did not understand. They all admitted that Berengaria was beautiful, but . . . The *buts* varied and, if viewed with sufficient detachment, could on occasion provoke a sour amusement. But she was cold, hard, stupid; she hadn't wanted to marry him; no, in sooth, somebody's aunt's brother-in-law had been in Italy long ago while Berengaria of Navarre had been staying with her aunt Lucia; there had been a young noble—of course an impossible match—Sancho had been furious and arranged the marriage with Richard

418

straightaway. Ah, but wasn't the real truth that Berengaria herself was queer? Joanna Plantagenet. That was why he, in a fury, had taken up with some man in Palestine, just his fun, his witty way of showing Berengaria how *she* was making a fool of herself; and you will note that it wasn't until Joanna had been married off again to Count Egidio that Richard had taken Berengaria back. Really, how strange, two women— two men ... But what? How? Why? On and on it went, tireless, pointless as our busy look, see, listen, roundabout at L'Espan.

And I would think: God's eyes! If only you knew, you gibbering, gabbling blind fools! And then again I would think: What a joke it would be, how it would fool you and serve you all right if—— But there I was bound to stop short because my sense of humour wasn't quite as keen or disinterested as that of St. Petronella.

Towards Berengaria Richard behaved impeccably now that he was on holiday and forced into her company. Courteous, attentive, kind. But there was no ease between them. Not even the flat, dull acceptance of one another that binds so many married couples. To my watchful eye they always seemed like a bride and groom—perhaps long betrothed, perhaps willing to make themselves agreeable to each another—but just newly thrust together, wary, distrustful, uncertain. When he joked with her at table she invariably looked anxious—now, now this is a jest, do I understand it? Ah yes, thank God—funny, yes, I see! And her laughter was always late. When he was attentive and kind there was a look in her eyes which said, Ah, if only this were real! She could pretend to the world; and to me she could make great angry speeches about false necklaces and pride and keeping up appearances— but it was plain to me now that I saw them together that she was really head over ears in love with him still and that her love constituted an almost fatal handicap.

However, on the whole, the holiday season was pleasant and ordinary until we came to Twelfth-night and were rioting our way through an uproarious game of forfeits. The whole point of this game is that the Lord of Misrule—who will tomorrow be reduced to his proper station in life—can be as tyrannical as he pleases and can dictate to everyone, choosing the forfeit which the victim must pay, with a special eye to the company's amusement. A shy young squire, for example, will be sent to kiss the haughtiest lady, the stoutest or the most pompous man set to going round the floor of the hall on his hands and knees, and so on. It is very simple. I never take part in the game because my participation embarrasses everybody, so on this evening I sat as I had on many another Twelfth-night, on a stool just behind the temporary throne from which the Lord of Misrule issued his orders. Now and again, as I had done many times before, I would suggest some particularly apt and amusing forfeit that occurred to me.

The fun was at its height; everybody was full of good meat and strong wine, bent on ending the festivities in proper style. Eddi, the jester, had proved himself an admirable Lord of Misrule, always amusing, always just tactful enough. One of the ladies whom I had overheard boasting in English had been sent to kiss the King just to see whether the touch of her lips held the magic that she imputed to it. And he had bussed her heartily and set her on his knee amidst great laughter.

Presently it was his own turn and he presented himself in good humble fashion and said the words, "My Lord of Misrule, what is it you will that I should do?" And Eddi, who may have been drunk or may have been bribed, or simply daring beyond belief, said in a low voice, "Get an heir for England."

I was the only one apart from Richard who could hear the words; not that there was anything strange in that, for the hall was full of din and sometimes the sentences in this game were whispered, especially if they partly concerned another person, so that that one might be taken by surprise. And only I, seated just behind Eddi's throne, could see Richard's face. It went quite black with rage. He lifted his hands, took Eddi by the throat, and began to shake him as a terrier shakes a rat. The merry, tipsy company, who had not heard Eddi's words or seen Richard's face, took this as part of the game and renewed their laughter. I got up from my seat and ran forward and took Richard's arm in as hard a grip as I could force my hands to and said, "My lord, desist! You'll kill him. The words were only said in jest." But he was past hearing. And my full weight on his arm could only weaken his grip, it could not break it. Without thinking, acting instinctively as an animal, I stretched my neck and set my teeth into the fleshy part of his hand and bit into it with all my might. With a muttered curse Richard moved his hand to shake me off as though I were a ferret, and Eddi, who, though he was thin and gangling, was too tough a fellow to be strangled by one of Richard Plantagenet's hands, shook himself free.

By this time the company was beginning to crowd down to

our end of the hall to see what was to do. There was half a minute when the whole thing hung in the balance. Then Eddi, recovering the quick wit which had brought him from herding sheep to entertaining kings, called out:

"My good people, that was a wasted jest and the best of the game. 'Get the Duchess of Apieta to bite you,' I said to this fellow. And most cunningly he did!"

"How could I know that?" I cried loudly in mock dismay. "I thought I was saving your life, my Lord of Misrule."

Richard, recovering his sanity, countered with, "How else could I have provoked her—when she wasn't even in the game? My Lord of Misrule, I claim privilege. The little she-cat sat apart, avoiding the penalties but, as you see, sharing the fun. Set her forfeit that she bind up the wound she has inflicted."

"That is but just," said Eddi, resuming his seat and the dictatorial pose. "You, woman, go with this fellow and bandage his hand with a piece of your best shift!"

Though slightly on the bawdy side, such an order was completely in tune with the spirit of the game. Richard and I left the hall together amidst a gale of laughter, with Eddi's voice bellowing through it, "Good people, who is next? Don't think to escape my orders. Who is next?" The game went on.

"I should have killed him but for you."

"I could see that. Otherwise I should have remembered my manners—and the fact that I prefer my meat thoroughly cooked."

"You showed great presence of mind. I always said you had the sharpest wit of any woman I ever encountered."

"And the sharpest teeth? Truly, Richard, I am sorry," I said, surveying the two half circles of holes my teeth had made on his hand.

"It's nothing," he said. "It was the surprise and the suddenness of the nip. You heard what he said to me, I suppose."

"Good advice is so often odious." I drew in my breath, took hold of my courage, and added, "It was good advice, you know."

He looked at me without speaking for a moment and then said briskly, "Come along, tie up my hand."

When I had done so he set his other hand under my chin, tilting my face; then, suddenly stooping from his great height, he kissed me, not in the hearty smacking fashion of the revels, but softly, slowly, almost like a lover.

"I shall have bussed every female out there before the

night is done," he said, as though explaining. "And that was a kiss of peace."

"Thank you, my liege," I said, forcing my voice to lightness. Father, on very rare occasions, had brushed my brow with his beard, but no man had ever kissed me before.

XVI

That Twelfth-night marked the end of the revels; some lords and ladies took their leave and I began to think, almost in homesick fashion, about L'Espan, but whenever I mentioned leaving Le Mans, Berengaria found some excuse to detain me. Finally, after some days of dalliance, I said:

"But you will be going back to Rouen yourself very shortly."

"Not until the Châlus treasure arrives. Richard is waiting for that. And surely, Anna, you who are so curious about all things remarkable would like to see a board and chessmen all made in gold that has been buried for five hundred years. They say it belonged to Charlemagne himself." She spoke as though the Châlus treasure were something that everyone knew about.

Buried in L'Espan, I had never even heard it mentioned and was forced to ask, "What is the Châlus treasure?"

"I told you. A golden chessboard and pieces. Had you not heard? A peasant ploughing on Vidomar's fields turned it out with his ploughshare. All the pieces are gold, but to distinguish them some are set with rubies and some with emeralds, and the squares on the board are also marked with jewels, one square being set with small diamonds and the next with sapphires."

"That," I said, "would be a very remarkable sight. And if Charlemagne ever possessed such a toy, every chronicle I ever read about him was at fault; he was supposed to despise such gauds."

"Well," she said, "wait until tomorrow or the next day and you shall see for yourself."

Later that day I mentioned the Châlus treasure to someone else and was told that one of Vidomar's ploughmen had uncovered the door of a secret underground chamber which, investigated, yielded six alabaster jars full to the brim with jewels.

Putting the two stories together, I found myself just able to believe that one of Vidomar's ploughmen had ploughed something of interest and possibly of value out of a field. It was worth waiting one day or two days to see what it was, particularly as Berengaria seemed to cling so ardently to my company.

Perhaps I was the only person who found that "treasure," when it did arrive, of any interest.

It was a jar of coarse red pottery with a lip at one side and a handle at the other, and when the clay was soft somebody had scratched on both sides the "fish" sign which abounded in the catacombs of Rome. I recognised the jar as one of those lamps which had shed a light upon those early Christians as they gathered underground for their worship—with Nero and his lions, Poppaea and her curiosity, Trachus and his spies almost overhead. Somebody faithful or sentimental had carried it northwards and at some time of crisis had buried it. There were twelve coins in it, six silver, six of base metal, and all so defaced by usage that they told me nothing.

Richard refused—or to be just—was completely unable to believe that this paltry bit of pottery, these few worthless coins actually constituted the Châlus treasure.

"If Vidomar thinks he can fool me thus——" he said, and breathed out threats as a dragon breathes fire.

He was, it seemed, a believer in the chessboard rather than in the alabaster jars of jewels, for the message he despatched to Vidomar ran, "Will you give up the golden chess set, or must I come and take it?"

Berengaria said to me, "Until he gets the answer, Anna, he will have no thought for anything else. I think I will ride back with you and spend a few days at L'Espan. I would like to see it and the women again."

I took it as a good sign that she should evince interest in something outside her relationship with Richard, and we set out in good spirits. Once I should have harboured doubts concerning the effect of her arrival on Blondel's peace of mind, but from the time of his return to the time of Richard's sending for her we had all lived together so pleasantly and peacefully that such doubts seemed now out of time and out of place.

They greeted each another with a warmth and pleasure which, despite their difference in rank, spoke of a steady affection. She said he must play for her a great deal during her visit because no other musician—and she had heard many in Rouen and Poitou—could make music half so well and sweetly as he did. She praised the appearance and design of the house which had grown up during her absence and gave him full credit for his work on it. I watched and listened and remembered how once a word of praise from her could bring a blush, a glow, a too ready word of self-deprecation. Now he listened and smiled and was pleased, but without anything pitiable about his pleasure.

When we were alone she said, "How old Blondel looks, Anna. And how ill!"

"He is older," I said; "we are all older. And he drinks too much."

"And what has happened to his arm?"

"It is withering. Like a half-lopped branch. Don't you remember, it was almost slashed through at the Battle of Arsouf?"

"Of course," she said, but I could see that she had either not known or had forgotten that trivial thing.

She was older now and kinder, less self-centred. And in a curious, almost ominous way, despite the elaborate hairdress, the fine newfangled gown and pointed shoes, the shining jewels, she fitted in with the peaceful, unworldly jog-trot life of L'Espan, that refuge for unwanted women. It was a pleasant, peaceful week that she spent with us; then the news came that Vidomar, Lord of Châlus, had returned Richard's message: "I see, my lord, that by demanding of me something I do not possess and have never possessed you are determined to pick a quarrel with me. I sent to you the only treasure-trove to which as my overlord you are entitled; anything else of mine that you covet you must indeed come and take."

Once Richard would have perceived the integrity of that answer, would have admired the sturdy spirit of the man who despatched it, and laughed and returned some witty, friendly answer. But he was older, too, and, under that genial, boisterous manner, soured and suspicious. He had chosen to believe in the golden chessboard, the jewelled chessmen, and without more ado he prepared to move against Vidomar and to besiege the castle at Châlus.

"I must go with him," Berengaria said, thrown into a flutter. "Now more than ever, I must be where he is." She looked at me earnestly. "Anna, I wish you could come with me—you are the only *friend* I have in the world—but I won't ask it of you because we shall be on the move, and L'Espan is so peaceful, so comfortable. I can see why you love it. But, Anna, if I ever want you, need you, will you come?"

"Of course I will. It is peaceful here, true, and I don't

424

particularly enjoy the company of your fine ladies—but now that the building is finished, L'Espan is likely to bore me. I'll come whenever you send for me."

As soon as she had gone I turned my attention to Blondel. I sent for him and he came and stood before me. It still lacked an hour to noon, but he was already drunk. Not reeling or helpless as in Acre—that stage was long past—but drunk nevertheless. I looked at him, puffy under the eyes, under the jaw, glazed pink over the cheekbones, his mane of hair, dead white now, too long and unkempt. His tunic, new for Christmas, was crumpled and stained, his hose dirty and in need of mending. The shrivelled small right hand he now carried, of habit, thrust into the front of his tunic.

And as he stood there I remembered with the greatest clarity the singing boy who had smiled at me in the market place at Pamplona—the taut slim figure, the lithe grace, the lovely intelligent face.

"Blondel," I said, "why do you do it?"

"Do what, my lady?"

"Drink," I said brutally. "Fuddle yourself with that damned wine. Look at yourself. You're still a young man, but you're beginning to look like an old soldier at a street corner."

"Well, I am an old soldier, am I not?" he asked amiably. "Of your charity, lady, kind lady, a penny for an old soldier back from the Holy Wars." It was good mimicry, and he laughed at the end of it.

"I'm not laughing," I said sternly. "I'm very much concerned about you, Blondel. Maybe I have been careless and unnoticing, but Her Majesty was quite shocked; she said how ill and how old you looked."

"Indeed?" he said, and tilted his head with something of his old merry look. Then he laughed again, not exactly bitterly or sardonically, but as though there were a joke in it, a joke known only to himself. "Did she now? And dirty? Did she say I was dirty?"

"No," I said, a little taken aback.

"She could have done, in good truth, but maybe she didn't notice that. For dirty I am."

"And why?" I asked passionately, crying out on my own hurt. "Why should you destroy yourself? You're young and healthy and immensely gifted. Maybe your life has gone wrong in one respect—or more than one," I skimmed on hastily, anxious to convey sympathy without knowledge, "but that is a very common fate. Only the weak and the silly—" I hesitated. I had meant to say "behave as you do," but something in his eyes gave me pause and I tried to find a more general, less offensive ending for the sentence.

"I am weak, I am silly. We have our uses, you know."

"You're not silly," I said impatiently. I could see that this conversation was leading nowhere.

We were standing near the little glassed-in window of my room, the window in which I took such pride, and although outside the garden was bleak and winter-bound and the trees still stark and bare, I could hear a bird singing, most piercingly sweet, confident in spring's coming. I fumbled for some thought that eluded me.

Then I said, "Really, Blondel, I didn't send for you to rail at you; it was just that I can't bear to see—— But we'll leave that. I wanted you, now that the house is completed, to turn your skill to another task." That was it! While the building was going forward he had been moderately sober; what he needed was to be busy, interested, engrossed. But as I said "another task" I hadn't in my mind the slightest shadow, the frailest seed of an idea of what I could set him to do. But I looked at him, saw the withering right hand, remembered that he could write with his left—write . . . write . . . Battle of Arsouf . . . Yes, I had it.

"The fact is," I said, "that monks who have never left their cloister and secular clerks who have never stepped outside their own rooms are pouring out accounts of this crusade as fast as they can scribble. Now you are a penman, maybe the only penman of any skill who went on the crusade and fought in the battles. If you would set down a record of personal experiences, all the little things, things the others couldn't know or guess at, it would be of great value. Could you face such a task? For instance—you were there, Blondel, standing just behind the Queen on that evening when the Marquis of Montferrat told us about the letter and the cake he had received from the Old Man of the Mountain. You heard with your own ears. Now at Hagenau they said that the Old Man was pure fable, and the scribes who know no better are saying that he has no existence—do you see? You could refute so many of their theories if only you would shoulder this task."

Between the puffy lids the eyes had brightened.

"I could write what I saw, what I know. I doubt whether it would rate as a historical record."

"It should shape well beside the account of Selwyn of Tours, who is so lame that he has to be carried from the scriptorium to the refectory and from the refectory to the dormitory," I said. "For some reason he feels himself qualified to write most didactically about the Third Crusade and why it failed. I understand that he—of course he is a monk—blames the women who followed the army and undermined the morale of the common soldiers."

Blondel laughed. "He's barking up the right tree, you know, my lady, but from the wrong side of the tree. Richard of England once said—and I am inclined to agree with him—that women were the root of the trouble. But one woman was more to blame than the others—and that was Her Grace, the Duchess of Apieta."

I gaped and goggled and said, "I? I'd like to know how you make that out."

"So easy, so plain. *You* sent me to Westminster. She would never have thought of it alone. Her mind only works on the small things. *You* sent me to Westminster. So Richard didn't marry Alys, and that made Philip his enemy; and Isaac of Cyprus insulted the princess who had refused him, so Lydia Comnena was taken prisoner and Leopold of Austria was affronted, being her uncle. You and I, my lady, though we do not figure in the chronicles, we are—what is the term?— mythical figures! Between us we ruined the Third Crusade!"

"You *are* drunk!" I said. "For God's sake, if you write, write in all soberness, not fantastic, wine-flown rubbish of that kind."

"I will write, and I will write the truth."

"I think Pontius Pilate said something like that."

"Ah no! That shows your mind to be a palimpsest. Pilate *asked*, 'What is truth?' and he *said*, 'What I have written I have written.'"

"I stand corrected. Well, will you begin at once?"

"This afternoon," he said.

XVII

He was still writing busily weeks later when Berengaria sent for me. A brief message, "Please, Anna, come. Blanche is here, gravely ill. I need you."

It was late March and the month had been dry and windy, so the mire had dried into dust on the roads and I made good speed to the manor house at Limoges where Berengaria had lodged while Richard besieged Châlus, twenty miles or so away. Châlus had proved a harder nut to crack than Richard had bargained for, and Blanche's husband Thibaut had come to lend his aid. Blanche had ridden with him, saying that it would be nice for her to be with Berengaria. Blanche had sought St. Petronella's aid in September, and I had wished her a fine big boy. But she had ridden hard for three days, keeping up with Thibaut and his men-at-arms, and the seven-month child she bore during the night after her arrival was rather bigger than most normally gestated children. The women and the midwives had done their best: there was careful stitching with black thread on her torn body, there were the open oyster shells under the bed, the bunch of hazel twigs on the pillow. But she died the day after I reached Limoges, and there were Berengaria and I linked in common grief again.

I chiefly remembered the serious, earnest way in which Blanche had sat by my fire and advised me about the administration of L'Espan. Berengaria's memory reached back to a time when they had both been small shy girls bidden on some occasion into impressive company and Blanche had taken the younger sister's hand and led her forward.

"I remember her hand was cold and not quite steady, but it comforted me and she marched forward like a soldier," Berengaria said, and wept.

"If she had been less brave she would have broken the journey. There are times when courage can be a disadvantage to a woman," I said.

"St. Petronella——" Berengaria said, and stopped.

And I thought it was 'better to talk about St. Petronella than to go on weeping, so I took up the theme.

"Blanche certainly asked for a lusty boy—and I've never seen a more promising baby. We can't blame St. Petronella. Thousands of women die every year in childbirth, even at the normal time."

"St. Petronella is harsh. She saw through Blanche too. Blanche was twenty-nine, Anna. Years past the age to have a first baby. But she asked for him and I suppose you could say her wish was granted. But it was a cheat, all the same."

"It gave Blanche seven months of great happiness," I ventured.

"Yes, I suppose so. I hope so. But it does seem such a pity."

For a moment it seemed to me that everything I looked at, everything in the world, seemed such a pity.

"You'll stay with me for a little while now, won't you, Anna? This siege goes on and on. Stay and spend Easter with me. They'll call a truce for the holy days and perhaps Richard will ride over."

But Richard had taken his last ride.

Sometime during the previous week he had succeeded in forcing the outer defences of the castle, but from an inner wall someone had taken deliberate aim at him and shot an arrow into his shoulder. No vital part had been touched, no great amount of blood lost; and although the arrowhead had broken off in the wound and the surgeon had made a clumsy job of cutting it out, Richard insisted upon treating it as a mere scratch and tried to keep as secret as possible the fact that he had been wounded at all. He had forbidden that the Queen—or anyone else who did not know—should be told. For two days he had gone about his business by directing the siege, which now promised to be quickly and successfully ended, and had managed to conceal the agony of the mangled wound. Then it had inflamed and he fell into fever and had been obliged to keep to his bed. Now he was out of his mind and raving, and his chaplain, Theobald, and Marcadie, the captain of his Flemish troops, had decided to take matters into their own hands and had sent for Berengaria and for Escel, who was in Brittany.

The news struck Berengaria into a dumb somnambulant state.

When she had said, "You will come with me, Anna?" she did not speak again until we were far on our way, riding through the mild early April day; then she said, "They say death always strikes thrice."

When we arrived she slipped down from her horse before anyone had time to aid her, shook out her skirts and, covered with dust as she was and with her hair falling loose about her shoulders, went straight to his bedside and there remained, replacing the covers as he thrust them off, smoothing back the tangled, sweat-soaked hair, ministering to his insatiable thirst, and sometimes, in quiet moments, holding his hand.

He did not know her. He lay propped on the pillows, staring straight ahead at the wall of the tent. His face was grey except for a patch of dusky crimson that looked as if it had been painted on each high cheekbone. His lips were cracked and blackened, and save for short intervals when his eyes closed and he seemed to doze for a moment, a constant stream of words flowed over them.

Chiefly he talked of Jerusalem. Sometimes he was actually storming the city, issuing vast stirring orders in a voice that was little more than a whisper; sometimes he was making preparations, reeling off lists of stores and equipment that had been consumed or abandoned or destroyed years ago, calling for men who had long been quiet in their graves.

"Go on, here I stand, aim straight at me, I'll not dodge. Nothing can touch me until I have taken Jerusalem. Shining in the sun, just beyond the hills; but not to be looked at. I shall never look at it until the moment when I lead my army against it.

"Walter is a better man than Longchamp, but he can't wring out the money as that ferret could. Anyway, England is milked dry. The golden treasure of Châlus should provide two hundred horses. You know, Raife, without horses there is no hope; if they'd left me the horses I would have risked it despite all.

"Water! Water! I've said a thousand times that they are to go round every hour. Every hour!

"But in the first place, I can't feed them. Hard on three thousand of them. I need my stores for the men who are coming to Jerusalem. Ask Leopold then, maybe he'll spare some of his sausages. Certainly not, Escel is using them on sores, a crazy notion, but by God's footstool, it works. Then kill the lot. Chop off their heads. Now we can go forward. Help, help for the Holy Sepulchre! Will you make way there? I promised to lay Philip's trinket to rest there. A present from Judas. Like the grey horse. When next I come I shall bring spare horses, hundreds of them. It irks me to see knights with armour dismounted, trundling about like little castles on legs, helpless, useless. And always thirsty; I know, everybody is thirsty, this is a thirsty land. They speak of it flowing with milk and honey, both bad things when you're thirsty: milk I never could stomach, and honey is best when made into mead as my barbarian English make it. Water is best, Blondel, mark my words; that stuff you guzzle will rot out your guts. For myself, I'd as soon drink horse's piss. If only we could find that well; it was clearly marked on the map. . . . Water!"

Then she would hold the cup to his lips again.

It went on all through the night and the next day. The April sun beat on the canvas, and the inside of the tent grew warm and stuffy. The stench of corruption crept about.

Escel arrived, carefully bearing a dish full of what looked to me like blue mould. He drove us from the bedside, and I led Berengaria away, saying, "This is the time for you to eat and drink and be strong." She swallowed what I offered. I

430

tried to make her raise her feet and rest them on a stool, for from long sitting in one position her legs and ankles had swollen until great rolls of puffy flesh hung over the tops of her shoes. But she went back and waited by the tent door until Escel emerged.

He was weeping.

"They delayed sending for me too long. And the surgeon was a clumsy butcher. He should have his own right hand cut off so that he never mangles another man!" He stumbled away, wiping his face on his sleeve.

There was another day and another night. I crept in and out. Berengaria kept her place by the bed. The low slurred voice had ceased its talk and Richard lay quiet with closed eyes.

The chaplain, with the wine and the wafer in readiness, hovered, waiting for the brief consciousness which often comes just before the end.

It came with the light of a beautiful morning full of bird song. Just such a morning as the one at L'Espan when Berengaria had ridden out to join Richard.

I was there, having carried Berengaria a strong hot posset, and I was persuading her to drink it.

Richard opened his eyes. They were no longer prominent and overbright, no longer blue, but dark and dull and sunken. And conscious.

He looked at us. With weary recognition. For a moment he did not speak. Nor did we, though Berengaria leaned forward so that he could see her more easily. Then he said:

"My mother . . . I have much to say—to my mother."

"She is on her way," Berengaria said, whether with or without truth I could not know. "But I am here, Richard. I could tell her—anything you wish her to be told."

The voice which, though slurred and weak, had run so glib in delirium now came slow and difficult.

"Tell her then—it must be John—not Arthur. If Constance had let me have him—I could have trained him, child as he is—but an untrained child—straight from his mother's skirts—could never—stand against John Iscariot and Philip Iscariot. . . . John, you understand, John."

"I understand, Richard."

Theobald, with the single-mindedness of all good priests, now moved forward and said, "My lord . . ."

With a flash of the old fire Richard said, "All in good time. Let us dispose of this world first. Fetch me Marcadie—and

431

the fellow who cut out the arrow that struck me. .... Is that Anna Apieta skulking in the shadow?"

I stepped forward. He closed his eyes as I approached and lay mustering his strength. Without looking at me, still with closed eyes, he said:

"She trusts you—and rightly. You are strong—competent. John will cheat her—the tin dues ... Look after her. You can reckon and write." He drew a gasping breath. "If more women were like you ..."

It flashed through my mind that I could reckon and write because I could never fulfil a woman's functions—and because a man more enlightened than other men had chosen to set me free.

It was nothing to my credit that I could be entrusted to deal with the dues from tin mines; any woman who at fourteen years of age had been put in charge of her own estate and revenues would have been, as he called it, strong and competent.

But he was dying, and this was no time for such thoughts. I said solemnly:

"Richard, I promise you that I will look after her and see justice done."

Then and only then did he turn his eyes to Berengaria and say, "I have been an ill husband to you, my lady—and you so beautiful and kind. But God makes us, you know, and He did not make me—a lover of women—it was not my choice."

"Oh, my lord," Berengaria said. And at that moment Theobald came hurrying back, followed by Marcadie, who pushed before him and then aside into a corner a tall young man with yellow hair whose hands were bound behind with a cord. And creeping behind them came the clumsy surgeon.

Richard closed his eyes again and breathed hard.

"This fellow first." He opened his eyes and looked at the cringing surgeon. "Always remember, you did the best you could. I set out to take Jerusalem, but I boggled it. You tried to cut the arrow out of me—you see! If you are to blame for the small thing ... I want you to take ten crowns from my purse and settle your mind, and God speed you in all you do. Marcadie!"

"I am here, my lord," said the Flemish captain, striding forward and brutally pushing the surgeon aside.

"You have the fellow who shot me?"

"He is here, my lord." He set a big brown hand between the shoulders of the young man and jerked him forward.

"Your name?" Richard asked in a failing voice.

"Bertrand de Gourdon," said the man, loudly, defiantly.

"And did I ever do you any ill?"

"You did, sire. Both my father and my brother died at your hand."

"Meet and just," Richard murmured. "I just wanted to know. Call quits, eh? Marcadie, I know I said—we'd hang—the whole—garrison. But let this fellow go free. And now, Theobald ..."

The priest, calm, sure in his office, moved forward. Berengaria dropped heavily to her knees by the side of the bed, and I joined her.

Outside in the camp Marcadie slowly and methodically flayed Bertrand de Gourdon before he hanged him side by side with the rest of the garrison.

The looters searched the castle for the golden treasure and found nothing.

Richard died. The April sun went down in splendour behind the thickly budded trees, and through the dusk the birds sang of spring.

XVIII

For once the superstition which Berengaria had mentioned was justified. Death struck his third blow while the tears for Richard were still wet on our faces.

It had been easier than I had expected to get Berengaria from the deathbed; she stood up obediently and would have let herself be led away, but her feet were now too swollen to allow walking and men had to carry her to the tent which had been made ready for our reception. There she lay on the bed, crying, but without tumult or bitterness. She was mourning the man whom, despite everything, she had loved, weeping for the tall red-haired young knight of the Spring Tournament.

We heard a commotion outside, the sound of some cavalcade arriving, and Berengaria rose on her elbow.

"Anna, that is Eleanor. Bring her straight to me. It is important that I give her his message before they start inventing things he said."

Once again I thought how far they erred who called her a stupid woman; and I thought that, properly treated and trusted, she would have made a good queen.

Outside in the dusk was a little knot of men on jaded

horses and in the middle of them a woman, hooded and cloaked.

As I pushed through the men who had gathered around the group I heard one say, "Madam, he is dead. He died within this hour."

I saw the woman's hands go not to her heart or her mouth, as is customary on the hearing of ill news, but to her belly. She swayed as she sat there on the horse. Hands reached to help her down, and as she gave herself to them her hood slipped back and I saw that it was not Eleanor but her daughter Joanna.

The Albigenses had risen against her husband Raymond, and she had left him, fighting for his life, and despite a well-advanced pregnancy had ridden to ask Richard to come to the aid of his brother-in-law.

The shock of the news killed her. We got her under cover; we did all we could—even Escel did his best to deal with a matter outside his scope, for miscarriages and the like were generally deemed to be beneath the notice of a serious physician—but no efforts were availing and she died next day.

She had asked to be buried beside her best-beloved brother, and we laid them together in the Abbey of Fontevrault, though Richard's heart, in accordance with a request he had made before he set out for Jerusalem, was taken to Rouen, his favourite city and the one which he had always regarded as his capital.

When that was done, Berengaria said to me:

"Now it is all over. You and I are alone together once more." She laid her hand on my arm. "Now that I look back, Anna, it seems that you and I have always been alone, really."

I looked back, too, and saw that there was some truth in that rather sweeping statement. Together and alone we had planned and plotted for Richard; together and alone we had waited for him; together and alone we had watched his passing.

But even as I laid my hand over hers which clasped my arm the treacherous thought went through my mind like a snake. We might live for another twenty, thirty years, alone together, entangled in a web of tapestry wool! Eyes on the page, ear cocked for the patient little sigh. The racking of the brain to bring to birth some comment or remark on a subject doomed to premature demise. Always before there had been a little hope of delivery—hope that Richard would marry

434

her, hope that Richard would return, hope that Richard would send for her. But now—twenty, thirty years of tapestry stitching and boredom. Long before that I should be praying for death to free me.

And from the women at L'Espan I had heard many stories of arrangements hastily entered into immediately after a bereavement. Pity could be a trap too.

L'Espan—where there were now seven women, most of them fond of tapestry work; where we had been making plans for a new well sunk in that underground forecourt . . .

In a voice that was so firm that it sounded brutal I said:

"I intend to go back to L'Espan, for a time, at least. If you care to come with me . . ."

"But of course," she said gently. "It was what I was thinking, that you and I should be together at L'Espan."

"But not alone," I insisted.

"In a sense, no, of course. We couldn't turn them away now. In fact, Anna—— Perhaps this is an idle thought. I haven't slept well since—— One has to occupy one's thoughts when one lies awake in the night. . . . We could make L'Espan bigger. There must be so many women like those there, like me. We might even"—she brought it out diffidently—"build a chapel and have a priest."

I saw then that, like many other women whom life has failed and disappointed, she was turning to Holy Church. And Holy Church, at least, would not fail her; with her it was simply a case of "Seek and ye shall find." And dimly, tentatively, I began to perceive how I could ease the burden off my unwilling shoulders onto those broad and accommodating ones.

"That is an interesting idea," I said.

And I thought: Holy Church—though they call her *she*—is strong and competent; she will deal with the Cornish tin mines and the mill dues from Le Bocage and all those miles of fishing rights. She will know what to do with women who come in with boxes of jewels.

Then I stiffened, remembering the little dog who was forbidden at the nunnery at Blois.

"If you make L'Espan into a nunnery, Berengaria, I shall insist—because, after all, I started it and it is supposed to belong to me—that part of it be reserved for women like me; women who could not bear to take vows, women who like little dogs."

"But you've never had a little dog in your life, Anna."

"You know what I mean."

"Yes. It's very strange that you should say that about making a nunnery. I had never said, had I, but I have been thinking——"

XIX

Women whose lives follow an ordinary pattern bear children, nourish and tend them, and start them on the road to growth, and for a while the child minds its mother's bidding; but inevitably there comes one day when it begins to follow its own will, and another day when, if not by word, by action, it says, "I can do without you now."

So it was with me and L'Espan. In the five years that followed Richard's death it grew and went its own way so inexorably that sometimes it seemed to me that the place had a destiny of its own, mapped from the moment of the turning of the first sod.

And the day came when the last stone was in place and I could walk around and see everything in order, with L'Espan pursuing its threefold life, no part of which concerned me.

There was the nunnery. Berengaria had hankered towards the idea of establishing a religious house, and subject to certain conditions, I was but too pleased to shuffle off the responsibility for the finance and administration. So now about L'Espan there were a dozen and a half nuns, soberly clothed, walking meekly with down-bent eyes, sedulously obedient to the orders of a tyrannical abbess whom they had chosen themselves in what I could only think was a passion for self-immolation. To me she seemed a terrible, detestable woman, but I knew that the establishment of the funds would be safe with her.

Then there was, in the old wing, what was invariably called the "Lodgings." It sheltered twenty women whose rights I had carefully guarded when I handed over my charge. They were the kind of women I should have been but for Father—unplaced, in need of a settled home, but lacking all sense of vocation. They moved more briskly, dressed more brightly in their shabby finery, had their pets, their playing cards, their tapestries, their ever-changing pattern of little alliances and feuds.

And in the newest part of the building there was the part which the abbess, who was German by origin, always called the "Kindergarten." There were housed a number of orphan

436

children and a few bastards and a few taken in charity from enormous families in overcrowded hovels.

I was, I must confess, as little at ease with the children as with the nuns or the ladies in the Lodgings. My appearance rouses only two responses in the young, stark terror or mockery. And although I liked to see them happy and well fed, I never had much feeling for children, except for two who seemed doomed never to be born—the boy who would look like Blondel, the girl who would be my god-daughter.

The one person who moved from part to part of L'Espan and seemed equally at home in each was Berengaria. She could help to tend the children in the Kindergarten and seemed happy when playing with them; she could move on and spend an hour or two with the ladies in the Lodgings, stitching a little, gossiping a little, eating cakes and sweetmeats; and then, at the call of the chapel bell, there she was, sinking easily and gracefully into place amongst the nuns. Affection, at times amounting to adoration, greeted her wherever she went; the children loved their gentle playmate, the ladies regarded her as one of themselves, the nuns looked on her as a saint and invariably referred to her as the foundress of L'Espan. And she was content, happy and tranquil as an old man, home after a long and disastrous war, basking in the sun. Armed with two weapons, great beauty and a stubborn will, she had fought for many years, losing every battle and yet emerging victorious, able to lay her weapons down, submitting her beauty to time, her will to that of God, now that the enemy, the loved one, was dead.

Gradually, but very surely, it became apparent to me that the will of God, so far as Berengaria was concerned, was conveyed through the voice of the abbess. The day came when that voice announced that I was free.

Madame Ursula and I concealed beneath a scrupulous politeness a cordial and reciprocal dislike. Probably she sensed that if it had been left to me L'Espan would have remained a purely secular establishment; and certainly the arrangements I had made, the protective measures I had taken for the happiness and security of the uncloistered inhabitants before I handed over the reins to her were justification for such a suspicion. So her dislike for me had sounder grounds than mine for her, which were based upon reasons less ponderable and more personal. Yet we had worked together very successfully during the long business of transition; she had a keen brain and, in any matter disconnected with the religious life, a sense of justice, a gift of logic. Professionally—and religion with its many ramifications was to her a profession rather than a vocation—she was unjust, illogical, dictatorial to an unimaginable degree, and unbearably superior. So armoured, so immune, that often words failed me and I longed with childish fury to smack her smooth plump face.

A few days after the last of the building was done she sent for me and brought into the open a subject which had lurked alongside for some time. The subject of Blondel.

I entered this passage of arms heavily handicapped from the start by, if nothing else, a sense of guilt; for it was a subject which I knew should have been faced and dealt with long ago.

Blondel had been at L'Espan when Berengaria and I returned there after Richard's death. He had finished his account of the crusade; no building was in progress and he was drinking steadily. His right arm was now useless, and it is admittedly difficult for anyone to keep neat and trim with one hand, however skilled that one may be. Not that Blondel now cared or took much trouble. However, I tidied him up to the best of my ability; he could still play his lute and he did a good deal to cheer Berengaria in those days, making her music and telling her stories and listening to those sad, reminiscent little speeches which are the voice of sorrow. And I, as always, took joy in his company. Sourness had sharpened his everready wit, and so long as I avoided remembering, eschewed sentimental backward-looking, all was well.

Then the spurt of new building, new planning had begun, and he had been busy and sober for longer intervals, and even the critical Madam Ursula had admitted his usefulness. Weeks and months had slipped away; now and again I had roused myself to say, "When were you last shaved?" or "Get your hair cut," or "That tunic is a disgrace," or "Come, let me cut your nails." But such cares were only like irksome little pebbles on a smooth and pleasant path. There were hours, especially during the winter when the evenings were long, which we could spend together in the room I had firmly reserved for myself, practising our English, reading together, or just talking. Such hours made up to me for being chained to L'Espan, chained by my promise to Berengaria, by my promise to Richard, by my self-exacted promise to Father. I would look after Berengaria, and where she was, there I would be; I could but be grateful that Blondel was there too.

Now here was Madam Ursula saying in her dry, rasping voice that he must go.

I restrained myself and was silent while she pointed out in nice order the strength of her position, the weakness of mine should I—that was the implication—be so silly as to make a stand.

The Lodgings' charter, which I had myself drawn up, stipulated that certain pets, capable of being kept within control, must be accepted. Not pages, servingmen, or minstrels—that was correct, was it not?

The women now in residence were of some long standing, women who remembered—doubtless with gratitude—all I had done for them and who would neither dispute nor attempt to share my privilege; but I did see—did I not?—that we must look to the future. Another generation of women would arise who, at need, could look back and say, "At one time the Duchess of Apieta lived here and kept her own lute player." Abuses so easily crept in, did they not?

And then, unfortunately, there was the character of the man.

I sat, resolutely dumb, while she pointed out that he was drunken and dissolute, a disgrace to any respectable establishment, even an entirely secular one. L'Espan was, of its very nature (and her glance accused me), a somewhat unorthodox place, and the task of any innovation was to prove itself at least as good as, and if possible better than, the thing it superseded, was it not? And think how misleading, how abominably misleading it would be if, when the bishop made his inspection, he met Blondel, dirty, unshaven, and drunk.

My silence at first encouraged and then finally disconcerted her. Silence from me was a new thing—but then we had never before talked openly about Blondel. I listened to her, to her irritating dicta and even more irritating questions, like bladders full of stones tied to curs' tails: "Is it not?" "Do you agree?"

Then I said, "Madam, what leads you to believe that the lute player is *my* appurtenance? So far as he belongs to anyone, he belongs to Her Majesty, does he not?"

That took her aback, but only for a moment. The professional side came into play. At one level there might be a difference between a disgrace belonging to the Duchess of Apieta and the same disgrace belonging to the Queen, the foundress of L'Espan. Madam Ursula gave that difference its due—a moment's silence. Then she was abbess of L'Espan, strong and armoured, and a disgrace was a disgrace, never mind its sponsor. The bishop on his inspection might not wait to have the distinction pointed out, and despite its unorthodox aspect L'Espan was going to gain a good report from the bishop if Madam Ursula had anything to do with it. (Was it not?)

"I did not realise," she said. "I am very sorry, in that case, to have troubled you in the matter, Your Grace. I will take up the question with Her Majesty."

Madam Ursula wasted no time. That evening after supper Berengaria took me by the arm and said, "Come to my room, Anna. I want to talk to you."

She fussed over me a little, insisting that I take the most comfortable seat, pouring me wine with her own hands, offering me small cakes cut into fancy shapes. Then she seated herself and lifted into her lap the heavy altar cloth which she was embroidering for the chapel. She stitched for a moment or two in silence, and when she spoke she did so without looking up.

"I had a conversation with the abbess just before vespers." She had taken lately to measuring the day in the cloister terms, and each time she did so I was conscious of a flick of reasonless, quickly suppressed irritation. I heard it sharpen my voice now as I said:

"About Blondel?"

She looked up. "Really, Anna, sometimes I think you must be a witch! How did you guess?"

"I didn't guess. She spoke to me this morning."

"She didn't mention that. What did she say to you?"

"Several things, many ridiculous and all unkind."

"And what did you say?"

"Absolutely nothing. I let her talk herself to a standstill and then referred her to you."

"Oh, what a pity. I would so much rather not have been mixed up in it."

I could see that the interview had disturbed her usual deep serenity; that and her attentiveness to me led me to the conclusion that Madam Ursula had launched a pretty shrewd attack and that Berengaria was now looking to me for support. I was prepared to give it right heartily, for my retreat that morning had been a tactical one, owing to diplomacy, not to reluctance or inability to fight.

"You were bound to be involved. And I thought better sooner than later. Whatever I had said this morning would have carried no weight at all. It is useless for me to argue or reason with her. She suspects my every motive and, unless we are talking business, discounts every word I say. So, though I had many good arguments, I thought they would sound better from you. She does at least listen to you—and with a marked degree of respect."

"Oh, Anna. You shouldn't say that. She is the abbess. She is the head of this house."

"Of the religious side of this house," I amended. "And if one of her nuns—God pity them—wanted to keep a singing bird, she would be entirely within her rights to say, 'No, you must drive it out to be gobbled up by a sparrow hawk.' But *we* have taken no vows of obedience. That was made perfectly plain from the first. I took particular pains to mark exactly the limit of her authority, and it stops at the door of the Lodgings. I always knew that one day she would poke her nose into our affairs, and I so arranged it that when she did that same nose could be given a sharp rap. I would have administered it myself this morning, but a rap from me would be beneath her notice; whereas one from *you* would be very effective. Mind you," I said rather warmly, "it cost me something this morning to keep a still tongue in my head. I so longed to point out to her that her moral scruples hadn't become troublesome while Blondel was planning and overseeing the building. They didn't sprout until the last stone was laid. So typical of her to overlook the disgrace so long as the usefulness lasted. Did you think to say that? Well, you can next time. In fact, in this fight I'll roll the stones up and you can fire them."

I then saw that over her poised and halted needle Berengaria was staring at me with some horror.

"But I agreed with her. I entirely agreed with her."

"What?" I daresay my face mirrored the horror.

"She is right, Anna. I agreed with her."

"You agreed that Blondel is a dirty, drunken, dissolute fellow, a disgrace to any respectable establishment?"

"Isn't it true?" She looked down and carefully threaded a pearl onto the needle.

So many thoughts rushed into my mind that for a moment I was speechless. I stared at her, seeing as though for the first time the smoothly dressed hair speckled with grey—that hair which had fallen in shining plaits over her shoulders, been gathered in the great rich knot at the back of her head, been twisted into fantastic fashionable horns on her brow; seeing the lips, once so richly curved, so ripely red, so like a rose, grown pale and narrow, grown prim and patient. As though

441

aware of my scrutiny, she lifted her head and looked at me, and I saw the sad, old woman's eyes.

And I thought of the tall redheaded knight, the valiant crusader, rotting in his untimely grave; killed not on some high emprise, some noble errand, but dead of avarice, slain in a sordid little squabble about a treasure which had no existence.

And I thought of Blondel, my beautiful singing boy, bloated, drunken, and cynical.

What dreadful destruction could be wrought by time, and what desolate ruin we did work upon one another. Past all bearing to contemplate.

What would she say now if I dared tell her the whole truth; if I told her that she had destroyed Blondel, made him what he was as surely as Richard had destroyed her and made her what she was?

For a moment the hot angry desire to do so was strong in me. Then I saw how useless and cruel such an outburst would be—merely a relief to my feelings at the expense of her peace. She was not to blame any more than Richard was to blame for spoiling her life, or Blondel for the smouldering fire in me.

"You can't say it isn't true," she said, and pulled the needle through, so that I realised that all this thinking had taken no longer than the firm stitching of a pearl into place. One drop of spleen forced its way through my self-control.

"He is not dissolute," I said loudly.

"Well, I am not clever with words. It was the one she used. And then, you see, since *your* conversation this morning, Anna, there was that most unfortunate occurrence during dinner."

"Nobody can be dissolute at dinner."

"Don't be ridiculous, Anna. It was a matter of discipline. Sister Elizabeth had occasion to punish two of the children, Marianne, the one with the curls, and that little cross-eyed girl—I forget her name. She said they were not to have any dinner, but, being merciful, she did not wish to torment them with the sight of the others feeding, so she stood them outside the door. When she went to recall them they were not there, and at last she found them in that little den which you fitted up for Blondel to write in. He had one on each knee and he was drawing things to make them laugh, and they both had crumbs on their faces—cake crumbs. You must see that such behaviour on his part makes it impossible for Sister Elizabeth to maintain discipline—and as the abbess says, Marianne is far too big a girl to sit on any man's knee."

"At last she has said something I can agree with! Too big and too heavy. But he lifted Catherine up to enable her to see what he was drawing, and Marianne climbed up uninvited. Her father has been dead not quite six months, Berengaria; probably he often set her on his knee, probably she thinks men's knees are for sitting on. As for the cake, I gave them that. I was there, you see. They said they had lost their dinner for making ugly stitches, and God knows I have made many such in my time."

"Then you are equally to blame," Berengaria said coldly.

I saw the spirit of the cloister, cold and irresistible as an evening shadow, move forward and engulf her.

"I agree. I'll go further and agree that a place where discipline is preferred before simple kindness, where, in fact, an unthinking kindness is regarded with suspicion, is not the place for Blondel—or for me."

She halted the busy needle then and looked up with the expression of one who half hears, doubts, and waits for a sound to be repeated.

"You said that as though, if Blondel were asked to go, you would go."

"And that," I said, "is precisely what I mean. Madam Ursula meant it too."

"That is nonsense, Anna. You talk about suspicion and lack of charity! She never mentioned your leaving. How could she? This is your home. But for you L'Espan would never have been built. There was never any suggestion—— Oh, why must you take this curious attitude? I never heard anything so ridiculous. One would think you couldn't live without Blondel."

"I should find it difficult to live without something that Blondel stands for, dirty, drunk, and disreputable as he may be. And that something doesn't flourish here, Berengaria. There's a taint—I've watched it spread and now I know you are infected. Only a short time ago, though you might have criticised Blondel yourself, you'd have been loyal and remembered the many services he has done you. You had only to say, 'He has served me faithfully and where I am he remains.' She would have accepted that from you. But you have caught the cloister cold-heart and you agree with her. So it remains for me to say, 'I have used him, and when he goes I go.' And that is what I am saying now."

"You're angry," Berengaria said with infuriating tolerance. "Don't be angry, be reasonable. Of course he has served

443

me—but he has always been fed and clothed and housed and been given presents. I'm fond of Blondel, but for years now he has been going downhill, getting dirtier, almost always fuddled with wine, and often rude." She pointed her needle at me. "Don't think that I was blind to these things until the abbess spoke. I've noticed. I've spoken to him repeatedly and he just laughs. If you'll just think for a moment you'll see, as I do, a dozen reasons why he should go, and not one why he should stay."

"I do. I see that with great clarity."

"Yet you are so perverse you must side with him. Just as you must give naughty children cake. You don't like the children; you never go near the Kindergarten; you said their singing sounded like the last wails of drowning kittens—but as soon as you see two being properly punished you must give them cake! And you agree that Blondel has no place here, but if he goes you threaten to leave too. It's so stupid."

"It was a promise rather than a threat," I said lightly. "L'Espan will be rid of two awkward misplaced people at one throw. Madam Ursula will be delighted." Not, I thought spitefully, that my removal would give her full rein; the Lodgings' charter was quite watertight, and if she tried to interfere with my women she would find herself reckoning not only with Sir Godric but with her own bishop as well.

"Anna, you don't really mean to go?" She looked at me and saw that I did. "I shall miss you—horribly. We've been through so much together." For a moment the memory of all our hopes and fears and schemes, merry times, sad times, journeyings and waitings were quick and vivid in the room. "So much," she said, and sighed, remembering. Then the cold shadow strode forward again and she said, "But it is useless to look backward—it's all over."

I saw her gaze drop to the little box of pearls. And I knew in a flash of perception that for some time now Blondel and I had been not merely perverse and awkward and out of place at L'Espan, but out of place in the new life she was building, constant uncomfortable reminders of the old life of stubborn self-will, fleshly passion, worldly scheming. She had turned her back on that life and on us. In a way our going would be a relief to her too. At that thought my heart leapt up like a bird inadvertently set free by a clumsy fowler. Yes, it was all over.

"But you have found peace—and happiness, of a sort—here, haven't you?" I asked gently.

She looked up, but her left hand moved to the box and blindly selected the next pearl.

"Oh yes, Anna. I've been happier here than at any time since—since I was a girl."

The happiness of resignation, routine, ritual, and faith. Very real; attainable to everyone—at a price. But the door to such a state of mind was so narrow that you must enter it alone, stripped naked; and so low that you must bend your head and say, "I agree," "I accept." Not for me—yet.

It was eight o'clock and a mild summer evening. Every pink rose on the little bush was open to the heart and some petals were already shedding; the white lilies were now in full bloom, filling the àir with a swooning sweetness. The garden was empty save for Thérèse, who, walking at a snail's pace, was taking her senile, obese little dog for its last airing of the day. The children were all abed, the ladies indoors. The stillness was broken only by the occasional murmur of a dove and the soft sound of the nuns at compline in the chapel.

I knew where I should find Blondel: in the place which Berengaria called his "little den." In the failing light he would be laying aside his reading or his writing, fitting a new string to his lute, or merely sitting and watching the night run in over the fields of the sky. He would not be sober. The wine jug would stand empty on the floor, the beaker, half full, be ready to hand.

His right arm, now withered to uselessness, would be tucked into the front of his tunic and the tunic would be dirty, stained, and crumpled. His face would be bloated, unshaven, cynical, kind.

I knew. What I should find; where I was going.

But you come in the end to the place where your heart is; that is, if you set your heart in an attainable place. And it occurred to me that of them all I was the only one who had done that. Now it would be easy enough to go to Blondel and say:

"Our work here is done; we are not wanted here any more. Come, let us go to Apieta and build *our* house."

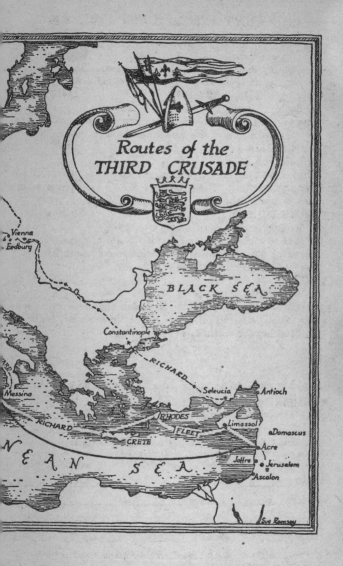

Routes of the
THIRD CRUSADE

BLACK SEA

Vienna
Eedburg

Constantinople

RICHARD

Seleucia • Antioch

Messina

RICHARD

RHODES

FLEET

Limassol

•Damascus

CRETE

•Acre

NEAN SEA

Joffra • Jerusalem

•Ascalon

Sus Romsey

CURRENT CREST BESTSELLERS